The Brothers Mecarnin

I0563514

Return to Aston Ridge

Book Two

Sarah Flanagan

Return to Aston Ridge

Book design by Sarah Flanagan
Photos and illustrations by Khala Carr unless otherwise noted

ISBN: 9781635220773

Printed in the United States of America
10 9 8 7 6 5 4 3 2 1

Rivershore Books
8982 Van Buren St. NE • Minneapolis, MN 55434
763-670-8677 • info@rivershorebooks.com

Two Months Earlier
Chapter 1

The sun was shining, a gentle breeze blowing across the golden grass. The mailman was whistling as he did his rounds, pushing mail through the slits of each house before going on to the next one.

There was nothing unusual about that particular morning, except the unusually bright sunlight and cooler air. However, a change was definitely to come sooner than the young mailman believed.

He was just pushing a handful of letters through one of the slits and as he turned to trot back down the front steps, he noticed that a dark cloud had gathered not far down the road.

"I had better head home," he mused aloud. "My round is almost done, and I don't want to get caught in that."

He hurried down the stairs and began to pick up his pace. He was just shoving the last few letters into the last house slit when he became increasingly aware that the sunlight that had been out just a second ago was now gone. Looking around, he realized that there was sunlight falling everywhere . . . except around him.

The man looked up; he was standing in the middle of the road, right in the path of the sunlight, but now the dark cloud hovered right above him . . . so close that he thought he could touch it. The young mailman was no fool, but he was also not a coward. So, when the dark cloud above him began to slowly twirl and swirl about, he didn't cry out and flee but stood watching with cautious glances about him.

The swirling cloud seemed almost ready to swirl itself out of existence when the man heard a voice behind him. Slowly turning around, he found that the only other person out that morning was standing right behind him. The man was unusually tall and thin . . . too thin. He wore a long black robe that fell to the ground and trailed behind him slightly. The robe was held closed by a black sash around his waist that had small spikes sewn into the lacy material.

A pale, almost gray-colored face peered from below paper-thin black eyebrows. His nose was rather long and slightly crooked, as was his thin mouth that was turned upwards in a wicked smile. That was all the man could make out of the narrow, sharp-shaped face, for the rest was concealed behind a large black hood.

After getting over his puzzlement at encountering this peculiar man, the mailman realized that the stranger was carrying something in his arms... a large bundle that, instead of being wrapped in paper, was wrapped in a black sheet and tied closed with red ribbon.

"Who are you?" the mailman inquired, suddenly finding that his voice was hoarse.

The stranger did not speak but took one step toward the man and bent over, laying the bundle none-too-gently on the ground. He took three steps backwards, away from the bundle, and made a mock salute with two of his long pale fingers.

For a split second the mailman's eyes fell on the bundle before him and when he lifted his eyes again, the stranger was gone and the cloud above him was slowly disappearing as if the sunlight was absorbing it.

In being a mailman, the lad was not unaccustomed to peculiar happenings. In the short three years he had been doing this job, he had encountered some vicious pets, funny noises coming from the houses on his run and even an iguana in a mailbox once.

Stepping forward, the man knelt down beside the bundle and touched it gently. It wasn't hard so possibly not a weapon. There was not a noise coming from it, so it couldn't be a bomb. Reaching over with one hand, the man cautiously began to untie the fancy red ribbon. The ribbon was of extremely heavy fabric but feeling that this wasn't a moment to be foolish, the mailman laid the ribbon to the side, intending to not discard them.

He folded back one end of the black fabric to realize that there were two layers. Folding back the fabric, he started in horror. Pulling the cloth back further, he unveiled a face ... of a child! Absolutely sheet white with no color or life in the child's face, it was obvious that the child was dead. Completely unfolding the black fabric, the mailman inspected the body and found no wounds. It was as if the child had been depleted of all life.

Folding the child back up in the cloth and tying it closed with the ribbon, the man picked up the dead child and hurried down the street toward his home.

People have always told me that you cannot buy the truth. Buying the truth only gives you lies and deceit. I never knew what this meant, and I don't think I have figured it out even now. I thought that my whole life had been completely deprived of lies and truth. I thought that there was nothing hidden and nothing to say. I realized what a fool I was for thinking that.

A time comes in every person's life when they are hit hard in the face with reality. The twins say that the day it will happen to them is when the stars collides with earth and we are bombarded by aliens. Deke avoids that kind of question because it actually makes him think in terms that he is not used to. Gene says that it will be like the day when Ivan nearly busted the guts out of his brain. I am not sure whether that was a yes or a no.

When I ask the girls, Seraphina just smiles, Eileen takes on a look as if someone stuck rotten fish up her nose, and Denise lowers her eyebrows at me. That is why, most of the time, I don't ask them. Neil is never helpful because he just says that it happens to him every day of his life. If he was referring to running around all day, then I would agree with him, but I get a strange feeling that wasn't what he meant. I have probably asked Oliver more times than the others, especially since he doesn't answer audibly but his eyes seem to answer for him. Once he even told me that he doubts that he will ever experience that. I don't know if that is good or bad.

I know one thing, though: if that day ever came for me, it would be a large handful of days. It would a week long remembered by us all, not just because of the truths that knocked us silly, but also the fact that it marked one of the hardest times in our lives.

It was a week before Christmas Eve, a terrible place to find yourself trapped in a box with sharp edges.

However, that is where we found ourselves . . . and I have to admit, most of us regretted it.

At the present day
Chapter 2

"*Let me grab my jacket,*" *Eileen called from the top of the stairs.*

She hurried down the hallway to the door which opened up into her room. As she stepped inside, she glanced down at her hand long enough to make sure she was still holding her bedroom key. She paused, her hand still resting on the doorknob as her eyes lifted.

A gasp shook her body and she pressed her back against the frame of the door, allowing her eyes to grow twice their normal size. Deke was standing in the middle of her room, his back to her. He was looking at what apparently was her bed but from the angle she had seen when she first entered, she knew that he wasn't just looking at her bed.

The boy didn't turn around but obviously knew she was there. "Funny," he remarked in a cool voice, "it happened literally five minutes before you guys came in the front door."

Eileen swallowed the lump that was growing in her throat and she forced words out. "Wha . . . What do we do?"

Deke finally turned around and his dark blue eyes showed no fear, no concern . . . No expression. "This is up to you, Eileen. This task was placed on your shoulders . . . What shall you do about it?"

"Deke," a voice called. "Deke . . . Where are you?"

Deke's eyes flew open to find the girlish face of Phillipa looking down at him. He rolled his head to one side and realized he had fallen asleep on the sofa in the library. Slowly rising to a half sitting position, resting on one elbow, he ran his hand across his warm face and through his hair.

His fingers brushed against the goggle-like glasses that rested on the top of his head. Fumbling with them, he pulled them down over his eyes. Phillipa tossed her head and grinned down at the boy. "Don't tell me that you need those to see!"

Deke smirked. He honestly rarely needed the water goggles unless he was reading or working with something small. However, when he first woke up from sleep or a nap, it made his eyes wake up to see things in a clear perspective.

Pushing them back, he shook his head. "No . . . what is it, though? Did I miss lunch?"

Phillipa arced an eyebrow in amusement. "You slept past dinner and breakfast this morning."

At once the boy sat up straight and looked around. Sure enough, the light outside was not the dim light of afternoon or evening . . . it was morning. Rubbing his hand back across his eyes, he groaned. "Oh, the gang is going to kill me!"

"You bet they are," Phillipa remarked. "Gene was furious when he couldn't rouse you. You were literally a stone! I had to slap you several times. Where were you, anyway?"

"In purgatory," Deke remarked sarcastically. "I was dreaming . . . At least, I was dreaming a memory."

Phillipa rose to a full stand and stepped to the side. "Suits you. But mark my words, if you don't get going, you'll be in a place much worse than purgatory or memories. Don't forget your coat; the snow is still falling out there."

Realizing that was true, Deke leapt from the chair. Phillipa grinned as she watched him stuff all of his things into his knapsack and hurriedly pull his shoes on that had been discarded on the floor the day before.

The boy had barely changed, unlike everyone else. He had barely grown, much to his chagrin, especially since he was now the shortest in the gang besides Zara. His dark brown hair was slightly longer now but kept moderately cut around the ears and the back of the neck. He always had his blue water-filled goggles which served as his glasses. He didn't wear the usual white, long sleeve, linen shirt underneath a brown, dark blue, dark green, or black jacket and clean pants that most boys wore. He wore a white starch shirt with a turnover collar and dark red necktie. Over that, he wore a dark brown leather jacket that Neil had given him. At first, the boy barely wore the jacket since he saw it as more an "athletic person's belonging," but after much persisting, Neil and Gene managed to get Deke so used to wearing it that he now always had it.

The boy's face had rounded out more in the past year, mostly because Cook was awfully fond of giving the four kids decent-sized meals. Not only because they were growing children, but also because when all four of them first moved into the house three years prior, they had all been sticks. Now, Deke was even beginning to show some meat on his bones, though he avoided any testing of their ability.

Deke paused long enough in the hallway to finish tying his shoelaces and slipping both straps of his knapsack onto his shoulders before heading out the front door. There was no barking greeting from Webstar since the young dog was probably with Neil. In fact, there was no doubt that Neil was exactly where she was.

Even though he had been asleep since the afternoon before, Deke didn't have to look far before he found the other boys. It was well known that the boys retreated to their hideout in the far reaches of Hichester. At the edge of the wood that encircled the small town of Hichester was a small grove. Surrounded by huge silver birch trees that were twice the age of Hichester, it was like a sheltered castle. The boys had stumbled upon it one morning on their way home from fishing. Truth be told, it was understandable that they found it, especially when Whip had tried to create his own shortcut through the woods rather than following the river. It got them slightly lost, but after finding the grove, they found home.

Since then, the boys had rehabilitated the grove into a true paradise (at least for boys between the ages of nine and thirteen). The girls contributed their own efforts, though they preferred to spend their time in more social areas and at the river rather than risking getting infested with ticks and chiggers in the woods.

The way that the boys remembered where the grove was located is personally confidential. Luckily, the only people outside of the gang who knew the location of the grove were Phillipa, Macaroon, and Mr. Wetherby. That was so if the kids didn't hear the calls of their parents or siblings, at least three adults knew where they could be found.

When you approach the edge of the forest, you are at once struck by the huge line of trees that seem to have the form of a strong battle line of soldiers. However, only one of these trees is a silver birch. Deke found said silver birch without difficulty, since it was directly behind old Mr. Res Schneider's house (which was a place the kids carefully avoided). Squeezing between the tight cluster of trees, Deke pulled himself out between the silver birch and the maple tree beside it into a semi clearer part of the forest. The trees were a perfect maze to an untrained eye. However, Deke's eyes were some of the few that were trained to recognize this clump of trees.

Taking a decisive far left, Deke pushed through the undergrowth and thick hydrangea bushes that grew in huge masses all over Hichester. As he approached two particularly large prickle bushes, he dropped to his knees. Reaching over with one careful hand, he grasped the bottom prickle tree branch that was purposely folded over the small, narrow tunnel that had been formed and shaped by the twins between and under the two bushes.

When they discovered the grove, they tried to find a way to protect it from prying intruders. However, the job was unnecessary, since a ring of prickle bushes and holly trees made a perfect perimeter around the far reaches of the grove. There were three ways to get through the sharp barricade, and only the gang members knew how to find them. Each entrance was a small tunnel (made by the twins) between and under two prickle bushes that were, most of the time, the largest of the lot. The way they recognized the particular bushes was the fact that on the left of each entrance grew a tree which had a long cut sliced into the dark bark (made by Neil) to distinguish its location.

Crawling on hands and knees (actually elbows, not hands), Deke pushed himself past the two bushes and inside the castle walls. The grove didn't take up the whole perimeter that the prickle bushes and holly trees created, but rather just the center. All the trees and heather that grew between the perimeter and the grove were allowed to grow thick and untamed to hide the location of the grove, should anyone venture past the walls.

Heading in a perfectly straight line toward the center, Deke pushed through the heather and bushes until he came upon the perfect paradise.

The grove was abuzz with life and energy. All the gang members, except the girls, were running around the place, leaping across the rather deep but narrow holes and ditches that made up the majority of the grove. There was a long rope in the center of the grove that hung from a branch high above the ground. This served as a swing that could carry you from any part of the grove to the other, rather than having to leap across ditches that were mostly dry but on certain days would fill with water.

Chapter 3

All eyes looked up as Deke entered and instead of returning to what they were doing, everyone hurried toward Deke or called out to him as he stepped inside.

"Where have you been, Deke? We thought you had died of a heart attack," Reed remarked glumly.

"You were out like a light! Did Phillipa finally get you up or did she have to force you?" Roy inquired, in a much more spirited attitude than his brother.

The twins were calling all kinds of questions from the far side of the grove. Oliver had looked up, once, from the book he was reading in the shade of a tree, but now he returned to it. Roy and Reed were dangling at different parts of the swing, trying to either knock the other off by kicking him in the face or trying to aggravate Oliver. Their attempts at the latter were useless.

Whip stood up from where he had been sitting beside Oliver. With a spring in his step, he walked over to his friend and clapped him on the shoulder. "Did you have time to think about what Mr. Wetherby said?"

Deke's mind raced to remember what Whip was referring to. Then he remembered; right before he fell asleep, Mr. Wetherby had offered to go with Deke to visit his maternal father, Steve Rasmussen, in Gerh that weekend. Deke had been invited to spend the week of Christmas there, but the boy had declined, saying that he wished to be in Hichester for Christmas. However, he was planning on venturing to Gerh that weekend to spend a few days with his father.

The boy shook his head. "Not really . . . I mean, it would make me feel better, but . . . I just don't know if I'm ready . . . even with the whole of Hichester behind me."

A smile touched Whip's lips and he ruffled Deke's hair. "If it was Gene saying that, it would make sense. However, you barely know half of Hichester. The other half don't wish to know you, especially since you nearly blew up the post office last year."

Deke grinned sheepishly. It had been a terrible mistake on his part to bring one of his inventions when he went to pick up a package for Mr. Wetherby. The invention had been bumped as he was leaving, setting it off, and it destroyed a huge pile of packages. Luckily, most of them weren't important.

Deke looked up at his friend, who was the exact same height as him. For a moment, Deke wished that it was Neil he was talking to. The boy always felt small beside Neil, but when he recalled how Neil had changed, he felt strangely secure. Neil wasn't the boy he used to be: mischievous, sarcastic, and even selfish. He was still mischievous and sarcastic but a good deal less exuberant. He was full of pent-up energy, but he used it in the right way: running. The boy was constantly on his feet, and it made grownups dizzy watching him run all over the place.

Unlike some of the other boys, who would get someone else in the gang to do things for them, Neil would do all the things himself, and most of them required running back and forth between town and wherever they were playing.

The thirteen-year-old boy was growing up . . . a little too fast. His voice was already matured, which made most of the fifteen-year-old boys in town jealous as they remembered how their voices had been girlish when they were Neil's age. He was an early bloomer, but instead of taking it for granted, he still cherished his childhood.

Deke had never believed that he could be proud of someone who was older than him. Naturally he was always proud of Gene, who made friends no matter where he went. The blond-haired boy was a natural peacemaker and sorted the situation out before using force, though the latter was always an option since Gene had become a much better fighter than even Neil.

Yet, besides the fact that Neil towered over Deke, he was much more athletic and was a year and a half older than Deke. Neil was a natural leader, which was one of the reasons why the gang had nominated him the captain of the gang when they discussed ranks the year before. He seemed to always have the answer and was the ideal older brother.

Neil was incredibly protective over his brothers and Eileen, but for some reason he seemed to have greater protection over Deke. Sometimes Deke got the feeling that the reason for this was that he was more vulnerable than Eileen and Gene. Truth be told, that *was* one of the reasons. Gene had no problem taking care of himself, and Eileen just avoided trouble, which always set Neil at ease concerning them. Deke didn't try to get into trouble and was rather good at avoiding it, but maybe it was a combination of his small stature, his vulnerability, and the fact that he was Neil's younger brother that made the older boy like a guardian to Deke.

Unlike Deke, everyone in the gang had changed in some way or another. Whip was still his mischievous self and, if anything, he had gotten worse. He did find a good enemy who disliked his form of disruption and that was Denise. Denise had suddenly taken on a curious, yet rather strict "keep to the rules" kind of behavior, which meant that she and Whip would find nothing in common except that they loved arguing with the other. The boy had grown slightly but wasn't able to live up to his father and his grandfather's height, meaning that Gene was soon taller than Whip. However, the only person Whip could say was shorter than him besides Zara was Deke.

Oliver . . . Well, Oliver hadn't changed at all. Still a man of few words, he kept quiet most of the time and was always reading. No surprise there. He had allowed his hair to grow slightly thicker, meaning that it would flop over his large glasses whenever he looked down and he was constantly brushing them back.

The twins had definitely changed. If Deke hadn't seen them in three years straight, he would have fainted after seeing how much they had changed. Lucky for him, though, he had watched them change gradually over the years, so it wasn't as surprising. Though for people who didn't see the two boys that often found it unnerving. Once rather harmonious boys, the boys had finally discovered their balance point which turned out to be the complete opposite of what everyone thought.

Roy was still spirited, cheerful, and rather strange in his crazy remarks. He was the typical geek who found everything fascinating. Honestly, most of the time no one understood a single word the boy was saying. Reed had gone completely down a different track, but it seemed to suit his slower form of things rather than Roy's. Reed wasn't as crazy or fast at doing anything as Roy but somehow kept up to him. He still lisped, but due to the fact that he didn't talk as much as before, it wasn't as noticeable. When he did talk, though, it was mostly concerning the negative, boring side of things.

Every single one of the kids had changed in at least one similar thing: their hair. Due to the fact that winter was coming along, and the weather was bitterly cold most of the day, the boys had been allowed to grow their hair a little longer so that it protected their ears and part of their necks, as well as their foreheads. Neil, however, kept his relatively shorter than the others.

A hand appeared from the inside of one of the deep pits, then another hand followed, grasping the side of the pit. The knuckles turned white as the person hauled himself out of the pit and over the side. The person, slightly soiled from being in the pit but moderately clean, looked as if he had just come back from a joy ride.

His blond hair was slightly wavy and slightly plastered in wavy locks by sweat but kept from sticking to his head by the fact that he looked windblown. His bright, glowing, turquoise-blue eyes were smiling, and his eyebrows held a mature fixture to them, while his smile and eyes carried the strong boyishness.

Gene was wearing a light blue shirt that possibly belonged to Neil since it was loose and relaxed on the slender, yet strongly built, young boy. The shirt was untucked, giving the air of relaxation, and the pair of brown pants he wore were soiled at the knees and rolled up slightly past his ankles.

"Hey, Deke, where have you been?" Gene's youthful, yet almost mature, voice inquired.

Gene's voice was already breaking toward a deeper version, which sometimes caused Deke despair. While his own voice was still childish, his two brothers—who were still too young to have mature voices—were already beginning to sound like teenagers. Gene's wasn't as noticeable as

Neil's, but it wasn't as squeaky and young as it had once been.

Deciding to ignore that thought, Deke answered his brother. "Phillipa had a hard time waking me up."

Gene smirked. "Never gets old, huh?"

Deke considered his brother a moment before furrowing his brow. "What are you even doing in that pit, Gene?"

His younger brother smirked knowingly. "Oh, I'm preparing for our next battle of Cops and Robbers. I told Neil that I would beat him this next round! He won't get away with hiding in a pile of leaves this time!"

Deke grinned. The only thing that Gene and Neil were competitive in was Cops and Robbers. It was a gang "tradition" to have a game of Cops and Robbers once a week, giving each team enough time to make up a plan. The week before, Neil's team had won only because Neil had hidden inside a pile of leaves the entire game, making it absolutely impossible for anyone to find him until the very end of the game.

"Anyway," Deke mused. "didn't you forget that Mr. Walker asked to see you at noon?"

Gene's eyes widened. "What time is it?"

Everyone looked down at their wrists, but only Oliver was wearing a watch. "Five minutes till noon."

"Ah!" the younger boy cried. "I've got to go!"

Everyone watched as Gene disappeared through the bushes, dusting his pants and shirt off as he went. When the sound of him crashing through the bushes died down, the twins turned to Deke.

"Do you know what that is all about?" Roy inquired.

Deke shrugged. "Maybe it has something to do with the fact that the council wants the society members to be in charge of Christmas preparations this week."

Chapter 4

The sixth-grade classroom was perfectly silent. Everyone's heads were bent over their books, silently reading their assignments for the last twenty minutes of school. It was the last day of school before Christmas break, which would last for about three to four weeks.

Mrs. McDowell, the sixth-grade teacher, was sitting at her desk, organizing all files and papers into folders so that she wouldn't leave a messy desk until January.

The only heads that weren't bent over their books were those of Oliver, Deke, and Denise. In fact, Denise's head was practically in her book since her face was squashed nose down into her books with her pile of red curly hair covering her whole desk. Her two skinny, pale arms were stuck up straight in the air, with the curved fingers showing impatience and annoyance. The last day of school before a break was always the worst for Denise to bear.

To her right sat Oliver, who had finished his reading long before the others; no surprise there. He was thus creating a paper airplane out of a piece of lined paper, which he was planning on flying straight into Denise's head. Deke, who sat on the other side of Denise, was trying his hardest to concentrate on his book. In truth, he was writhing inside with worry, excitement, and the feeling of having not eaten all of his breakfast.

His eyes kept wavering off the page to all the other faces in the room. He wondered how long it would be before he saw them again. He didn't know if his father would have him stay in Gerh after the first visit. In truth, Deke hoped not, especially since Hichester was like a paradise to him and all his friends and family were here.

Deke quickly allowed his eyes to waver over to Oliver. He knew that nothing escaped the tall, gangly boy with wild orange hair and large spectacles. Oliver's gray eyes were concentrating on the airplane that he was preparing to toss at Denise's pile of hair.

He saw the eruption even before it happened. Oliver's eyes shot straight across the room to the schoolroom clock that hung above the chalkboard. They blinked once, then a smile appeared on the quiet boy's face. Just as this happened, the bell calling for the end of the day went off.

Denise's head shot up and she just narrowly missed being hit by the paper plane that Oliver let loose. Instead of hitting Denise (due to the fact that she had moved), the plane glided across the table to Deke and struck the inkwell that stood atop a small pile of books.

At the same moment, Oliver and Denise leapt up from their chairs, but Oliver forgot that his legs were long, and they got entangled with the underneath of the chair. His chair toppled over and struck Denise. The girl immediately lost balance and was falling back onto the ground.

A hand appeared out of nowhere and grabbed her fallen chair, setting it up in one swift motion so that Denise fell right into a sit back in the chair. Oliver had managed to get himself out of his predicament just as Deke's inkwell was caught.

The three slowly turned around, hoping beyond hope that it wasn't one of the teachers or grownups. They knew that if it was, they would get it tough especially in causing such a ruckus on the last day of school.

Standing there, towering over the three, even slightly taller than Oliver, stood Neil. His hair was no longer spiky, though it did have its own energy. He kept it brushed out of his forehead, caused probably by the fact that when he ran (which was all the time) his hair would get in his eyes, so he resorted to keeping it out of the way. His eyebrows were still firm but full of expression and energy.

His eyes, one gray, one green, hadn't changed except they seemed to go deeper . . . deeper down into people's souls when he stared at them. Before, you felt annoyed when Neil would stare at you or look you straight in the eye. Now, when he did that, you felt either at ease or worried, depending on what Neil was discovering by staring into your soul.

Neil's once pursed and firm lips had relaxed and had smiles, grins, and smirks ready to throw all over the place. His nose had rounded out slightly (everyone thinks it was because of how Cook demanded he eat healthier, bigger foods), and his body had grown into his slightly large ears. Now, it was obvious that they had never been large; his face had just been small before.

However, the only thing that had come as a shock to everyone was Neil's skin tone. Before, he had been slightly fair skinned like Gene and Deke but over the course of two to three years, his skin had taken on an almost tanned color. Deke's suggestion was that it had been caused by his being constantly out in the sun. However, the slightly deeper skin tone wasn't caused by tanning, but rather just by natural genetics. That was clear because even his shoulders and legs were like that, even though he kept them covered all the time. Kids found it hard to believe that Neil was Deke and Gene's brother because his skin was at least two to three times darker than theirs, but after studying their eye shape, face shape and other traits, it was recognizable that the three boys were related.

Denise let out the big breath of air she had been holding in and Deke's shoulders relaxed. Oliver smiled once but then resorted to gathering his books. He missed the wide grin that appeared on Neil's handsome face. Few people knew it, but a smile from Oliver was enough to last a lifetime. His smiles were rare, and he saved them for people whom he cared for the most.

Surprising or not, Oliver and Neil had become best buddies in the past few years, not only because they were the oldest boys of the gang but also, they found a balance between the two of them and found that they could relate to each other.

Neil found that in being the oldest of the three brothers, he could only talk with Gene and Deke about certain things. Other things, he had to go to Oliver about, especially if it had to do with his age. Oliver similarly found it relaxing talking with Neil about things that he never really brought out into the open. Neil was probably the only person Oliver spoke to more than once a day with more than one word in his sentences.

"Where did you pop up from?" Denise demanded, trying to not act gracious on purpose.

"Through the chimney," Neil replied sarcastically with a grin to match. "I came through the door, Denise. The seventh graders were let out early if we finished our reading early."

"What are you guys planning the rest of the day?" Denise inquired, looking directly at the two brothers.

Deke exchanged a sort of worried, anxious yet slightly excited look with his older brother. A smile appeared on Neil's face and he realized that he had better answer Denise before she suspected treachery.

"The gang and I were gonna go skating on the river. Gene said something about having a meeting with the headmasters later about Christmas assignments, so he won't be joining us. You know, I don't recall past Christmases being this . . . this much work!"

Denise shrugged. "I don't expect less. I mean, Deke just found out that he's not a Mecarnin and he'll be leaving tomorrow to visit his dad whom he's never met, and Christmas is just a few days away!"

Deke twitched, obviously unnerved by the first thing she said. It was true that he felt nervous, but he also felt slightly excited. Christmas was coming, and everyone was going to be returning to Hichester for the holidays. Denise's little siblings were coming, and Destiny, Silver, and Emma were getting back from Hintwini. It would be great!

Just as they were about to step out into the hallway, Seraphina, Eileen, and Zara set on them like a pack of wild wolves.

"Guys, did you hear?" Seraphina squealed. "Oliver wrote a play on scenes from the Old Testament, and Whip is in charge of leading it."

"Who thought that was a good idea?" Neil inquired, pulling his coat on. "Don't tell me that the twins will be part of the cast."

"Actually, yes," Eileen pointed out. "They'll be playing the roles of Adam and Satan in the Garden of Eden."

Deke blinked several times before speaking. "Surprisingly, I wouldn't disagree."

"Hey, Zara," Denise remarked as she pushed past the boys into the hallway. "Who's this with you?"

Zara stepped to the side to reveal that there was another girl with her. The girl was about Zara's size but possibly a year or two older. Her dark brown, almost black hair was cut short and came to her chin, cut in layers. There were several light blue highlights in her hair that stood out like a light in the dark. Her eyes were large, round, and violet colored. She was surprisingly pretty with a pointed chin, petite nose, and bright smile.

"This is Drew Driscoll. She just recently moved here from Catasbanel," Zara explained.

Neil held out a hand politely and shook the girl's hand. "I'm Neil Mecarnin."

Drew's smile expanded as everyone shook her hand and introduced themselves. "It's a pleasure to meet you. My parents were members of SOHE, and they thought that living here would open many opportunities for me. However, I'm not a changeling myself."

"You're not?" Denise inquired, almost disappointed.

Drew shook her head. "No. My brother is, though. I was kinda cut short so to speak."

"I was just showing Drew around," Zara explained. "I was going to introduce her to the twins, but I couldn't find them."

Neil smirked. "Didn't you hear? The twins escaped from class three minutes before it was let out without anyone noticing. Anyone can guess where they ended up."

Chapter 5

Sure enough, they were able to locate the twins in the field that separated the edge of the woods from the edge of town. The snow was like a perfect white blanket, untouched by any human hands . . . that is, except for the two sets of footprints that trailed all over the field.

The mound of snow that appeared in the center of the field was what the twins had dubbed "the snow fort." It was really just a pile of snow that had been pushed off the streets and the kids had hollowed out.

As the gang and Drew approached, they saw that the twins had busied themselves building a snowman out of a particularly high part of the snow pile. Reed was leaning against one low side of the wall, his hand keeping his head up while he handed Roy rocks one at a time.

"Come on, Mr. Scrooge," Roy was saying as the gang approached from behind. "Christmas isn't a time for lazing around doing nothing. Today starts Christmas break, and it'll be quite a break! Deke and Neil are leaving tomorrow for Gerh and we are in charge of assisting Whip in the Christmas play. We'll also have to think of some pranks to play on poor Gene. He's got to deal with Christmas preparations at SOHE this year!"

Reed grunted and handed him the carrot. Roy snatched it up and began to grind it into the snowman's face with difficulty. "We're the mighty twin squad! Nothing can hold us back! We are fugitives of lost people!"

Even though the carrot was just beginning to slip into the snowman's head, Roy removed it and held it like a sword, pointed at Reed for a moment. "Fear us! The spirochetosis that you will get if you come between us is immense!"

Reed rolled his eyes and laid his head back, closing his eyes and ears to the sound and sight of his brother. Just as Roy got the carrot on the snowman's upper forehead, he discovered that his twin wasn't paying attention.

"The mighty twin squad should not go into a slumber."

Realizing that Reed wasn't prepared to listen to Roy's dreamy rantings, the cheerful boy returned to his snowman. Just as he turned around, however, the large round head of the snowman swiveled around to look directly at him and somewhere from within the snowman came a deep voice.

"You done yet?"

The gang had the view that Roy didn't: a perfect view of Whip, who had appeared stealthily from the woods and had grasped the head of the snowman without Roy realizing. At the sound of Whip's disguised voice, Roy's eyes literally bulged, and he would have run off in horror if he hadn't tripped over his twin and if Whip hadn't laughed out loud.

"Merry Christmas, guys!" Whip called as he set the snowman head back down.

The gang hurried over and climbed into the hard, hollowed-out pile of snow. Whip was still laughing as Zara and Drew approached the mound.

"Who ith thith?" Reed inquired in his slow, drawn-out voice.

Drew's face lit up and she held out her hand to the boy. "I'm Drew."

Reed shook it slowly, and if Drew thought he wasn't interested, she forgot once Roy gave her a bone-breaking handshake. She held out her hand to Whip and gave him a smile, but the boy gave her a smirk.

"What happened to your hair? Did the bargemen manage to kidnap you for a few days?" he inquired sarcastically.

Seraphina and Neil tried desperately to give Whip signals to not push it, but Drew's face was already turning from cheerful to furious.

"I can see that you know nothing of hairstyles, shorty," Drew snapped back, causing Zara to jump. "If we're going to judge hair, don't forget to point out that yours looks like you just came out of a hurricane!"

Whip's face turned from a fair complexion to crimson red. He pushed past the twins to stand facing Drew, his hands clenched. "You cut yours like a boy!"

"Yours is so long someone could mistake you for a girl!" Drew retorted.

The twins were looking over their shoulders at the two with worried expressions on their faces. Denise was covering her mouth to stifle a laugh while Zara and Gene bit their lips to not let anyone see that they were smiling. Neil, Deke, and Seraphina were just staring at the two nine year olds going head to head.

Whip grinned mischievously as another retort rose into his mind. "It's a shame people would mistake you for a boy but not realize that you wouldn't even be able to take care of yourself."

With that, Whip took a step backwards, so he was slightly hidden behind Reed. Drew's face burned red and she rolled up her right sleeve as if threatening to beat him up.

"Oh, really, you half-pint scarecrow!?"

"Yeah, really," Whip added, preparing to say more.

Luckily for Whip, Neil felt that it was about time someone stepped in. From the look of things, they would be going at it with their fists within the next three minutes.

"Okay, you panthers, cool it off," he remarked, placing a hand on each of their shoulders. "Whip, I'm sure you and the twins had better head over to SOHE. I think they'll be discussing roles shortly. Seraphina, you and Gene had better go too, since you'll be helping. Denise, if you could help Zara show Drew around and maybe you three could go visit the bargemen, that would be great. Oliver and I are going to help Deke pack."

* * * * *

"All right, everyone," Quintin called out loudly in his high-pitched voice, pushing his huge spectacles back onto his long pointy nose. "Let's try the confident strike."

Neil glanced up from the notepad in his hand. He was carefully observing everyone's movements and reactions to each of Quintin Quaker's calls. Neil never understood why someone who seemed so elusive as Quintin would have been chosen as the Suppression of Physicality teacher. That class was what Viggo Walker believed to be the most important of all the classes at SOHE.

Neil watched as half of the students strode across the room toward the other half. The first half were pretending to be humans approaching a group of concealed changelings. The other half had to control their desires to worry about being revealed and act calm and submissive. The "human" half also had to aggravate the other half so that they could practice patience and concealment through mentality. Neil grinned when he saw that Vivian had the whole confident strike down pat while Zara was itching to just pounce one of the "humans" who was pushing her patience.

The boy scribbled down some notes before realizing that Gene was not part of either group. He was sitting on a bench near the door, watching the whole scene that was occurring in Steeple Hall. Picking himself up, Neil made his way over to his brother and sat down beside him.

"What's on your mind?"

"You don't want to know," Gene remarked. "Or all your brain files would be full and overflowing."

Neil grinned as he continued to watch the other students. "So did Mr. Walker give you a job?"

Gene nodded. "He did: decoration . . . But that's not what's on my mind. It's Quintin Quaker."

"Anyone would get tired of watching him push his glasses back on his nose. I think he needs a smaller pair," Neil mused aloud.

"It's not that," Gene objected, almost snappish. "He doesn't speak for himself! He says everything that Iris Opal tells him to!"

Neil could right away tell that the mood of the conversation had turned from bored to aggravated. Iris Opal was the new headmistress of SOHE who had joined a year earlier. She had an iron fist and wasn't afraid of keeping everyone on close tabs. If anyone missed a day without having a reasonable alibi, she would literally sue! However, Neil felt that Gene's aggravation toward the woman wasn't that.

"Everything she says, and thinks, is: concealment, concealment, don't let anyone know! For crying out loud! If I had better sense, I would suggest she just have leather stitched to all of our backs and be done with it!" Gene groaned. "I can just hear her speaking through Quintin's words."

"That's pretty deep, man," Neil remarked. "I never see you complain about any classes here."

Gene rolled his eyes. "Except the one that doesn't make any sense! In Robert North's psychological appreciation class, we mentally accept and appreciate our gifts and learn how to use them in useful ways. Mrs. Schneider teaches us aerial development and techniques; Principal Wadsworth has the Substantial Education and Progression and then there's the Individual Derivation Ancestry class with Mrs. Keith . . . but this class doesn't fit in here!"

Neil laughed. "You should tell more people about it. From the look of things, half of the students have lost their nerves trying to hide behind their shirts. I feel bad for you aerobeasts. I don't know how you do it."

"It just doesn't make sense, Neil," Gene continued as if Neil hadn't spoken. "If we hadn't used our gifts three years ago, Emma and the rest would be dead and Hichester would probably be attacked by underbeasts. We didn't accomplish anything by concealing who we really are!"

"And what exactly are we, Gene?" Neil inquired in a soft voice.

Gene slowly looked back at his brother. He was prepared to answer when Quintin let out a shrill cry which announced that the class was over and now it was on to Rana Keith and the Individual Derivation.

Chapter 6

"You guys didn't have to come and help me pack," Deke pointed out from his bed.

Neil nodded as he handed his brother a pile of pants. "I know, but I got the feeling you were kinda let down."

Oliver grinned in agreement as he folded several pairs of socks and brought them to Deke.

Deke took the pants and socks, tossed them in the trunk then slumped on his bed. "I just . . . I don't understand why my dad never expressed any interest in me until now."

Neil raised an eyebrow. "I wouldn't say that, Deke. He might have not known where you were . . . or that you even existed. No one knows what happened between Mom and your dad . . . the only one who possibly knows is your dad."

"You're coming, right?" Deke inquired, sudden fear glinting in his eyes.

Neil grinned. "I wouldn't miss it for the world."

Deke smiled as his small multicolored cat, Dusty, climbed onto his lap. "I also feel guilty . . . guilty that we're leaving Gene all alone here with Whip and the twins."

"We're taking Eileen and Denise with us," Neil pointed out. "That will give him two less people to worry about."

Deke gave his brother a pathetic stare, which told Neil that he didn't find it funny. "You know what I mean. Gene just turned nine and he has all these responsibilities on his shoulders. Shouldn't we be supporting him more? Isn't that what brothers are for?"

Neil smiled, sitting down on the other side of the trunk. "Deke, if it was too much work for Gene, he would let people know. He was able to participate in a full school rescue mission when we saved Emma three years back. If it wasn't too much work for him at six years, this will be a breeze."

"I just don't want him to feel left out—"

Neil quickly interrupted him with a scoff. "Deke, that boy is never bored a day in his life! The twins and Whip will keep him busy, and Zara, Seraphina, and the rest of the gang will be here to help him. It's not like he'll starve! Cook, Phillipa, and Macaroon will be here too. Besides, he doesn't need your talent in the kitchen. You can barely boil water!"

Deke was brought out of his gloom almost immediately. "I can boil water! It's just when it starts bubbling, I lose control."

"Right, like the time you heated cereal on the stove because you thought it was soup," Neil remarked, half to himself.

"I will have you know that the virtuosity of cuisine is not my region of proficiency, but the datum of the complication is that it isn't yours either," Deke snapped.

Silence followed that was probably too quiet to even be silence. Neil immediately turned to Oliver, who had been watching the scene with a grin.

"The Catasbanian translation, Oliver?"

"Cooking isn't either of your area of expertise."

* * * * *

Gene suddenly became aware that a head was peering over his shoulder. Slowly glancing up from his notepad, he saw Jerry Wadsworth looking at him from the desk next to him. Jerry Wadsworth was Principal Wadsworth's fourteen-year-old son and someone that Gene had grown to admire.

One of the strongest and most practical of the society members, Jerry was a perfect woodpecker aerobeast. Bright red hair slicked back smoothly on his pale face, the boy always wore dark cloths to match his changeling gift. Jerry was not a bad-looking boy with shockingly black eyes that darted back and forth with extreme curiosity.

"What are you working on?" Jerry whispered.

Gene glanced down at the students below them. This was one of Gene's favorite classrooms in the whole society. They were at present waiting for Mrs. Keith to return from the bathroom before they continued their classes on changeling ancestry.

In the Mt. Kyvers hall, all the classrooms were the same. With glass floors and glass ceilings, the kids could see into the classrooms above and below them. However, in being on the first floor, all they could see was the water below the building. The desks were, needless to say, peculiar.

A huge iron tree was erected in the center of the room with small niches in the trunk so that one could climb up as easy as climbing a staircase. Each branch ended in a large curved almost cuplike fashion where each student would sit comfortably cross-legged and get the feeling of constant weightlessness.

This feeling that the kids experienced every day at four p.m. sharp was just what they needed to lift their spirits and clear their minds before they hurried off to their separate development classes.

Gene glanced down at his notepad which he had drawn from his knapsack. He had scribbled a bunch of words, letters, and definitions that probably only Deke would understand.

"I'm trying to figure out an answer," he whispered back.

Jerry cocked his head to the side, resting his arms and cheek on the side of his levitated seat. "Answer to what?"

"Suppression of Physicality," Gene hissed.

A huge grin appeared on Jerry's face. "That again? You know how many times you have tried to figure out an answer for that?"

Gene looked down at his notepad, then back at Jerry. "I don't know . . . I lost count."

"Fifteen," Jerry hissed. "This will be the sixteenth since Iris Opal joined the clan!"

"That obvious huh?"

Jerry nodded, grinning down at the boy. "And you haven't yet mentioned your encounter with those two underbeasts in the smothering marshes."

"She would kill me if she found out," Gene hissed sharply. "I will only reveal that if I have no other choice. I'm trying to do this professionally."

"Then you should hire Deke," Jerry remarked, a little too loudly.

"He has enough on his mind already," Gene objected. "Now shush and go back to your books! I don't want to get behind on the ancestry quiz like last week and then have to miss Aerial Development."

Jerry nodded in understanding. "Know the feeling. Ever since Quintin Quaker got his own class, we barely get Mrs. Schneider more than three times a week!"

"You're telling me!" Gene remarked. "I'm just glad I learnt how to actually fly before Iris Opal showed up or I would never have learned how to spiral."

"We're doing land navigation and recognition today," Whip whispered from below. "So pay attention!"

Mrs. Keith suddenly reappeared and clapped her hands loudly. Gene always felt small in the presence of Rana Keith. Though she was a petite woman, she held great power both physical and mental. Extremely clever and sharp in replies, no kid in ancestry classes could get in a smart remark without Mrs. Keith having the final word.

Brushing her shortly cropped black hair out of her face, the woman began to consult the huge book before her. Mrs. Keith reminded Gene of a karate fighter. Her short hair framed her pointed, smooth face. Her skin was slightly dark, just barely lighter than Livonia's but had a shimmer to it. She was strongly built, slender with powerful legs, arms and shoulders. Gene wondered why she hadn't been chosen for the Substantial Education and Progression class of Physical Education.

Leaving the book behind on her desk, Mrs. Keith began to walk across the glass floor, considering the children above and about her. The woman was in her late sixties, but you could barely see it to look at her till you heard her speak. Gene wondered what her voice had sounded like when she was young. Probably powerful and full of energy. Now it was croaky and always full of pain.

"Many people believe," she began, "that there is always an ancestor that they can blame or loathe for something that happened in their lives. Can someone give me an example?"

Seraphina's hand shot up and Neil took note of her quick reaction. Neil was always allowed to sit in the classes to act as scribe for the teachers as well as the students.

"Miss Schneider?" Mrs. Keith inquired.

"Everyone believes that Bentley Hichester's heirs would greatly loathe him. Of course, it's only one male from each generation who is plagued with the curse, but many people find that enough reason to blame him for his pride."

Everyone leaned forward, waiting to see what Mrs. Keith would say to that observation. What she did wasn't what anyone expected. Her face turned an unusual paleness for someone with such dark skin and her hands began to shake.

"I guess people would think that . . . Though I doubt that his heirs would blame him . . . if they knew who his children and grandchildren were like . . . ."

The woman slowly shook her head and clapped her hands loudly. "Class is dismissed. Aerobeasts, please report to Mrs. Schneider in the Observatory, merbeasts to the aquarium with Mr. Nielson, and werebeasts to the viaduct with Mrs. Fischer."

Chapter 7

"Just drop that box there, Zara," Gene called from across the room.

Zara set the box down, making note of the "Fragile" sign on the side. Brushing her shoulder length light brown hair out of her eyes, Zara got a good look at the Hall of Organization. The huge open room was on its way to being prepared for the huge Christmas Party that would take place on the evening of Christmas day.

Gene was organizing the large cardboard boxes that were being pulled out of the storage closet from the theater. Several were piled by the door and from the weight of them, they were garland and Christmas lights. The other boxes were slightly heavier and almost all labeled "fragile," indicating that they were tree decorations.

The tree wouldn't be brought in till the next morning since Mr. Schneider, Mr. Wadsworth and several other men had to venture out of Hichester to find a tree.

"So, what's the plan for the week?" Zara inquired in a loud voice since Gene was a good twenty meters away from her.

Gene opened the lid of one box, checked the contents then placed it to the side. "Well we can't decorate the tree till tomorrow, so we'll start on the garland and other decorations first. Tomorrow will be mostly tree decorating . . . then we have to go and prepare the outside . . . we'll save that for Christmas Eve. The rest of the week before then we'll be busy helping Whip with the play."

Zara nodded half-heartedly. The play consisted of four different scenes from the Bible. The first was the Garden of Eden and the fall of man. The second was the story of David and Absalom. Third was the Annunciation and lastly was the Nativity.

Almost every one of the gang members had a role in the play that is except Deke. Deke had tried to audition for some of the parts, but he had horrible stage fright, as did Whip so Deke stepped down and the directing job was given to Whip.

Naturally the twins had the rolls of Adam and Satan, no one knowing which twin played which part while Seraphina played Eve. She was the only girl who was willing to play in the same scene as the twins. Neil and Emma had the rolls of Mary and Joseph, while two other boys would play David and Absalom. Due to the fact that everyone wanted a part, Zara was given the roll of the younger Mary in the Annunciation scene while Gene had the role of Gabriel since he was the only one besides Seraphina who had angel colored hair.

"... But how could this be? I am not yet married ..." Zara muttered to herself.

Gene glanced up from the box he was examining, a smile appearing on his boyish face. "Don't tell me you're having second thoughts on your role."

Zara looked up, not realizing she had spoken aloud. "Oh no ... I was just going over my lines ... have you gotten yours?"

Gene shrugged. "Mostly. I mean, the Annunciation isn't exactly the least known event. I'll wager that everyone here knows it by heart. I'm just concerned about Oliver."

"Why is that?" Zara inquired, pushing her hair behind her ears. "I would think we didn't have to worry about him."

"You do realize that Oliver is playing David and he is supposed to have a pretty lengthy conversation with Eileen about Absalom's death. When have you ever heard Oliver speak that much?" Gene inquired.

Zara thought about that fact. It was true. Eileen had offered to play the male role of Joab since Deke couldn't even get on stage long enough to kill Absalom. Zara wasn't too worried about Eileen. Eileen was shy of course but she wasn't practically mute like Oliver!

"I get your point," Zara mused. "That does pose a problem."

Just at that moment, the hall door flew open and Roy poked his head in. "Yo Gene, we need your help out here!"

Gene looked down at the boxes in his arms. He was halfway through sorting them and Zara could tell he was contemplating telling Roy to get lost. However, knowing Gene, he was fighting that urge.

Setting the boxes down, Gene followed Roy out the door with Zara close behind. Gene made sure he was out of the hall before he expressed his annoyance. "I'm on a schedule here in case you hadn't noticed Roy. What is going on?"

Roy led the two across the gangplank to Steeple Hall where there was a large crowd of SOHE students in a circle. For a moment Gene thought it was another fight and was prepared to break it up when everyone stepped back to let him see.

Lying on the cold, frosted platform was a boy of about fourteen. His bright red hair was crusted in snow and dried blood, his lip was bleeding terribly, and his face was bruised. His eyes were closed, and he was shivering uncontrollably.

Gene recognized him as Jerry! An older boy was just laying a blanket around him when Gene hurried over and fell on the cold platform next to him.

"What happened?" he demanded, feeling the boy's face.

His face was deathly cold, and his lips were turning purple.

"We found him like this on the bank of the lake," the older boy replied. "He was hidden among the reeds and we can't wake him up."

Gene noticed a movement beside him as Zara fell to her knees beside him and grasped the boy's wrist. "He's probably unconscious. He's practically frozen! We need to warm him up slowly, so he doesn't get hypothermia!"

Gene reached a hand under the boy's head and lifted the boy's head off the cold floor. "Can you help me Zara?"

Zara grasped the boy's legs and the two lifted him off the ground. The crowd followed them like a herd of geese while several kids ran ahead to open up the apothecary door.

Livonia was just hanging a wreath above the mantel when the door flew open and half of the SOHE students blew in, shielding Gene and Zara who were carrying Jerry.

"Livonia, we need your help!" Gene cried.

Pushing past the other students, the tall woman carefully guided the two kids to a sofa near the fireplace where they placed the boy gently. Zara sat down beside Jerry's head and began to rub his hands between hers in the attempt to warm them. Gene didn't pause to sit but hurried out of the room, followed closely by the sound of running water.

"There are blankets in the cabinet over there," Livonia called to a nearby girl.

A pile of wool blankets was thrown on the floor beside the couch and Livonia began to wrap the boy.

"We need to get him into warmer clothes fast!"

Gene soon returned, carrying a bucket of steaming hot water. He passed it to Zara as Livonia instructed him to help her carry Jerry to a private room. There were about five less people in the apothecary room, but their disappearance was soon answered by the arrival of the gang.

"What happened?" Seraphina asked the moment they burst in.

"Jerry was found beaten up and hidden in the reeds," several voices replied.

Denise, Seraphina and Drew hurried over to Zara who was waiting outside the door with the hot water. She was giving Gene and Livonia enough time to dress Jerry in warm clothes before she entered.

"I don't know what happened," she whispered. "Gene and I were in the hall organizing when Roy brought the news."

"What can we do?" Neil whispered.

Zara gave a meaningful look over her shoulder and immediately Oliver and Neil took the message. Kindly telling everyone that they would keep them updated, they shooed the crowd of kids out of the apothecary till there was no one else there but the gang and Drew.

The door of the room opened, and Gene appeared. Taking the hot bucket of water from Zara, he ducked back in the room but left the door open. The kids carefully peeked around the corner to see that Jerry was lying beneath a mound of blankets and quilts, color slowly beginning to reappear in his face.

"Seraphina, there you are," Livonia remarked, relief evident in her voice.

Seraphina had been training underneath Livonia in the healing arts, so in a way she was an assistant to Livonia. Slipping into the room with the rest of the gang behind her, Seraphina sat on the other side of Jerry.

She ran her warm hands through his cold icy hair and began to ruffle it gently, trying to melt the ice and snow.

"What do you think happened?"

"He obviously got into a fight," Livonia pointed out. "There are hand and finger marks all over his face and arms. It looks like he hit his head on something hard, causing him to black out. However, from the look of it . . . he might very well be in a coma."

Neil slowly stepped over and placed a strong hand on Jerry's pale one.

"What can we do?"

Livonia shook her head sadly. "Nothing till he wakes up . . . just pray."

"And hope that this doesn't continue," Gene added in a whisper, gaining agreement from the others.

Zara turned slightly at the sound of Gene's voice. There was something in the way he spoke that sounded different. It wasn't pity . . . or worry . . . well the worry was evident in his eyes, but the sound of his voice dripped with fury.

Chapter 8

"Don't forget to write us regularly," Gene added.

Deke raised an eyebrow through the open car window. "It's not like we'll be gone for months! It's just a few days! Besides, you'll be too busy to want letters from us!"

"In that case," Whip remarked, trying to keep the spirit light. "We'll write you often since you'll obviously be too bored to do anything but read letters!"

Neil laughed out loud as he tossed Deke his suitcase. He closed the side door and walked around to enter the other door. Turning slightly, he found Gene standing behind him, a slight look of worry on his face.

Neil grinned as he placed a hand on both his brother's shoulders. "Don't tell me you're going to miss me!"

Gene shook his head. "Nah, like Deke said, we'll be too busy to miss you."

Smiling, Neil gave his brother a quick hug but kept a firm grip on his shoulders. Leaning over so that he was eye level with his brother, Neil could sense something was up.

"What's wrong then?"

Gene shrugged. "Maybe it's just nerves . . . but it feels like things have been too peaceful lately. There hasn't been any underbeast sightings or attacks for three years! I don't know . . . I guess I'm just guessing that they'll choose a perfect time like this to cause trouble."

"I guess it's possible," Neil remarked. "But the more you think about it, the more chances it will happen. Don't let Nohte get in the way of your Christmas spirit brother."

Gene smiled and lifted his eyes to show Neil that he understood. Patting his brother on the back, Neil stepped into the car and pulled the door closed. Gene stepped out of the way and stood between Whip and Seraphina.

Mr. Wetherby put the car in reverse and began to back up as Eileen and Denise stuck their hands out the windows to wave farewell. The black car trudged through the snow, a black glare on the pure white landscape.

For the longest time, Seraphina, Zara, Whip, Deke, the twins, and Oliver just stood there watching the car roll along until it disappeared around the first bend. Slowly the kids made their way toward bay 93.4. It was the only bay open during the holidays since the river was frozen and the bargemen had to bring out the bobsleigh. Either that or you had to ice skate back.

"Why don't we drop by and wish Sister Anne a Merry Christmas?" Seraphina suggested, realizing that the silence was one of gloom.

The others agreed without much of a fight and soon they were stamping their feet free of snow as they rapped on the door of the cabin.

As they stepped inside, the snow began to trickle off their wraps and onto the floor. Three faces looked up from where they had been working over sewing machines.

"Hello there," Sister Anne called. "Just seeing Deke and Neil off?"

Seraphina nodded. "We wanted to warm up before we had to skate back."

"Be my guest," Sister Beatrice remarked, waving a hand toward the glowing fire. "We're just working on the new wraps for next fall."

"You start them this early?" Whip inquired, suddenly intrigued.

The three sisters nodded. "Absolutely! It doesn't just take a month to design new wraps then make them especially since we have to make some hundred or so."

Zara let out a shiver as she placed her back against the warm stones of the fireplace. "We were wondering if you have heard from Emma or the Nielsons."

Sister Anne cocked her head to the side. "The Nielsons just went through bay 93.4 after you arrived. You must have missed them . . . we were expecting Emma yesterday, but she hasn't arrived."

At once, several heads popped up and exchanged confused looks. Emma was always reliable and was never late. Destiny and Silver had returned two days ago with the news that Emma would be an extra day . . . but they never said she would be another two days!

"That doesn't sound right," Zara pointed out.

Sister Anne nodded. "You're right . . . it doesn't sound right at all."

* * * * *

"Gene Mecarnin," Robert North called from the other end of the platform. "If I could have your full attention sometime this week, it would be wonderful."

Gene quickly stuffed his notebook back into his bag and resorted to listening to Robert. The man was barely twenty-one with a keen desire to show off. The only reason he was placed in the

Psychological Appreciation course was because it limited how much he could show off to the kids younger than him.

"Good," Robert remarked, pretending to take on a Catasbanian accent which made him sound only more ridiculous. "Now would someone like to explain how our knowledge of marine, aerial and land animals would aid us in our lives?"

Several hands shot up, but Robert's eyes were locked on Gene's. Last week he had asked this question and Gene had come back with a stunning remark that it would aid them in understanding certain concepts that underbeasts and other enemies didn't understand. This would give them a greater advantage in a battle. Robert had fairly flown into a rage at the very beginning of Gene's answer and had sent the boy to Mr. Walker's office for ten minutes as punishment.

"Gene," Robert called sharply. "Would you care to answer that question?"

The boy slowly stood up and nodded. "The knowledge of marine, aerial and land animals will aid us in our lives because it far surpasses the usual understanding that humans have of a world that is foreign to them but native to us."

A ripple of giggles followed that only caused Robert North to go redder in the face.

Those were the exact same words Robert had used the week before in reply to Gene's smart remark to the question.

"Well . . . Yes . . . " Robert stammered, clearing his throat loudly. "Now if you'll all take out your notebooks and write down a list of reasons why this knowledge would aid us. Silently please. These notes will help you write up a presentation next week after Christmas."

At once all heads bent over their notebooks. They knew that when they had a paper due and Robert was kind enough to tell them, it was obviously important. Unlike in school, their papers weren't graded or marked wrong. They were carefully diagnosed and either pinned up on the bulletin board in the Hall of Organization or if they had a suggestion, they were taken into consideration.

Robert headed back into the building, leaving the members to their writing in the outdoors. Once he was gone, Gene carefully crawled on hands and knees almost entirely to the front of the group of kids until he was sitting directly behind Oliver.

"Psst, Oliver," the boy hissed. "I need your help with something."

"What about Deke?" the boy inquired, not allowing his pencil to stop.

"Deke already had a lot on his mind," the younger boy whispered back. "What would be a good word for 'group' or 'gang'?"

Oliver's pencil paused a moment on the notepad. "Don't tell me you're thinking of changing the gang's name."

Gene grinned. "No, the twins would revolt. It's for my paper."

Oliver slowly pushed his glasses back onto his nose and considered the remark. The last time they had a paper that was assigned to them by Robert North, Gene had written down a list of knock-knock jokes. That was mostly because the paper had been due on April Fool's. It had taken Robert almost the entire year to get over that embarrassment until recently.

"Well . . . there's assembly, clutch, faction, component, division, element . . ."

"Thanks," Gene hissed, cutting Oliver off halfway through the next word before scuttling back to his place.

Oliver returned to his list but couldn't help but wonder why Gene wanted to know something like that.

Chapter 9

Zara and Seraphina pressed against each other to keep each other warm. The snow was piling up around their ankles as they trudged down the street. They were heading over to visit Destiny and Silver, hoping that Emma had arrived. They had given it another twelve hours before they ventured to check to see if she had gotten in.

"If this snow doesn't stop falling, we'll have to leave our houses through the chimneys," Seraphina panted, shivering. "We can barely open our front door! Rodge can't stand it! He says the snow where he stays never gets this high."

"He'll live with it," Zara panted back.

"Gene just flies around the place instead of walking. That's why he's never late because of snowdrifts like the rest of us. I don't know how he can fly in this weather."

Zara shrugged. "I guess he just has stronger resilience to the cold. His immunity is probably . . ."

Seraphina glanced over at Zara when she didn't continue. Zara was looking around, her eyebrows furrowed down. "What's wrong?"

Zara shook her head. "I don't know . . . I just thought I heard something."

Shaking the thought out of her head, Zara continued to trudge along. However, Seraphina couldn't help but wonder if something had actually been there. And the more she thought about it, the more she felt that strange feeling that something was watching her . . . but what?

The door of the hall of organization blew open and the sound of whirling snow entered the warm room.

"Close the door!" Several voices hollered.

Zara pushed against the door and it slid closed. Seraphina began to unwind the scarf from her face, realizing that it was almost frozen to her cheeks. Light flooded the hall, and everyone was standing by the flights of stairs where the tree was set up.

Seraphina's dad had returned with a huge tree, about fifteen feet tall. It was perfectly shaped with billions of branches and a perfect shaped trunk. A crowd of people were standing around the tree now, attempting to decorate it.

Roy and Reed were halfway up the stairs, fitting ornaments about three fourths up the tree. Oliver was carefully fitting the star on the top by standing on the balcony just above the tip of the tree. Rodge, Vivian and Phillipa were standing on ladders and chairs, trying to reach the empty spaces. Gene was standing off to the side, trying to untangle a pile of tree lights.

"I think you need to put more ornamenth higher Philippa," Reed remarked as he studied the gigantic tree.

Roy made a pitiful look on his face. "We need more snowflakes! A Christmas party will not work without snowflake decorations!"

"Don't forget wooden decorations! They spark up the place," Philippa pointed out as she stood on the top rung of the ladder to reach further up the tree.

Rodge studied the tree out of the corner of his eye and made a confused look. "Most of the ornaments are wooden or cloth, we need more glass and marble ones."

This at once gained him a distressed look from Phillipa who raised the inward ends of her eyebrows in agony. "You get the rainbow ornaments!"

Gene slapped his head and shook his blond hair in exasperation. "So there will be no ordinary decorations?"

There was a long pause in which the decorators studied their work, then the work of each other. "NO!"

Sighing, Gene went back to his lights. Zara and Seraphina stepped over, considering the scene.

"Looks like it's going well," Zara pointed out.

Gene groaned. "I'll be glad when we're done, and Whip will be in charge of the play. Then I won't be the casual observer! They absolutely refused to let me help decorate once I got out the red balls! What happened to classic Christmas decorations?"

Seraphina smiled but there was worry in her eyes. "Gene . . . we just came from Emma's . . . there is no sign of her. The weather is getting really bad and Sister Anne just came down to ask if Emma arrived, but she didn't . . . she didn't even check in at Break Neck yet. There is no sign of her."

Gene looked up from his work and his blue eyes shimmered with concern. "That is so unlike Emma . . . something must have happened."

Seraphina nodded but Zara interrupted the exchange. "That's not all that's wrong Gene. Whip and Drew are on the verge of murdering each other! Drew offered to help Seraphina with the scenery and Whip fairly knocked all the paint cans over because he refuses to work in the same space as her! Then Drew almost tar and feathered him when Macaroon arrived thankfully! We left him to keep an eye on the panthers, but he can't be there forever. Those two need something to happen before they kill each other."

Letting out a distressed sigh, Gene sat down on the bottom step of the stairs. "This is just great. Neil and Deke have barely been gone ten hours and already I've been fired, there are no Christmas lights that aren't tangled, Emma is missing again, and my best friend is preparing to murder someone!"

Zara grinned and decided to lighten the mood. "Maybe you should invest in pest control."

Gene looked up long enough to show that he wasn't amused. "I would agree if there were no lights or missing friends involved."

Seraphina sat down beside Gene and put a hand around his shoulders. "Maybe . . . maybe we should go visit my grandfather Res. He's been through crazy times like these . . . maybe he could help out."

Gene nodded. "I could certainly use the help. Especially advise on how to deal with human pests."

* * * * *

There was another knock at the door, followed by the doorknob jiggling. "Gene . . . if you're in there tell me! My hands are full."

"I'm in here," Gene remarked from his desk.

The door opened this time to admit Eileen. She was balancing a tray that carried two mugs and a plate of cookies. She set the tray down on the end of the desk, a good distance from Gene's pile of papers and notes.

"I brought you some cocoa. Cook demanded that if you didn't want to eat dinner, you had to at least get something in you before bed," Eileen remarked. "And I advise you to eat something. It's almost midnight."

"Yeah," Gene remarked absently. "Sure . . ."

The girl set one of the mugs next to him before taking the other in her hands. She sat down on the chair next to Gene and glanced at the messy pile of papers. "What are you doing anyway?"

"My paper," Gene replied.

Eileen slowly raised one eyebrow suspiciously. "What, did you suddenly decide to become the next Deke Mecarnin? The Gene I know wouldn't spend until midnight writing a paper that is never seriously taken into consideration considering what you did last time Robert gave you an assignment."

"This one is important," Gene remarked.

Eileen was about to ask how it was important when Gene spoke up. "It all makes sense Eileen. I guess no one ever really thought about it this way. But after Christmas I am going to present this paper in a way that will cause people to look at it differently every time."

The girl glanced down at her feet to realize the strange feeling against her leg was Webstar. Webstar was a lovely Shepherd mix that Neil had rescued two years earlier. He had named her Webster, thinking she was a boy. However, a week later Phillipa revealed the dog's true gender so they changed the spelling of her name to W-E-B-S-T-A-R to make it seem more feminine.

Eileen leant over and scratched the dog behind her ears. Webstar had gotten past looking like a skeleton almost three weeks after Neil rescued her. However now, she was starting to look a little overfed.

"Look at what differently?" Eileen inquired softly.

"Changelings," Gene almost cried. "In case you hadn't noticed, not one of the headmasters are changelings."

Eileen held up her finger, about to speak again but Gene already saw it coming. "I know Mrs. Schneider, Mrs. Keith and Mr. Nielson are as close to changelings as humans get but they are always silent on the matter!"

"Gene . . ." Eileen started. "Are you saying that humans are ignorant in the ways of changelings?"

"Of course not," Gene replied, slamming his pencil down. "I'm saying they don't see what's coming."

Eileen furrowed her brow seriously. What was coming? What was causing Gene to suddenly get all riled up? Before she could ask, Gene had placed his mug back on the tray and ushered the girl to the door.

"You know, I think I will hit the hay now," the boy remarked. "Goodnight Eileen."

The girl was just halfway through her reply when Gene closed the door, leaving Eileen standing in the hallway with the tray of cookies and two mugs . . . both still full.

Chapter 10

Gene considered the house cautiously. He had never met Mr. Schneider on more than a few occasions and on those, he felt that there was something about the man to be cautious about. Maybe it was the seriousness in his voice . . . or the pain in his eyes or even the fury that played through the way he moved.

Seraphina slowly took a step forward and grasped Gene's hand. The boy looked up into her smiling eyes and felt his confidence return. Following the girl and Zara up the stairs, Gene brushed the ice from his coat and ruffled his hair which was damp from the snow.

Zara rapped gently on the door and they were greeted by the sound of footsteps as if someone had seen them walk onto the porch and was just standing inches from the door. The knob turned, and the door swung open to reveal the towering figure of Res Schneider.

If Gene ever encountered a person who knew first-hand what pain felt like, he believed that he would look like Res. The man's dark black hair was brushed out of his eyes and fell smoothly against his neck. His dark eyebrows were firm and full of expression. His lips were full but showed no sign of smiling while his nose was rigid and sharp. The man was incredibly handsome for his age, but it was evident that he didn't feel the joy that was spreading through the Hichester air.

"Seraphina," he remarked in his slight Gerhenian accent. "Come on in. It's good to see you, Zara and you, Gene."

The kids slowly ducked into the house as the tall man stepped back. Res reminded Gene incredibly of an older version of Rodge. Of course, Rodge was much younger and had a lighter and more joyful character but the slender, tall build, the proud head and confident features were the same.

Hanging their coats and hats on the hallway hooks, the three treaded silently down the dim lit hallway to the sitting room. Gene had never been inside Res Schneider's house in person, but he had heard descriptions from Whip and Seraphina. True to their word, it was dreary and dim. Everything had dark rustic colors of brown, black, grey and dark crimson. If not for the red, Gene would have thought that it looked like a funeral home. However, with the red it almost gave off a secretive air.

Once the three were seated in armchairs in the sitting room, Gene began to feel himself relax.

Res was quiet, that was obvious and not your usually cheerful and jolly sixty-year-old grandfather type figure. Res began to pour tea into tall red mugs and Gene caught a slight glimpse of gray hairs appearing above Res's ears.

Res didn't exactly look his age. In fact, he looked much younger, but it was evident he carried a burden; not a burden on his face, looks and actions but in his eyes. The burden was there as plain as day.

"So, what brings you three out and about on a day like this?" Res inquired, handing out the mugs of hot tea. "I would think you would be up to your necks in preparations."

Zara and Gene exchanged looks. Res wasn't exactly "in the world" so to speak but he wasn't ignorant of common sense.

"Actually, that's why we came to visit you," Seraphina explained. "We're more over our heads than up to our necks . . . And we thought you might be able to help us . . . at least giving us advise as to how to handle it all."

A twinkle appeared in Res's eyes, but it didn't reach the rest of his face. "For that, you should go to a party planner."

Zara hastily shook her head. "It's not just Christmas preparations sir. Everything is . . . Erupting . . . for lack of a better word."

"It's Whip sir," Gene finally admitted. "He's . . . not really getting along with one of our other friends and it's getting pretty ugly. Besides that, we have to all work together and we can't when he's . . . being him."

Zara actually thought she saw a ghost of a smile light on Res's face. She began to blow silently on her tea but forgot to warn Seraphina that it was hot, and the other girl took a big swig and immediately went pale.

"Well you most certainly can't make Whip stop being himself," Res pointed out. "The least you can do is just find a way you can fix the situation by using Whip's character in the process. Find a balance where Whip can be himself, but he'll be limited on how much he can cause trouble with this other friend. That's what happens many times . . . at least once in everyone's life."

Zara located the pitcher of cream and handed it to Seraphina who poured almost the whole pitcher of cream into her cup and took a quick drink. Immediately Seraphina relaxed and let out a sigh but considered her now white tea in distress.

"Did you ever have that kind of encounter?" Gene inquired, completely ignoring the two girls who were barely paying attention.

A faraway look appeared in Res's eyes as he slowly nodded. "Aye . . . aye Gene I did. That encounter was what made my life what it is now."

Seraphina and Zara looked up from Seraphina's cup, suddenly just hearing the last part. Seraphina had a slight suspicion of what her grandfather was saying since she had heard part of the story, but Zara was clueless.

"What happened?" Zara and Gene asked in unison.

The pained look that lit upon Res's face almost made the two completely regret asking but the man obviously saw their curiosity.

"I was a young man . . . full of life and I lived with my older brother and his family. There was a girl, Alanna, whom I had known for years and was hoping to marry one day. However, Alanna chose another man over me. I was able to live with it for about a year until something happened. Alanna's husband, Sebastian, had a sister by the name of Maria. She was a good woman but wasn't exactly on good terms with her brother Sebastian. One day while Sebastian was off on business, Maria hired someone to inform Alanna that her husband had died. Alanna went into mourning for three weeks but finally Maria encouraged her to remarry as soon as possible and knowing how I felt toward Alanna, she suggested me. Alanna and I were married but it was evident that Alanna still mourned Sebastian. Three days after we were married, Sebastian returned, and Alanna realized that she had been tricked. Thinking that I was part of the whole set-up, Alanna left with Sebastian and I never saw her again."

Seraphina bit her lip. She had heard bits and pieces of that story but the way her grandfather told it, she felt like she was part of the whole story.

"Two years later, Sebastian appeared and presented me with Alanna's only child . . . a boy. She had died in childbirth and the child was about a year old. Sebastian told me that the child was mine and Alanna's from our short time together. He left me with the child and I never saw Sebastian again. I raised the boy, Michael, to the very best of my abilities. When he was about five, I remarried to your grandmother Agnes, Seraphina. Two years later Sebastian the second was born. We named him after Alanna's husband."

Gene's tea hadn't been touched. He was so enraptured in the whole story that he didn't notice Zara pouring some more tea in his already full cup.

Res had lowered his head and his eyes as he told the last part. Now he lifted his eyes to reveal that tears were streaming down the sides of his face. "The diary . . . that Silver gave you Gene. It was where I wrote my songs and compositions. I was a musician back in the day. The only complete song in that journal was the one I wrote for Alanna the day we were married. I almost destroyed that diary after Alanna left . . . but when Sebastian brought Michael . . . I would hear the child singing the song to himself. I never knew if Alanna taught him that song, or if by some miracle, Michael always knew it."

Seraphina set down her milky tea to realize that tears were appearing in her own eyes. Wiping at them with a napkin, she quickly gulped and sniffled back the tears.

"In answer to your question Gene," Res continued. "Maria knew that I cared for Alanna and used it to her own advantage to make Alanna and Sebastian miserable. Sebastian also knew that I would raise Michael to the best of my abilities because of my love for Alanna. Maria used my character for the wrong reasons while Sebastian used them for the right. You just have to find the balance with Whip."

Gene slowly cleared his throat, nodding. "That's . . . . that's exactly what I needed to hear Mr. Schneider . . . . Thank you."

Res smiled just barely and nodded his head to show that he accepted Gene's thanks. However, he saw the look on Gene's face and prepared himself for another question.

"What if . . ." Gene started. "What if I neglected to tell my older brother something purposely because I didn't want him to worry? Would that be justified?"

Res considered this a moment before replying. "It depends on your reasons."

Chapter 11

"You didn't tell Neil what!?" Whip cried.

Gene cringed. Obviously, his day could have been going a whole lot better. "I didn't tell Neil that Webstar is expecting puppies because I didn't want him to get all up tight and try to either take Webstar or stay."

"So, you obviously want Webstar, but you don't want Neil to come home?" Roy inquired from where he and Reed were studying their script.

Gene glowered at the two long enough for them to cringe before looking back at Whip. "I just didn't want Neil to try and lug a pregnant sheep dog with him to Gerh and I didn't want him to remain behind either when Deke dearly needs his support!"

"What I want to know ith if Webthtar will even take care of her pupth once the realizeth that they're half great Dane!" Reed mused.

Seraphina, Zara and Whip all lowered their eyes at Reed. The last thing Gene needed was another thing to worry him. After all, it was kind of the twins' fault that there was this new dilemma. This was because when they went off for a skiing trip two weeks back, they had left their Great Dane, Chopper, with the Mecarnin's since they didn't want to take him along and that's when everything happened.

In truth, none of them could blame Gene for not telling Neil because they knew the boy would have nearly killed the twins, especially once he found out that it was partially their fault for not telling them that Chopper was a boy until they returned. Naturally, none of the brothers had found it disturbing that the twins had forgotten that part in the whole explanation, but once Neil found out what his darling sheepdog was going through, he would find it less disturbing and more infuriating.

"Webstar will have the same urge to stay with her puppies," Seraphina replied, "no matter how different they are in species. Just like a horse who was bred with a donkey and has a cross colt."

Gene gave Seraphina a quick smile, glad that at least that part of the conversation was over. However, Roy raised an eyebrow and looked up from his script. "So who would be the donkey: Webstar or Chopper?"

Zara would have wrung his neck if the theater door hadn't opened and admitted Destiny and Silver, bundled up to their noses and covered in snow.

"Getting worse out there?" Gene inquired.

The two girls nodded as they shook their clothes off and sat down with the others. "We can't stay long. We promised Mr. Walker that we would help clear the snow off of the SOHE platforms. However, we have a message from Mr. Schneider."

Whip and Seraphina lifted their heads, wondering what their dad had to say.

"Your dad wants you to go look for Emma, Whip," Destiny explained. "Lyle will give you a ride to Break Neck but from there you'll have to go on foot. It's getting too crazy out there for cars and until the snow settles, you'll have to look on foot. He wants you to scour the woods around Break Neck and if you find nothing, begin to make your way to the train station. If you can't find her there, figure out if she arrived on any trains the past few days. If nothing, we'll have to wait till the snow's out. That's all we can do till this blizzard settles."

Whip nodded, at least glad to get away from the problems that were arising in Hichester. Just as he was about to rise, Silver spoke up. "Oh and one more thing. He wants you to take someone with you, so you don't get lost as well."

Whip rolled his eyes to heaven, but he knew that it was only logical. He was about to select Oliver or Gene when Destiny spoke up again. "He already chose your partner. He wants you to take Drew."

All heads snapped up and Drew's eyes grew twice as wide as her face. Whip merely stared at the two girls, believing that they were bluffing but then seeing the earnestness, his eyes expanded.

The two pulled their mittens back on and headed back to the door. "See you later!"

And with that, the two girls were gone, leaving Drew and Whip with nothing to do but obey. As the two began to slowly bundle up, the others exchanged worried looks. They waited of course till the two were out the door before speaking.

"Is your dad nuts?" Roy hissed. "They'll murder each other before they even reach Break Neck!"

Seraphina shrugged. "I don't know why he thought that was a good idea. I mean, I told him about Whip's problem with Drew and about Emma's disappearance . . . maybe he wanted to just combine two problems."

"Or he had a good reason," Oliver pointed out. "By putting the two together, he might force them to get along."

Gene nodded and considered the closed door behind them. "I hope so."

* * * * *

"Okay, places everyone please!" Rodge called from the stage.

There was an eruption of shocked shouts and screams as everyone hustled about to get ready. Seraphina cringed from her seat in the back of the theater. Rodge had allowed her to attend rehearsal only because she didn't have anything else to do and also, he was nervous since Gene had put him in charge of the rehearsal at least until Whip returned.

"Can I have the third Wiseman on stage please!?" Rodge hollered toward the back stage, giving the other two Wisemen (Reed and Oliver) aggravated looks.

Roy finally emerged from the back of the stage garbed in an elaborate outfit of purple. Reed and Oliver had managed to gain the golden and green outfits, leaving Roy with the more girlish color much to his chagrin.

Roy skidded to a stop in front of Rodge, readjusting his crooked paper crown. Rodge lowered his eyebrows at the boy long enough to express his annoyance before speaking. "Roy . . . . Where might I ask is your chest? Gold, I presume?"

Glancing quickly at Reed and Oliver, Roy saw that he was indeed the king who brought gold. However, he shrugged innocently. "If I am to play the lead Wiseman, I cannot mess with trifles you know."

Seraphina could see Rodge roll his eyes before groaning. "I might point out that the real Wiseman didn't consider his gift of gold a meager trifle. Besides without it your scene will fall flat."

There was a momentary pause while Roy considered this before realizing the logic: "Oh!"

The boy hurried off and Rodge returned to speaking to Reed and Oliver. After giving them specific advice and once Roy returned, Rodge confiscated their script and stepped to the side. Just as he was about to give the signal to begin, Bobby Clymer poked his head out from the back stage.

"Psst . . . Rodge. Your two busy bees from society have arrived for the decorations," the boy hissed.

Rodge slowly raised an eyebrow. "Busy bees? We're not doing Noah's Ark, no one ordered bees . . . ."

Bobby was about to disappear back stage when Rodge realized what he had said.

"Society? Oh . . . tell them they'll find the boxes in the red cabinet."

Bobby nodded and hurried to relay the news to Zara and Gene who were doubled over in laughter at the joke they had managed to pull on Rodge.

Chapter 12

"Hi dad . . . . Hello father . . . . I'm Deke, hello father . . ."

Neil looked away from the frosted window to look at Deke. The boy was gnawing his lip almost till it bled, his feet fidgeting with the floor of the car. Denise was sitting silently between the two brothers, trying to not take any notice of them.

"What are you doing Deke?" Neil inquired, leaning over to look at his brother.

Deke looked up and shrugged. "Just trying to think of what I'll say when I meet my dad . . . ."

"Don't think too hard about it," Denise advised. "Or we'll be waiting an hour before we get through introductions."

"Just speak from your heart, Deke," Mr. Wetherby suggested from behind the wheel. "Just say the first thing that pops in your head . . . unless it's something rude."

"Like what?" Deke demanded, getting desperate. "It's not every day I meet my true father who also happens to be really important. What do I even do around him? It's not like I can pull out the gears to his clock!"

Mr. Wetherby smiled, remembering the time not long ago when Deke took apart the hallway clock to figure out how it worked. Macaroon had been okay with it, but Cook had gone into a rage.

"Well in my day we um . . . . We . . . we um . . ." Mr. Wetherby started, suddenly losing all train of thought.

"Hunted dinosaurs?" Neil inquired, receiving wide eyed looks from Eileen and Denise.

"That's right," Mr. Wetherby replied, not realizing what Neil had said. "We hunted dinosaurs . . . . What? No, we didn't! I'm not that old Neil!"

The two girls quickly smirked while Neil managed a wide grin. However, Deke didn't seem to get the joke. "Uh . . . isn't that it?"

Mr. Wetherby slammed on the brakes, having not noticed the street sign. "Yes, it is . . . . Thanks Deke. Out we go."

Grabbing their coats and pulling them on, the four kids and one adult filed out of the car onto the snow-covered sidewalk. Slowly lifting their eyes, they looked up at a huge stone town house that stood before them.

Neil could practically hear Deke swallow beside him. Placing a hand on his brother's shoulder, Neil leant over to his ear. "You've got this bud."

When Mr. Wetherby knocked on the door, it was answered by a woman in a crisp blue and white uniform. She took one look at the man and the children before stepping to the side and letting them in. She took their coats and hung them on the wall before leading them down a hallway lined with portraits and candles on the walls.

"The master will be with you shortly," she explained in a thick Gerhenian accent. "I will go fetch him."

She guided them into a sitting room and disappeared. Slowly the kids and Mr. Wetherby took seats on the light brown leather couches. Deke sat on the edge of his, almost afraid to sit down. He admired the clean red carpet, the huge windows and the glass top tables.

Deke's lips began to move as he imagined what he would say. Neil noticed this and draped an arm over his brother's shoulders. "Don't worry bro, everything will be fine."

Deke glanced at the girls and realized that they offered no support. Denise was rolling her eyes, obviously exasperated at why Deke was so worried. Eileen was giving him a look full of pity . . . obviously she felt nervous too. Maybe that was her acute spy skill of disguising what she really felt.

Neil caught this exchange and shook his head. "Honestly Deke. You're eleven years old and you'll conquer this! It's not like you're meeting the king of Catasbanel! You've got it _made_ man."

Deke lowered his eyebrows, finding no comfort in those words. "Underlining certain words in your sentences doesn't automatically elucidate their meaning."

"Would you like me to spell it out?" Denise inquired, slightly fed up with the boy's negative mood.

Deke was about to give her leave to do so when the door opened again, and the maid reappeared. This time, she stepped to the side to admit another person. The five guests rose to their feet and Neil gently pushed Deke slightly forward, but the boy didn't move further than Denise.

Steve Rasmussen entered the room and he was the last person any of the kids expected. Practically a giant, the man towered slightly over Mr. Wetherby. He was built just like Mr. Wetherby, powerful, bulky with huge stature and good six-foot six-inch height. Massive arms and massive hands added to the giant of a man. Dark brown hair was brushed slightly out of his face and was thick and slightly long like Deke's. His eyes were dark brown, almost black.

The man's eyes scanned the faces, landing on Mr. Wetherby. "Chris, so good to see you again."

Mr. Wetherby strode forward and shook the man's hand and gave a polite bow of his head. "It's been a long time."

After shaking each other's hands and exchanging some words, Mr. Wetherby turned and motioned to the children. Eileen and Denise stepped forward first as Mr. Wetherby placed a hand on their shoulders.

"This is my adopted daughter, Eileen. And this is Denise Nielson, you may remember her father."

Steve nodded. "It's a pleasure to meet you girls. I know your father well Miss Neilson. In fact, I may ask you some questions later about him. "

Neil slowly took a step forward and Steve's dark eyes widened. The man didn't say a word so Neil extended his hand for the man to shake. "I'm Neil . . ."

The giant man slowly shook the boy's hand but there was something in his face, the way he stared at Neil that told the boy that he was either shocked, not interested or horrified. Neil took a step backward and turned to Deke.

He gave Deke another nudge and the boy slowly took a step forward. Steve's eyes locked on the small boy and sized him up. His brown hair all over the place, wearing a white starch shirt and dress pants underneath a brown dress coat, Deke looked like he had come out of a whirlwind.

Deke gulped and was about to use Neil's simple introduction for himself when something strange happened. Steve covered the distance between them and scooped the small boy up in a bone-breaking bear hug. Deke could barely breath when he found that he was losing all air and possibly some ribs.

"Hello little man!" Steve Rasmussen roared in a thick Gerhenian accent.

Chapter 13

Gene nudged the door open with his elbow and pushed through, carrying the cardboard box. Zara followed close behind, carrying the small sheepdog in her arms.

"You're sure Deke won't mind?" she inquired as Gene set the box down on the bed.

Gene stuck his hand in the box and drew out a small dog bed. "Of course. Besides, Deke's door already has the kitty lock, so that means that if Webstar needs to get out I won't have to be here to let her out."

True to his word, Deke had created a button on the floor beside his door that was out of the way of people's feet, but he had made it so that it connected to the doorknob so if someone tripped the switch, the door would open. He even went so far as to teach Dusty how to press the button to get out.

"Also," Gene remarked as he began to set up the dog bed in one corner. "It's already covered in animal hair and Webstar will have a roommate."

As if knowing that it meant her, Dusty lifted her head and eyed the three with her green eyes. Seeing that none of them made the move to grab her, she laid her head back down on the bed covers and went back to sleep.

Zara raised her eyebrows, considering the cat. "I would say Deke practically spoils that cat."

Gene nodded. "You don't know the half of it."

He finally finished setting up the dog bed, so Zara set the small dog down in the cocoon of blankets and old pillows. Webstar curled up and buried her face in the blankets, blocking out the noise of chatter.

"Why don't we clean up in here while we're at it?" Zara inquired. "It looks a mess!"

Gene considered the room and realized that Zara was far from wrong. Clothes were scattered all over the floor and the desk. Books from the school year were piled in heaps on the floor below the desk since the desk itself was covered in inventions and tools. The bed was unmade and looked like someone slept in it and then just crawled out without even flattening the blankets.

"Not a bad idea."

The two set about cleaning the room. First of all, they couldn't really turn on the bright light since both Dusty and Webstar were asleep. In that case they just turned on the dim desk light and began to tidy up. They folded all the clean clothes and tossed the dirty ones into the hamper. They lined up his shoes in the closet and piled his books neatly on his desk chair where they wouldn't get stepped on.

Zara set about organizing his tools while Gene tried to make his bed without rousing Dusty. Zara considered the largest invention on the desk. "What exactly does this do?"

Gene looked up from behind a pile of pillows. "Oh that is supposed to be a back massager. He was trying to make it for Dusty, but it was too loud for the cat's liking."

"What are these?" Zara asked after a moment.

She was peering into a cardboard box that was full to the brim with small little contraptions that looked like flashlights.

"Oh, those are pretty cool. Deke made a flashlight that will shine but also has a small pencil on one end, a pocket knife on the other and a screwdriver on the side. He offers one to whoever comes over for a sleepover. You can take one."

Zara considered the box. They were all black colored. Typical. Drawing one out she realized Gene was right. There was a small button on the top that switched on the small penlight. On the other end was a small cap that unscrewed to reveal a freshly sharpened pencil tip. On the side was a small crevice where a knife was situated and on the other side, a larger crevice with a small screwdriver.

The girl heard a protesting yowl as Gene moved Dusty to the other end of the bed so that he could put the pillows back on. Zara was just turning the light off and pocketing the object when Gene spoke up.

"Huh . . . that's odd."

Zara turned around to see that Gene was just placing the pillows on the bed when he had found something. He was holding a small notebook in his hand and considering the front.

Zara hurried over and saw that the front had Deke's name scribbled on the front. Obviously, his journal.

"What's odd?"

Gene set the pillows down and touched the front of the journal. "This . . . I got this journal for Deke two weeks ago . . . but there wasn't this burn mark here."

Zara squinted her eyes in the dim light to see that a large black burn mark covered the whole left side of the journal, covering part of the D of Deke's name.

"That looks too big to be a candle mark," she mused.

"And Deke never uses candles," Gene pointed out. "He only uses flashlights because he is horribly afraid of fires."

Gene was about to place the unopened diary back under the covers, but Zara's curiosity won. She knew Gene wouldn't tread on his brother's private thoughts, but Zara couldn't help it. Deke was never the secretive type, but he went so far as to not tell anyone about a huge burn mark on his brand-new journal and he kept it hidden under his covers. Snatching up the diary, Zara flipped through the pages.

"Hey Zara!" Gene cried. "Deke won't appreciate that!"

Zara ignored him and flipped to the middle of the book. "Deke writes a lot in the course of a few weeks," she remarked.

Considering the pages, she realized that most of them were diagrams that looked strange. Obviously, invention ideas. She flipped further to see that in between every other diagram was what looked like a diary passage.

"This is peculiar," Zara remarked, hurrying over to the light of the desk lamp.

Gene followed and tried to take the diary from her prying eyes, but his own caught sight of what Zara had seen. There was a contraption that looked like a helmet, but it was too large to be a humans from the scale measurements and the shape wouldn't fit a human . . . more like a horse!

"What is that?" he asked.

Zara shrugged. "I don't know but look at this."

She flipped to the previous page to show that both were covered in dates and beside each was a checkmark.

"What is with all those dates?" she asked. "It's not every day or every other day."

Gene considered the page, leaning against Zara's shoulder as he did so. "Well . . . it looks like he puts the date of every seven days . . . wait, this date says December 5th . . . . That was a Wednesday."

"And this one is December 12th, that was a Wednesday too. What does Deke do every Wednesday?" Zara demanded. "And after every date is one word: Aston Ridge . . ."

Gene looked away from the page to try and think. "That is the ridge that separates bargeman village from the river . . . why would he go there? Other than school and society . . . he works up here . . . . No wait . . . every Wednesday Neil and I go to the field to meet you guys, but Deke never comes."

"Are you sure he is always up here when you're gone?" Zara demanded. "After all, Eileen never comes either. Maybe they do something together on Wednesdays."

Gene shook his head. "Whenever I leave, both of them say they're going to stay home. When I get back, they're exactly where I left them."

"Unless they leave the instant you do and time it so that they get back before you," Zara pointed out. "Do you think Phillipa or Macaroon might know?"

The boy shook his head again. "I doubt it. Wednesday is when Phillipa does shopping for Cook and Macaroon has the day to himself. Most of the time he leaves Hichester on Wednesday to visit Break Neck and stuff . . . . But Cook might know."

About two minutes later, Zara and Gene were standing in the kitchen, watching Cook while she chopped carrots for the dinner soup. "What is it you want?" she demanded. "If you're hungry there's prunes in the cabinet."

Gene was very partial to prunes but he was on a mission. "We need to ask you something."

Cook looked up to realize that both were staring hard at her. "Don't look me directly in the eyes. Maybe I'll answer you."

"It's about something Deke might or might not have done," Zara explained.

The knife didn't stop but Cook began to speak. "What might that be?"

"Does Deke leave the house on Wednesdays after I go to the hideout?" Gene inquired.

"Why do you ask?" Cook demanded.

Gene almost wanted to call her bluff. Cook never answered a question with a question unless she had her own suspicions. "Because he always says he doesn't, but I get the feeling he does."

"He might," Cook remarked, moving more carrots onto the cutting board. "He and Eileen head out about five minutes after you leave. I don't see them for a good hour just before you get back."

"When did this start?" Zara inquired, remembering that the first date in Deke's diary was the first Wednesday after he got the diary.

"Oh, several months ago," Cook replied. "Quite a while ago actually . . . almost a year. The first time they left they were in kinda a hurry. It was a Tuesday though, so I went up to get the laundry. Eileen's room was a perfect mess! Clothes were everywhere, and the bed looked like it had been shredded by a dog!"

Zara and Gene exchanged looks. Eileen was very neat, and her room was always spotless, especially on Tuesdays which was laundry day.

Also, Webstar couldn't have shredded the bed because she was always in Neil's room or out in the back yard and Eileen always had her door locked.

"Anything else?" Zara inquired.

Cook shook her head. "I did find a burn mark on the floor. I guess she must have set a candle on the floor or something."

Immediately Zara saw Gene's eyes grow wide. "They didn't . . . did they?"

"Of course, they did," Cook remarked, scraping carrots into the pot then stopped. "Wait . . . what did they do?"

However, when she looked up, the two were gone.

Chapter 14

"You know, when it comes to privacy, you're not much better than me," Zara pointed out. "This is like breaking into a bank."

Gene raised his head long enough to give her a grin. "Eileen's room isn't a vault, though she locks it like it is."

Gene turned back to the key he was trying to turn. All of the bedroom doors had a spare which hung downstairs in Mr. Wetherby's office. After pretty much breaking and entering the office, the two had found the key to Eileen's room but the door wouldn't open.

"She might have put an eye and hook on the door so people like you couldn't break in," Zara pointed out.

The boy looked up from the keyhole and grinned. "Thanks for letting me know."

With that, he reached into his pocket and drew out one of Deke's flashlight contraptions. Pulling out the pocket knife, he wedged the blade into the crack between the doorframe and the door. Slowly sliding it from the bottom up, he listened carefully. Presently, he heard a little jingle and something small bouncing against the door.

"Bingo!"

He turned the doorknob and pushed into the room. Zara followed cautiously and switched on the light. It was as clean as a pin with books piled neatly on her desk, all the clothes put away, her backpack hanging on a hook on the wall and the books on her shelf in alphabetical order.

The bed was made and there was a small note on the pillow. Taking a quick look at it, Zara saw that it was a reminder for Cook to not wash her favorite blue blouse with the other light clothes, so it wouldn't bleach out.

"What exactly are we looking for?" Zara inquired.

"This," Gene announced, emerging from the closet carrying a knapsack.

Stuffing his hand inside he began to fish around. "Eileen told you about that egg her father placed in her care, right?"

Zara nodded. "Very confidential information. She only told Denise and Seraphina as well. She swore us to secrecy."

"Well," Gene remarked. "This is where she always kept it . . . and there is no other place it could be . . . . But it's not in here!"

Turning the knapsack over, Gene shook the contents onto the bed. Old rags and scarfs fell onto the bed. Just when Gene was about to stop shaking the bag, something small and hard fell out. The two bent over it like it was a gold nugget.

"What is that?" Zara inquired, lowering her eyebrows in concentration. "It looks like a piece of pottery."

Gene picked it up and ran it over in his fingers. "No . . . it's too thin and fragile to be pottery . . . . It's an egg shell."

* * * * *

"They jutht left the other day," Reed pointed out. "I don't think they really want a letter from you Roy."

His twin shrugged as he pushed the door of the post office open. The little bell above the door jingled as the twins stepped out of the snow. Shaking snow off their boots and swinging their arms to warm themselves, the two closed the door.

The snow had finally stopped falling and lay almost to their knees. Everyone was busy shoveling snow off the roads and the platforms at SOHE. It truly looked like a winter wonderland.

"A lot has happened in the past two days," Roy pointed out. "It's best to keep them updated so they don't worry."

Hurrying over to the counter, Roy poked his nose over the side to see that Mr. Chester was on duty. Peering over his glasses at the boy, Mr. Chester set down his notebook.

"Excuse me," Roy remarked. "I can't see over the side of the counter!"

It was true. Roy and Reed were not exactly the tallest ten-year olds in town. In fact, they were incredibly short and were only slightly taller than Zara. The post office counter wasn't the lowest either since only parents really came to mail something.

"Oh hi," Mr. Chester remarked, leaning over so the boy could at least see his face. "What do you need?"

"I want to mail this letter," Roy announced, handing him a letter that was wrinkled, and all beaten up from being in his coat pocket.

"Who is it to?" Mr. Chester inquired.

"I don't know, find out," Roy suggested, causing his twin to roll his eyes.

"Well how can I mail it without knowing who it's to?" Mr. Chester inquired, pointing out that there was no forwarding name on the envelope.

Grumbling, Roy quickly scribbled the name on the envelope and handed it back to the man. The man looked over his glasses at the name, then back at Roy.

"It's to Neil?"

Roy nodded. Mr. Chester spun in his chair and grabbed a stamp. "Well, that won't be hard. Everyone knows Neil."

"Alright, can you please mail it?" Roy demanded, starting to get impatient since he needed to use the outhouse.

"Let me get my checkbook," Mr. Chester replied, getting impatient as well.

Roy's eyebrows shot up and he bounced up to see over the counter. "No just mail it!"

"You need to pay to mail it," Mr. Chester explained, returning to the counter.

Reed allowed a smile to appear on his face as his brother gulped. "What? I didn't bring any money with me! Here . . . ." Reaching over to his brother and pulling a hair from his brother's head. "Here is a royal hair!"

Mr. Chester scrunched his nose as Roy held the black hair out to his face. "It smells like fish oil."

This guy would fit in with Whip, Reed thought to himself.

"I had fish sticks this morning."

"Why would I take a hair?" Mr. Chester inquired, beginning to warm up to the kid.

Roy's eyes widened as if the man had just asked who George Washington was. "I'm a friend of a royal family! I am the Roy!"

"Roy?" Mr. Chester inquired, deciding to play along with the game. "The Roy?"

Reed's eyebrows shot up in confusion but realized that Mr. Chester was smiling mischievously. Reed smiled as well, realizing that Roy was falling right into a good prank.

"Yeah!" Roy replied impatiently. "Just mail it! Wait . . . . THE Roy? People know about me? Ooh! Tell people I dropped by so they will come looking for me. I'll put a bounty on my head, so they'll come from afar as well . . . that will be interested . . . . Just mail the letter!"

"Alright," Mr. Chester remarked, placing the letter in an already overflowing box and stapling the lid shut.

"No wait I want to write something on the envelope!" Roy squealed.

Mr. Chester grinned. "Sorry, it's already in the box."

"OH!" Roy groaned, letting out a pitiful groan that sounded like a goose.

When the twins exited the post office, Roy was in a worse mood than Reed was daily.

"What a rip off," Roy groaned. "I forgot to mention that Emma was missing!"

"That'th the biggetht part and you forgot that?" Reed inquired.

Roy nodded. "It was already five pages long."

His twin raised an eyebrow. "What could you have to thay that would take five pageth?"

"Well I used the first three pages to tell about Whip and Drew's problem and that Webstar is having puppies and Gene is losing his mind . . ."

"What about the latht two pageth?"

Roy considered the question before remembering. "Those were spent expressing my deep wish that they'll return happy and healthy."

"That took two whole pageth?"

"Two pages and five sticky notes. I was running out of room," Roy replied. "What?"

Reed had been looking at his brother with a peculiar look on his face which was a mixture of confusion, amusement and surprise. "You really have problemth! Though I can't thay that the whole letter thing wath ath bad ath mailing it!"

Roy bit his lip. "Was it really bad?"

Reed nodded. "I thought Mr. Chethter wath going to burtht to bloodvethel."

"Was it as bad as the time I put salt on a homeless snail and put it in Denise's tea cup?" Roy inquired.

114

Reed grinned, remembering how Roy hadn't been invited to Denise's next birthday party (or any birthday party for that matter) after that. "I think it wath ath bad ath the time you exploded the refectory when you lit a flammable liquid and then thaid that it wath a fire-breathing tarantula that had laid eggth in your bed and ath punishment you had fed it an onion which cauthed itth gall bladder to shrink and explode."

Roy grinned, remembering that day which had been exactly three days after he had promised not to cause any problems during dinner hour at society. "That one never worked well."

"Well you had better think of a better excuthe for your bad mood," Reed remarked. "Becauthe here cometh Zara and Gene."

Roy looked up just as the two skidded to a stop in front of them. "Hey there people," Roy greeted but didn't get far when Zara stuffed a handful of letters into his hands.

"Get those to all the gang members," Zara instructed. "Tell them to meet us as soon as possible!"

"Where do we meet you?" Reed demanded as the two spun on their heels and disappeared as soon as they had appeared.

Gene turned to call over his shoulder. "The notes will say! No time to lose!"

Chapter 15

"Alright from the top," Rodge called, raising his hands to the small group of singers.

Seraphina was jolted from her sleep when the theater was filled with chorus singing. She relaxed once she realized that the fire alarm hadn't gone off.

She did however see Bobby Clymer reappear from backstage and whisper something to Rodge.

"Your two busy bees have sent two stray lambs from Fischer with an urgent message," Bobby whispered.

Rodge slowly rolled his eyes, almost fed up with Bobby interrupted rehearsals. "Fischer? Oh great!"

When the boy arrived in backstage, he found Roy and Reed standing there with peculiar looks on their faces.

"What in the world are you two doing back here?" Rodge demanded. "I thought I told you to take the day off, so we could clean up your last mess before you made another one!"

"It's important," Roy pointed out.

Rodge groaned. "Of all that is good on this earth. We're halfway through the David and Absalom rehearsal. The Israelites will be here soon to put their clothes on!"

"We have urgent letterth from Gene and Zara," Reed interrupted.

"For the last time . . . ." Rodge started but froze. "Urgent letters? What happened?"

"We don't know," both twins replied. "They gave us letters to give to you and then left in a hurry."

They handed the letter that had been written to Rodge who quickly tore it open and read the letter in a heartbeat.

"Go and grab the bobsled," Rodge instructed urgently. "Whip left it behind our house. If you run into any of the other gang members, tell them to meet us at the bargeman village and Bobby, tell Seraphina I need her!"

* * * * *

"You know Deke, this isn't too bad once you think about it," Neil remarked, squinting to take aim with his pool pole.

Deke was leaning on his pole, not really concentrating on the pool game, giving Neil a better chance to win. "I just find it unnerving is all! My dad and our mom divorced after I was born for a reason that my dad won't tell me. I mean, dad was all kind and jolly during lunch, but he refused to explain the most complicated part about why my mom split up with him! Besides that, he hasn't mentioned how he found me or why he didn't visit me before this."

Neil looked up from his pole for a second to give his brother a grin. "Maybe you're thinking too hard about it. Maybe it's a personal grown up matter and he wants you to be older before he tells you. You know, marriage is something neither of us knows about very well yet. I don't have any wish to know much about it until I'm twenty anyway!"

The boy went back to studying his aim just as Eileen and Denise came hurrying through the door to him. The two had been admiring the library not two seconds ago and from the looks on their faces, they had something ridiculous or extremely important to say. They were practically bouncing on their feet like they had to use the restroom.

"I don't care what it is about, but I will finish this game," Neil remarked without raising his eyes.

The two girls stood there, perfectly content on waiting but at last the urge was so great that Neil stood up and groaned. "Oh come on, out with it!"

Both girls started talking at once which caused the two boys to frown. What could be so important that Denise and Eileen, who were usually serious and quiet, were pretty much exploding.

"We just overheard Mr. Wetherby and your dad talking about how Deke seems a little aloof and kind of nervous around your dad. Mr. Wetherby suggested you spend the whole day with your dad tomorrow while the three of us keep ourselves busy," Eileen explained. "He said that he thinks it might relieve some of the tension and nervousness."

"Uh, I just found out that my dad isn't Neil and Gene's dad and he isn't the person I expected. I also find out that he knew of my existence but never tried to find me till now and I have millions of questions he won't answer. Why wouldn't I act aloof?" Deke snapped.

Denise shrugged. "I guess they know that, so they want to help relieve some of it for both of you. But there's another thing . . . Eileen just realized something that never dawned on us."

"And what might that be?" Neil inquired, realizing that this conversation wasn't enough to keep him from his game and returned to aiming.

"Didn't you find it strange that Deke is younger than you Neil, but you have different parents? How could Mr. Rasmussen and your mom have Deke, then your mom marries Frank Mecarnin and have you and Gene if you are older than Deke?" Denise inquired.

Neil had just taken a strike but missed the ball entirely when he absorbed the question. He looked up to see both the girls looking at him as if expecting him to have the answer. In truth, that had never dawned on him and now he thought of it, there was a question waiting . . . how could he be Deke's older brother if Deke's father wasn't Gene and Neil's?

Chapter 16

"Watch out for that catch," Zara called back.

Gene quickly swerved on his skates to avoid a chunk of ice that would have surely caused him to fall face first on the ice. Once he got back to his steady sprint, he saw that Zara's pace was beginning to lag as the hill began to level out and their endurance began to wear off.

"What if they refuse to tell us?" Gene demanded.

Zara shook her head. "We were able to convince Cook to tell us. We can surely convince Lyle and the rest to tell us. Besides, we have Deke's password."

Gene's mind raced back to earlier just after they found the egg shells in Eileen's room. They had gone back to Deke's journal to find out that one of the first date entries he mentioned going to the bargeman village and there was small handwriting in one corner in Gerhenian which Gene had deciphered as: Password: Just scouting the area.

"It may have nothing to do with the bargemen," Gene pointed out. "He might have just swung by the village that particular Wednesday."

Zara didn't stop skating but flapped her arms to keep them warm. "Well, it's the only mention other than dates and diagrams in that whole journal! We might as well find out what we can. If nothing comes of this, the gang will be ready to help us ask around town. Someone had to see Eileen and Deke at least one Wednesday. Cook said it's been going on for almost a year. Someone was bound to see them."

Gene considered that and was prepared to agree in word when he thought he heard something . . . something that sounded increasingly like the crunch of snow. Yet again, it might have just been a small animal or the sound of his skates. However, he couldn't help but notice that the hair was standing up on the back of his neck. Not knowing why, Gene opened his eyes wider and began to scan the area for any peculiar movement.

His uncanny bird aerobeast sense of danger was one that Gene had grown to appreciate the past few years and he never took for granted. Even if he didn't see or know of any danger, he respected the fact that his unique changeling senses picked up things long before his human senses did.

Gene's eyes scanned the rolling white hills . . . nothing. He looked back ahead at Zara who was about six feet in front of him. He looked back at the ice to make sure he wasn't about to trip over a chink when he caught sight of what looked like a water glare on the ice. However, as his keen blue eyes squinted at the shape . . . he realized that it was moving at an incredible speed toward Zara and had more of a definite shape than just a water glare.

That was when it dawned on him. Gene's eyes flashed up and his voice cracked loudly the moment his eyes caught sight of the danger. "Zara look out!"

It was too late. As Zara tried to brake and turn to see what Gene was calling about, a black shape appeared from the sky at incredible speed and slammed into her shoulder, knocking her clear off her feet. Zara's wings were pinned beneath her coat, so she couldn't regain her balance easily but catapulted toward Gene.

The moment Gene's senses began to become more alert, Gene had loosened the zipper on his coat just in case and the moment his eyes caught sight of the dark shape, he had thrown his coat off to release his wings.

Gene's eyes didn't miss a thing as Zara came flying at him, head over heels with no way of regaining her feet in time. Gene leapt into the air the moment she would have struck him and grabbed her hand as he took off.

By catching her hand, Gene slowed her fall enough for her to regain her feet as she skidded to a kneeling position on the ice. Gene released her hand because he knew that in a fight, your opponent doesn't wait for you to catch up. The black figure was almost on him now, but Gene wrapped his wings around his body and spun, kicking his foot free and striking the attacker's thigh with his boot.

The attacker crashed toward the ice but saw that Gene had been caught off guard by his foot naturally reacting. The boy had lost control of his flight and had landed on his knees slightly to the right of the attacker in the snow.

Zara had been watching the two fall and now had a perfect glimpse of their attacker. Dressed from head to foot in black, the attacker didn't look very tall . . . barely a few inches taller than Gene. Nothing of his face showed except the golden eyes that stared out from behind dark rimmed lids. The attacker had no weapon and wore black leather gloves. For a moment Zara thought he was a ninja but taking one good look at the jet black, nasty looking wings, she knew he must be an underbeast.

As the creature lifted his wings, Zara realized that the attacker's left wing seemed disabled because it hung limp and he didn't try to fly. Gene must have sprained it when he knocked him from the sky.

The attacker rose to his feet and seeing that Gene was slightly busy getting untangled from himself, began to approach Zara. The girl hadn't had time to recover since it had taken just two seconds for Gene to warn her and the whole scene to happen. Her wings weren't free, and she had no way to defend herself against this attacker who looked twice as strong as her and was a good half head taller.

Deciding that she had nothing to lose, Zara reached up and began to unzip her jacket as fast as she could, but it wasn't fast enough. The attacker was on her and reaching back a hand to strike when something struck Zara, knocking her out of the way and onto her side.

Someone was on Zara and as she turned her face to the side, she saw that Gene was lying on top of her, his wings spread out and almost protectively shielding her while he looked over his shoulder. Zara peered around Gene's golden wings to see that the attacker had been knocked to his back when Gene's wings struck him in the face.

He was now rising to his feet and reaching to his belt. Zara thought she could feel the blood begin to boil in Gene and his body tensed. She felt like a single muscle was on top of her because the boy tensed so much, lines appeared on his forehead and his jaws.

Wrapping his arms around Zara, Gene leapt to his feet in a single motion and took three powerful leaps, practically dragging Zara in front of him. As they leapt into the air, Zara's ears drummed with the incredibly loud sound of Gene's wings pounding.

She had never seen Gene move this fast or with this much ferocity. It was like all the hate, love, joy and sorrow in Gene's body was erupting through every beat of his wings. Within seconds they were out of reach of the attacker and flying at incredible speed back toward the town.

"What are you doing?" Zara demanded. "He'll follow us!"

"No, he won't!" Gene yelled, almost breaking Zara's eardrums. "He's a suicide attacker!"

Zara furrowed her brow. "What does that mean?"

Gene's turquoise eyes met her dark blue ones and Zara could see a series of tangled and twisted fear in the boy's eyes. "He is going to kill himself in the attempt to kill us!"

"How do you know?" Zara demanded.

After all, Gene had barely given the guy two seconds to even recover from getting hit in the jaw by a pair of wings. In fact, they had barely been in his presence more than half a minute and had just left him behind about eighteen seconds ago.

"Because that was a bomb he was grabbing!" Gene yelled just as a louder noise erupted.

Zara couldn't see back the way they had come but the sudden gust of wind that knocked at them and the horrid explosion noise was enough to tell her that she had just narrowly escaped being eliminated from the world.

The after wave from the explosion was too much for even Gene's well-muscled wings to fight and the two found themselves hurling from the sky toward the snow below. They landed feather light in the snow, but the wind was knocked out of them as ashes fell from the sky and sprinkled the white ground about them.

Chapter 17

Deke opened the door of the bedroom where he had been for his stay in Gerh. It was across the hallway from Neil and down the hallway from Denise and Eileen which was great, so he didn't feel out of place. However, as he stepped out to find that it wasn't as stone silent as usual, he felt uncomfortable.

Heading down the hallway, the sound that had been coming from the first floor grew louder. Deke placed his hand on the large railing of the long staircase. The staircase had three short flights that turned so the railing made a decently large spiral.

When they had first arrived, Denise and Neil had charged up the stairs to try sliding down the railing. Eileen had watched with calm silence while Deke had watched with amazement and admiration. Watching the two zip down made it look so easy but when he had tried himself, he had thought that the railing looked a little too narrow and long.

Deke considered the empty stairs and the long railing. The sound of voices from below were enticing and helped cover up Deke's concern.

Laying on his stomach over the railing Deke pushed off from the top step and went sliding down. For the first few feet he went slow but as he neared the curve, he sped up. He was glad that the bottom of the railing ended in a downward curl or he would have hit his side hard.

He came sailing off the railing and stumbled to catch his footing. When he got his footing and looked up, he saw a maid and butler watching him with amused looks. Deke managed a sheepish smile and waved.

"Just between us master," the butler remarked. "I have tried that myself."

Deke felt his nervousness disappear and he smiled brighter. "You don't have to call me master. Deke is fine."

The butler and maid's eyes widened as if afraid to use Deke's name. That was when Deke realized that the two were grasping boxes and suitcases. Glancing around the two, Deke saw that there were other piles of boxes and suitcases down the hallway.

"What is going on?" he inquired.

The maid's eyes lit up. "You didn't know? The master has ordered the return to Hanalona. He only came here to Gerh to welcome you."

"Hanalona?" Deke asked. "What is that?"

Again, the maid and butler's eyes expanded which caused Deke to frown. "I am surprised that your father never told you sir," the butler remarked. "Hanalona is your father's estate. This is just the house he rented for the two days that he was waiting for you."

Deke raised his eyebrows. "You mean father is not from Gerh?"

The maid smiled. "He was born and has lived in Gerhenia his whole life. He is pure Gerhenian. He just came here to fetch you personally. He wishes you to come home to Hanalona as soon as possible."

"Oh," Deke said, deciding to end it there. "Does that mean my friends will be returning to Hichester sooner than planned?"

"Not at all," a voice remarked from behind him.

Everyone turned as Mr. Wetherby strode down the hallway toward Deke. "You and Denise will be going with your father to Hanalona for the rest of your vacation. Neil, Eileen and I have other arrangements."

"Are you three returning home?" Deke asked, suddenly afraid of losing his two supporters.

Mr. Wetherby smiled. "Au contraire. I have a friend here in Gerh that I have agreed to visit during our stay here. We'll meet you back in Hichester before Christmas."

Deke quickly swallowed the saliva that was building in his mouth. He felt a shiver run down his spine but shook it off. He was going to be strong . . . even if it took all of him.

*　*　*　*　*

Zara's eyes cracked open. The world swam before her blearily. *This must be what Deke sees without his goggles*, she thought. Slowly, the dark shapes before her began to take more definite shape and stopped shaking. The closest shape was the head of Seraphina who was sitting either beside or behind her, supporting her in a sitting position.

Other shapes became obvious: Destiny, Silver . . . Oliver. Oliver's back was to her and it looked like he was kneeling over someone. Gene! Zara's eyes flew open and she tried to sit up, but her head racked in protest. She fell back limp against Seraphina's supporting arm.

"What happened?" she asked groggily.

"The twins delivered the messages and we started for the bargeman village. We were almost there when we saw the explosion and found you two. You were kinda out of it for a moment,"

Destiny explained seriously. "What was that bang all about?"

"A suicidal bomber," Zara groaned. "Gene saw it coming . . . . Where is Gene?"

"He's okay," Seraphina replied. "Oliver's got him taken care of. Rodge has gone to fetch a bobsled. We'll get you two back soon."

"What is a suicidal bomber doing in Hichester?" Silver demanded. "I thought the war was over."

"Well there is still crime in the world Sil," Seraphina pointed out. "What I would like to know is why he was after you two."

Zara sat up slowly and rubbed her head. Seraphina backed up a bit to give her air. "He was an underbeast . . . or an aerobeast of some kind. His wings looked like crow . . . or buzzard. I barely got a glimpse of him. It all happened so fast, but he was fast . . . and strong."

"Well he's gone now," Destiny sighed. "Even if he wasn't a suicidal bomber, Gene said his wing looked sprained, so he couldn't have gotten away fast enough even if he wanted to."

"Zara?" a voice inquired from a distance.

Everyone looked over their shoulders as Oliver stepped to the side and Gene limped over. There was a cut on his forehead, but the blood had dried. The boy stumbled over to Zara and fell down in the snow in front of her.

"Are you alright?" he asked.

Zara slowly nodded. "Yeah . . . thanks."

Gene let out a relieved sigh and wrapped his arms around Zara's shoulders, hugging her close. Zara was surprised at this motion of relief, but she felt just as relieved, so she let Gene hug her. When he released her, Zara suddenly felt like she could do with another hug.

"Where are the twins?" Gene asked, trying to break the silence that had followed his friendly gesture.

"We thought it best to leave someone behind to explain where we went if anything happened. The messages sounded urgent enough, so we didn't know how long we'd be," Silver replied.

As if almost on cue, they became aware of the sound of ice skates behind them. Turning, they saw Rodge skating toward them, pulling a bobsled behind him with the twins pushing from behind.

"Woah guys," Rodge cried, hurrying over to the crowd. "Is everyone alright?"

Rodge had just recently turned twenty but had the spirit and energy of a teenager. He was incredibly fond of the gang, especially Gene and Zara. In being the oldest, he probably saw a younger version of himself in the two of them since they were the youngest of the gang but had most of the fire.

Several heads nodded in agreement and Rodge immediately relaxed. He ran his hand through his dark, almost black brown hair and sat on his heels. "That makes one less thing to worry about."

Seraphina raised her eyebrow at her brother. "What is that supposed to mean?"

Rodge nodded over his shoulder at the twins. That was when everyone saw that Reed wasn't standing but sitting on the end of the bobsled, his head bobbing as if he was ready to fall asleep. However, his dark tanned skin was deathly white.

"What in the world?" Seraphina cried, hurrying over to the boy.

"You'll never believe what happened, Seraph!" Roy panted. "We were just going to join Rodge after telling your parents where you were . . . and we were attacked by this guy and his accomplice!"

"What?" Destiny demanded.

Silver's almost white eyes widened. "What?"

"Wait what?" Gene and Zara asked together.

Rodge raised his eyebrows in amusement. "That's a lot of lightbulb measurements in a row."

No one payed heed to his joke since it wasn't the time to think of that.

"They stopped to get a snack at the grocery store on their way to meet me and by the time they joined me, Reed felt sick. He *says* that all he ate was an apple," Rodge explained.

"You said you were attacked by a guy and his accomplice," Gene pointed out.

"Yeah," Roy nodded. "Reed ate the apple."

Realizing that they were treading on a very delicate conversation, Seraphina tried to keep calm. "Was he foaming at the mouth?"

When she said this, everyone realized what she was thinking. Possibly the apple had a worm in it or something like that and the twins being the way they were, wouldn't have found it suspicious. Foaming would be a possible indication of poisoning.

Roy scratched the back of his head. "Who? The apple?"

Zara's eyes widened while Gene tried to not smile. However, Destiny was prepared to knock Roy silly. "Reed!" she hissed through gritted teeth.

"No," Rodge admitted. "He just got serious stomach pains and kept thrashing about furiously."

Seraphina was feeling the boy's head and hands. Suddenly she stopped and placed her hand on Reed's neck. Turning the boy's head to the side, she revealed that there was a bright red line on his neck. "Did you hit your neck on something Reed?"

The boy slowly shook his head. "I doubt it was anything dangerous . . . probably a worm. He should be fine with rest and plenty of water to flush out his system," Seraphina finally mused.

"Oh, and there is another thing," Roy pointed out.

Gene lowered his eyebrows. "How did I know you were going to say that?"

Roy locked eyes with Gene but the humor had been depleted from the boy's dark eyes. "Funny you should be the one to say that Gene . . . because it's about you."

Gene's eyebrows lowered more. "Still not surprised. What is it?"

"Everyone who was supposed to help put the garland up outside dropped out," Roy pointed out.

Gene's eyebrows lifted but the frown was evident in his eyes. "What for? We only have four days till Christmas and we're not even done inside! Since Whip is gone, I'm in charge of the play and that will take up three good full days!"

"Half of the crew dropped out of the play too," Reed remarked groggily.

"But why?" Destiny snapped, fed up with all these half answers.

The twins exchanged looks before looking directly at Gene. "Because there are rumors going around that you were the one who beat up Jerry and left him for dead."

Chapter 18

"You know..." Drew panted, taking every few seconds to gasp for air as they trudged through the snow. "If we had .... a hunting dog ... we would have found Emma .... Long ago."

Whip pulled his foot from three feet of snow only to put it back down again. "We're almost done," he retorted. "After that we can search the road to the station. The roads have been cleared so it won't be so stressful."

"I'm not saying it's stressful," Drew retorted, leaning against a tree trunk. "I'm saying that it's taking a while and all this trudging in our old footprints isn't exactly good education. All I've learned is that stepping in your own footsteps doesn't make mountain climbing easier."

"We're not mountain climbing," Whip pointed out. "We're walking through a snowy forest which turns out to not be that hilly, thank you very much."

Drew lowered her eyebrows and took another two steps before answering. "Then how do you explain the steep decline that we're encountering? And don't even say that a decline is easier to deal with than an incline because the last decline we encountered left us soaking wet in the pants and bumped and bruised."

Whip had to admit, Drew was right. They had encountered a sharp decline a while back and thinking that the decent would be easy, they didn't prepare themselves when they slipped on the slippery hill and fell the whole way down. Their pants had dried a while ago, but they were cold and slightly crusted in the areas where the snow seeped through their clothes.

Shrugging, Whip decided to make a quick reply so that Drew didn't think that she hit a weak spot on him. "Well . . . if anything, the work out will help us lose some weight!"

Drew's eyebrows went down. "I've lost two pounds . . . .in the last year."

Whip stopped in his tracks long enough to look back at the girl and smile slightly. Drew wasn't exactly skinny nor was she overweight. Slightly on the plump side but Whip had seen girls who had more to complain about.

"What do you do, exercise and then add on more weight by eating?" Whip inquired.

"I will have you know smarty pants," Drew snapped. "That talking about weight isn't exactly a topic to joke about especially when you're talking with girls. Guys will take it fine, but girls are sensitive about their weight especially since we have to worry about keeping up with you guys in the long run!"

Whip prepared to say something snotty back when he thought he heard voices. Stopping in his tracks, he turned to Drew and put a finger to his lips. Drew didn't find it necessary to listen to him and kept trudging loudly through the snow. Once she reached Whip however, the boy clamped a hand on her mouth and held her still.

"I heard something . . ." he whispered.

Drew tried to muffle something through his mitten but decided that if she was quiet, he might let her go sooner. Then it dawned on Drew that she was working with an aerobeast. One of the first things Zara warned her about was that aerobeasts have exceedingly keen sense of sight and hearing. Perhaps there was a good reason for Whip's change in behavior.

Listening quietly, Drew realized that she too could hear the sound of voices . . . but ever so faintly. Whip's head snapped around to the left as if he knew where the faint noise was coming from.

"It's over there," he whispered, beginning to shed his outer coat.

"What are you doing?" Drew demanded, knowing that if someone is shedding their coat on a day like this, they're either mad or up to something.

"We'll have to fly over there," Whip whispered. "I don't know who it is, but I don't want to reveal our position and walking there would block out the voices."

Drew watched with curiosity as Whip tied his coat around his waist then reached to a zipper that ran from his shoulder blades down to the small of his back. Zipping it down expertly, Whip shook his wings free of their cage and flapped them once to warm them up.

Staring in awe, Drew wondered at how Whip could possibly hide those wings inside his jacket. They were long and slender, dark brown and smooth; the wings of a whip-poor-will. Before she knew it, Whip was turning to her and holding out his hand.

Drew suddenly came out of her trance and gave the boy a scowl. "I am not taking your hand," she snapped.

Whip was in no mood to start a lengthy argument, so he reached out and grabbed the girl's wrist. Ignoring her grunting protests, Whip pulled her onto his back and took off running toward the sharp decline. Drew managed to keep her squeal down as they surged over the sky and

Whip carried them a safe distance from the tree tops.

"Why didn't we do this earlier when we were looking for Emma?" Drew demanded.

"Because the sky doesn't have footprints dummy," Whip pointed out in a hiss. "now be quiet."

Drew could barely see over Whip's shoulders, nor hear over the sound of his flapping wings. In that case, she waited until Whip began to just hover over a particularly crowded part of the forest.

"See them?" she hissed.

Whip nodded. "They're down there . . . hold on."

Drew knew better than to start an argument on the move, but when Whip began to plummet straight toward the trees, she almost began to list the possibilities that they would die.

Whip, naturally, ignored her and continued to plummet. He swerved expertly through the tight branches and then stopped sharp just as his feet struck a thick limb of a spruce tree. Drew slowly cracked open her eyes when she realized that they had stopped.

The boy pulled her off his back and planted her on a branch below him, so he could keep a good eye on her in case she fell. Grasping the branch above her head, Drew peered through the thick snow-covered branches at the ground. It was a long way down!

She looked up at Whip, hoping that he was as nervous as her, but his eyes were firmly fixed on a scene about twenty meters from their tree. Squinting her eyes, Drew was able to make out what Whip saw and caught her breath. She could make out the shapes of two people: girls. One was tall, slender with dark brown hair underneath a dark green slouch hat: Emma! The other looked completely different with black shortly cut hair, dressed in a prim boarding school outfit. From the looks of the nice leather boots and wool lined sleeves, it was a rather well-to-do boarding school uniform.

Drew let out a sharp gasp when she felt Whip wrap an arm around her waist and lift her off her feet. "Let's get a closer look," he hissed in her ear.

Not bothering to put her on his back, Whip dropped from the tree as silently as a mouse. Drew found the snow incredibly close to her face as Whip held her around the waist. The boy bent low, extended his wings out slightly to conceal most of Drew and began to hurry through the snow so light footed that Drew was surprised that he had been trudging loudly earlier.

Whip pulled to a harsh stop behind a snow-covered bush. He let Drew go and immediately she pushed away from him, almost hitting the bush. However, she knew that they were close to Emma and the other girl, so she stayed still and quiet. Finding a small opening in the bush to peer out, Drew realized that they were about ten feet away from the two girls now!

"You know very well why I'm here," the strange girl was saying in a snappish tone. "Four years ago I was sent to Williams and you stayed here with your pathetic little family."

The two concealed eavesdroppers could see Emma swallow down her pent-up fury and speak calmly. "Come on Styl. I most certainly can't go back and change the past and neither can you."

"Oh, so you're going to start that whole 'I am innocent and you're the one who is powerless' is that it? You're just as bad as me Emma if not worse. You're no angel," Styl hissed angrily, taking a step or two around Emma as if interrogating her.

"No one is an angel, but I am just asking you to accept the fact that I cannot change the past. All I can do is ask you to be the good person I know is in there somewhere and let go of the things that hurt you," Emma pleaded. "I don't want anyone to get hurt, least of all you."

Whip's eyes were locked on Emma, trying to figure out what was going on, but Drew saw a slight movement from Styl. When she looked back, she realized that the girl's left arm was hidden behind her back.

"Oh, I'm not going to get hurt," Styl retorted, causing Whip and Drew to cringe at the sharpness of her voice. "If anyone is going to get hurt, it's you. You ruined my life! You stole the pity that should have fallen on me! I am the one who was wounded by the pains of our parents, not you. You gained mercy when you did not deserve it!"

Whip and Drew could see that Emma's face was going pale, but she was fighting to keep herself composed. "Styl, let's not start an argument. I am sorry that you lost the thing you wanted the most. I know what it feels like. But trust me, if you just let it go and try again, everything will be alright."

The dark-haired girl spun around, and her eyebrows knitted almost into one. Drew grasped Whip's arm in fright without even realizing it. "This is it Emma. I am going to end this little charade of yours once and for all and no one will be the wiser."

With that, Styl's concealed arm shot out and a huge tree branch flew right at Emma's head.

The girl reacted to its appearance but not quick enough. She avoided the sharp brambles on the branch, but she couldn't avoid the heavy weight it laid on the back of her neck.

Whip held Drew down as Emma crumbled to the snow. He wasn't prepared to reveal their position to someone like Styl until he was sure the coast was clear. He watched as the dark-haired girl considered the unconscious Emma before turning on her heel and hurrying back through the snow.

The moment Styl was out of sight, Whip released Drew and the girl leapt over to Emma. The girl was face-down in the snow and limp. Drew turned her over and cupped the girl's head in her lap. Whip skidded to a stop beside them and felt Emma's pulse.

"She's just unconscious," he breathed in relief. "But we'd better get her back home as soon as possible."

Drew glanced over her shoulder at where Styl had disappeared and a scowl appeared on her pretty face. "If she had killed Emma, it would have been murder in cold blood! The little meanie, what was she thinking? What was that whole argument about anyway?"

Whip shook his head. "We didn't hear the first part . . . but from the sound of it, they've known each other for a while. Apparently Styl lost something that either went to Emma or something along those lines. What I don't know is what would be so important that she would hurt someone like that!"

Drew bit her teeth together hard, making a grinding sound. "If I get my hands on her . . . . oh, it will be a dark day!"

"You mean it will be a dark day for you," Whip pointed out. "Don't let revenge take hold Drew. That will lead to hate and that will definitely make a dark day."

Chapter 19

Deke pressed his nose against the windowpane of the carriage. If he had known that they would be taking carriage to Hanalona, he would have asked to ride outside. It was hot and stuffy inside the carriage, even though it was just him and Denise inside while his father rode outside on horseback.

Denise had been leaning her head against the dark blue cushioning of the wall and had drifted off to sleep. Now she lifted her head and blinked sleepily. She saw that Deke's skin looked rather pale and dry as if he was healing from sunburn and his skin was peeling. That indicated that something was on his mind or troubling him. As a merbeast, Deke suffered from something that was known as "anti-sweat hormones." Unlike humans or other changelings who were not merbeasts, Deke didn't sweat when he was upset or nervous but dried out.

"What is troubling you?" Denise inquired.

Deke jumped at her voice, having not known that she had awoken. "Oh . . . nothing."

Denise lowered her eyebrows. "I hope you don't think that I'm a fool Deke. I know when you're upset, and you are right now."

Deke huffed and covered his face with his arm, but he knew that Denise could still sense his worry.

"Are you afraid of your dad?"

Deke slowly lifted his eyes and Denise saw pure fear playing across his young face. "It's not just my dad that scares me Denise . . . it's the nightmares."

A cold hand clutched Denise's heart. She had never heard Deke crying out in the night. "What nightmares?"

A shiver ran down Deke's spine. "Every night since we left Hichester . . . I've been having nightmares. They're perfectly horrible Denise! I am standing on the edge of a cliff with Neil and Gene . . . both of them smiling when the ground crumbles beneath Neil and he falls . . . Gene doesn't cry out but just looks at me as I scream. When I begin to step toward Gene . . . a huge ball of fire appears out of the sky and strikes the ground between us . . . and through the flames I see Gene fall over the cliff as well and I can just stand there . . . doing nothing to save them."

Denise honestly didn't know what to say to that. She had never dreamt that Deke was going through those types of things in his sleep. She had always assumed that he slept like a rock.

Deke returned to pressing his nose against the window but only for a moment before the carriage pulled to a harsh stop.

The voice of the driver called out from above. "We're here sir."

Deke reached over to the window and pushed the curtains back. They had been kept closed to keep the heat in but now as he opened them, his eyes grew wide. Miles upon miles of land spread out before him. They were atop a perfectly white hill of snowy grass. Fences, barns, houses, villages and forests spread out as far as the eye could see. Deke felt his mouth slowly opening in surprise when Denise spoke up from the other side of the carriage.

"Uh Deke . . . you had better come see this."

Deke turned around and hurried over to Denise who had rolled down her own window and was looking out the other side of the carriage to the north. Deke squeezed his head and shoulders out but stopped short before he could get his hands out.

The largest hills that Deke had ever seen rose up from at least three miles off in the distance. They were obviously mountains but weren't as rigid, hard and snow-covered as Deke had expected mountains to be. Nestled at the foot of the mountains was a huge hill covered in trees and freshly fallen snow. Directly between the carriage window and the mountains rose the largest building that Deke had ever seen.

In fact, it wasn't a building . . . but a castle! With a soft cream, almost golden-brown hue, the castle was gigantic. It wasn't your typical medieval castle with a drawbridge and walls. There was a wall that went all the way around but there was no drawbridge. The front of the wall rose three times as high as the rest of the wall into what looked like a building. It was far larger than any of the town houses in Gerh.

Within the castle walls were several buildings. Two looked like large, slightly wide towers which were the tallest points of the castle. The other buildings were about the size of huge townhouses. The largest was a massive building, almost as tall as the tallest tower which stood at least four hundred feet. It was the largest, widest and longest building of the whole castle and stood out from the others. That was the foyer. There were two tall, smaller towers on either side of the building and connected to it like horns.

Denise and Deke exchanged shocked looks as the carriage slowly began to move down the road. They kept their heads sticking out the window as the carriage traveled down the hill and toward the entrance gate of the castle.

As they neared the castle, the two suddenly felt incredibly small. The huge walls got nearer but even those didn't amount for the feeling that the two experienced as the carriage rolled through the huge gates into the courtyard of the castle.

The buildings within the wall rose up all around the large town square. People buzzed around in the square, hurrying about, dragging children or themselves through the snow. Ankle deep snow lay across the courtyard and piles of snow lay on ever windowsill.

Denise and Deke felt the carriage jolt as the driver hopped off and opened the door for them. Wrapping their cloaks around them to block out the harsh cold that they barely felt, the two slowly stepped out into the courtyard.

"Okay, I knew your dad was important but this . . . what is he? An emperor?" Denise whispered.

Deke didn't answer but stared in stunned amazement. The clomping of horses drew him out of his daze, and he turned to see his father ride up into the courtyard. There was a great murmur and joyous greetings from the people nearby. Deke's father waved kindly and smiled as he pulled his horse to a stop and dismounted.

He approached the two kids immediately and placed a hand on both of their shoulders. "Welcome to Hanalona."

Denise furrowed her brow. There was something about that name that seemed familiar, but she couldn't place it.

"Sir . . . is Hanalona it's full name?" she inquired.

Steven Rasmussen smiled as he ruffled his son's brown hair. "I thought you might ask that Miss Nielson. You probably heard your parents speaking of it. The full name of my grandfather's creation is Hanalona Montecarlen."

Deke didn't recognize that name, nor did he understand the pale and shocked look that crossed Denise's face until he heard her faint squeak of shock.

"But that means . . . this is the castle of the king of Gerhenia!"

* * * * *

"Ugh! Open up!" Whip called, ramming his shoulder against the apothecary door. "There is an emergency out here! Open the door! Open in the name of us!"

Drew tried to kick the door with her foot, but she was already bracing herself against the weight of Emma in her arms. The tall girl was being held between the two of them and in being several years older than them, Emma wasn't an easy load.

"If you don't open the door in five seconds, I'm going to completely lose it!" Whip hollered.

Slowly the door began to open. Drew and Whip were almost prepared to barge in when they realized who had opened the door. Standing in the open doorway was one of the twins, possibly Reed, wearing a bright pink bathrobe and huge blue bunny slippers. His hair was rolled in purple hair curlers, he carried a hot steaming mug of tea in one hand and his eyes were covered by cucumber slices.

Reaching up with his free hand, Reed picked the cucumber slices off his eyes and considered the two kids with no expression. Emma was dangling in their arms and the two were panting from exertion and covered in snow.

"Guyth . . . the pantherth are home . . ." Reed started in his slow voice.

He was interrupted by the appearance of Seraphina and Zara who pushed the boy to the side and hurried over to Whip and Drew.

"Oh my gosh!" Zara cried. "What happened? We were so worried when you didn't get back earlier!"

Seraphina held the door open as they pulled Emma inside. "Set her on the couch. Tell us what happened! You two are a sight!"

"It's a long story," Drew gasped. "We'll need Livonia to take a look at her. She was hit over the head with a pretty large stick."

Seraphina and Zara looked at the two in puzzlement. "Why did you hit her with a stick?"

"We didn't!" Whip cried, waving his arms in innocence. "There was this girl, Styl, who was talking with Emma when we came upon them. They were arguing so we listened in and then Styl clobbered Emma over the head with a stick before running off."

Zara cringed while Seraphina stared. "Well," the blond girl remarked. "I'll try to keep her still and warm. Livonia went out for a break. More relatives are arriving at the riverbank and Livonia went to welcome them."

"It'th probably betht we thtayed here then," Reed remarked, stepping over.

Whip considered the boy in stunned shock. "What happened to you?"

"An encounter with a drugged apple," Seraphina replied. "You're supposed to be in your room Reed."

"Roy kicked me out," the boy replied. "He wanted a moment of peace and quiet, tho he made me leave tho I wouldn't dithturb him."

Whip scanned the room, finding Oliver sitting at the counter. "Where is Gene?"

Zara and Seraphina exchanged quick looks before Oliver replied from the counter. "He's with Vivian. They're trying to finish the scenery."

Drew lowered her eyebrows. "But they were halfway through when we left. Why aren't they done yet?"

Again, the two girls exchanged looks and finally Whip couldn't stand it any longer. "Okay, what happened while we're gone? It's not good is it?"

About thirty minutes later, after Seraphina and Zara had told the story about three times in several different forms, Whip and Drew were shooed out of the apothecary along with the now recovered Reed, Roy and Oliver. They were trudging through the thick snow, breathing up steam with their warm breath.

"That is really strange," Whip remarked. "Everyone knows Gene and trusts him! I mean gosh, the headmasters at SOHE even put him in charge of practically everything for the Christmas Party! If you ask me, it might all be some prank someone is playing just to make Gene's life miserable."

"Well maybe after a while we can sort it out," Drew suggested. "At least Vivian is with him."

The others nodded in agreement. Just then, Whip lifted his eyes to see a crowd of people up ahead. "Hey, there is the welcoming party. Why don't we go say hi? Maybe Deke and Neil are with them."

"They're not supposed to get back for another three days," Roy pointed out.

No one payed any heed to what Roy said and hurried over to the crowd. Most of the crowd were grownups but there were a handful of kids and teenagers as well, stretched out near the riverbank, chattering to people that were climbing out of the bobsled.

"Hey Lyle!" Whip called to the tall bargeman.

Lyle looked up from behind his thick wraps and smiled. The bargeman always wore their full outfits in winter and most of the time, the gang wished that they were bargemen because the outfits looked far warmer than hats, mittens and coats.

"Salutations," the tall man called, making a mock salute.

Drew hurried over to pet the four huge furry horses who pulled the sled while the twins tried to climb up into the driver's seat next to Lyle.

Oliver stood off to the side, watching it all while Whip joined Drew by the horses.

"Hey Sugar," Whip greeted, petting the nose of the furry white horse. "And Bucker . . . Dancer. Hey, who's this Lyle?"

Lyle looked up from where he was helping the twins up to see Whip petting the furry black horse who led the sleigh next to Dancer. "That is Sef. He's a new one."

Whip grinned and stroked the noble horse's ears. He loved the way the horses' hooves clinked on the snow with their spiked horseshoes and the jingle bells that lined their harnesses. He would often go down the river with Gene to visit the bargeman village just to check on the horses. There were about eight of them and during the warmer months when the bobsled wasn't used, they were allowed to ride the horses up and down the river for exercise.

"You're a big guy," Whip was saying to the horse. "Take care of Dancer, she's a biter!"

"Psst Whip," Drew hissed.

Whip looked slightly over at the girl who was petting Sugar. At once he stopped smiling and stroking Sef when he saw the paleness on Drew's face and the horror in her violet eyes.

"What is it?"

Drew slowly nodded over her shoulder but didn't speak, point or turn around. Instead, she continued to pet Sugar as if trying to not draw attention to herself. Whip looked at where she nodded, and his throat clamped shut. Livonia was chatting with several grownups who had just piled out of the sledge . . . and between two of the grownups was none other than Styl!

"What is she doing here?" Whip hissed.

Drew shrugged and pressed her face against Sugar's white neck. "I don't know, but obviously Livonia knows her because I saw them smiling and chatting together! If she sees Emma in the apothecary . . ."

Whip felt his blood boil and he stepped away from the horses. "Stay here and keep an eye on her. I'm taking Oliver back to the apothecary to warn the others. Keep the twins out of trouble."

Drew nodded automatically as Whip charged up the slope, grabbing Oliver as he went.

Chapter 20

"So . . . ." Eileen remarked from the back of the car. "This Bruce guy . . . why do people find him strange?"

Neil glanced away from where he had been staring listlessly out the window and Mr. Wetherby looked at the girl through the rearview mirror.

"Well," Mr. Wetherby began, turning the car down the next street. "He's what you might call a genius. He graduated from high school rather early, but he wasn't accepted into college because he was so young. In that case he decided to just study science and continue his own experiments at home. He lives with a foster family since he lost his real family when he was little. I guess people find him strange because he sticks to himself . . . . Honestly I don't know."

"I thought you knew him," Eileen pointed out.

Mr. Wetherby grinned, always finding Eileen's bluntness amusing. "Well I do but it's been about two years since I saw him. When I saw him last, I did find him strange . . . but that was only because whatever he said I couldn't understand."

Neil and Eileen exchanged looks that spoke volumes of concern. "Uh oh," both whispered under their breath.

"Ah, here we are," Mr. Wetherby remarked, interrupting their thoughts.

The two lifted their heads to see that they had appeared in front of a small neighborhood house. Huge bushes grew out front, all trimmed neatly except for one near the gate that looked like something had eaten a huge hole out of the center but from the look of it, it was probably burnt.

Mr. Wetherby parked the car on the curb and as he turned it off, the two kids slowly piled out. The house was deathly quiet as they climbed out but as they started up the walk, they heard a noise that sounded like a cat who had just been blown to smithereens.

Eileen and Neil froze in their tracks, shivering in concern. How bad exactly was this Bruce guy?

Mr. Wetherby was knocking on the front door by the time the two finally made their way slowly up the front steps. The door was opened by an elderly lady who looked even older than Mr. Wetherby. Her white hair was piled on the top of her head, her blue eyes full of energy and there were a few wisps of hair that looked like they had been singed.

"Hello Mrs. Menisci . . . we're here to see Bruce," Mr. Wetherby explained.

The woman took one look at the two kids and Mr. Wetherby before stepping to the side. "Please come in. I was hoping you would come by sometime soon Chris," the woman remarked in a croaky voice.

"Is everything alright?" Mr. Wetherby inquired as he stepped inside.

Mrs. Menisci shrugged. "I just think the boy needs some new surroundings. He's been really quiet ever since he blew up the oven last week. I told him it wasn't a big deal, but he wouldn't be sidetracked."

"Well maybe we can talk to him," Neil suggested, trying to sound helpful.

The woman turned to look at the boy as he spoke, and her eyes grew wide. Her hands began to shake as she slowly took a step back from Neil. Neil didn't see this, but Eileen did. She was about to bring it to attention when she noticed Mr. Wetherby giving her hand signals to not speak.

Mrs. Menisci composed herself long enough to lead the three down a narrow hallway to the back bedroom at the very back of the house. Once there, she knocked on the door that had cuts and scorch marks all over it. On the doorknob hung a sign that said: ***enter at your own risk.***

"Who is it?" a voice from inside inquired.

"You have some visitors Bruce," the elderly woman croaked. "Mr. Wetherby and two friends."

The door slowly opened to reveal that the interior of the room was pitch black. Standing in the doorway before them was a person about Neil's height wearing a long brown leather apron that fell to the floor, large work gloves that were too large for his hands and a bandana around his forehead.

"Mr. Wetherby!" the person remarked, reaching up to remove the stuff from his face. "So good to see you again!"

The boy stepped to the side as he removed his goggles to reveal bright blue eyes. The three slowly stepped into the dim lit room while Mrs. Menisci excused herself.

Closing the door behind them, Bruce took off the bandana and switched on a light. The room was immediately flooded with light to reveal that all the walls were lined with tables. There was one single chair in the room, and it was on wheels, so he could move from table to table. Each table was full of microscopes, tubes, boxes, bags and loads of books.

Under one desk was a small door that looked barely large enough to fit Eileen. The door was open to reveal a small closet space about five by five feet. Inside was a floor bed which was covered in blankets that weren't folded and books as if the boy didn't sleep but read instead of slept.

While Eileen and Mr. Wetherby took in the room, Neil's eyes locked on the boy who stood before him. The boy was about ten, two years younger than Deke and barely taller. A headful of wild brown hair came down his neck and stuck out above his forehead. On his head was what looked like huge glasses that helped his ears see rather than his eyes.

Reaching up with both hands, the boy pressed a small button that sat snuggly behind his left ear. A small whirring sound followed, and the headset seemed to move. The lenses rotated so that they were hanging right in front of Bruce's eyes now rather than above his ears.

The glasses made his blue eyes look huge, too large for his face. A cheeky smile appeared on his young, thin face as he removed his gloves to reveal long, thin and bony fingers.

"You must be Neil and Eileen! Mr. Wetherby wrote me yesterday and told me about you! I'm Bruce."

Neil could do nothing but stare at the boy. There was something about those eyes, the wild hair . . . the smile that reminded Neil of someone.

Eileen meanwhile seemed vastly interested in the whole thing.

"So . . . is this your lab?" she inquired.

Bruce smiled. "Actually this is the inventor's corner," he explained. "the lab is in the loft."

The boy hurried across the room and pulled a string that hung above one of the desks. The sound of gears could be heard through the walls and a small ladder appeared from where it had been concealed on the ceiling. The ladder revealed a small trapdoor in the ceiling which it leant against.

"Would you care to come up?" Bruce inquired.

"I'll stay down here," Mr. Wetherby remarked. "I'll go and say hello to Mr. Menisci. You kids go ahead."

Neil and Eileen readily followed the genius up the ladder and into the darkness of the loft. They could hear Bruce fumbling around on the wall until he found the switch and turned on the light.

The loft was barely larger than the bedroom but truly amazing. Cranes were attached to the walls, dangling from the ceiling. Huge glass jars, tubes and containers lined shelves that covered most of the walls. A huge table sat in the middle of the room, empty and clean. There were bookcases and shelves that lined the walls but no chairs.

"This is my lab," Bruce explained.

Neil and Eileen didn't hide the fact that their jaws were dangling from their mouths at the sight. Bruce began to whiz about the room expertly, checking on the colorful liquids that filled the jars, tubes and containers.

The two slowly began to walk around the room, admiring every jar and container. Eileen found a large fish tank that was full to the brim with a red liquid.

"What is this?" she inquired.

Bruce buzzed over and grinned at her. "This is what I call *Uthanium*. It's a specific mixture of liquid chemicals and acids that will build off of specific metals. Watch."

The boy reached into a drawer below the fish tank and drew out a small piece of metal. He grasped the metal in a pair of long tweezers and inserted it into the red liquid. He waited for about three seconds before drawing it out and the metal had now expanded to twice the size with a different shape. There were crystals growing off of it and they looked sharp.

"That is so cool!" Eileen admitted as Bruce placed the object on a piece of paper near the tank.

"The crystals are incredibly difficult to break. You cannot melt or blow them up. You have to go in there with razor sharp knives that are incredibly thin and take it apart bit by bit," Bruce explained. "It would make a cool blade."

As Bruce hurried off to inspect a jar of bubbling green liquid, Eileen touched the crystal. It was dry but razor sharp . . . it would make a cool blade for sure!

"Hey Bruce," Neil called from the other end of the room. "What does this do?"

Eileen and Bruce hurried over to see that Neil had located a small jar on a shelf that was full of water and floating in the center was a small blue object that looked like a ball.

"Oh, this is my favorite," Bruce replied. "I call it *mehnthis*."

Bruce unscrewed the cap of the jar and sticking tweezers in, he drew out the blue ball. Placing it on a plate next to the jar, he dug through the pile of tools on the table until he located a small chisel and hammer. After about five minutes of work, he managed to scrape the tiniest bit of the blueness off the ball till it fell onto the plate in a neat little curlicue.

"This single piece," Bruce explained, holding it in his palm. "Is enough to make someone go crazy!"

Neil and Eileen exchanged confused looks, but Bruce wasn't done explaining.

"If you eat it, dissolve it in water and then drink it, this will make whatever your thinking become too much to bear. If you were greatly nervous about an upcoming test or something like that and then you took this, you would outright freak out and express your nervousness."

"In words or in actions?" Eileen inquired, suddenly startled.

"Depends on what you're raving about," Bruce replied. "If it is a physical thing, probably in actions. If it is a verbal or mental thing, then usually in words."

Suddenly, Bruce's features changed, and a smile appeared on his young face. "There is an experiment I'm working on. Maybe you would like to help?"

Both nodded their heads vigorously. Bruce put the *mehnthis* back in its water jar before heading to the center table. The two followed him as he began to bustle around. He brought over several books, three jars full of different colors liquids, two that contained solid objects, testing tubes, tweezers and syringes. Lastly, he brought over a small paper bag.

"This is more an investigation than an experiment," Bruce clarified. "A neighborhood down the road was attacked with hidden explosives last week and was burnt to the ground. I went along with a bunch of other volunteers to help clear the rubble and I found this."

Bruce turned the paper bag upside down and out fluttered a small piece of cloth that was about the size of his hand. "This was in all the rubble, but I kept it, hoping that I could figure out what the explosives were made of. However, while I was testing, I found out that this piece of material isn't from Gerhenia."

Eileen lowered her eyebrows. "What does that have to do with anything? The cloth might have come from another country; that's perfectly normal."

Bruce nodded. "But there is something else . . . this material doesn't match any type of man-made or natural organic material known to the world."

The two kids froze. Realization dawned on them. "What are you saying?" Neil hissed.

"I'm saying that this piece of cloth . . . . it's not of this world."

Chapter 21

"Seraph!" Whip shouted as he burst into the apothecary.

He skidded to a stop with Oliver practically colliding with him. Seraphina was sitting next to Emma on the couch, brushing out the girl's dark brown hair. Zara was pacing back and forth in the back of the room, fingering her mouth thoughtfully with her eyebrows down.

"Whip you'll never believe what happened!" Zara cried, rushing over to the boy and shaking his shoulders.

"Oh no, not again," Whip sighed. "Will things never stop happening? I have something I need to tell you too."

"Well this is more important," Zara replied, not giving the boy a moment to speak. "The headmasters at society found out that Gene fought off the suicide bomber and used his wings in the process and they're really heated! They're considering keeping Gene on restrictions for a few weeks!"

Whip's eyebrows flew up. "Restrictions? What does that mean?"

"It means he won't be able to use his wings or even let them open for a certain amount of time," Seraphina replied. "They're punishing him for using them to defend himself and Zara!"

Whip let out a disgusted scoff and rolled his eyes. "That is absurd! If Gene hadn't used them, he and Zara would have been blown to smithereens! What are their reasons?"

Seraphina shrugged. "They said that it's against the society rules. No one is allowed to use their changeling gifts to fight any living thing."

"But we used our wings to fight the underbeasts three years ago when we rescued Emma! We all did!" Whip pointed out.

Zara quickly bit her lip as she closed the door. "Well . . . the only one who actually used his changeling gifts to fight someone was Gene. The rest of us just used our human gifts. You used your hands to drop those rocks on the sentries . . . not your wings. The only reason they never mentioned this before is because we never brought up the fact that Gene fought off the underbeasts . . . we left that part out of the story because we didn't want anyone to worry."

"And you're telling me we never revealed it in the past three years?" Whip almost snapped. "Besides that, why can't we use our changeling abilities to defend ourselves?"

"I don't think they see it that way," Seraphina pointed out. "They see it as 'attacking another human being.' I believe they fear that if they allow changelings to use their gifts to physically fight . . . they think it might lead to all the wrong ideas such as revenge and war. Of course, they're right but defending yourself against an attack is different than starting the fight yourself."

* * * * *

There was another knock at the front door and three heads poked out of Bruce's bedroom. They saw Mr. Wetherby head out of the sitting room and down the front hallway to the door. They could hear the doorknob turn and the door creak on the hinges.

"May I help you?" they heard Mr. Wetherby ask.

There was a pause before a voice spoke. "These are for Neil Mecarnin."

Eileen and Bruce both looked at Neil in surprise. They had no idea how anyone knew the address that was needed to reach Neil. They had received a rather lengthy letter from Roy yesterday, before they left Gerh.

There was another long pause before the door closed and Mr. Wetherby appeared down the hallway. He held a small handful of letters and he fingered them thoughtfully. He lifted his eyes and saw the three kids watching him. He raised the letters and wagged them.

"They're for you Neil," he remarked. "I contacted Livonia and gave her our new address so the kids could write you."

Relieved that there was no suspicion there, Eileen and Neil emerged from the room. Bruce ducked back into the bedroom, not the social type. Once Mr. Wetherby handed them the letters, Eileen and Neil headed into the room that Eileen had been given to sleep in during their short stay there.

They plopped down on the bed and Eileen switched on her light.

"This one's from Gene," Neil remarked, opening the first letter.

Dear Neil, I hope you are having a good time in Gerh with Deke. After reading your letter this morning, I guessed that I shouldn't burden Deke anymore by telling him what's happening here. It's gotten kinda busy but nothing we can't handle. Whip and Drew were sent out to find Emma because she was late, and they eventually found her. Whip and Drew have finally started to get along . . . slightly. I went to visit Res Schneider with Seraphina and Zara earlier today. He told us about his earlier years . . . honestly, it was kinda cool! I wonder what it was like back in the 630's! Christmas preparations are going alright, just busy. I hope you guys are having a nice time!

See you soon! Love, Gene.

"Well it sounds like things are going well," Eileen remarked from the other couch where she was opening one of the other letters.

Neil shrugged but considered the letter a moment. "Gene always writes long letters going into detail . . . this one is short and right to the point . . . it's almost like he's in a hurry. Besides, Gene doesn't like to worry us . . . I wonder if he was including everything."

Eileen looked up from the letter she had opened, her face going slightly pale. "Neil . . . listen to this one. It's from Whip."

"Uh oh," Neil groaned. "Let me guess, it's a list of knock-knock jokes?"

Eileen shook her head. "the complete opposite . . ."

Neil's eyes reflected concern. Whip always wrote letters full of jokes . . . what could possibly get that boy worried?

Dear Neil,

We need help here! It's a riot! Knowing Gene, he probably told you that everything is cool and calm . . . . It's not! Drew and I had to go hunting for Emma because she was two days late. When we found her, this stranger: Styl, beat her up and left her for dead in the woods! We managed to get Emma back home but then Styl arrived in Hichester! Luckily, she didn't recognize Drew and me, so we're keeping Emma hidden till we can find out what is up. Also, Gene and Zara got attacked by a bomber on their way to bargeman village! I don't know why they were going that way, but if Gene hadn't reacted in time, the guy would have killed them. Now the headmasters are mad at Gene because he used his wings to defend himself and Zara! What's worse, there was a small rumor that Gene was the one who hurt Jerry! The poor boy is still unconscious but luckily the rumor didn't stay around for long. But the rumor left a scar and now people are dropping out of the play and Christmas preparations! Neil we're in a crisis of the century! Oh, I've got to go, Emma just woke up! See ya soon!
Sincerely, Whip.

Neil blinked several times as Eileen repeated the last sentence. "Okay . . . that does not sound like the usual Whip letter," he pointed out. "But he was right about the first thing, Gene made his letter sound really calm and everything great!"

"But why would someone hurt Emma?" Eileen demanded. "And who would think that

179

…rry! Jerry is such a nice person
…y fond of him!"

…more concerned about that attacker,"
…marked almost absently, his mind
…ntrating on what he had just heard, "and
…ny would the headmasters blame Gene for
defending himself?"

"What's the next one?" Eileen inquired. "Hopefully we'll get some answers."

Neil looked down at the envelope in his hand and saw that it was from Zara. Opening it, he read it aloud hastily.

Dear Neil, whatever you do, don't believe a word Gene says. He is trying to not worry you or Deke especially now but there is plenty for you to worry about! There have been attacks all over Hichester! First the suicide bomber who attacked Gene and me, then Reed ate a wormy apple and got sick! They'll exaggerate in their letter but it's pretty close to the truth! Emma just woke from her coma, but things aren't good! Apparently, this girl Styl has a grudge against her and Emma won't tell us . . . at least not yet. Whip and Drew are really put out about the whole thing and are determined to figure out whole story and do something about it. Lucki the two have gotten along a little better but that is the only thing that has worked in the past two days! Things are falling apart and all of them are falling on Gene! I don't know how he can handle it and write a calm letter to you! He is losing weight and sleep . . . this is taking a toll on him! Please tell me what to do! Respectfully, Zara.

"Is it just me," Neil remarked. "or are they getting worse by the letter? Gene's was suspicious to start off but then Whip revealed the flaw . . . and now Zara is adding to it! This is starting to look really bad Eileen!"

The girl nodded. "this next one is from the twins . . ."

"From seeing what Whip had to say, I'm almost interested to see what those two have to say."

Smiling but with concern evident in her eyes, Eileen opened the letter and began to read.

NEIL MECARNIN! SAVE US FROM THIS CRISIS! Okay, this is Reed, I had to confiscate the pen and paper from Roy before he filled the whole paper with capital letters. In truth, he is partially wrong and partially out of his min . . . NO I AM NOT! NEIL, IT IS A RIOT BACK HERE! YOU'VE GOT TO SAVE US! REED WAS ALMOST POISONED EARLIER TODAY AND . . . And that boy definitely has problems. Things are kinda piling up out here but nothing to go and use caps all over the paper. In case you didn't know . . . PEOPLE ARE SAYING THAT GENE IS BEGINNING TO DEFY THE SOCIETY BY DEFENDING HIMSELF AND OTHERS ARE SAYING HE LEFT JERRY FOR DEAD! NEIL YOU'VE GOT TO DO SOMETHING BEFORE REED COMES BACK FROM THE BATHROOM AND TAKES THE PEN FROM ME AGAIN! I'M DOWN ON MY KNEES HERE! PLEASE SAVE US NEIL! Oh boy, I think we had better go Neil. Actually, Roy was practically kneeling while writing that last part. Anyway, we still have to truck through the waist deep snow to the post office. Oh, that's another thing, the snow won't stop falling and before long, no one will be able to come or leave. See ya. Sincerely yours, Reed. HELP US NEIL! YOUR DYING FRIEND, ROY!

"Okay this is definitely getting worse," Eileen admitted. "I know Roy can sometimes go crazy but even Reed admitted that things are going crazy . . . even though he was kind of ignorant about it. Also, I thought Whip and Zara's explanations of the attacks and the rumors about Gene were bad but when the twins add to it . . . it's starting to sound worse than I thought before."

Neil nodded. "Let's see what Seraphina has to say. If she is concerned, then there is definitely something to worry about."

Eileen cleared her throat and began to read the letter, her face changing colors as she reached the middle before she began to read aloud.

Dear Neil, I think it's about time you just heard the honest truth. We're all worried Neil. It's not just the fact that Emma just woke up from a coma and pointed out that Styl (who happens to not know that Emma is here in Hichester) has a grudge against her that seems to be a little more serious than just a grudge especially since she left Emma in the woods where she could catch hypothermia. Luckily Whip and Drew found her but that is not the worst of it because both of them are determined to do nothing till the whole mystery with Styl and Emma is figured out. Whip even dropped out of leading the play and the only other person who could possibly handle the twins is Gene . . . that boy doesn't need another thing to worry about and now he has to lead the play with half cast since most of them refuse to be around Gene. Also,

Webstar is preparing to have puppies any day. Gene didn't tell you because he was worried you would be concerned the whole time you were gone. Besides that, Zara is concerned about all the attacks as are the rest of us, but I'm also worried about Gene because every time we turn around there is another thing that piles up on Gene's shoulders. Honestly Neil, things are getting worse and I don't know how long we can handle this. Please pray for us Neil that we'll be able to figure this out. True to the twins' point, we're in a dilemma. Have a good time in Gerh but please don't worry Deke about everything happening back here. It's the last thing he needs. Love, Seraphina.

There was a long silence as the two sat there, drinking in what Seraphina had just written. Setting the letters down firmly, Neil rose to his feet.

"Well that settles it. Seraphina wouldn't write a letter full of that much concern unless it was absolutely necessary," he pointed out as he started for the door.

"What are you going to do?" Eileen asked, worried even more by the look in Neil's eyes.

The boy spun on his heel long enough to give her a firm look. "I'm going back to Hichester tonight!"

"Tonight!?" Eileen squealed. "But what about Deke, Denise and Mr. Wetherby? Wont they worry when they don't find us here?"

"We'll leave a note for them," Neil explained. "But Gene needs us more than we're needed waiting here for the others to join up with us."

Eileen considered the pile of letters about her on the couch. "You do have a point Neil . . . but we came to support Deke. I don't think leaving him to go home right now would be much support."

"We're not offering any support sitting around here for two days," Neil protested. "Besides, I can't support Deke when I know that Gene is having trouble. Gene was always there for me when I was having trouble when my wing was removed. It's time that I repaid that debt."

Chapter 22

Bruce held out his hand and Eileen put the vial on his palm. Bruce took one look at the vial before handing it back. "The blue one Eileen. That one is the potassium."

Eileen quickly grabbed the correct vial and handed it to him. Bruce bent back over the small cage he was working over. His hands were stuck into rubber gloves that allowed him to work inside the cage without letting any air or germs into the glass cage.

The girl glanced at Neil who had been inspecting a particle of the cloth through a microscope. The boy had looked up long enough to give her a cheeky grin. Eileen had practically no idea what the two of them had been saying for the past two hours so she did her job for the experiment by handing them things.

"Have you figured out the particular part of Falfi the particle was from?" Bruce asked without looking up from his job.

Eileen had ventured to watch Bruce mostly because his work was a little more interesting. He was pouring all sorts of things onto the particle, causing it to turn color, change form or even blow up slightly inside the cage. Neil was just looking at another part of it through the microscope, writing down things and checking in the log books.

"Yeah . . . just a second," Neil replied.

The boy hurried from the microscope and grabbed another book from the shelf. Flipping through the pages, his eyes scanned it.

"Kesroc," Neil remarked.

The two spun around to face him as he looked up from the page. "It's from Kesroc Falfi."

"But that's the capitol," Bruce pointed out. "Strange . . ."

Eileen turned back to the boy. "Why is that strange?"

Bruce shrugged. "Mostly because the people in the neighborhood there . . . were far too poor to make a journey all the way to Kesroc Falfi."

"So, it was obviously an outside job?" Neil inquired, putting the book back on the shelf.

Bruce nodded. "I'll have to do further research on the origin of the explosives."

However, the three would have to hold up because Mr. Wetherby's voice broke the silence. "Kids! It's time to go! We still have to stop by Gerh before you two head to Break Neck!"

"Coming!" Eileen hollered. "Come on Bruce."

Bruce grinned as he began to switch off the lights and other things in the room, leaving it completely dark. The three slowly descended the stairs as Bruce closed the hatch behind them. After turning all the lights off in the inventor's room, Bruce grabbed his backpack and they hurried out to meet Mr. Wetherby in the car.

* * * * *

Denise had her arms clasped in front of her as she walked back and forth in front of the door. She could hear the sound of water swishing inside the washing room. She had just finished her own shower and was all clean and dressed. She had immediately been given a dress that fit her surprisingly well. She had been told that there was an abundant amount of spare clothes in the guest bedroom wardrobes, but it was uncanny that these clothes fitted her as if they had been handmade for her.

Some of the dresses that had been placed in her room for her didn't work with her hair. They were light or bright colors that would have better suited dark hair rather than red. The one she wore at present was a dark blue one that fell to her feet and covered the black flats she wore. The sleeves were slender until the elbows where they became long and huge. When she let her hands hang by her sides, her hands would disappear into the sleeves.

Denise stopped pacing when she heard the water stop rustling and the door opened. Deke emerged from the room, followed by the butler who had been assigned to help him wash.

Deke's hair was slightly damp and almost looked curly. He was clean that was for sure and smelled a lot better than usual. He wore a pair of dark brown pants that were tucked into knee high leather boots. He also wore a long sleeve white linen shirt, tucked into his pants and over the shirt he wore a short dark brown leather jacket.

The embroidery on the jacket was exquisite and careful work of silver and golds. There were matching designs on the boots and along the belt of the pants.

"You look . . . different," Denise remarked, not sure what to make of this new Deke.

Deke had been holding his goggles and pushed them onto his eyes. He studied Denise a moment through his blue goggles before pushing them back onto his head.

"You look like you were meant to live here."

Denise couldn't help but smile but quickly pushed it off. "You do live here."

Deke quickly cleared his throat and started down the huge hallway, Denise following close behind. "No Denise . . . my dad lives here."

"I don't know," the girl mused. "It seems that he's looking toward having you stay here with him. I mean, it's not every day that you find out that your dad is King Steven Rasmussen of Gerhenia!"

Deke didn't answer but stared straight ahead as they walked. Of course, Denise could tell that his skin was going dry and there was an astonished look in his eyes. Grinning to herself, Denise decided to push it further.

"You know, that also makes you a prince!"

Deke stopped short and spun on the girl. "Wait what?"

"Didn't you know?" Denise inquired, pretending to act innocent. "When your mother or father is king or queen, you are a prince or princess . . . and I don't think you're a princess."

Deke opened his mouth as if prepared to object with Denise's perfect logic when a door down the hallway opened. Golden light flooded the dim lit hallway and a butler stepped out.

"Your Highness, Miss Nielson. Dinner is served."

The butler did a low bow and held out his arm toward the open door. Deke waited long enough to give Denise a distressed look, but the girl had a smug and excited look on her face as she walked bravely through the door. Deke hesitated only a moment before following her.

They stepped into a huge open room that looked like it could be a grand hall. There was absolutely nothing in the gigantic room other than the tapestries that lined the walls and the huge wooden table in the center of the room.

The king was standing at one end of the room but as the two kids entered, he strode toward the table and held out a hand toward them. Denise walked forward, obviously more accustomed to these things than Deke and took the man's hand.

Leading Denise around the table, Steven seated her at one of the only three chairs at the huge table. By then, Deke had appeared at the chair across the table from Denise and was waiting for his father to sit. He waited until his father was sitting down before he seated himself.

The moment he sat down, the door of the dining room opened and five serving girls entered with trays of food as if there weren't already dozens of platters of food already on the table.

"So how do you like life in Hichester, Deke?" Steven inquired as he began to carve the huge ham before him.

Swallowing a mouthful of saliva, Deke began to wonder where he should start. How was he to know his father would be pleased when he heard about his friends and family back home? Or about what he did in his spare time. Obviously, he wouldn't tell his father things that he wouldn't even tell Neil or Gene. That wouldn't make any sense since his two brothers could take any news without dying.

"It's great," he replied before he realized he spoke. It was like his voice was speaking for him. "I've made a lot of friends there . . . and I've been inventing stuff in my free time."

Steven looked up as he set his carving tools down and began to help Denise serve her helping of ham. "Really? What kind of things do you invent?"

Thank goodness he didn't ask about my friends, Deke thought. It wasn't that Deke was ashamed of his friends, but he would have to mention Whip and the twins, and he didn't know how his father would take hearing about them . . . . Especially the twins.

"Oh, just random stuff . . . I made a door contraption for my cat, so she can let herself out of my room without my being there . . ." Deke started, serving himself some green beans and asparagus. "I'm trying to make a clock that has a heartbeat rate and body temperature part to it. I've got most of the temperature part down, but the heart beat is hard."

Steven considered his son a moment before glancing at Denise who was being served pudding by one of the serving girls. "Mr. Wetherby says that your brothers are part of a Christmas play this winter."

Deke didn't look up, but he duly noted the fact that Steven used the term "brothers" when he meant Gene and Neil. Okay so that erased Deke's worry that Neil and Gene might not even be his half-brothers.

"Yeah," he replied. "I was going to be part, but I have terrible stage fright. So, I'm going to help set up stage between scenes. To be honest, I prefer watching plays than acting in them. Neil is much better than I am."

Steven smiled but didn't look at Deke this time. "Everyone has a fright of something. Stage fright is nothing to be ashamed of. Many people are afraid to just talk to one person but are okay with acting in front of an audience."

Deke's eyebrows went down immediately, and he couldn't concentrate on his food even though there were only vegetables on it so far. It was like his father would start a conversation that might or might not have to do with Neil and

Gene, but then the moment Deke started talking about his brothers, his father would drift off of the first subject. Deke couldn't even remember how they got talking in the first place.

"Well, Neil has no fear of people that's for sure," Deke remarked, trying to see how far he could get talking about Neil before his father changed the subject. "He'll jump into arguments to solve the problem. He's not afraid of audiences and he excels at being a leader. I mean, I even get kinda nervous talking with some of my friends on matters that make me nervous but with Neil, I don't."

The smile seemed frozen on Steven's face which roused Deke's suspicion. There was no smile in Steven's eyes anymore and he was obviously not looking at his food . . . or at least not concentrating on it.

"Eileen seems really nice," he started. "How long have you known her Denise?"

Deke found his eyes expand at the fact that his father had ignored him and changed to talking to Denise. However, when Denise glanced in his direction, he pretended to not be hurt.

"Oh . . ." Denise started after taking a bite of ham. "I've known her for about three years. She is a real sweet girl."

Steven nodded and a kind smile crossed his face. "How about your father? I hope everything is going well in Pyralani."

"Oh yes," Denise remarked, warming up to the conversation and forgetting her food all together. "There was an outbreak of objection against a new campaign that my father is involved with but after a while it died down."

Deke lowered his eyebrows a moment before speaking up. "Denise . . . I thought your dad was a doctor . . . how can he be involved with a campaign?"

Denise slowly looked over the platters of food at Deke and it was evident that she had something she was afraid to say. "Actually Deke . . . my father isn't a doctor. That is what he wants everyone to believe because of his work. He works hand in hand with the king of Pyralani in different campaigns which limits the people he can reveal his position to . . . Also, I didn't want you all to treat me differently because of who my father was."

She cut off there and Deke was staring at her, mouth slightly open and obviously confused. Steven cut the silence by clearing his throat, getting Deke's attention but not Denise's.

"Deke . . . Denise's father is the earl of Pyralani. His cousin is the king of Pyralani. I work with them regularly . . . that is how I knew Denise."

Deke slowly turned and looked back at Denise who was looking at him in distress. He had never seen that look of concern or worry on Denise's face but now it revealed a whole list of things.

"You . . . you knew my father . . . even before we got here . . ." Deke slowly started.

There was a dreadful silence in which Denise looked down at her plate and away from Deke's gaze and in which Steven began speaking again.

"About that play," Steven remarked hastily. "What is the genre? Was it written by a friend of yours . . ."

Deke caught him off mid-sentence by placing his hands down on the table and looking him straight in the eye. "Dad, I need to ask you something."

Steve glanced up from his food, not sure what his son was going to ask but thinking it might be associated with Denise's heritage since that was what they had been talking about when Deke interrupted. "What is it son?"

He was no longer Deke, the tongue-tied-too-scared-to-start-the-conversation kid. He was thinking of all those days when Gene would look him directly in the eye and encourage him to keep going. All those days when Neil's strong hand would grip his shoulder and help him get his mind back on track. Neither of them was here but he was going to do this for them. He was going to speak his mind without hesitation for the first time in his life because he owed it to them.

"How is Neil related to me?" he asked bluntly and in a stronger voice than he was prepared for.

Steve was shocked and actually snapped his head back slightly in confusion. His son had talked almost half to himself the past two days and hadn't come out with a blunt question like that. Deke was probably more surprised than him especially at the firm tone in his voice. He actually sounded like Neil when he was trying to break up an argument.

"I don't see how that exactly has to do with me," Steven began. "We are in no way . . ."

Deke shook his head vigorously and placed his hand firmly on the arm of his chair, gripping it to get control of himself. "No. I need to know. How. Is. Neil. Related. To. Me?"

Steven's dark brown eyes met Deke's and he could see the defiance and determination in the boy's eyes. Steven didn't have much experience with kids, but he could handle his own son surely.

He was the adult in this conversation. If he said the word, Deke would hush up and nothing else would be said on the matter. Isn't that how it always happens?

"That is none of your concern," Steven replied, preparing to look back at his food.

The last word of his reply was barely out of his mouth before Deke stood up so fast that the chair jostled slightly. "Yes, it is something of my concern. I just find out that I am possibly half related to the only family I've ever known. My whole life I thought I was the son of Morgan and Frank Mecarnin only to find I am the son of Morgan and Steve Rasmussen. The son of a king no less! I also find out that one of my best friends is the daughter of an earl, the niece of a king and a friend to my father and no one ever told me. Yet, there is the fact that I have an older brother and a younger brother who I am related to in some way but the only parent I seem to have will not tell me how I am related to my brother!"

"What if Neil isn't your brother?" Steven snapped, his voice rising.

Deke almost faltered . . . was that it? Was Neil really not his brother? Was he just a distant cousin . . . or just a kid picked up along the way? No . . . no that couldn't be! Neil had their mother's green eyes . . . or at least one of them. He

had the nose and mouth shape of their mother . . .
he was definitely related to him in some way.

"Even if he isn't my brother by blood, he is
one of the only two people who have ever been
true family to me! Mr. Wetherby was always like a
grandfather and Eileen is like a sister, but Gene
and Neil have been the only family that have been
there for me since I was a kid! Now I know I
cannot trust things my mother and Frank
Mecarnin taught me because it was obviously all a
lie! The only people I know won't lie to me are
Gene and Neil! They have a right to know just as
much as me about WHAT HAPPENED!"

Steven met the glare of his son. Full of
fire . . . blue fire. He knew Deke had poor
eyesight, that was one of the first things the boy
had revealed. Yet, Steven felt a strange sensation
that Deke wasn't looking at him with his eyes . . .
he was looking at him with his soul . . . full of
concern, fury, joy . . . and confusion.

He had better get it over with because
those blue fire eyes were beginning to burn
Steven's brown ones. When he replied, he half
expected Deke to stare and fall back into his chair
and they could continue their meal. However,
Deke's facial features didn't change. He pushed
the chair back roughly with his foot and strode
directly to the door without looking back,

slamming it behind him, causing the serving girl to jump. A moment later Denise excused herself and followed Deke hastily through the door.

What Steven didn't see was that on the other side, Denise found Deke in the hallway and at once his face went a full shade paler than pale and his lip began to tremble. Denise could barely hear the words that left his mouth but later, she wondered at how he had even gotten those few out:

"We all have the same mother . . . . But different fathers."

Chapter 23

"Why?" Deke's voice whispered so hoarsely that Denise thought it would crack. "Why didn't you tell me? You knew who my father was the moment you heard his name! Why didn't you . . . tell me?"

Deke's voice was so slow and quiet, Denise felt herself feel hot and cold at the same time, kind of like when she broke something that was vitally important. She shuffled her feet nervously, but it was in vain for her long skirts muffled the sound.

"I . . . I was sworn to secrecy Deke."

Deke looked up and his blue eyes flared like blue flame. "You were sworn to secrecy to keep the truth from me?! I find out that my dad is not Neil and Gene's dad and that we are all half-brothers while for the past twelve years I have thought that we were full blood brothers! I find out that I cannot trust one of my friends with the truth and not even my dad! Mr. Wetherby is the only one who doesn't lie to me!"

Denise wondered at the perfect timing of Deke's observation. It was ironic that he would mention Mr. Wetherby at that moment.

"Deke . . ." the girl slowly started. "Mr. Wetherby was the one who . . . swore us to secrecy."

Deke had turned away after his last outburst but now he slowly turned back. "Who is 'us'?"

"Me . . . my family . . . Seraphina, Emma . . . Whip, Oliver . . . the twins, Eileen, Father Fischer . . . everyone. We were all sworn to secrecy by Mr. Wetherby and Matilda's request," the girl replied in a voice that was even quieter than Deke's.

Deke slowly considered this fact. The fact that everyone knew of these secrets but had kept them . . . did that mean that . . .

"What about . . . ." He started but Denise cut him off.

"Gene and Neil don't know . . . you three are the only ones who don't know," Denise replied. "It was for your own good."

"For our own good?" Deke inquired, his voice rising. "It was for our own good that the truth was kept from us! Our true heritage hidden and the matters of life concealed?"

"We didn't want you to be afraid . . ." Denise started.

This time, Deke was the one who cut her off. "Afraid of what? Tell me! What am I supposed to be afraid of?"

Denise's eyes slowly grew until Deke suddenly realized that this wasn't a joke. "You . . ." she started. "You really don't know?"

"Of course not!" Deke snapped but at once regretted it because the girl jumped. "What am I supposed to know?"

Denise slowly extended one hand as if hesitant to touch Deke. Deke didn't move but stared in surprise as Denise reached forward and took his hand. Never in his time of knowing Denise had the girl ever taken his hand and it sent a tingle up his spine. Her hand was gentle but fiercely strong.

"I need to show you something," she whispered.

Leading him after her, Denise grasped the front of her skirt with one hand and lifted it out of the way of her feet. Picking up the pace, she hurried down the hallway that was deemed too fast for a lady but much to slow for a girl.

Denise's mind was set on hurrying and making sure to not get lost. Of course, she couldn't since she had visited this castle before when she had accompanied her father on business trips. Deke was following close behind her like a puppy, apologizing to anyone they bumped or startled and throwing out "pardon us" and "excuse us" remarks all over the place.

After leaving the tangle of hallways behind them, Denise lead him down the high, railing-less stairs that curved down into the great hall. This room had surprised Deke, but the stairs had frightened him. There was one set of stairs in this room that curved like an "S" from one side of the room all the way up to the door that led up into the tangle of hallways and doorways of the upper half of the foyer.

There were no railings on that staircase, and it was solid brick so there was no chance that it would break but the top of the stairs was almost fifteen feet from the floor of the great hall and without railings, Deke believed that there had been someone at one point who had fallen.

Denise hurried down the stairs as if they weren't stairs at all while Deke bit his lip in concern that their speed would prove their downfall. However, they managed to reach the bottom of the stairs alive and Denise hurried across the huge, open and relatively empty hall to one of the doors across from the stairs.

The hall was used for large occasions such as banquets, dances and ceremonies and that was when tables and other things were brought out.

However, on a regular day to day basis, it was used more as the common room where people had room to move around and talk.

Denise pushed through the huge oak doors as they groaned on the hinges. She led Deke down the stairs within the door which lead down to the kitchen. The stairs were beginning to darken until Denise pushed open the kitchen door and the two charged into the room.

All the cooks and maids stopped short as the two flew through the door and down the small flight of stairs. Denise didn't stop to explain and while Deke waved to the women with a sheepish smile, Denise dragged him through the kitchen to a door that led out of the kitchen.

Deke hadn't had time to really explore the castle other than a few rooms and the most important rooms such as the dining room and the great hall as well as the library which reminded him of the one at SOHE.

This door that Denise lead him through opened up a series of unknown places. The door lead to a narrow dark staircase that seemed to go down forever, twisting and turning this way and that. Soon the stairs began to become flat and almost uneven.

Deke had no idea how Denise could see but he followed her loyally as she led him farther down. Just when Deke was getting fed up with stairs, a light appeared up ahead. Denise slowed down and released Deke's hand for the first time since they had started their venture.

She took a few steps forward toward a torch that was hanging on the wall. Lifting it off the hook, she grasped it expertly in her hand and stood to the side. She looked back at Deke who hadn't moved, and she moved her free hand toward the place beyond her that was dim lit.

Deke slowly moved forward, not knowing what to expect. As he passed Denise, he realized that the glare of the torch lit up a small metal plaque that was drilled into the hard stone of the dead end. There was nothing there other than the plaque, so Deke leant forward and squinted.

Denise moved closer and held the torch near the plaque so he could see better. Pulling his goggles over his eyes, Deke considered the plaque. Etched carefully into the fine, rather ancient metal, he could make out a small paragraph which he read aloud:

Herein lies the place known as the Missing Piece. None shall enter but those divined. All else who strive to enter will encounter great distress and no success on their attempts. Insert your password to the label and discover that which you wish to know but be warned: this is only a piece.

Cameron II S-----r on the 643 of the Golden Age

Deke slowly lifted his eyes and looked at Denise. "Who was he? His name is missing."

Denise nodded. Only the first and last letters of the last name were there because the years of rust and dampness had eaten away at that name.

"He was a good man. He, along with several other special people put this place here to keep the enemy from finding all the answers, should they discover the Scoih."

"The Scoih? Like in Cochin Scoih the country?" Deke inquired.

Denise smiled. "Correct. There is an underground world in Cochin Scoih that only a few people know of and even fewer people have seen with their own eyes. No one knows where it is . . . only a few people do."

"Who . . . . Who are those few people?" Deke demanded, suddenly intrigued.

Denise didn't answer in words but reached into her sleeve. She pulled out a small chain that Deke had seen her wearing around her neck, but he had never seen what was on the end of the chain. As she drew it out, Deke felt his heart stop when he realized that a tiny piece of blue crystal hung from the end. The crystal was not your ordinary crystal. Shining beyond the brightness of the torch, it lit up the dark passage. It was so smooth and perfectly shaped but barely bigger than Deke's tiny finger.

Deke might have not known who Cameron II was or about the things Denise had been acquainting him with, but he was no stranger to well-known legends, myths and tales and this particular one he knew was true: the tale of the Guardians of Corlan, also known as the HUDGE members.

"Denise . . . don't tell me that . . . . That . . . that thing is . . ." Deke stammered.

Denise smiled and nodded solemnly. "Indeed it is Deke. It is one of the eight crystals of Uhffer Toah."

Deke knew well of the legend of Uhffer Toah. About how at the very beginning, when redemption for all mankind was promised by the Lord, another promise was made. The promise was that when man's need was dire between the beginning and end of time, there would always be someone to fix the wrong in the world . . . someone to protect those who truly believed in the Lord.

Deke also knew very well that the Guardians of Corlan were part of that promise, better known as the promise of Uhffer Toah. The guardians defeated evil that had reigned through the world for centuries. They gave home and a second chance to man. Better yet, they had answered many doubts and questions.

This crystal . . . the crystal that Denise now held was one of the eight crystals gifted to the guardians when they began their mission to save the Faith. The crystals were a gift from God, a sign of His love and that He truly entrusted a wonderful mission to the guardians.

"My grandfather . . . Timber Nielson gave this to me," Denise explained. "After . . . . after the other guardians died, he couldn't bear to keep it, so he gave it to me. He said that it will not do miraculous things like in the legends, but he said that it is the password."

"Okay," Deke remarked. "So I get the fact that the guardians were the few who saw the Scoih . . . but what does this passage have to do with that and who in the world is Cameron II?"

Denise saw that she had gotten off topic, so she held the crystal close to her while she spoke. "After the guardians . . . or most of them died, Cameron and many other people went to the Scoih and removed several parts of it and brought it here. They buried it down here and put such strong locks here that nothing could enter the chamber. They did that so if anything happened to the Scoih, not everything would be lost."

Deke rapped his knuckles on the plaque and a deep, thick sound echoed through the dark passage. "It doesn't look like they did anything but put a plaque on a wall of stone."

Denise smiled and stepped forward, past Deke. She lifted the crystal, lighting up the wall and the plaque: "Insert your password on the label," she read aloud in a low voice.

Deke had crossed his arms over his chest and was impatiently tapping his foot on the stone floor. He was losing his patience with Denise's peculiar, mysterious and almost secretive behavior. He watched with no expression as Denise lifted the crystal toward the plaque and placed it on the two words: *Missing Piece.*

She held the crystal there for what seemed like forever but was really only three seconds. Deke thought he heard a chinking noise like a stone falling from the ceiling. He glanced over his shoulder, expecting to see someone behind them but the passage was empty other than the glaring torch on the wall.

When he turned back toward Denise, he realized that the dead end and the plaque on the wall were gone. There was now a huge open hole before them, and Denise was lifting the blue crystal to light up the dark entrance.

"What in the world?" Deke hissed. "What did you do?"

Denise glanced over her shoulder and held up the crystal. "Cameron didn't make it impossible to enter this place . . . only impossible for those who did not have a crystal of Uhffer Toah."

Deke furrowed his brow. "So it wasn't by coincidence that Timber gave you that crystal before we came here?"

The girl shook her head. "It wasn't a coincidence. He knew that by coming to visit your father, we would end up here and eventually the truth would be presented before you. He thought it best that we have the key. He was considering giving it to my parents but when he heard that I was coming with you, he gave it to me."

Without another word, the girl ducked her head and stepped into the dark doorway, leaving Deke to follow hesitantly.

Chapter 24

As Seraphina headed back into the room behind the stage, she found Whip and Drew sitting in straight back chairs, their chins in their hands. Both of them had their eyebrows down, furrowed in thought.

"What's on your mind?" she inquired as she sat down beside them.

Before the two could answer, the twins hurried in and slammed down into sitting positions. "They're trying to think of a way to prove Styl's guilt in the crime," Roy explained.

"They want her to admit to her guilt," Reed clarified.

Seraphina raised her eyebrows. "Why would you do that? Maybe it's none of our business what is going on between Emma and Styl."

Whip lifted his head and shook it hard. "Sorry sis but this is different. Styl struck Emma unconscious and left her in the woods. She didn't think there was anyone around and if we hadn't been there, Emma would have froze to death! Besides, Emma was in a coma for almost three full hours! It's more serious than just a grudge. This is . . . more like revenge on the highest level!"

Drew nodded in agreement. "See Seraphina, we cannot leave Emma on her own with Styl running around. If that girl finds out that Emma is here in Hichester, safe and her act didn't go unnoticed, someone is going to get hurt and chances are it'll be Emma."

Seraphina glanced at the twins who were more than prepared to back the two up. She turned her concerned eyes to Zara who just appeared, but the girl was also nodding her head in agreement with Drew and Whip's reasoning.

"They're right S," Zara admitted, sitting down beside Drew. "I hate to admit it, but they are."

"Well," Seraphina remarked in defeat. "Did either of you come up with a plan then?"

"Oh yeah," Roy replied, interrupting Whip's answer. "We were going to have Whip pretend to faint but that would never work in his case even though it would have been marvelous to see!"

"I preferred the Drew-playing-kick-the-can-with-Thtyl-and-bet-on-Emma'th-releathe-then-punch-Whip-and-lock-up-Thtyl idea," Reed admitted.

Seraphina turned her eyes to her brother to see Drew and Whip glowering at the twins. "Were you seriously going to do that?"

"Of course not!" Drew cried. "We don't have a plan! Do we just go straight up to Styl and reveal that we know what she did to Emma? She would have our heads! In case you didn't notice, she is much older than us and probably stronger."

"Drew has a point," Whip added. "Hey Seraphina . . . what if you pretended that you saw the crime? You're bigger than Styl and you could take care of yourself. Besides, the grownups would believe you more than they would believe the two of us."

"I can't do that, Whip!" Seraphina almost shouted. "That would be lying! I never saw the accident and only heard it from you two and Emma. Emma can't do it because she's still recovering, and we need to keep her as far from Styl as possible. I can't bear false witness for something I didn't see."

Immediately, all their faces fell. The twins, Whip and Drew had all been thinking of what Seraphina could say to Styl but once they heard the last part, they knew she was right.

"Then that means . . ." Drew gulped. "Whip or I have to do it . . . we were the only witnesses in the case."

Zara nodded. "Or you could both do it. Or flip a coin if you want but the more witnesses, the better."

"But how do we bring the culprit to justice?" Whip demanded. "The only ones who know of this whole thing are the six of us, Gene and Emma. Styl is on the other side. We can't just reveal it, she'll have our heads but also, we need to help her see her fault. It wouldn't do to accuse her without helping her repent."

"Spoken like a true changeling," Seraphina remarked, smiling at her brother. "We'll have to think of something . . . two girls get into an argument because one is jealous of the other while the other tries to mend the broken bond between them. Instead, the jealous one betrays them . . . that's tough."

"Why does that sound so familiar?" Zara inquired.

Everyone shrugged. It sounded familiar to them as well, but they couldn't place it.

Presently, they were awoken from their hard thinking by the appearance of Rodge. His face was red, and he was panting.

"Guys . . . something's happened . . . and it's not good!"

"What do you mean?" Seraphina asked, leaping to her feet.

Rodge shook his head, his dark eyes showing fear. "Everyone dropped out of Christmas decorating!"

"The cowards," Roy snapped. "I thought that rumor was just a mean joke, but it's gone too far this time!"

"Yes, it has," Rodge admitted, "and the headmasters are prepared to throw Gene out of the society."

"WHAT?!" Zara cried, running over to Rodge and grabbing his arm, shaking it. "Why would they do that? Gene is one of their best students!"

"Well, Zara," Rodge panted, "after what they heard a few minutes ago . . . they don't think he is the best student anymore."

Zara and Seraphina's faces immediately went pale. The whole thing with the suicide bomber and the rumor had been going on for several hours so it couldn't have been that.

"What did they hear?" Whip whispered in a hoarse voice. "What?"

Rodge sighed and ran his hand through his dark hair. "Destiny arrived at the society about twenty minutes ago with Bobby Clymer and Victor West. She and Victor said that Gene appeared and attacked Bobby . . . knocking him into a coma."

* * * * *

Deke stumbled over a chinking in the floor,
reaching out to grab something and found a wall.
Keeping his hand on the wall, Deke looked over at
Denise who was walking around the room, shining
the blue crystal all over the place.

They were in a large open room, not much
bigger than a master bedroom but connected to
the room where three arch doorways, each leading
to different directions.

In each arch was a gate of different design
and material. Directly to the left of the passage
entrance was the first of these gateways with a
huge golden gate. It didn't look that strong and
had more design to it than depth. One could easily
slip through the fancy designs or even bend the
metal but from the look of it, the gate was made of
gold so it would be virtually impossible to bend it
by hand.

To the direct right of the passage entrance
was another gateway with a solid black gate, made
of solid iron. There was no design on the gate and
reminded Deke of a black hole. Directly opposite
the passage entrance was the third and final
gateway. This one was made of strong bars of
silver. It had no fancy curly Q's, nor was it solid

and grim looking but halfway between almost like a prison door.

"Where do these lead to?" Deke inquired.

Denise slowly turned to look at the boy, her face lit up by the blue crystal in her hand. Without a word, the girl lifted the crystal high above her head and walked to the center of the room. That was when Deke became aware of a small chandelier that hung from the center of the relatively low ceiling.

The chandelier looked more like a glass ball that hung from a thick silver chain rather than anything else. Denise stood on tippy toe till she could touch the chandelier. Lifting the crystal, she touched the glass with the blue gem, and everything changed.

Three shoots of pure white light shot out from the glass and sped off in three different directions. Each struck a part of the wall directly above each gateway. Deke hastily pulled on his goggles and squinted at the bright light that lit up the walls above each arch.

Above the solid black iron gate was a word that was barely decipherable, but Deke could make it out as ancient Rechuedian: Charity.

Deke spun around and looked at the word above the silver gate: Hope. The single word: Faith shone bright above the golden gate as well.

"What do they mean?" Deke whispered hoarsely.

Denise smiled as she stood on tiptoe again and touched the glass a last time. The light seemed to grow just faintly, and a fourth shoot of light left the glass and sailed toward the passage entrance. In the white light, Deke could make out a few pale words:

The Room of Righteousness

"The Room of Righteousness," Denise read aloud. "This is where the legends come to reality Deke. Each of these chambers represent different time in history, the present, past and the future when these three virtues play a major role."

Deke slowly followed Denise as the girl strode over to the golden gate. The girl touched the bars gently with her hand and it seemed to glow a brighter gold until it was shining almost brighter than the crystal in her hand.

"The chamber of Faith. It is where the prophecies of the guardians dwell. This chamber holds the answers to what they were assigned to do and how they did it," the girl whispered.

Not even bothering to open the gate, the girl led Deke over to the silver gate. This time she didn't touch the gate but pushed Deke toward it. The boy slowly touched the silver metal and it began to glow. It became almost too bright to look at, then . . . the light subsided for a half second before the gate gave way. It slowly creaked open and swung into the chamber.

Denise grasped Deke's hand and placed the crystal in his hand. She gave him a gentle nudge toward the interior of the chamber, but Deke hesitated.

"What about you?"

Denise shook her head vigorously. "That chamber is for your eyes only. Yours and the eyes of your brothers."

Deke paused to see if he could convince her otherwise, but Denise stepped back, out of the bright glow of the crystal. Turning to look over his shoulder, Deke took a deep breath and stepped further into the chamber.

The chamber stretched out long, not curved or with other passages. Deke presently reached the dead end and saw that the chamber was only about eight feet wide and twenty feet long. Deke took a few steps back toward the gate, but his eye caught something . . . a faint glimmer from the wall.

Squinting through his goggles and lifting the crystal, Deke saw that there was a small hole chiseled out of the wall. Laying in the long, narrow hole was a small scroll. Reaching out with one hand, he grasped the scroll and jolted.

The material of the scroll was made of the softest paper he had ever held, and it sent a sudden warmth through his body. Letting the crystal hang by his neck, Deke unrolled the scroll slowly. There was a single golden word in the center of the page: Understanding.

Furrowing his brow, Deke rolled the parchment back up and placed it back into the hole. Just as he did so, the parchment began to glow a faint glow of red, blue and green. The glow swirled around the parchment and then spread onto the stone wall surrounding the hole. Deke watched as the three glowing colors leapt up the wall and then struck a metal plaque on the wall above the hole and the light faded.

Grasping the crystal around his neck, Deke lifted it into the air and peered at the plaque:

When almost all hope was lost, the three arose from the depths. They defeated doubt and skepticism and turned to each other for support.

December 3rd, 720

Deke cocked his head to the side, that was the date when they rescued Emma from the underbeast lair three years prier. He took note of what was said on the plaque before turning away.

He stopped short when something caught his eye. Lifting the crystal higher in the air, he saw

223

that there were multiple plaques on the walls with holes beneath them. Six of them to be exact, three on each side of the chamber.

Crossing the chamber, Deke grasped the next scroll but realized that it was blank. He turned it over but there was nothing written on it. Glancing up at the plaque, he saw another writing:

The wind was silent, the fire blazed firm but the three knew that the other was worthy and stuck through the night to battle the dark who invaded their home and their life.

There was no date on that plaque either which made Deke frown. He looked at each of the other four plaques, none of them making sense and none of them having dates. All four of the other scrolls were blank as well and when he put them back in their holes, they didn't glow like the first one had.

After a moment, Deke left the chamber and handed the crystal back to Denise. "I don't get it."

The girl smiled as she slipped the crystal into her sleeve. "Few do. The chances of you understanding that chamber before everything is completed is rather low. I will tell you this Deke: these chambers were not made lightly. They were made by steady hands who worked at the bidding of the Lord. Every time you or your brothers learn something new that brings hope to the world, it will become clearer and clearer."

Without another word, Denise took Deke's hand and led him out of the room. She turned and touched the plaque on the door again and it slowly closed. As it did so, Deke caught a glimpse of the light in the room fade to darkness again.

Denise turned and taking the torch, began to walk back up the stairs. Deke stared at the plaque on the wall for a moment before charging after her.

"What about the other two rooms? The one belonging to the guardians and the other one?" he demanded.

Denise shook her head. "The guardians' chamber will only be opened by them themselves. The day you see the interior of their chamber is the day when you and your brothers complete what you were meant to do. The third . . . I honestly don't know . . . it's of the future."

Chapter 25

"Are you done writing that letter Neil?" Eileen called. "The car is waiting!"

"Just a second!" Neil called back.

Dear Deke, Denise and Mr. Rasmussen,

Don't worry about the two of us. We're going straight home to help Gene because it sounds like he needs help back there. We'll be fine, and we'll write as soon as we arrive. Have a nice visit at Hanalona. Mr. Wetherby has decided to wait in Gerh with Bruce till you return. Love, Neil and Eileen.

Neil wrapped up the note, placing it in the maid's hands. "Don't forget to give it to them the moment they return."

The maid nodded and smiled as she handed Neil his hat and coat. "And don't you forget to stay warm. The snow is coming down out there."

Neil clamped his hat on and began to pull his coat on before Eileen appeared and dragged him the rest of the way. Steven's personal chauffeur was behind the wheel and smiling at them. When the two revealed their need back home, the man had offered to drive the two kids home since Mr. Wetherby and Bruce were staying behind a while longer to wait for the others.

Eileen pushed the boy into the back seat of the car and climbed in, closing the door behind her. Mr. Wetherby appeared at the window and Eileen rolled it down, so they could hear him.

"Martin will see you to Break Neck without fail," he reminded them. "He won't be able to take you farther since I'll need him back here to help the others back when they return."

The two kids nodded, and Neil smiled just as the car started off. "Thank you."

Just as the car neared the first turn, Neil heard someone call his name. Spinning in his seat he turned to see Mr. Wetherby cupping his hands around his mouth and yelling something. All he could hear was:

"You're not the only one . . ."

Eileen looked at the boy quizzically as Neil sank back down into the seat. "What was that all about?"

Neil shook his head, black hair waving back and forth. He would need a haircut soon. He was starting to look like Deke the day before haircut week. "I don't know . . . but something about his tone told me that it was important."

About an hour later, Neil found himself being shaken awake by a very alert and not usually quiet Eileen. Her dark blue eyes were wide with shock and her hair was slightly crusted from snow as if she had left the car for a moment.

"What is it?" Neil moaned, protesting against her rousing him.

"We're stuck Neil!" Eileen cried.

"No, I think we got my foot unstuck from the buckle about three minutes before I fell asleep," Neil retorted, half asleep.

Eileen shook him hard, causing his head to knock against the door handle. "Not that stuck! The car is stuck in the snow!"

"We'll just walk the rest of the way," Neil said groggily as he sat up straight.

Martin turned around in his seat and considered Neil a moment. "It's another thirty mile walk to Break Neck Creek son."

Neil was immediately awake and looking about him from his seat. Snow was piled up in front of them but not too bad from behind. "Isn't there anything we can do?" his voice cracking in worry."

"The only thing we can do is turn around and head back," Martin replied. "That's the only direction this machine is going."

Neil bit his lip hard, causing it to turn white. He couldn't turn back! Gene needed his help back home badly. By the time the snow was cleared it would be time for Deke to come home for Christmas Eve and who knows what would happen between now and that time.

"There's . . . no way to get home . . ." Neil started, fearing to ask it louder than a whisper.

Eileen was about to object to Martin's point and was prepared to walk the thirty miles when Martin spoke up. "Maybe this kind gentleman will know how we can get there."

The two kids sat up straight in their seats to see that through the front window, a man was walking toward them in the snow. He was dressed in a long overcoat, a hat pulled down over his ears but reddish blond hair showing around the sides of his face and a shortly carefully trimmed beard and mustache made him look in his forties when he was probably in his late twenties.

Martin opened his door and slowly climbed out. Eileen opened her door which wouldn't open more than halfway since the snow was piled beside the door about knee deep. The two climbed out and shivered in their overcoats and hats.

The man approached and considered the car. "Before you ask, this isn't the first time this has happened," the man remarked in an obviously Catasbanian accent. "We got a delivery truck stuck right here last year. This place really piles up with snow in the winter."

Right away the kids and Martin relaxed at the kindness in the man's cheerful tone. "Trying to get home?" the man continued.

The three nodded. "I'm trying to get these two to the west side of the Smothering River," Martin explained, carefully avoiding the mention of Break Neck since the man might not even know what it is.

The man nodded. "We've had several pass through here on their way there. I can tell you this, if you don't get that car out of there now, you'll be stuck here overnight."

"Oh boy," Neil groaned.

The stranger considered Neil and Eileen, obviously noticing the dampened hope and obvious worry in their eyes. "Well, the roads should be clear by tomorrow once the plows come through in the morning. However, it it's just the two you need to get there, they can stay with me until the morning and then my chauffeur can take them to their destination."

Martin tensed slightly, obviously not liking the idea of leaving his charges in the hands of a stranger and possibly a replacement chauffeur. He obviously was very proud of his job.

"That's very kind of you . . ." Eileen started, not sure whether to accept or refuse since they didn't know the man well.

Just when the two kids were about to refuse, a man bundled up in a wooly coat and a thick hat hurried through the snow toward the first stranger. This new person was heavy set and slightly short compared to the tall, slender man.

"Sir Charles," the man panted, blowing steam from his warm breath. "Your wife just wired from the Church. She'll be home shortly from the Confirmation meeting."

The first stranger, Sir Charles, nodded thanks to the man who hurried off back the way he had come. Even before Sir Charles looked back at them, Neil and Eileen had exchanged knowing looks and smiles. If they needed any encouragement to accept the invitation, the mention of Church and Confirmation was all they needed to know that they were safe.

"We would be honored sir," Eileen said, pretending to finish her sentence. "We hope it will not be too much trouble for you."

Sir Charles waved his hand and smiled. "None whatsoever. We love to have you stay with us even if it is just for the night. My brother-in-law and daughter just returned from boarding school for the holidays and I'm sure they would love the company of youths."

Neil and Eileen smiled at this remark and saw that Martin also seemed eased. Sir Charles then set about helping them draw out their bags and close the doors. Neil and Eileen gave Martin messages to relay to Steve Rasmussen before the man backed the car out of the snow and headed back down the road of matted snow and ice.

Sir Charles began to head off the road and as the two followed, they became increasingly aware of a tall Victorian house that rose up from the snow-covered pine trees. The drive was covered in snow but the gray-and-cream stone house with its dark gray shingles gave an almost wintery look to the frosty hillside.

* * * * *

There was a small herd of people who were following Deke down the stairs. Denise was one of the number, but she wasn't chattering like a bird as they walked. Most of the people were young maids, pages and a few squires whom she and Deke had gotten to know over the day and night they had been there.

"Do you have to go sir?" a young page inquired. "You just got here!"

Deke smiled faintly but the smile wasn't in his eyes. "It is a two-day journey to Break Neck and I cannot miss getting back home before

Christmas. If I do, my brothers will have my head."

"Just tell them that you are the prince of Gerhenia," a maid suggested. "Then they won't be able to complain."

Denise looked over at her companion to see that a faraway look had appeared in Deke's eyes. "Actually . . ." the boy started. "I'm not going to tell anyone about that."

"WHAT?!" the group of young people demanded.

Denise found herself staring in surprise at Deke.

"Okay, Seraphina and Whip and the rest might know who I am but I'm going to make sure they don't tell Neil or Gene. I don't want them treating me differently because of who I am. Just like Denise said."

Denise felt a smile appear on her face at those words, but a young squire stepped forward as they reached the courtyard. "But what of Miss Seraphina and Master Whip? They wouldn't treat you differently."

Deke stopped to set down his knapsack of things and wrapped his cloak closer around his body as they stood in the blistering cold. "What are you talking about?"

As the squire began to explain, Denise wished dearly that she could just disappear from the face of the earth.

"Didn't you know sir? Miss Seraphina and Master Whip are the children of the Duke of Catasbanel. They go way back with your father and Miss Denise's father."

Denise was relieved when Deke didn't go pale or freak out. Obviously with everything that Deke had found out in the past twenty-four hours, nothing surprised him anymore. After they got back from the Room of Righteousness, Deke asked Denise further questions about her life as the daughter of an earl and found out that she had frequently visited Hanalona.

After that the boy had gone to sleep and had awoken at precisely six in the morning to tell Denise and his father that he wished to return home to Break Neck. Naturally this was understandable because the journey back to Gerh would take a full day so they would spend the night at the hotel where they had first met Steven before traveling to Break Neck which would get them home before Christmas.

Steven had tried to convince his son to stay longer but from the almost defiant way that Deke persisted, Steven gave up two minutes into the debate. Denise merely followed Deke's advice, packing and preparing to leave within three hours.

"Is that so?" Deke inquired of the squire, giving Denise a look that said, *You might have told me sooner.* "I'll be sure to keep that quiet as well."

The carriage finally arrived in the courtyard and the driver opened the door. Denise quickly stepped in out of the cold and Deke placed his bag inside. He paused and turned to look at the world he was leaving. The huge snow-covered courtyard was silent, watching him and the carriage as if mournfully. He could see the tall, rigid shape of his father at the top of the foyer steps, watching the scene.

Slowly turning back to the carriage, Deke stepped in and closed the door behind him . . . not bothering to look out the window until they were almost out of sight of Hanalona Montecarlen.

Chapter 26

"I doubt that would be the best idea," Emma pointed out from her position on the couch in the apothecary living room.

She was seated between the twins while Drew and Whip sat across from her. The four had been left in Emma's supervision while Seraphina and Zara went to speak with Destiny about the whole incident from earlier and hopefully get information from Gene as well.

"Well I most certainly can't take over leading the play," Whip pointed out. "Drew and I are already over our heads in trying to figure out . . . . Stuff."

Whip got a quick glare from Drew who had told him to not reveal their plan of Styl's injustice to Emma since they still weren't sure what to do about it.

"Well Gene seemed to be doing fine leading the play, preparing Christmas decorations, taking care of Webstar, and getting you two to get along just fine by himself until everyone ditched on him," Emma pointed out.

"I honestly don't know how he did it without going stark raving mad," Drew admitted.

"And I don't like the sound of the past news Rodge brought us . . . I don't know Gene well, but I don't think he would do something like this."

Roy cleared his throat. "Could we get back to the conversation on who is going to lead the play?"

"Well we most certainly won't put you in charge," Drew pointed out to the boy. "You would get holidays mixed up and have the stage hands wear bunny ears instead of Santa hats!"

"What about Reed?" Emma suggested, trying to pacify the four.

Whip and Drew were prepared to object when Roy interrupted their response. "I wouldn't put him in charge. He hasn't showered for the last month."

Almost immediately Drew's mouth dropped open, Whip's eyes grew wide, and Emma instinctively scooted farther away from the boy who acted as if no one had spoken.

"Should I be concerned or impressed by that observation?" Drew inquired, her violet eyes not moving from Reed.

At that moment the door of the apothecary opened, admitting Seraphina and Zara who were chatting angrily with each other. They were so in-depth in their talking that they barely took notice of the five kids watching them.

"It's absolutely ridiculous!" Zara pointed out. "Destiny was always on our side. Okay, yeah, I know that Destiny is always the kind of harsh one of the two, but she doesn't hate Gene! Why would she be so determined to spread that horrid rumor?"

"Well she said that Gene started out by acting normal then just out of the blue hurt Bobby . . . though she did say there was something strange about him," Seraphina pointed out.

"Strange indeed!" Zara snapped. "She's the one acting strange! What I would like to know is who spread the first rumor about Gene. The one where they said he was the one who hurt Jerry."

Reed let out a loud grunt which caused the two girls to stop and turn to him. "Actually . . . I know who it wath."

The boy's twin stared at him in stunned silence. Obviously, Roy hadn't expected his brother to know something he didn't.

"Let me guess . . . it was Barret?" Whip suggested.

Slowly the boy shook his head. He opened his mouth to give the fateful answer when the door of the apothecary opened and in strode Oliver, grasping a large book in one arm and his knapsack in the other. Everyone turned to acknowledge his entrance but the look on his face was enough for them to worry.

"It was me," he said. "I told the twins about it, but a bunch of other kids overheard us. I was the one who spread the rumor."

The silence that followed was so dense that you could hear Roy's jaw drop. Drew and Emma instinctively put their hands across their mouths, but their eyebrows showed their distress. Whip merely stared, no expression on his face while Zara and Seraphina lowered their eyebrows.

"Why would you do that?" Zara snapped. "What reason do you have to say that Gene would do something like that?"

Oliver slowly shook his head, distressed enough at the looks his friends were giving him. "I have nothing against Gene, Zara. None whatsoever . . . but I saw him with my own eyes . . . he hit Jerry and dragged him to the lake."

Slowly Whip's head began to shake back and forth ever so slowly. "Only someone as smart as you would do something so foolish! Don't you know what this means? Now the society have to reasons to think that Gene has problems and that adds on the fact that he is defying the overly strict rules of SOHE! This is just peachy!"

"Well Oliver," Roy remarked harshly. "You'll have to go out there and defend Gene!"

All at once, Whip and Drew shook their heads violently. "He can't do that," Drew objected. "He is a witness of the crime. If he went so far as to defend Gene's innocence, then people will begin to think that he is lying about one or the other. Besides that, he can't let his friendship with Gene get in the way of what he knows is right. What happened was wrong and if Gene was involved, then Gene was in the wrong. Oliver cannot defend the wrong thing."

Whip nodded in agreement but kept it minor since he saw Emma giving Drew a suspicious look. However, Emma wasn't thinking about Drew's reply.

"By the way . . . . Where is Gene?"

* * * * *

"Have you considered just telling Styl out in the open about the whole thing?" Drew inquired.

Whip looked up from where he had been writing down ideas. His head full of mad brown hair bounced atop his head. "What? That is ridiculous! Do you know what would happen if we did that? One word: D-E-A-T-H!"

"I think you're over exaggerating," Drew objected. "It's not like Styl is a murderer. Besides we don't even have any right to barge in on their personal problems."

"Are we going to go back all over again?" Whip groaned. "We agreed that the only decent thing to do was to give Styl justice, bring out her conscience and hope for the best."

Chapter 27

"This is awfully kind of you sir," Neil remarked as they stepped out of the snow.

The two children were engulfed in the warmth of the front hallway. Sir Charles stamped the snow off his shoes before hanging his hat and overcoat on a hook near the wall.

As the two began to take off their own coats and hats, Sir Charles bent down to untie his galoshes. "Don't mention it. I wouldn't dream of sending you two back when your spirits seemed so set on reaching your destination. Besides, I wasn't going to deny you hospitality especially at such a late hour. Why it must be nearly ten!"

Eileen shook her head, snow and ice falling from her dark hair. Neil ran his hand through his own hair, ruffling it slightly, and rubbed his eyes which were beginning to feel crusty.

Sir Charles kindly took their coats for them and hung them up. However, as Neil drew his hat off his head and rumpled his hair, the man's blue eyes changed extremely to one of shock. Eileen saw this strange look but decided against bringing it to light.

As they set their wet and cold galoshes against the wall, Sir Charles led them down the warm carpeted hallway. Presently they came upon a flight of stairs and Sir Charles waved his hand toward them.

"There are two spare rooms upstairs. Take the right at the top of the stairs and they'll be the first two doors on the left," he explained.

The two nodded their thanks as the man turned and headed through another doorway. Neil began to head up the stairs, but Eileen glanced up to catch sight of three young people looking through the railings at them. One girl with reddish blond hair wore a light blue winter hat and had a cherry colored blanket wrapped around her shoulders. Her large blue eyes stared at Eileen and Neil in shock.

There was another girl sitting on the step below her, most of her body wrapped up in a pale gray blanket but bright green eyes slowly nodding closed. On the step above the two girls sat a boy wrapped up in a green checkered blanket, letting out a long yawn. Obviously, they weren't supposed to be out of bed.

As Eileen started up the stairs, the three leapt to their feet and disappeared from the railing. Once Neil and Eileen reached the top of the stairs, Eileen looked about for any sign of the three but only caught a glimpse of a bedroom door closing in a rush.

Neil had located the two empty bedrooms and was just entering one when Eileen stopped him. "How long will you be?"

Neil considered himself before replying. "Just need to change into clean cloths . . . maybe wash my face . . . . About ten minutes?"

Eileen nodded and entered the opposite room without another word.

Exactly ten minutes later Neil heard Eileen knocking on the door, whispering his name. Opening it, Neil found Eileen wearing a clean dark blue blouse, a long dark blue skirt that came from above her waist to her ankles, white stockings and dry shoes. Her hair looked dry and she had brushed it back into a braid that ran down her back.

"You look done enough," Eileen remarked, interrupting Neil's protest. "Let's go find Sir Charles."

Neil subsided but took the time to pull on a dry pair of shoes before following the girl downstairs. Thye tried the room that Sir Charles had entered earlier but that only led to the library which was empty.

They began to make their way down the hallway when they head chatting and laughing from a room down the hall. Peering into the room, they found themselves looking into a cozy living room with a blazing fire. Sir Charles stood by the fireplace, smoking a pipe while a tall, elegant woman sat on a couch nearby.

Sir Charles lifted his eyes and caught sight of the two standing in the doorway. "Ah there you are! I hope you find your rooms satisfactory?"

Eileen nodded and smiled brightly. "Yes indeed. Thank you, sir."

"Just call me Charles lass," the man replied with a grin, then waving a hand toward the woman. "This is my wife Crystal."

Eileen turned her smiling face to the woman and held out her hand for a handshake but froze. The woman was tall, slender with fair complexion. Her face was all points, pointy nose, slanted eyes and high cheekbones. She was incredibly beautiful but her auburn hair, pulled up into a bun made her look older than she really was. But those eyes . . . those pure gray eyes made Eileen's hand begin to go numb.

The woman stood up and smiling, shook the silent girl's hand, apparently not noticing Eileen's shock or choosing to ignore it. Still smiling, the woman turned to shake Neil's hand, but her expression changed as fast as Eileen's had. Her face went deadly pale and her eyes grew wide as the boy came over and shook her hand, clueless as to why the woman and Eileen were staring.

"Please take a seat," Sir Charles remarked, breaking the silence. "Would you care for tea?"

"Yes please," Neil answered, knocking Eileen from her daze by giving her a nudge.

The girl sat down as if in a trance as Neil plopped down beside her, nevertheless smiling. Sir Charles began to pour tea into delicate white china cups from an iron kettle.

"So," he began. "I don't believe I caught your names when we first met. We're the Maciborski family as you know."

Neil nodded, remembering hearing that name when Sir Charles first brought them in. "I'm Neil . . . . Mecarnin and this is my friend, Eileen Gerasimov Wetherby."

Sir Charles raised an eyebrow as he handed the two their cups of tea. "Rather long last name lass."

"I was adopted," Eileen explained. "Three years ago, Gerasimov is my original last name, but my new last name is Wetherby."

The man smiled. "What about you Neil? Just a family friend?"

Neil suddenly became aware that Crystal was watching his face persistently, listening to every word he said with bated breath. It almost made him fidgety.

"Actually . . . I'm a ward of Eileen's father. My two brothers and I were offered the choice of taking on the name Wetherby, but we chose the option of wardship. Partially because we wanted to remain strong for our parents . . . who died . . . rather terribly when I was five."

Sir Charles nodded, a sad look crossing his face. "I am sorry."

Neil shook his head. "Don't worry about it . . . . I actually don't know my real father at all. I didn't find out until this week that I am only half related to my brothers."

"Is that so?" Sir Charles inquired, cocking his head. "How is that?"

"I'm not sure," Neil replied honestly. "I heard that my true father died . . . . And my mother remarried and had my brother . . . I don't know what happened between them though because they separated then had my little brother. It's kind of complicated honestly."

Sir Charles smiled. "Indeed it is . . . but that isn't the first time I've encountered someone with a complicated family past. Crystal also had a rather puzzling past as well."

Eileen snapped her head around to look at the woman who was still deathly pale and staring at Neil. "You did?"

The woman nodded slowly. "I married when I was very young . . . against my parents' wishes. After that our relationship was . . . rocky to say the least. My brother Cole was in an accident and fell into a coma for two months. I guess I was just too upset by everything that was happening that I blamed his accident on my parents . . . ."

Neil's eyebrows shot down and he furrowed his brow. "That name sounds strangely familiar . . . don't know where I heard it before."

Sir Charles still had no clue that something strange was going on and continued to speak. "So Neil. You said you have two brothers. Are you two heading back to see them?"

"In a way yes and no. Gene is back home and that's where we're headed. He's really got his hands full with stuff. Deke however is up in Gerhenia with Denise and his father. He'll be joining us back home in a few days," Neil replied, turning to look Crystal directly in the eyes.

When the teacup crashed on the floor from Crystal's hands, Eileen didn't even jump. She had suspected that something was up and when Crystal's face went a terribly sick shade of white and her hands began to shake, she wasn't even surprised. Neil and Sir Charles turned to her however and saw the alarm in her eyes. Crystal's eyes were locked on Neil's and were growing wide by the second. Slowly her shaking hands went up to cover her mouth as a single word escaped her.

"Deke!"

This was the last thing Eileen expected so she frowned in confusion. However, her questions that were piling were soon answered as the woman removed her hands from her mouth and spoke in a barely audible voice.

"You once said that good will always win . . . why is it losing now?"

Eileen looked up at Sir Charles, but the man was just as clueless as she was. She was about to look to Neil for an answer but when she looked at where Neil had been sitting, the boy was no longer there . . . he had completely slipped from the seat and was lying on the floor, his eyes staring forward but they were no longer green and gray . . . . They were blue!

Chapter 28

Neil's vision swirled before him. Everything around him . . . Eileen's face . . . Sir Charles's hair . . . the ceiling . . . it all blurred before him and swirled out of vision. He felt like there was a glass before him that he couldn't move or see through . . . . Then something did begin to come into focus . . . a hand.

A hand was reaching out to him where he lay. Neil slowly turned his head and saw that he was looking up into the hazel eyes of a young man. He looked to be about sixteen and was incredibly handsome. Dark brown wavy hair was swept up from his eyes and forehead. His features were sharp but kind with a straight nose, firm jaw and smiling firm mouth.

He wore a long white robe that came to his knees with a red sash around his waist and across his chest. Light seemed to shine from him and reflect out of his eyes. He was barefoot and as he walked, it was like fire licked up from wherever his feet touched.

Neil slowly took his strong young hand and the young man drew him to his feet with surprising ease. The man's hand felt incredibly warm and as Neil stood, he saw that he came to the man's shoulder but just about an arm's length from him he felt like he was inches from a burning fire. There was heat radiating off of the young man.

"Don't be afraid Neil," the man spoke in a mature teenage boy's voice that was clear and strong. "I'm here to show you some answers."

Neil watched the young man for a long time. What was it about that hair . . . those eyes . . . that handsome face that was so familiar that it burned his mind? The young man put an arm around Neil's shoulders and drew the boy toward what looked like a mirror.

The mirror was larger than anything Neil had ever seen. It seemed to go on forever. That was when Neil realized that he was in complete nothingness . . . there was no ground . . . no sky, no plants or anything . . . he was standing in complete whiteness other than the mirror which had a bluish tint to it.

As the man drew Neil toward the mirror, the younger boy realized that he couldn't see the reflection of the young man even though he was standing right next to him . . . he could only see his own reflection. However, his reflection didn't stay long as it began to blur before him. Neil almost thought that he was going to blank out again but instead . . . the mirror began to show a different picture than his reflection.

The picture that the mirror showed him was more a scene than a picture. It showed a street in a silent city at night . . . a young mother and father are running down the street. The woman is carrying a small baby girl who barely looks to be more than a year. Another girl is running with them . . . a young girl with auburn hair who was carrying a small child herself and from the look of it, the girl is pregnant. Two small boys of about the same age were sprinting beside them.

Just when the small group reach the end of the street, the father turned, said something to the mother and began to head back the way they had come. The mother began to scream at him at the top of her lungs, but the teenage girl and the two small boys held her back.

The father ran back the way they had come and began to talk as if he was speaking to someone. A single noise broke the silence and Neil cringed as he recognized that sound as a gunshot. The father froze in his tracks . . . then crumbled to the ground. One of the two boys began to sprint over to his father and to hold the man's face in his hands.

The second boy hurried over and tried to drag the first one away from the unmoving body of their father. However, the first boy refused and continues to sob bitterly over the body of the man. The second boy lifts his eyes and it was obvious he had spotted something. He placed himself in front of his brother and Neil had to close his eyes as another noise rang through the air. He couldn't open his eyes again . . . the sight was too terrible that he could even see it in his mind.

Neil continued to close his eyes until the young man tapped his shoulder. Neil looked back at the mirror to see that the scene had changed. The young boy who had been crying beside his father's body was now sitting on the edge of a cliff. His face looked calm and peaceful but a pain evident in his eyes. The small little baby girl from earlier was running about happily.

The scene seemed uncommonly friendly and happy . . . until Neil saw the path that the little girl was taking. For a split second the boy looked away and the small girl ran straight for the cliff . . . and disappeared over the side.

"NO!" He heard himself cry but realized that it was the boy in the scene who had cried.

The boy rushed to the edge of the cliff and looked over. Neil became aware that he could see the small girl, holding onto a large root that was protruding from the side of the cliff. The breath in Neil's throat caught in his chest as the boy tore off the jacket he wore to reveal a set of beautiful black blackbird wings!

Neil watched as the boy lifted into the air and soared over the side of the cliff. Choosing his path carefully, the small boy landed on a small ledge next to the girl and grasped her around the waist. He pulled her off the root and the girl clung to his neck in fright.

"It's alright Sara," the boy whispered. "Nothing will happen to us if we have faith."

The boy was just about to take off when the ledge he was standing on began to crumble. Looking about him, the boy loosed his sister's hold on his neck and tossed her into the air. The girl flew up into the air and landed down on the grass above the cliff, safe and sound . . . but not for the boy.

The ledge crumbled the moment he tossed his sister. He tried to take to the skies, but a huge rock came falling down on top of him and struck one of his wings. Neil's eyes snapped shut as the boy went plummeting out of sight. He didn't open them again till he felt the stranger tap his shoulder yet again.

Neil felt tears stinging his eyes as he opened them to see the boy in the scene lying on his back at the bottom of the ravine. His eyes were closed . . . his body was spread out . . . and he had only one wing on his back . . . the other one, broken and smashed to bits lay beside him. Neil didn't want to look any longer, but he realized that the face of the boy began to change . . . it was as if he was losing age . . . getting younger again.

Neil watched in silence and shock until the face of the small boy transformed into the face that Neil knew . . . . It was his own . . . but he was younger . . . much younger! Probably barely five years old . . . he was the boy in the vision . . . he had a family, a life . . . an accident . . . a sister.

Neil turned his eyes from the mirror as the vision slowly disappeared and the mirror began to only show his own reflection. He looked up at the young man beside him. He was smiling at Neil with a sad look in his eyes.

"Why . . . why did that have to happen?" Neil demanded.

The young man shook his head. "Only God knows Neil. Things happen for a reason though it takes a long time for us to realize. I was in a family I loathed, and I never knew why . . . until I met someone whom I wouldn't have met if I hadn't been where I was at the right moment . . . at the right place."

Neil was about to turn his face back to the blank mirror when he suddenly realized that the man began to take several steps back from him.

The boy watched as the stranger continued to step back and as he did, he seemed to fade away into the whiteness that surrounded them. Just when he was completely gone, Neil heard him faintly say something:

"Until next time."

"Neil!" a voice called from far off.

Neil turned, and it was as if the whiteness dissolved into blurry colors. Things began to make sense as someone kept calling his name. Gradually the voice got louder, and the blurry landscape began to focus . . . . Neil was lying on the floor in the living room of Sir Charles's house . . . Eileen was leaning over him while Sir Charles was fanning him with a book. Crystal was standing nearby, her face pale and her teeth biting down hard on her lower lip.

"Neil?" Eileen asked again, shaking the boy one more time.

Neil let out a groan which caused the girl to stop shaking him. "Yeah I'm awake . . . ."

"You were out like a light!" Eileen remarked grinning, you must be really tired.

Neil slowly shook his head as he sat up with Eileen's help. "I wasn't asleep . . . I . . . I saw . . . It was so clear Eileen . . . I saw my past! I had a family! Had . . . had a sister . . . and my dad . . . he . . ."

There was a long silence during which Sir Charles and Crystal exchanged looks that Neil and Eileen didn't catch. Neil was choking on his own words but as Eileen's hand snaked around his shoulders, he got control of himself.

"There's something else Eileen . . ." he started, his eyes suddenly flashing with amazement. "You'll never believe who I saw!"

Eileen furrowed her brow. How could he have seen someone in the three minutes he had been out? She hadn't left his side . . . then again, he said he had witnessed a vision. Perhaps that was where he saw someone. However, the thing that came from his mouth was the last thing she expected:

"Why?" he demanded. "Why did mom change my name? And what happened to the baby?"

Chapter 29

"You are going to do what!?" Seraphina cried.

Whip cringed. He had barely told her the plan he and Drew had come up with about ten minutes ago and already she had blown out his eardrum. They had all split up to go in search of Gene with Oliver staying with Emma for the evening.

"We're going to reenact the scene of the crime in the play," Whip explained. "Drew and I heard most of the argument and it was most unique. Not your usual argument. We'll reenact the whole scene and Styl will recognize it and possible prove her guilt or think better of her past decisions."

"I don't know Whip," Seraphina replied, scanning the area for Gene. "Where are you going to put that in the play without anyone suspecting something's up? Besides, how do you know it will hit the right cord and not the wrong one? It might remind Styl so much of her grudge against Emma that it might get worse."

"We've got to risk it," Whip retorted. "Besides, the two guys who were going to play

Absalom and Joab fell out remember? So, Drew and I will play the parts."

"Which will be Absalom? Styl or Emma?"

Whip rolled his eyes. "Emma obviously! If we put the part of Styl into the part of Absalom, she'll probably think we're threatening to kill her! Besides, Styl did strike Emma just like Joab killed Absalom."

"But she didn't kill Emma," Seraphina pointed out, trying to find a way to convince her brother out of the risk.

"That's what you think," Whip remarked. "To Styl, Emma could be dead or lying around somewhere in the middle of the woods dying of the cold."

"But . . ." Seraphina began when presently she spotted a figure ahead of them.

Small, slender wearing a black leather coat, white flannel shirt and a gray school boy cap, the two were more than certain it was Gene not only because of the pale hair that was visible beneath the cap but the way he walked.

"There's Gene," Whip whispered.

"Remember," Seraphina added in a low tone. "Don't act like you're wary of him. Act like nothing has happened . . . nothing at all! But I wouldn't mention Oliver's involvement with the rumors. Just talk about your plans for the play."

259

Whip raised his eyebrows in surprise. "I thought you didn't approve of them."

"Well it's either that or mentioning something else that might trigger something. Just do it," Seraphina hissed.

Gene continued to approach and the two lifted their hands in greeting. Gene returned it and quickened his pace as he approached.

Whip was about to run over and give the boy a hug, to hide the fact that he was concerned but when Gene approached, he held back. There was something about Gene that wasn't right . . . maybe it was because he kept his head almost low so that the cap he wore shadowed his face . . . or maybe it was the paleness of his skin and the minor amount of color in his cheeks and mouth . . . he was barely dressed for the weather, but his hands weren't even red from the cold.

"Hey Gene," Seraphina remarked in a bright tone.

"Hey," Gene replied, causing the two to suddenly go on alert especially since the reply seemed almost blank.

"We were just looking for you," Whip explained. "Destiny said you would be around here somewhere."

Seraphina almost jogged her brother, warning him to not bring up the rumors but then again, if Gene reacted to it, it might prove something.

Gene's eyebrows lowered, and his mouth pinched into a scowl. "What does she want?"

Whip started at Gene's suddenly sharp tone, but Seraphina composed herself faster. "She was worried about you."

"I'm sure she is," Gene snapped. "You tell her to mind her own business!"

Seraphina quickly gave Whip a look to tell him to bring up the play conversation. "Uh . . . we found out a way to bring out Styl's conscience, Gene."

Gene's facial expressions didn't change. "Why would you bring out Styl's conscience? I thought it was Emma who caused the problem."

Whip and Seraphina exchanged fully confused and puzzled looks. They completely missed seeing Gene quickly reach behind his back. However, when they turned back to him, they thought they heard a strange almost clinking noise.

"Well . . . we'll see you later Gene," Whip began, beginning to step past the boy.

The strangest thing followed that movement. The moment Whip stepped within two feet of Gene, the boy flat out flared and raised his hand. Whip wasn't prepared for the sudden violence from his friend, but Seraphina had seen the boy tense and had flown forward. Seraphina pushed her brother out of the way and Gene's hand slammed onto her head. Seraphina crumbled to the snow and lay still.

"Seraphina!" Whip cried, falling to his knees beside his sister. "Gene what did you do?"

The boy looked up at Gene only to realize that there was no expression on the boy's face. It was like he didn't even see them there. Slowly Gene began to run off past them, but kept his shoulder pointed toward Whip. When he was almost out of sight, he turned around and ran off at incredible speed for someone who was running through the snow.

"Seraphina," Whip whispered, turning his attention back to his sister. "Wake up . . . come on wake up!"

Seraphina didn't move a muscle and Whip began to panic. Desperate times require desperate measures. In that case he pulled off his coat and allowed his narrow wings to unfold. Grasping his sister under the arms, he hauled her with difficulty onto his back. His knees began to buckle beneath the weight . . . he had to get into the air.

Taking a running leap, he left his jacket in the snow and took to the skies. It wasn't until he was a good fifty feet from the ground that the weight on his back wasn't as painful.

"We've got to get to Zara's," Whip panted. "They'll know what to do."

Zara had just stopped at her house to ask Vivian to help in the search for Gene when she heard a loud thud land on their front porch. Zara was still dressed in her winter garments while Vivian wore a clean light blue dress, white cotton stockings and her button-up boots.

The two hurried to the door just as Whip climbed from the pile he had created on the front stoop, dragging Seraphina with him. "Guys! I need help!"

The two girls immediately flew out the door. Of course, Vivian had to take time to throw on some galoshes over her socks before she could help the two drag Seraphina inside.

"What in the world happened?" Zara demanded.

The three dragged the unconscious girl into the living room and laid her on the couch. Vivian set about getting a bowl of warm water and cloths.

"It was Gene!" Whip almost yelped. "We ran into him over by Swamp Road! We were just talking about my plan for the play and he fairly flew at us! He almost got me, but Seraphina pushed him out of the way. Then he just left. He didn't even look upset or even angry!"

Zara's blue eyes widened with concern. "That doesn't sound anything like Gene! You must have been seeing things Whip."

The boy shook his head hard. "No, Seraphina recognized him too. It was Gene, no doubt about it!"

Vivian returned from the kitchen and sat down on the couch beside Seraphina. She began to push the long blond locks out of the girl's face when she stopped and drew her hand back.

"She's bleeding Whip."

Whip and Zara hurried to Seraphina's side. Sure enough, there was a deep gash on the side of the girl's head, running from her left jaw, all the way up the side of her face and to her hairline.

"Oh, heavenly Father!" Whip cried, grabbing one of the damp cloths and pressing it against the wound. "Where did that come from?"

"Is that where Gene hit her?" Zara demanded.

Whip nodded. "But there was nothing in his hand!"

Zara's eyebrows went down in confusion but the other two were busy cleaning the wound and stopping the bleeding.

"What are we going to do about this?" Vivian whispered. "It's going a little too far."

Whip nodded firmly in agreement. Zara looked from her sister to Whip. Those two were probably the most loyal to Gene besides Deke and Neil. If those two don't believe in Gene's innocence and aren't determined to defend him . . . Gene was done for.

"I'll be back," Zara replied. "Keep Seraphina here till she comes to. If she doesn't wake up in another hour, better go find Livonia. I won't be back till late."

The two barely heard her as she grabbed her coat and charged out the door. She stopped long enough to look back at the house. This was not the most efficient way to go about it but there was nothing else she could do.

She didn't have time to explain the whole thing to Drew in person, so she taped a letter to the door when she dropped by. She hurried out of the snow-covered lawn and tore off her jacket. Letting her wings open, Zara tied the jacket around her waist and began to pump her wings to warm them.

Drew's mother was just coming out to see who had been knocking when she saw the girl leap into the air and disappear from sight almost within three seconds.

"Mom?" Drew's voice called from down the hallway. "What was that?"

The woman pulled the note off the door and held it out to her daughter. "I think I just saw Zara fly off a second ago. She must have left this on the door for you."

Drew grabbed the letter and tore to her room. If Zara left her a note at this time, it must be urgent. She leapt onto her bed as she opened the envelope and unfolded the letter:

Dear Drew, I don't have much time, but I need you to do something for me. Whip and Vivian don't believe in Gene's innocence, not after he supposedly hurt Seraphina. I need you to find Gene as soon as possible and keep him away from the gang. Do whatever you must but keep him still till I get back. I've gone to get help . . . the only ones who can help. Love, Zara.

Drew's violet eyes grew wide. There was no one here in Hichester that could possibly help Gene if Whip and Vivian were against him . . . no one except Deke and Neil. She couldn't have! She would die of exhaustion if she did!

Drew charged down the stairs, calling a quick explanation to her mom before grabbing her coat and hurrying out. She had left Gene at the society barely ten minutes ago. Hopefully he was still there.

When the girl arrived at the society, she found him sitting in the apothecary with Emma. Oliver was nowhere to be found.

"Where have you been?" Drew cried the moment she entered.

Gene's eyes grew wide as he looked at her in puzzlement. "Right here . . . why?"

Emma nodded her head. "He's right Drew. He's been here since you guys left to look for him."

Chapter 30

"This is too weird," Eileen remarked. "You two are siblings?"

Crystal and Neil nodded together, not exactly startled by Eileen's second outburst that morning. They had woken up rather early to the sound of Crystal and Neil talking downstairs in the living room. No one but the two, Charles and Eileen were awake as they sat at the breakfast table.

"Yes Eileen," Neil assured her. "I thought it was weird too but now it begins to make sense after hearing what Crystal told me. When I fell, our mom decided to put the whole thing behind her, so she changed my name, but Crystal never heard about it because she left with Charles and her kids before I even woke up."

Eileen shivered. "So weird!"

Neil turned back to Crystal and his eyes got serious. "Last night you said you would explain about the little girl in the vision . . . who was she?"

Crystal slowly set down the piece of toast she was buttering and ran her hand through her loose auburn hair. Turning to the maid who had just walked in with fresh porridge, she spoke.

"Olivia . . . could you rouse the children and ask them to join us?"

The woman nodded and quickly hurried from the room. Crystal turned back to Neil and continued to butter her toast. "I guess it's best to show you . . . rather than tell."

Neil and Eileen glanced at each other uneasily across the table. They were in a hurry to get home, but they were also intrigued about this whole encounter. It was more than a coincidence that the place they happened to strand in front of also happened to be where Neil's sister lived!

A few moments later, the dining room door opened, and a small girl charged in. She looked to be about Neil's age but rather small for her age. Her light auburn, almost blond hair was all over the place and her blue eyes full of energy.

"Good morning mama," the girl chirped, rushing over to Crystal and throwing her arms around the woman's neck.

"Good morning darling," Crystal replied, hugging the girl back.

The girl slowly turned and caught sight of Neil and Eileen. Her blue eyes grew wide and without a single word, she turned on her heel and charged out of the room.

"That was my daughter Annabelle," Crystal explained. "She's awfully shy. She'll be leaving later this morning to join her older sister up in Catasbanel. They spend every other Christmas up there with Charles's family."

Neil's eyes widened, realizing that he was in fact an uncle to a girl who was practically his age. After all, considering the fact that Crystal was in fact nineteen years older than him (seventeen not counting the years he lost) it was perfectly possible that she could have had a child the year he was born.

Annabelle had barely left the room when two more children appeared. Eileen recognized them as two of the children she had seen by the railing the night before. Annabelle had been the other one.

Eileen caught a movement out of the corner of her eye and saw Neil tense as he looked at the two children. The girl was about ten years old with long jet-black hair that fell to her shoulders, pulled back by a headband. Her large green eyes were the same color as Neil's left green one. Her face was all points just like Crystal and she was incredibly pretty. The boy was about nine with wild auburn hair, the same color as Crystal's but as wild as Deke's, if not more. His eyes were the same silvery gray as Neil's right one. His face was rounder and more boyish than the pointy features of the girl's. His nose was round, and his face was just pure boyish.

"Good morning Crystal," the girl replied in a sleepy voice.

"Morning Sara," Crystal replied, smiling. "Morning Clint."

The boy waved to the woman as he charged for one of the empty seats. Naturally, it was the one next to Neil. Plopping down next to Neil, Clint began to serve his breakfast.

"Hello . . . I'm Clint," the boy remarked with a large grin.

Eileen caught Neil looking at her with bated breath. He could see the resemblance between Clint and Crystal just as much as she could. Neil quickly ducked his head so that no one could really see his face except perhaps Clint.

Sara sat down beside Eileen, opposite the two boys. "Be polite Clint," she warned in a soft girlish voice.

"It's alright," Neil replied in a low voice. He turned and held out his hand to the boy. "I'm Neil. It's nice to meet you Clint."

Clint's face lit up as he shook Neil's hand. "You're the first boy older than me who actually replied! Most boys I meet at the boarding school and stuff just snub me. I like you!"

Sara let out an obvious groan at her brother's bluntness, but Neil's face lit up. Eileen smiled to herself. Clint was definitely made of the same stuff as Neil and his brothers.

"Lighten up Seraphina," Clint observed.

Eileen and Neil's heads both snapped up at that name but only Crystal caught it.

"Your name is Seraphina?" Eileen inquired.

The girl nodded. "My full name is Seraphina, but I prefer to be called Sara. It's simpler, shorter and not as unusual."

A huge smile spread across Neil's face as he heard those words. "I actually know someone who's name is Seraphina too. She's a good friend of mine."

Sara's face at once perked up. "Does she go by Sara too?"

Eileen shook her head. "No, but we call her Seraph sometimes. Funny, now we have to Seraphina's!"

Clint had been listening to the conversation but feeling suddenly left out, he spoke up.

"Olivia said you guys got stranded last night," Clint continued, his mouth half full of fruit. "Where are you headed?"

If Clint had asked him yesterday when they first arrived, Neil wouldn't have told the particulars. However, he knew he could trust these people . . . they were his family after all!

"Break Neck Creek," he replied.

Crystal and Charles snapped their heads up at once. "You didn't mention that last night Neil," Charles pointed out.

Neil shrugged. "I didn't know . . . what to think."

Charles immediately smiled, understanding the boy's reasonable caution. "Don't mention it. I would do the same."

"Break Neck huh?" Clint inquired. "I've heard of it a little . . . not many people talk about it. They say it's haunted! But some say that town nearby is really nice . . . what is it . . . Hichester? Yeah that's it! I've always wanted to go there! It sounds so cool! At least we get to spend Christmas here with Crystal! Sara doesn't really like boarding school, but I guess . . ."

"Clint," Sara warned. "Maybe Neil would like to eat."

The boy instantly looked like a wounded puppy but quickly whispered an apology to Neil. The older boy however smiled and lifted his head enough to look Clint directly in the eyes.

"Don't worry about it. You remind me of my brother Gene. He's kinda talkative too."

Clint's face lit up as he heard Neil's words. He looked up at Neil to thank him for the compliment when suddenly he froze. "Woah! You have different colored eyes!? That's so cool!"

Eileen glanced at Sara . . . no different expression. Obviously, Crystal hadn't told them that much about Neil.

"Mom!" a voice called from the hallway. "I'm ready to leave!"

Crystal, Sara, Charles and Clint hurried from their seats into the hallway with Eileen and Neil following. Annabelle was standing there, wrapped up and ready to go with a suitcase in each hand.

"Make sure to keep your hat on until you're inside," Crystal reminded her. "And tell your sister we said hello and we'll see her for Easter."

The girl nodded as she gave her parents a hug and a wave to Sara and Clint. "See ya!"

They all lifted their hands in farewell as the girl hurried down the snowy steps to the waiting car out front. They stood there waving and blowing kisses until the car was far out of sight down the snowy road that was mostly cleared. Even then, the kids stepped out into the snow to relish in the beauty that the white snow spread across the countryside. Sara was still waving at the side of the road when Clint suddenly spoke up.

"Hey Neil! Don't you love snow? I love it because it is white, and it doesn't turn your fingers colors!"

Eileen smiled, thinking of Seraphina back home. The girl would probably not agree since she loved having her fingers dirty with paint and dye.

Neil shrugged as he picked up a snowball and threw it at Eileen who squealed. "I like it alright . . . though I'm not the biggest fan."

"Why not?" Clint demanded, preparing another snowball to throw at his sister.

"Well," Neil replied, grabbing more snow. "When I was little I fell off a cliff and was in a coma for a long time. When I fell into the ravine it was full of snow and I almost caught pneumonia. I guess it left a scar."

Eileen furrowed her brow. Neil loved snow and was always asking for snow during the hot days of summer. Then again, she realized that he was trying to break the truth to his siblings slowly.

Clint didn't seem to find anything strange about that remark, but Sara practically froze where she stood by the street. Slowly turning around, she stared at Neil in stunned silence.

The boy smiled almost sheepishly as he balled the snowball into a hard rock and tossed it at Eileen again. "However, *nothing can hurt us if we have faith*."

That broke the dam that had been threatening to overflow. Sara charged across the snow-covered lawn and catapulted herself into Neil, almost knocking him over. She would have knocked him into the snow if Neil hadn't expected the reaction she had.

Clint stared in confused puzzlement as Sara buried her face in Neil's shoulder and continued to blubber cries between sobs as her shoulders shook.

When Sara finally let her brother go, Neil was grinning from ear to ear and the girl's face was streaming with tears. "We thought you were dead!" she cried. "When Crystal found us at the orphanage Mom left us at . . . she said that she believed you to be dead!"

Neil grinned. "I guess the Lord had other plans for me."

Sara was about to hug him again when a small body slammed itself into Neil, fully knocking him into the snow.

"You're Cole!" Clint squealed. "Crystal never mentioned that you changed your name!"

"Well actually mom changed my name," Neil replied as he slowly climbed out of the snow.

He squatted in front of the small boy and looked into his eyes. He had never met Clint but there was their mother in him . . . the hair . . . the face shape . . . all of it. Clint was practically bouncing in his galoshes with joy.

Sara pulled Neil into another hug and laid her head on his shoulder while Clint clung to Neil's leg. Neil could barely see so he didn't notice Eileen looking up toward the sky until she pulled him out of the way.

A soft thunk sounded nearby and everyone released Neil to see what had made the noise. There, lying on the snow was a young girl with her light brown hair covered in snow and a pair of strong wings hanging limply from her back.

"ZARA!" Neil and Eileen cried together.

They charged over to the girl and drew her to her feet. The girl was deathly pale and breathing heavily. Her eyes were falling closed and her wings looked like the muscles were screaming for a break.

"Mr. . . . . Rasmussen . . . . Said you'd be here . . ." she panted.

"Zara Salerno!" Eileen scolded. "What are you doing all the way here? Not even Gene could make this trip without dying of exhaustion! What were you thinking?"

"I . . . needed . . . . Neil's . . . . help . . . quickly," Zara panted. "It's . . . . Gene . . ."

"What about Gene?" Neil and Eileen asked in unison, their faces going pale.

Zara shook her head, shaking snow and ice from her hair. "The gang . . . . Are beginning . . . to turn . . . against him . . . they think . . . he hurt . . . . Seraphina . . . Gene . . . . Will be thrown out . . . of Hichester . . . ."

Neil looked up and his eyes locked with Eileen's. "That settles it," he remarked firmly. "We're   leaving   now!"

Chapter 31

Denise pressed her cheek against the carriage window, rather enjoying watching life speed past outside. Besides that, Deke was fooling around in his backpack, trying to find something to read.

"Deke we'll be there in another fifteen minutes," Denise pointed out. "That isn't enough time to read anything."

"I'm not looking for a book," Deke objected. "I just suddenly thought of something and I'm trying to find it."

Denise's ears perked up at this announcement. "What is it?"

Deke continued to hunt around in his backpack, failing to answer the girl until finally he drew out a small object. Denise had never seen it before, but she did remember Neil mentioning it once. A large dark blue envelope.

"Isn't that a peculiar color for an envelope?" Denise inquired, cocking her head to the side at the sight of the envelope.

"Apparently not here in Gerh," Deke pointed out. "I actually asked the maid at my dads' about it and she said that father always uses these blue envelopes. This one wasn't brought by my dad but by a guy named Alec. My mom and . . . . Step-dad seemed really put out when he brought it. I don't know what happened to my step-dad or Alec, but my mom was killed shortly afterwards by underbeasts."

"Are you sure they weren't killed as well?" Denise inquired, having been told in detail (by Neil) about Deke's past.

Deke shrugged. "Why would the underbeasts kill my mom and leave her body but take the dead bodies of Mr. Mecarnin and Alec?"

Denise considered the envelope a moment. It was crumpled, wrinkled and slightly torn in certain places. The name on the front was completely gone from old age and the envelope seriously looked old. However, the thing that surprised her was the fact that it wasn't opened.

"You have never opened it?" she almost squealed.

Deke looked down at the closed envelope and shook his head. "I kinda forgot about it after we moved to the house for the homeless . . . then in Hichester I was so busy with school and SOHE I never thought about it until dad's lawyer mentioned it . . . and also the fact that Alec is my uncle."

"Do you think that letter is from your uncle?" Denise inquired, suddenly warming up to the mystery.

"Could be," Deke admitted. "But I don't know why my mom and step-dad seemed to hostile toward him."

Denise scooted closer and jabbed Deke with her elbow. "Well what are you waiting for? Open it."

Deke carefully open the letter, realizing that the envelope was so fragile that it was ready to crumble. The letter inside was made of the exact same material as the letter Deke had received a month earlier, declaring that he was to visit his true father.

Almost velvet like, the letter was thin . . . a single sheet which was barely covered in small letters. Deke had to pull on his water goggles to read in. Reading it silently, Deke's lips moved as he read until his eyes slowly grew. The water goggles made his eyes even larger than comfortable, causing Denise to lean over and read the letter:

Dear Deke,

You may not know me and being such a small lad, you might not understand. In that case, I will make it as simple as possible. My name is Alec Rasmussen and my dear brother Steven is in fact your real father. Frank Mecarnin is merely your step-father. Your father does not know this, but I have been trying to return you to him for many years. No matter what it takes, I will see you reunited with your father. I must go for I am pressed for time but all I can add to this is that you're not the only . . . . . .

The rest of the letter was smeared, except for the simple handwriting of Alec at the bottom of the page.

"That is strange," Denise remarked aloud. "Why would your parents seem so adamant about not letting you meet your father? It seems like your uncle was pretty determined . . . . I wonder why. Do you suppose your Uncle Alec; your mom and your step-dad had gotten in an argument? What if your uncle went too far in trying to get you together with your dad?" Denise suggested.

Deke's brown hair slowly swished as he shook his head. Slowly pushing his goggles off his eyes and onto his head, Deke closed the letter and held it in his shaking hands.

"The look on my parents' faces weren't that of anger . . . . But of fear. It was as if they were afraid of Alec . . . or of what he was doing . . . but why?"

Deke slowly looked at Denise for an answer and the sheepish, almost guilty look on her face told Deke that she had the answer. "What do you know?"

Denise shook her head. "Not much . . . but according to Mr. Wetherby and Matilda . . . your father found out that Neil wasn't his son and that your mother had been married before she married your father . . . so they split up. After that, your mother refused to even hear the name of your father and your uncle persisted. He was the only one who knew where you were and was constantly trying to get you back to your father. Naturally, your mother got so tired that she led your father to believe that you had died so that he wouldn't keep sending Alec to find you . . . but Alec knew the truth."

"But . . . . Why was my uncle so determined to have me back?" Deke demanded. "And why did my step-dad seem afraid of him too?"

Denise stopped for a moment and bit her lip. "Because your uncle really wanted you to be the heir . . . . If you hadn't returned, someone else would have inherited the kingdom of Gerhenia and Alec was determined to not let it be anyone but you."

Chapter 32

Eileen couldn't help smiling as the sleigh jingled through the snow. Clint was seated in the front seat next to Lyle, constantly asking questions of the bargeman as they drove along. Sara and Crystal were constantly telling their brother to shush up, but Lyle didn't seem to mind. He was grinning from ear to ear, answering all of the boy's questions.

Sara, Crystal and Charles were looking about them in interest, constantly giving Neil nervous looks as the boy was half hanging over the side of the sleigh. Eileen grinned, knowing that Neil was more than ready to get home and this long sleigh ride was all that was keeping his impatience from erupting.

"I haven't met Gene before," Crystal remarked aloud. "Is he much like mother?"

Neil shook his head. "Other than the light hair, he's nothing like her. He gained his height and features from . . . his dad and his eyes."

Crystal smiled and leant back. "Deke was just a baby when I left . . . has he changed?"

Neil was about to shake his head again when Eileen spoke up. "Well he's certainly not a baby anymore."

Sara let out a bright snicker at that, especially when Neil rolled his eyes teasingly. "When will we get there?"

Neil seemed just as puzzled himself since everything was white around them. However, Lyle called back from the front. "We've just arrived."

Both Eileen and Neil cocked their heads in confusion at this. They couldn't see the Rivershore, just the snow covering everything. That is, until they saw two figures that seemed to be floating in the air. It wasn't until they were close that they realized that the two figures, the twins, were actually sitting on the huge piles of snow that lined the river.

"Hello the sleigh!" Roy hollered.

Reed waved once but didn't do the whole Can-Can dance with it like his brother did. Neil looked quickly at his siblings, only to see them all grinning at the twins.

Slowly the sleigh pulled to a stop and Clint was pretty much prepared to leap out right then and there. Neil and Eileen were the first to leap out and help the others down. Gradually a small crowd began to build around them, consisting of the whole gang, minus Emma and Seraphina along with Vivian, Drew and Rodge.

Eileen escaped the clutches of the twins by hurrying to greet Drew who was bouncing up and down. She shook the girl's hands, making sure to steer a good distance from the twins. Rodge of course made sure to greet Neil first so he could hurry over to greet Eileen.

"I'm so glad you're back!" Roy squealed as he hurried over with Reed in tow. "We're practically drowned!"

"In terms of snow, I certainly believe you," Neil remarked, considering the piles of snow lining the river.

He turned around to help Zara and Sara from the sleigh. At once, all the boys except Rodge perked up at the presence of another girl. Neil was prepared to roll his eyes, but introductions were more important.

"This is my sister Sara," he explained. "And so is Crystal. Clint is my brother."

The girls, Oliver and Rodge were able to keep straight faces but the twins and Whip allowed their jaws to drop. There was no doubt considering the resemblance between the four siblings, but it was the last thing they expected Neil to bring home two days before Christmas.

"Speaking of siblings," Neil remarked but Whip interrupted him.

"Gene," he remarked through gritted teeth. "Will be along shortly. He got stuck helping at SOHE."

Zara gave the boy a warning glare but the tension in his voice immediately hit Eileen and Neil. Zara quickly caught Eileen and Drew's attention and slowly the three girls drew the gang a good distance off, leaving Neil to stand at the river's edge with Clint and Sara.

There was what sounded like an eruption from far off, followed by the sound of a jet. Neil felt all the air knocked out of him as a hard object struck him square in the chest and another shape tackle him by the legs. Once he had composed himself, he had been knocked entirely on his back with Webstar pawing at his feet excitedly and Gene pulling him to his feet.

"Great to have you home man!" Gene cried, pulling Neil up before giving him a football tackle hug.

A grin spread across Neil's face as he hugged his brother back while trying to pet Webstar as well. When Gene had released him, Neil considered the boy. He seemed alright . . . other than the fact that there were large bags under his eyes, and he looked under nourished.

The dog meanwhile looked the complete opposite. Neil knew that her outrageous size was not because of overeating but she looked rather spirited for someone in her condition.

"You must be Gene," Sara remarked, stepping over and holding out her hand to the boy. "I've heard a lot about you. I'm Sara."

Gene shook the girl's hand but halfway through, he froze and looked from Sara to his brother then back again. Clint could barely stand the suspense and finally blurted it out. "We're his siblings!"

Gene was just absorbing this when he noticed something else. "Where's . . . . where's Deke?"

"He'll be following shortly. He went to visit his father's . . . . house . . . he'll be along shortly?"

Neil had been gone from Gene's presence for so long that he had almost forgotten the familiar looks in his brother's face. However, the look that his brother now took on was completely mysterious. He didn't know what had happened till Zara leapt over and grabbed Gene by the shoulder just as the boy went limp.

"Oh shucks!" the girl muttered, grasping the boy beneath the arms. "I knew he was too weak to be out! He hasn't eaten in two days!"

Chapter 33

Eileen shivered as she trudged through the snow toward the apothecary. The snow was still falling and piling up on the platforms of the society even though they had just been cleared the day before. Honestly, she couldn't complain especially since she had chosen of her own free will to head to the apothecary.

She could barely stand Neil and the rest of the gang talking about Gene's behavior. They had obviously concluded that they shouldn't let Gene know that they suspect something in the hopes that they might figure out the problem. Of course, right from the start Neil had expressed his opinion about how Gene would never do such outrageous things especially hurting Seraphina, but Whip and Vivian weren't going to be swayed easily.

The girl stomped her feet loudly outside the apothecary door before heading in. The front room was much warmer than outside, and Livonia was sitting behind the desk. Emma was calmly sitting by the fire, reading a book with the still unconscious Gene lying on the couch behind her.

"Eileen!" the older girl chirped as Eileen pulled off her coat and hat. "I didn't know you had gotten back!"

"Neil thought it was a good idea to come back early," Eileen explained as she hung up her things before joining the girl by the fire. "How are you feeling?"

Eileen considered the older girl a moment. Her dark brown hair pulled high in a bushy ponytail, bangs hanging all about her face. She wore a perky rusty pink dress that came a good length past her knees, along with lighter pink stockings and her boots.

The girl was obviously in higher spirits than Eileen who was dressed in a dull gray sweater, light purple dress, stockings and her boots.

"So . . . what do you think of everything that's happening?" she inquired.

Emma fairly flew out of her skin and leapt from her chair. Rushing across the room she snatched up a small piece of paper that was lying on Livonia's desk and hurried back to Eileen. Plopping back down in her seat, she shoved the paper at the younger girl and began bouncing in her seat as if too excited to wait for Eileen to read it.

"Vivian just finished making the Christmas Party fliers!" the girl chirped.

Eileen slowly looked down at the flier and realized that Vivian had quite outdone herself this time. Scrawled in fancy letters across the front page was:

Hichester District Annual Christmas Celebration

Opening the flier, Eileen saw that there were at least five pages in the flier and the front one was dedicated to "contents." Sighing to herself, Eileen decided to not read the whole rather dense flier and just scanned down the list of contents:

1) Annual Christmas play
2) Main course meal
3) Dances. 1st, parents. 2nd, children
4) Presentation of school and SOHE graduates
5) Talent Show
6) Dessert and refreshments

Eileen finished reading the contents before she noticed that Emma was waiting for her to read the whole flier. The girl quickly pretended to read the whole flier, only scanning over the brightly decorated pages with fancy handwriting. She did pause to see who had been put down as the play director. When she saw that it was Rodge, she relaxed, knowing that it would be one less thing for Gene to worry about.

When she came to the last page, her eyes lighted on something that caught her attention. In neat writing in the bottom corner of the last page was a small notice:

Please join us on December 26ᵗʰ in the Hall of Organization at SOHE for the presentations that will be read by the third, fourth- and fifth-year members of SOHE. Thank you.

Eileen felt her face go red. Was this Robert North's idea of trying to make Gene even more nervous about the presentations and papers? Emma seemed to sense what the girl was thinking and at once spoke up.

"Don't worry Eileen. I asked Vivian where she got all the information and she said that it was Mr. Walker's idea. She said that Robert had no idea about it until after he saw the fliers."

She handed the flier back to Emma and leant back in her chair.

"So, what did you want to tell me?"

"Did you see the part about the dances?" Emma demanded. "Well there is only one dance for the adults and one for the kids and students. There'll be music playing and all, but we only get really one chance to dance with someone."

Eileen felt her comfort zone disappear at this. She had to dance with someone?

"Who are you going to dance with?" the girl inquired.

She didn't know why she asked that, but Emma acted as though she was glad she had. "Ivan naturally," the girl remarked.

Ivan and Emma had been dating for the past year and seemed to everyone in the gang to perfectly "suit each other." Both were calm, energetic but with natural common sense.

Eileen was about to comment on this when something struck her mind. Ivan was a rather good-looking young man and she knew that when he began dating Emma, a lot of girls at school were disappointed that he hadn't chosen them. Could it be that Styl envied Emma because of Ivan? That was one possibility and the only possible reason that had arisen as of yet.

"Have you thought about what you're going to do with your hair?" Emma asked, breaking Eileen's train of thought.

Eileen raised one of her eyebrows. "Why would I do that? I'm not playing Absalom."

Emma let out a bark of laughter and at once Eileen was glad that she hadn't let slip Whip and Drew's plan. If she had, she was sure Emma would have something to say to the two.

"I didn't mean that," Emma remarked. "You cannot go to the party with your hair down! I've even convinced Vivian and Zara to do something new to their hair."

"Good luck with Denise," Eileen mused. "You'll only have today and tomorrow to convince her."

Emma smiled. "Oh I have a plan all worked out. I'll catch her in a really good mood and offer to do something for her if she agrees to let me style her hair."

"Well good luck with me too," Eileen remarked. "Now that I'm warned, you'll have a harder time."

The girl hadn't noticed that Emma had risen to her feet. When she did notice, Emma had returned carrying a brush and a comb. She positioned herself behind Eileen and thrust the comb into Eileen's long hair.

"What are you doing?" Eileen demanded. "Combs get stuck in my hair!"

"Whoops," Emma remarked. "It'll take me some time to get it out."

Eileen could sense the sarcasm in Emma's voice and knew that she had done that on purpose. Rolling her eyes, she crossed her arms

"Oh fine! Don't make it crazy though! It better be easy, so I can do it again tomorrow."

A grin lit up Emma's face and she began to work carefully with the long black locks. "Look at it from a brighter prospective Eileen! We can chat while I'm doing it."

Eileen pursed her lips thoughtfully. "Like what?"

"Oh, just the fact that Denise and Deke will be getting back in another five hours.

"About time," Eileen remarked. "It's Christmas Eve!"

Eileen didn't see Emma lower her eyebrows in confusion. It was so unlike Eileen to seem this negative that it had Emma suddenly all worried.

Chapter 34

"You'll find no mercy from me," Whip taunted. "You ruined my life and you'll pay for it."

"No, no, no," Drew objected. "You sound like a villain! You're playing a character who has a deep grudge against another person, but you aren't out for blood shed or to creep the living daylight out of the person."

"So, did that sound okay or bad?" Whip inquired, not sure where Drew was getting at.

The girl slowly brushed her hair behind her ear and sighed. "Just say exactly what we heard Styl say in the woods."

Whip looked pitifully at the others who were sitting at the other end of the library, watching the two rehearse. Whip had called an emergency meeting with the gang at the Mecarnin's house due to several reasons. The first reason was that Deke and Denise had just returned and needed to be caught up on things happening. Second, Whip wanted everyone to give their info on how the play sounded at least during their scene.

"Don't make it too obvious," Denise suggested, considering her copy of the script. "Or

Styl will get suspicious. Most certainly don't make eye contact with anyone during the scene and try to not say their names instead of 'Absalom' and 'Joab.' It would be terrible if she heard you do that."

"Yeah," Roy mused. "You wouldn't need to pretend to kill each other in the play, Styl would take care of that for you."

Whip and Drew lowered their eyebrows at Roy but what Whip said was far worse. "Or we could ask Gene to the play and let him take care of it."

Seraphina could feel Neil's body go as tense as an angry dogs. His eyebrows went completely down, and the hair practically stood up on the back of his neck. The girl was glad though that Gene was upstairs taking care of Webstar or it would have been worse.

"Whip Schneider that is quite enough," Zara snapped, giving the boy an angry look.

Whip merely shrugged but stopped mid shrug when Neil rose hastily to his feet and strode quickly out of the room. Whip was about to ask what that was all about when he saw that Seraphina, Zara, Sara, Clint, Bruce and Denise were all glaring at him.

It was dark outside. The sun was completely hidden behind the houses as Neil sat on the front stoop. Webstar wasn't sitting beside him as usual since she had been confined to Deke's bedroom permanently till after her puppies arrived. Deke hadn't taken kindly to having a new roommate when he had arrived earlier with Denise, Bruce and Mr. Wetherby. It took almost a full hour for everyone to convince him to let the dog stay. Clint and Bruce had agreed to bunk up in the room across from Neil while Sara slept with Eileen, giving Crystal and Charles the other guest bedroom.

The door of the house opened, and Sara slipped out, closing it behind her. She sat down silently next to Neil and drew her knees up to her chin.

"Something's troubling you," she remarked in a soft voice.

Neil nodded. "Everything is troubling me."

A smile appeared on Sara's face. "That's an awful lot."

"You don't know the half of it," Neil remarked, almost practically speaking to himself. "I'm really worried about Gene. Everyone trusts him! He is the person I probably trust more than myself but now it seems that almost no one believes in him."

Sara slowly nodded. "Rumors can do that to ya."

"That's not what everyone seems to think," Neil grumbled. "Whip, Vivian . . . the twins . . . even Denise!"

"Well their suspicions are understandable," Sara pointed out. "Whip and the twins personally witnessed injuries . . . Vivian is easily influenced, and Denise is . . . . Denise."

Neil felt a strong urge to smile at that last part but managed to keep a serious look on his face. "That's another thing! Who is it that keeps attacking everyone, disguised as Gene? I mean, either the whole gang are terrible at recognizing Gene or someone posing as him or this is all a ruse."

"Don't tell me you doubt Gene," Sara snapped.

Neil's eyes blazed as he turned to look at her. "Are you kidding? Of course, I believe Gene! That boy deserves more trust than we can give him! If it wasn't for Gene, I wouldn't be here right now . . . . None of us would be. He taught me what it means to feel like I'm someone when I was no one."

Sara waited until she was sure Neil's breathing had relaxed before she wrapped an arm around his shoulders. "I don't know Gene well . . . but I can tell he means a lot to you. If it's any comfort . . . I'll be here to help you defend Gene if it gets worse. I know Bruce and even Clint would probably do the same."

Neil was about to reply to this when a loud crash was heard from inside the house. Both spun around to look at the door which soon flew open. The front stoop was flooded with light as the twins crowded toward the door.

"Neil! You need to come quick! Webstar is having her puppies!"

The boy was just leaping up when Sara grabbed his arm and held him back. "You act as though she was about to explode!"

The twins quickly exchanged confused looks before looking back at Sara. "Didn't you hear a word we thaid?" Reed demanded.

Sara rolled her eyes. "Yes I did and if I were you, I would leave the poor dog alone for crying out loud! She knows more about these things than you do!"

Roy was about to lift his finger to object when Reed poked him in the ribs. "She has a point."

Chapter 35

"Everybody's in place for the play!" Roy declared to Rodge from behind the curtain.

Rodge quickly made a hand signal to Neil across the stage. The younger boy began to pull back the curtains just as Rodge stepped out amidst cheers and applause from the audience. Neil wondered at how the boy could be so calm in front of a huge audience like that.

When the applause and noise had died down, Rodge clasped his hands behind his back and began to introduce the production. "For the past several . . ." He didn't get much further since a rather noticeable and loud noise cut him off:

"Psst," Roy interrupted. "We can't find Reed. Stay here and stall for time; I'll be right back."

Rodge's eyes widened as the boy hurried off in no way silently. Slowly shaking his head, the boy turned back to the audience.

"For the past several years the Society of Hichester Enterprise has held this Christmas gettogether along with their annual Christmas pageant," Rodge began, making sure his voice carried clear to the back of the theater.

Neil cringed to himself as he heard Roy's loud voice cut the short silence from backstage:

"REED!" the boy hollered. "Oh Reed!"

Rodge pretended he didn't hear the loud boy (even though he was sure everyone else could) and continued. "Most of the time it has been the traditional Christmas pageant of the Nativity . . ."

"Reed, where are ya?" Roy's voice called from a different part of the backstage, sounding rather far off but still noticeable.

". . . and this year everyone agreed that we would alter the plan slightly and present you with a different Biblical pageant," Rodge persisted, his voice showing volumes of annoyance.

"REED FISCHER are you hiding?" Roy called from off in the distance.

Suddenly there was a scream which Neil guessed came from the girls' changing room when Roy probably barged in on them in search of Reed. Neil could hear the boy quickly apologize before closing the door so loudly that Neil jumped.

"The first scene of this play is from man's fall from grace," Rodge continued, gritting his teeth tightly.

"Oh Reed!" Roy hollered.

Rodge stopped as the sound of knocking followed by Roy's voice and the sound of water that could be heard.

"Who ith it?" Reed said in his croaky voice loud enough for it to carry to the audience and Rodge.

The sound of Roy entering the room could be heard and the sound of running water increased.

"Reed, it's me Roy," Roy said in a voice that was so fast it was almost inaudible. "You're on under thirty seconds. Hurry!" he remarked before slamming the door behind him.

"WHAT!?" Reed cried, then they could hear the sound of a curtain opening. "You've got to be kidding me I'm not even drethed!"

Roy poked his head back out from back stage and gave Rodge a thumbs up, completely ignoring the glare that the boy was giving him. Rodge was almost at his wits end and decided to cut to the chase.

"Ladies, gentlemen and children; I am pleased . . . . To present to you the first act of our play: The Garden of Eden."

Once Rodge escaped from the stage, he hurried back down the hallway to the dressing rooms. He couldn't get angry with the twins at present since they were on stage.

When he came bursting into the boys' changing room, he found everyone ready and in their costumes, lazing around. That is, everyone except Whip and Drew. The two had their heads bowed, staring at the script before them.

"No, we have to say that part or Styl will get suspicious," Whip was saying. "If we don't mention Joab not following David's orders than everything will fall apart."

Rodge walked over and placed a hand on their shoulders, causing the two to jump clear out of their skin. "I thought you figured this out yesterday. Why are you so jumpy anyway?"

"I'm not jumpy," Drew replied. "Whip is the one who is afraid that Styl will come and eat us alive."

Whip lowered his eyebrows though no one could really see it since his hair practically covered his eyebrows. "Weren't you the one who said that you had a dream that Styl broke into my house and hung me upside down from the clothesline?"

"You know I never understood how that got into my mind," Drew remarked, trying to get out of the conversation.

"Just be ready in another ten minutes," Rodge whispered. "I had better go see how the devil and our first parents are doing."

Whip and Drew didn't quite get his joke until after he left the room. By then it was too late for them to comment. Rodge had barely gone when Neil poked his head in so fast that the two leapt.

"You're on in three minutes," the boy whispered.

Whip saluted weakly before following Drew out the door. The two stood behind the curtain, staring out at the bright stage and the audience that filled the theater.

"I have butterflies in my stomach," Whip complained.

"Did you eat any caterpillars?" Drew inquired, even though her own hands were shaking. "Just remember . . . reenact the scene of the crime."

Whip nodded so rapidly that Drew thought his head would fall off. Luckily Neil gave them the signal and they walked onto stage. The curtains were closed while the props team (Oliver, Destiny and Silver) changed the scenery for the next act.

The first scene of the act went well since it was mostly conversations that Drew (playing Absalom) and Ivan (playing David) had with their military captains about the fight. As the curtains closed to give the team time to change to the next scene, Rodge came out to help Drew get tangled up in the fake tree.

They had placed a box underneath the tree so that Drew could stand on it and pretend she was dangling, while a fake bush stood in front of the box, concealing it. As the curtains opened, Drew began to wriggle as if trying to free herself from the tree when in truth, she was wiggling in nervousness.

Whip came striding a little too confidently onto the stage and the boy could almost feel Styl's eyes on him. Neil had told him that the girl was sitting with a bunch of other kids in the first row on the far-right side.

"Oh Joab," Drew whimpered. "Please help me down from here! I feel that my brain strings are about to snap!"

A small ripple of laughter ran through the audience but Rodge and Neil both slapped their faces. It was obvious that wasn't her line, but it served the purpose.

"I have not come here to help you," Whip snapped angrily, so angrily that Drew suddenly felt afraid.

"Then why are you here Joab?"

Whip felt his blood boil as they began to step into the reenactment part. "You know very well why I'm here."

"Come on Joab. I most certainly can't go back and change the past and neither can you," Drew whimpered, wondering dearly what Styl was thinking at that specific time.

"Oh, so you're going to start that whole 'I am innocent and you're the one who is powerless' is that it? You're just as bad as me Absalom if not worse. You're no angel," Whip hissed angrily, taking a step or two around Drew as if interrogating her, just as Styl had done with Emma.

Drew swallowed the saliva that was blocking her voice. "No one is an angel, but I am just asking you to accept the fact that I cannot change the past. All I can do is ask you to be the good person I know is in there somewhere and let go of the things that hurt you. I don't want anyone to get hurt, least of all you."

Whip pretending to scoff loudly but his eyes had just caught sight of the tall, slender girl in the audience and he had stolen a glance that direction. He could barely make out her features, but he knew that someone else could.

Down amidst the audience, Deke was sitting down the row from Styl, making sure that he stole several glances in her direction. The girl had seemed relatively calm and passive during the first three minutes of the conversation, but the moment Whip said the line: "I am innocent and you're the one who is powerless," Deke was sure he saw her eyebrows go down.

"Oh, I'm not going to get hurt," Whip remarked from the stage. "If anyone is going to get hurt, it's you. You ruined my life! You stole the pity that should have fallen on me! I am the one who was wounded by the pains of our king, not you. You gained mercy when you did not deserve it!"

Deke could see that Styl's face was going pale, but she was fighting to keep herself composed as Drew continued: "Joab, let's not start an argument. I am sorry that you lost the thing you wanted the most. I know what it feels like. But trust me, if you just let it go and try again, everything will be alright."

Whip spun around to face Drew and pulled out his fake sword, raising it above his head. "This is it Absalom. I am going to end this little charade of yours once and for all and no one will be the wiser."

The moment Whip struck at the side of Drew, the curtains closed and the two scurried off the stage. Neil and Rodge clapped them happily on the back, congratulating them on being so convincing. Everyone else hurried from the changing rooms to congratulate them as the next scene began.

Whip and Drew were just starting back to change when Deke came sprinting up to them. "Whip . . . . Drew! That was great!"

"Thanks bud," Whip remarked. "What was Styl's reaction?'

Deke shook his head. "It took her a moment but then it was obvious that she recognized the last half of the conversation."

"Did she say anything . . . do anything?" Drew asked, suddenly curious.

"She frowned the whole time . . . didn't say a word," Deke began. "But then the moment you said your last line Whip, she left."

The two stopped short. "Left?" they asked in unison.

Deke nodded. "Yeah left . . . as in departing."

Drew and Whip slowly looked at each other only to realize that both of them were pale. Deke didn't know what happened but the two grabbed their coats and ran off with no explanation. He decided it was best not to ask, though he did inform Neil and Rodge of their departure.

Chapter 36

"I still don't understand why you didn't allow me to come and see the play," Emma complained.

"Oh, you didn't miss much," Neil admitted. "The twins were horrendous. At least the parents thought it was funny. Rodge was prepared to skin them afterwards though."

Eileen smiled but quickly erased the smile from her face when Neil looked in her direction. The two had hurried to the apothecary to fetch Emma, whom they had banned from appearing at the party until they were sure Styl wasn't anywhere to be seen.

"The dance will be starting soon," Neil admitted, opening the door for them.

The two girls hurried into the Hall of Organization with Neil following close behind. It was dreadfully cold outside due to the fact that it was getting dark but also because the snow had turned to ice.

The room was a buzz with noise. People were walking around, chatting with friends and family. Kids were running around, trying to steer clear of their parents while catching up with their friends.

Ivan soon appeared out of the crowd and grinned brightly at Emma before turning to Neil. "I hope you don't mind if I steal her for a while?"

Neil grinned back at the boy and gave Emma a teasing push forward. "Be my guest!"

Ivan and Emma were about to leave when Emma stopped and turned to Neil. "Who are you going to dance with?"

Neil's eyes instantly grew wide and the color drained from his face. "I . . . . I don't know . . . I have to ask someone?"

Emma and Eileen exchanged exasperated looks while Ivan grinned. "Yeah man! It's tradition! Don't you remember last year? Oh wait . . . you were sick last year so you don't remember."

"Just go up to a girl and ask her," Emma suggested. "Always works."

Ivan was just about to object when Emma spoke up again. "What about you Eileen? Has someone asked you?"

Neil snapped his head around to consider the girl. Eileen was almost a sister to him. If anything, she was his wardmate. He hadn't heard the girl speak of anyone asking her to dance, nor had he heard her speak about boys for that matter; at least not in the way of dating and such.

Eileen couldn't exactly hide behind her long black hair as she usually could since Emma had managed to pull all her hair back into a semi down, semi up fashion. Eileen's true facial features had been revealed and had almost frightened everyone.

They never seen anything of her face outside of her eyes (partially), her mouth, nose and part of her forehead. Now they could see that she was in fact strikingly pretty. She was always pretty but with her hair out of her eyes, it was more obvious. She had high, sharp cheek bones, rounded chin and long slender eyebrows.

Eileen tried her hardest to not reply but soon the answer arose when her dance partner appeared through the crowd. Neil felt himself tense as Rodge stepped over and grinned at Eileen.

"You . . . . I mean . . . I thought . . ." Neil stammered, looking from Rodge to Eileen.

The grin on Rodge's face grew wider. "I hope you don't mind Neil."

Emma and Ivan shot Neil concerned looks. It would ruin the night if Neil expressed a dislike for Rodge dancing with Eileen. After all it was just one dance and nothing like a date. Neil was still looking from Eileen to Rodge with wide eyes. Slowly he shook his head and the other four silently relaxed.

The music began to kick back up and the four quickly left Neil staring after them. About halfway through the dance, Neil was able to relax and noticed he wasn't the only one who wasn't dancing. Deke wasn't dancing, and neither were Roy or Reed. The twins were helping a handful of grownups bring out refreshments while Deke watched the dancing from the other side of the room.

Neil continued to scan the crowd, looking for the rest of the gang. Whip and Drew had still not returned but that was a relief in certain respects. Seraphina was still in a serious coma at the apothecary, so she wasn't around. Zara was dancing with Gene, typical, while Oliver was dancing with Denise. It was a miracle that Oliver convinced Denise to dance though after a moment, Neil realized that Denise would only accept Oliver because he wasn't annoying.

Suddenly Neil's eyes fell on tall, handsome, blond haired Luke who was dancing with Vivian. The boy felt his face get red but managed to control it. He completely understood why Vivian would find Luke attractive, but it made the boy writhe inside for not having considered the dance before now.

The music ended abruptly, followed by a roar of applause from the dancers and the adults who were watching. Everyone was at once called to attention by the loud booming voice of Mr. Walker who stood at the top of the stairs on the other side of the hall.

"Ladies and gentlemen please gather around," he called, waiting until everyone obeyed before speaking again. "I want to thank you all again for coming. Now we will be presenting our school and society graduates."

There was a loud roar of applause and everyone, especially the kids, tensed up with excitement. Mr. Walker lifted his hands to calm down the uproar and didn't speak till every last trickle of applause had disappeared.

"First we will begin with our high school graduates," he announced, drawing out a small piece of paper. "First off, Roster Denver. He will be moving to Catasbanel where he will attend the university before returning here to Hichester where he hopes to take up teaching and professorship here at the society."

There was a loud cheer as slender, slightly short Roster hurried up the stairs to receive his diploma and a firm handshake from Mr. Walker before quickly descending the stairs. There were about five other students who had graduated and were leaving for college or staying in Hichester. It was a good ten minutes later before Mr. Walker finished the last announcement.

"And last but not least: Eric Octavian. He is planning on being apprenticed to Mr. Nielson here at the society where he will learn to teach members and hopefully become a professor here at society."

There was an uncommonly loud cheer as the boy hurried up the stairs. Deke couldn't remember why that name sounded familiar but once he saw the boy hurry up the stairs, he knew. Eric was one of the most popular but kindest boys in Hichester. He was a tall, sturdily built and strikingly handsome boy with straight brown hair.

Once Eric had descended and disappeared into the crowd, Mr. Walker began to speak again.

"Now we will move onto the society members. There are no new graduates this year but there are quite a number of new members and students moving up."

All the members tensed noticeably. It was rare that anyone got bumped up to the next level in the society. For your first two years you were in stage one. You followed orders, did loads of chores and did well in your classes. After that you began to have a possible chance of being bumped up. At present there were eighteen stage one students, eight stage two, six stage three and only four stage four.

Stage two was everyone's favorite after stage one because that meant less chores, more time to explore and work privately on your projects. You also got the privilege to spend extra time in the aquarium or the observatory. Stage three was practically a nightmare. Just like eleventh grade in high school, stage three was full of extra homework, double the usual amount of classes and very little time to spare for the observatory or the aquarium mostly because you spent most of your afternoon in the library.

Stage four was never reached until you were a junior or senior in high school. It was much more intense, physical endurance wise with not the greatest amount of homework or classes. You began to help by teaching and aiding the younger students, acting as examples. You had a load of time to yourself and was in a way a more mature version of stage two.

At present, everyone in the gang was in stage one other than Seraphina and Emma who had been bumped up to stage two three months ago. Oliver had been bumped straight up to stage three, completely skipping stage two. Everyone pitied him but Oliver practically adored stage three, mostly because of the homework but no one was surprised.

"First I will announce all the new members to the Society of Hichester Enterprise," Mr. Walker remarked, interrupting Deke's thoughts. "Scarlet Wheeks, Hahn Nielson, Hadwin Nielson . . . . Lurdes Nielson, Hilary Kent and Sara Catalani."

The whole gang perked up in surprise as Scarlet and Hilary, two dark skinned girls, hurried up the stairs. Following closely were Hahn, Hadwin and Lurdes, Denise's brothers, with their curly hair bouncing. Hahn and Hadwin were the twins with black hair while Lurdes was red haired. Lastly, Sara hurried up the stairs much to everyone's surprise.

"I didn't know Sara was a changeling too," Eileen whispered to Neil.

The boy shook his head. "Neither did I."

Once they reached the top, the six kids lined up on either side of Mr. Walker who began to speak about each in turn:

"Scarlet is eight years old and just recently discovered that she is a gifted panther werebeast. Hilary is also eight and has come from a long line of changelings. She however is the first person of her family in eighty years to be a crane aerobeast."

There were cheers and applause as the two girls waved and quickly descended the stairs. Mr. Walker then turned to the three boys, obviously finding it difficult to tell them apart.

"Hahn and Hadwin Nielson are six years old, Lurdes is five and are all three . . . Werebeasts? Hahn is a racoon, Hadwin a leopard and Lurdes a green tree frog."

There was a small ripple of laughter as the three boys skipped down the stairs, leaving Sara at the top of the stairs with Mr. Walker.

"Last but not least, Sara is ten and a surprisingly gifted wolf werebeast."

Every member of the gang turned to look at Neil in surprise who was just as surprised as they were. When the girl joined them on the floor, she merely grinned at them and pretended that nothing had happened.

"If I may have your attention please for another few minutes," Mr. Walker remarked. "There are a few students who are being moved up a stage in the society."

The silence that filled the room was so dense that people's ears began to ring. Mr. Walker drew out a small sticky note and pulled on his glasses to see better.

"New candidates for stage two: Whip Schneider, Roy and Reed Fischer, Neil Mecarnin and Zara Salerno."

Neil felt all the life drained out of him as his brothers clambered to hug him. He was glad though that he didn't have to walk up the stairs, but he felt bad that Whip wouldn't hear it from Mr. Walker himself.

"Candidates for stage three," Mr. Walker called out. "Emma Wagner, Ivan Olsen and Barret Stevens."

The gang hurried over to clap Emma on the back who was grinning from ear to ear but shivering from the realization that she was now in stage three. Oliver of course wrapped an arm around his sister as comfort which brought another smile to her face.

"Finally, new candidates for stage four: Oliver Wagner . . ."

There wasn't time for him to continue right away because the whole place erupted in cheers. Everyone knew Oliver and how talented he was, especially the fact that he was the first member to completely skip stage two. The gang practically smothered him till Neil pushed them off before Oliver fainted.

". . . And . . ." Mr. Walker hollered. "A second candidate for stage four: Gene Mecarnin."

When Roy and Reed had been pushed off of Oliver, they had resorted to hugging Zara, pretty much lifting her off her feet. When they heard Gene's name mentioned however, they completely dropped the girl.

There was no applause or cheers that followed . . . just a dreadful silence. Gene was barely nine and the youngest stage four member ever was sixteen. Everyone's eyes turned to Gene who was standing between Deke and Neil, going deathly pale.

"Is this a joke?" someone asked in a low voice but loud enough for Gene to hear.

"He's not even in high school. He completely skipped stage two and three," another remarked.

Neil had turned to look at Oliver and Emma for guidance, but both were staring in confusion. As he turned to look back at Gene . . . he was gone.

Chapter 37

"Just don't blow the place up okay Bruce?" Sara inquired.

The boy lowered his eyebrows as he pulled on his glasses. "Don't be ridiculous! I know what I'm doing."

The girl nodded slowly. "That's what I'm afraid of."

It was now time for the talent show that Bruce had offered to do. When Vivian had received word about Bruce's intelligence, she had insisted that he have a few demonstrations. The boy was now setting out a few boxes on an empty table at one end of the hall where everyone could see.

"Could I have your attention please?" he called.

All eyes turned to him and many kids crowded around to get better looks. Bruce drew out the first box and turned it over into a bowl. Everyone waited with bated breath to see what was inside. When he lifted the box, they weren't prepared. In the bowl was a pile of bright pink moist, powdery, almost flour like substance.

Several kids made disgusted or shocked noises. Some laughed while the rest remained silent, waiting to see what would happen. Sara glanced in Eileen and Neil's direction, only to see the two grinning knowingly. Apparently, they knew what this stuff could do.

Bruce stuck his hands straight into the stuff and a soft squishing noise followed, gaining some more disgusted noises from the crowd.

"This stuff is a secret mixture of organic substances and chemicals that I concocted. I call it Hand Clay. It is strangely attracted to any form of body heat. When I stick my hands into it, the warmth in my hands causes it to stick to me."

With that, Bruce began to lift his hands and the substance began to ooze as it continued to stick to his hands like glue. Sara was just thinking of how messy this would be to clean up when Bruce continued speaking.

"It looks like a real mess, right?" he asked, lifting his hands high, making a peculiarly shaped trail of the goo. "But wait until we pour water on it. Sara?"

Sara quickly grabbed the pitcher of water that rested on the table and lifted it up. She turned to Bruce for guidance, but the boy just nodded. In that case she slowly began to pour the water onto the goo. She was expecting it to start to dissolve like most gooey stuff but instead, this stuff didn't move.

When she poured all the water on the goo, it settled in the bottom of the bowl. Bruce stepped back from the substance and drew his hands out. Instead of the goo falling back into the bowl, it stayed where it was as if it had frozen.

"The water causes the substance to crystalize," Bruce explained, tapping the now hard goo. "The only way to un-crystalize it is to boil it on the fire in water."

Several kids hurried over to touch the goo. Sure enough, it was rock hard and had now created a rather impressively strange shape.

"Do another one!" a kid hollered from somewhere in the back of the crowd.

Bruce then resorted to showing the *mehnthis* and explaining its talents. Several kids asked for a demonstration, but Bruce said it was very strong and could be rather dangerous. Finally, he drew out the last box and pulled out a glove.

The glove wasn't normal, that was for sure. It looked almost metallic and had a whole bunch of buttons and dials on the palm.

"This is an invention I did a few years back. It can tell all sorts of things about you just by reading your pulse, feeling your body temperature and everything else in your hand," Bruce explained. "Who would like to volunteer?"

A small girl hurried from the crowd and planted herself right in front of Bruce. The boy carefully slipped the glove onto her hand and began to press buttons and dials.

"I am going to call out what the glove reads, and you tell me if it's true alright?" he asked the girl.

The girl nodded as Bruce began to punch more buttons.

"You are nine years old?" he inquired, gaining a rapid nod from the girl. "You were born August second, 713?"

The girl nodded again, her eyes growing wide. Bruce continued to read the screen on the palm of the glove. "You are A negative blood, allergic to all nuts except peanuts and are of Cochin Scoih descent?"

The girl's mouth practically fell open at the last few parts, but it was followed by roars of laughter and applause from the audience.

Deke had been standing with Sara and Denise, watching the scene. When Bruce called out those announcements, he felt himself grinning.

"We'll have to get Bruce to show Clint that thing," Sara remarked. "He was so determined to stay home with Webstar. But he doesn't realize what he's missing out on."

Deke nodded in agreement. However, his eyes caught sight of something else that drew his attention from the talent show. Gene was standing at the other side of the room, watching the show. Deke suddenly noticed his younger brother wave to a kid nearby and say something in greeting. What surprised Deke was that the kid didn't return the greeting but gave the boy a deep glare.

This caused great concern in Deke. Gene had always been a friendly person and had befriended everyone he met. It was completely unlike people to not like Gene and this wasn't the first time Deke had seen someone glare at his brother since his return. Something was definitely up.

Deke noticed something else as well . . . Neil was talking with Oliver and the twins about eighteen feet from Deke. He was also a good distance from Gene. The four were talking cheerfully when Deke noticed someone approaching Neil . . . Barret!

"Oh, not good," Deke whispered aloud.

Denise and Sara prepared to ask him what he meant but they had just caught sight of what Deke had seen.

"What does he want?" Denise almost snapped under her breath.

What they couldn't hear was what Barret was saying to Neil:

"Hello there man," the boy called, stepping over.

Oliver, the twins and Neil tensed but didn't allow the anger in their eyes to cross the rest of their faces. Barret was trouble, no doubt. He was constantly picking fights and bullying people. For the first few months that Neil and his brothers had lived in Hichester, he had bullied them nonstop.

"Enjoying the party?" Barret continued.

Neil nodded. "Yes, we are actually."

Barret either didn't hear the anger in Neil's voice or chose to ignore it. "Glad to hear it. Have you tried that new red punch they put out? It's really good!"

He held out four glasses to them which were halfway full of punch. The twins naturally leapt at the drinks. Neil almost had an urge to tell them to not drink it, but he couldn't accuse Barret of something without proof. Maybe Barret just wanted to act nice to start off before saying something unkind. Or maybe he was just in the mood to be nice.

The twins downed their cups and when Neil saw that nothing was happening, he relaxed.

Oliver took one of the cups, trying to be polite and nudged Neil to take one as well. Barret held out the last cup to Neil who took it slowly and drank it quickly, trying to get over with it.

Barret smiled brightly. "Told you it was good," he remarked. "Can't wait till desserts! By the way Neil, I didn't see you dancing earlier."

Neil shrugged innocently. "I didn't have time to find a partner. Besides, I'm not the best dancer."

Oliver at once noticed the change in Barret's features. The boy's eyes changed, the smile at once turned to teasing and his eyebrows lowered. The boy looked ready to pounce.

"Bet you were angry when Vivian accepted Luke's invitation to dance," Barret remarked.

The twins and Oliver exchanged puzzled looks as Barret continued to grin. Neil meanwhile, suddenly felt strange. His vision wavered and was no longer clear. He couldn't focus on Barret, Oliver or the twins . . . he couldn't focus on anything at all and it all seemed so dark and dim. His head felt hot and his hands were shaking.

He slowly began to turn around to look at the others, hoping that Oliver would see his distress. However, as he turned, he realized that there was one thing he could focus on . . . one thing that didn't look dark: Vivian.

Neil spun on his heel and looked angrily at Barret. "What are you talking about?"

Barret's grin grew at the sound of Neil's infuriated voice. "Oh, you know how Vivian didn't dance with you but danced with Luke."

Oliver didn't quite know what Barret was getting at. He wasn't saying anything too outright mean. Naturally it was rude of him to say those things to Neil, but Oliver couldn't quite understand why Neil was suddenly so angry all of a sudden. He hadn't seen Neil get upset in almost over a year.

The sweat was dripping from Neil's face, his eyes were wide with fury and his hands were clenched so tight that they were turning white. Neil took another step toward Barret and Oliver suddenly felt panicky.

Bruce had noticed a disturbance in the back of the crowd and had glanced up from his demonstration. What he did see clearly was Deke and Gene sprint through the crowd expertly and hurry toward Neil.

Neil grabbed a hold of Barret's shirt and twisted it in his hands. "I will tell you one thing Barret Olsen! Vivian wouldn't have danced with Luke if you hadn't set this whole thing up!"

Everyone had turned from the talent show to the boy who was now practically screaming.

Luckily half of his words were muffled by the sounds of Oliver and the twins trying to calm him down. Every time they tried to loosen his grip on Barret, he lashed out.

When Deke and Gene appeared through the crowd, Neil crumbled to the ground limply. If they hadn't seen Oliver clop the boy over the back of the head with his fist, they wouldn't have known what had happened.

"Good going Olly," Deke remarked.

The two boys hurried to their brother and picked him up from the ground. Hauling him onto Gene's shoulders, Deke helped his brother balance Neil as they hurried toward the side door that led to the offices.

"Mr. Nielson can we use your office for a moment?" Deke called.

The tall, elderly man waved in reply as the two boys disappeared through the door, carrying their brother. Oliver followed close behind and closed the door firmly behind them before giving the twins strict instructions to not let anyone through.

"What about the gang members?" Roy demanded.

"Anyone but Vivian," Oliver replied. "Whatever you do, don't let her in here!"

Chapter 38

Bruce shook his head angrily. "That downright scoundrel! I shouldn't have demonstrated the *mehnthis*! He probably stole a smidge when I did the demonstration and then dissolved it in the punch before giving it to Neil!"

"What I want to know," Denise remarked. "Is how Barret knew that Neil is crazy about Vivian."

At once, everyone in the gang turned and looked at her in surprise.

"In case you hadn't noticed," Emma pointed out. "For the past three years, since Neil gave up on Vicky, he has been practically over his head for Vi. It's obvious to everyone except Vivian."

Zara rolled her eyes. "I just don't understand teenagers!"

Denise smiled at the girl, feeling the same way.

"An uncomfortable turn of events," Roy remarked, approaching the group.

Everyone snapped their heads around to see that the twins were not on guard at the door anymore!

"What are you doing over here?" Zara demanded.

"Oh, Vivian thaid that you guyth were talking about thomething cool tho we came over to thee," Reed replied. "Why?"

Zara, Denise and Emma turned to look at the hallway door, just as it closed behind Vivian.

Vivian had been dying to know what was going on. When Deke and Gene had disappeared into the hallway with Oliver and Neil, she had tried to get an answer from the rest of the gang but none of them would tell. She had noticed them talking amongst themselves and she suspected that they just didn't want to tell her. When she had noticed that the twins were on duty, she quickly made an easy removal of them before slipping inside.

The hallway was empty, and all of the doors were closed. She did however hear a noise coming from the furthest door from the hall. It sounded muffled but almost like someone was screaming . . . a masculine scream.

She was halfway to the door when it flew open and someone collided with her. Vivian groaned inwardly as her head hit the carpet as the person ran into her. As she opened her eyes, she realized that Neil was the one who had collided with her.

The boy's hair was everywhere, and his eyes were wild, blood shot and staring at her in sudden shock. His face was deadly pale and sweating uncontrollably.

"Vivian!" the boy almost cried.

The girl was going to greet the boy when his mix matched eyes rolled into the back of his head and he crumpled to the floor. When Vivian sat up, she saw Oliver running toward her with a firm look on his face.

"Vivian get out of here!" the boy practically yelled, grabbing Neil and charging back toward the office.

Gene and Deke were close on his tail and had to spin on their heel quickly to keep up with him as he hurried back into the room.

* * * * *

"Gene can you hand me that pillow over there?" Oliver asked from his position on top of Neil.

The only way they could keep the boy down was to sit on him, but his yells were enough to break their eardrums. Gene tossed the pillow to Oliver who buried his own face in it to drown out some of the noise.

"How much longer will it take for the *mehnthis* to get out of him?" Gene yelled to Deke, over the noise of Neil's screams.

"Another fifteen minutes," Deke yelled back. "I just hope Barret didn't use an overdose or we could be here for hours. Bruce said it was strong."

Gene groaned. "Oh please spare us that! That is the last thing we need right now!"

Deke lowered his eyebrows and rolled them sarcastically, something quite out of character for him. "If you hadn't hurt Seraphina, Jerry and Bobby, things wouldn't so difficult right now!"

Gene stared at his brother in shock. Deke had barely spoken to him since he had been back which greatly disturbed him, but this was not the Deke he knew.

"What are you talking about? I didn't hurt any of them! I don't know where people are getting these ideas, but Jerry and Seraphina would be the last people I would hurt. Besides that, I barely know Bobby!"

"Then how do you explain everyone's dejection toward you?" Deke snapped. "Everyone, even Whip, Vivian and some of the gang members are starting to believe it! Even Eileen is starting to believe it!"

"I didn't do it!" Gene cried. "I would **never hurt** them, and I don't know why you want to accuse me! Besides, why would the society move me to stage four if they thought I was guilty?"

"Maybe you bribed them," Deke retorted.

Gene made a face and scoffed. "What would I have to bribe them with? Extra chores? I was as surprised as you when they moved me up! I had nothing to do with these attacks and I had nothing to do with my promotion."

"Right," Deke remarked. "Then why is it that Oliver was the one who witnessed you hurting Jerry?"

Oliver had been hearing muffled cries from the two boys through the pillow but hadn't really heard most of the conversation. However, he did hear that last part and snapped his head up, despite Neil's rantings.

Gene slowly turned, his eyes wide, the blood gone from his face. His eyes locked with Oliver and at once the boy felt a moment of doubt. He hadn't been up close, but he had been more than sure that it had been Gene. That look in Gene's eyes though held something that scared Oliver . . . a fear . . . a fear so great that Oliver hated himself for having told anyone about his seeing Gene hurt Jerry.

"Gene I . . ." the boy started but Gene had already disappeared through the door.

Chapter 39

The noise finally died down. Deke was sitting in a chair, covering his ears with his hands. Gene was nowhere to be seen.

Neil slowly lifted his head and eyed Oliver who was still sitting on him, his head buried in a pillow.

"What happened?" Neil inquired, looking from boy to boy. "I don't remember anything after Barret gave me that punch."

Deke was still trying to untangle his fingers from his ears, so Oliver replied. "You began to freak out . . . and all your common sense left you. I was actually afraid you were going to tell Vivian . . . you know that you have a crush on her. We've been in here for over half an hour trying to keep you away from earshot of the others. I don't want to know what everyone would have thought if they had heard what I've heard in the past forty minutes! I'm going to ban Bruce from doing any demonstrations in Barret's presence again!"

Neil glanced at Deke. "I was that bad?"

"Without any doubt," the boy assured him, rubbing his ears. "I'm actually glad you have enough common sense to not say all that in that tone and with that much . . . Oh, what should I call it . . . energy."

"It was almost like mad furious love ranting!" Oliver corrected. "There's no other way to put it."

Neil leaned back and shivered. "Thanks . . . for keeping me back here then."

Deke grinned. "I'm just glad Barrett didn't give you too much of that *mehnthis* or we would still be back here. First though I think we need to test you before we release you. What's the first thing that comes to mind?"

Neil shrugged. "Webstar . . ."

"Second thing that comes to mind?"

"Changelings."

"Third?"

Oliver glanced at Deke, wondering how far he would go before he would get an impatient reaction from his brother.

Neil raised his eyebrow, getting agitated now. "Christmas . . ."

"Fourth?" Deke pursued, speaking faster and giving Neil less time to think.

"Kill Barrett," Neil replied, his eyebrows narrowing in anger.

Deke grinned. "Fifth?"

"Get lost Deke Rasmussen!" Neil snapped, finally losing his patience.

"Atta boy, you're sane again," Deke remarked, nodding his head in satisfaction.

When the three boys emerged from the hallway, the hall was practically empty. There were a few grownups and kids cleaning up but other than that, it was empty. Emma, Zara, the twins, Denise, Sara and Bruce however were waiting for them and hurried over as they emerged.

"You okay bud?" Emma inquired.

"I'm so sorry," Bruce whimpered. "I'll never bring out *mehnthis* again!"

Neil grinned. "Don't worry about it. I'm just glad Oliver had enough sense to knock me out."

The gang grinned brightly but Neil furrowed his brow as he looked around. "Where is Eileen and Gene?"

"Oh, Gene ran off home," Zara replied, showing confusion. "Don't know why but Eileen offered to follow him."

* * * * *

Neil twirled the pencil on his finger again. This time he stopped it mid spin so that the sharp point was pointed downwards.

347

"There is still no evidence," he remarked aloud.

Mr. Wetherby looked up from where he had been working quietly in the library. He had barely noticed that Neil was in there but now he saw that the boy was deep in thought.

"Evidence for what?" he inquired.

Neil woke from his apparent daydreaming and locked eyes with the man. "Oh . . . the rumors about Gene. You've heard them, right?"

Mr. Wetherby nodded solemnly. "I have . . . and I must admit that I am disturbed. It is most unlike Gene to do such a thing, but it is also unlike so many people . . . reliable people, to make things up like this. I want to believe Gene, but then there is the fact that even his closest friends don't and many of them have been witnesses to attacks."

Neil nodded. "But there is no evidence that it was Gene. No one has been able to confirm what time the attacks happened and because of that, we cannot be sure of whether Gene has an alibi."

"You would make a good lawyer Neil," the old man mused aloud before returning to his book. "What are you planning on doing about it?"

Neil lowered his eyebrows, obviously not in the mood for joking. "I am going to prove the Gene is innocent."

A scoff came from somewhere nearby and the two turned to see that Deke had just entered the room.

"Good luck with that. While you're at it, why don't you prove that rain can turn to sugar," the boy remarked sarcastically.

Neil lowered his eyebrows. "What is your problem?"

"My problem? In case you hadn't noticed Neil, there is no way you can prove that Gene is innocent. It's not like you can keep him under your supervision all the time and then if an attack happens you can be sure it wasn't him. That is practically ridiculous!" Deke snapped.

Mr. Wetherby's eyes turned to Neil, realizing that the boy was staring at Deke with a growing smile. "Deke," the boy began. "You may accidently be a genius."

Deke furrowed his brow in surprise. "I thought I already was."

"No," Neil replied. "You were already an architect. Oliver has the genius part down pat."

Deke slowly turned to Mr. Wetherby and gave him a pitiful look. "Translation?"

Mr. Wetherby grinned. Neil and Deke were probably the funniest to watch when they were having a conversation. Deke always talked like he had swallowed a dictionary and Neil would ask for a simpler explanation. Naturally, when Neil spoke almost in a one-sided way, Deke would need a more complicated translation. Gene naturally could understand both of their languages and was usually the interpreter. This was one of the reasons why Mr. Wetherby was so fond of being a sort of protector over a group of wards.

Eileen of course was his adopted daughter, but Neil, Deke and Gene were like children under his protection but not entirely under his influence. He believed greatly in giving them freedom, even if it meant interfering with each other's business. He had learnt long ago that boys learn faster the hard way rather than the easy way.

"I honestly don't know either Deke," the old man replied.

"I'll keep Gene here all day tomorrow," Neil proclaimed. "Whip said that there have been reports every day of Gene either bullying or beating up someone. Well, tomorrow, if there is such an encounter, we will know it's not Gene."

"And what if there isn't?" Deke demanded.

Neil nodded. "Then I will admit to suspicion but until I have evident proof, I will not blame Gene of such a crime."

Deke slowly rolled his eyes and groaned. "Fine . . . oh and by the way. The reason I came down was because Clint wanted me to tell you that Webstar is ready for visitors."

The boy didn't know what happened, but Neil was up from the chair in a second and out the door. Deke honestly felt a gust of wind as his brother ran past. Deke glanced at Mr. Wetherby who was just as surprised as he was.

"When did Neil get that strong?"

Clint, Bruce, Sara, Eileen and Gene were wondering the same thing when Neil came bursting into Deke's bedroom two minutes later. They were all sitting in a circle around Webstar's bed and cooing over the puppies. They made room for Neil beside Webstar, so he could see the litter.

Five puppies to be exact: one black, a white, a brown, a cream colored one with specks of black and brown and one that almost looked reddish. They were all small, slightly hairy but not as hairy as their mother. They looked just like their mother in shape other than the fact that they were rather large for puppies and their muzzles which were slightly rounder than Webstar's sharp nose.

Neil leant over and picked up the black one with one hand and held the pup to him. The pup was about the size of his hands, plus Oliver's hands put together. The pup was slightly damp but clean, thanks to Eileen and Gene's interaction with the event.

"Have you named them?" he inquired.

The kids shook their heads. "We wanted you to have the say."

Neil considered the pups before answering. "Well there are five . . . How about Bruce, Clint, Sara, Eileen and Gene choose the names since I practically named Webstar."

The five kids lit up at this offer and began choosing which pup they would name. Naturally Eileen captured the black one from Neil while Sara chose the white one.

"What do you say to Chopper Jr.?" Eileen inquired.

Sara raised her eyebrows. "I thought the senior Chopper was brown."

Eileen nodded. "That's how we'll tell them apart. We can call him Junior for short. What about you Sara?"

The girl considered the puppy before replying. "Blizzard. She was practically born during a blizzard and she looks like one too."

"I'm settling for Peanut," Clint announced, picking up the brown one.

No one argued with that name but of course they objected to Bruce's name for the multi colored puppy: Duke.

"That one's a girl Bruce," Neil pointed out matter-of-factly.

Finally, he settled for Duchess after much convincing from the others that she was indeed a female puppy. Gene found it rather difficult to name his puppy. He had never had a pet before and suddenly found his mind blank.

"Could I just call him Bud till I think of one?" he inquired.

Neil nodded, smiling at his brother. He knew how hard it could be to name something. He had taken almost three days to name Webstar.

"Hey guys," Deke's voice called from the doorway. "Who took the doorknob off the door? It was here the last time I was here."

Everyone looked around at each other until their eyes fell on the doorknob in Neil's hand. The boy slowly handed it to his brother and grinned sheepishly. "Sorry bro . . . a little excited when I came in."

Deke took the doorknob but couldn't help noticing that his brother's voice seemed strangely uncertain. He also felt uncertain himself. When had his brother been this excited that he tore off doorknobs?

Chapter 40

"You won't be able to keep Gene in there forever Neil," Eileen pointed out. "He's going to need to leave to use the bathroom and stuff."

The boy rolled his eyes. "I know that! I'll just keep an eye on him! But giving him an excuse to not leave the house today is step one. You just need to keep your ears open for news of attacks today."

Eileen sighed. "Right. Well, I had better go or the girls are going to kill me."

"Where are you off to today?"

"We were going to see if Seraphina, Jerry or Bobby have woken up," Eileen replied. "If not, we were going to go ice skating on the lake."

Neil grinned and gave a mock salute. "Give everyone my best!"

Eileen considered the boy, sitting against Gene's bedroom door with Webstar asleep beside him and the puppies in his lap. He looked like he wasn't going anywhere soon.

When the girl left the house, Deke, Sara and Clint were waiting. Bruce had revealed that he wasn't one for snow and had begged to stay home. As the four headed out of the gate, they saw the rest of the gang hurrying toward them.

Emma, Zara and Vivian immediately looped their arms through Sara and Eileen's, making a link between them while the boys ran ahead.

"Does Neil really think this is going to work?" Vivian inquired. "If nothing happens today, it could mean anything. And if something does happen, it still doesn't prove that Gene isn't involved. He could have told someone to do all these things, so he could set up an alibi for himself."

Emma nodded but didn't seem too sure. "I don't know. Gene is so young . . . I don't see what he could gain from doing this, other than mistrust from his friends. If Jerry, Bobby and Seraphina had done something unkind or unfair to Gene then I would possibly understand but even then, it is out of character for Gene to hurt anyone outside of self-defense."

"But what about Gene's defiance of the society rules?" Eileen insisted. "Gene has never been that type. He has always respected rules and regulations and never questioned them."

There was a momentary silence before Zara spoke up. "But doesn't it seem kind of understandable, considering that almost everyone in the society is almost rebelling silently in a way to the new development?"

The girls had to admit, that was a fair point. If anything, Gene was just expressing what they were too afraid to, but they were thinking it in their minds. Gene was a very open-minded person so in a way that wasn't out of character for him, but it happened at just the wrong time.

"What about the promotion?" Sara inquired. "I don't know much so far about the society but from the sound of it, that has never happened before other than Oliver. Besides, Oliver just skipped one stage, not two! On the other hand, it was understandable in Oliver's case because he excelled beyond expectation in stage three and everyone could see it even before he was promoted. Gene however is not even ten and he got promoted to four. Oliver didn't reach third stage till he was twelve!"

"It's only a three-year difference," Emma pointed out. "But that is a good point. I wouldn't expect it from the professors, especially Iris Opal! That woman practically hates anyone who defies rules and Gene has been doing that a lot lately and then out of the blue they promote him to fourth!"

Vivian shrugged and stamped her feet to keep warm. "Maybe they decided to promote him before the suicidal bomber attack, and it was too late to change the promotion."

A silence fell over the four girls and they stopped dead in their tracks. The same thought all came to their minds and as they looked at each other, they realized they had all guessed it.

"What if . . ." Eileen started. "What if the suicidal bomber was the same one who has been initiating all these attacks?"

The other girls nodded. "The attacks started increasing after the bomber . . . and it's possible he might have survived," Emma admitted.

Vivian slowly shook her head. "I doubt it. The guy was wounded. There is no way he would have survived that explosion unless he was immortal. But they might be in cahoots."

What the girls didn't notice was that Zara sunk down into deep silence as she ran all these possibilities through her mind.

Meanwhile, inside the house, Neil was getting himself comfortable sitting against the door. The puppies were yawning loudly and making gurgling sounds through their noses. Neil carefully picked up Blizzard and scratched beneath her chin. She grunted happily at that, causing Neil to smile.

As Neil placed her back on his lap, he saw that Peanut and Duchess had located each other and were trying to start a squabble. Neil put a hand between them, but they soon managed to climb over his hand and continue bickering.

"Now, now guys that's enough," he remarked.

He wedged both hands between them and just barely pushed them apart. However, the two pups went skidding off his lap and about a foot down the carpet from the movement. Neil's eyebrows at once went down in confusion. He had barely touched them, and it was as if he had boxed them straight in the nose!

The boy glanced over at Webstar to see the dog watching him carefully. Swallowing, Neil shrugged off the whole thing and went back to fondling with the pups. It wasn't long before Peanut began to fight with Junior and this time it was a little more heated since they were both boys.

Neil didn't dare try to push them apart, even though he felt that his mind was playing tricks on him. In that case, he gently told them to stop. When they didn't listen, he furrowed his brow at the two, trying to see if just looking firm would make them stop.

Surprisingly . . . it did! Both pups stared at him in stunned shock and slowly curled up with pitiful looks on their faces as if their mother had just scolded them. Neil was trying to figure out how that could have happened when he heard what he hadn't heard before . . . a soft growling sound. It was the type of guttural growl that he had heard several dogs, including Chopper senior and Webstar use when trying to act fierce, firm or angry.

Neil looked over at Webstar, only to see that she was staring at him just as surprised as the pups. He soon realized that all the dogs were looking at him. Neil's eyebrows lifted, wondering if they were afraid of his frown and the growling stopped . . . This at once caused Neil to recoil in confusion. He felt his eyebrows and moved them up and down . . . nothing. So, it wasn't his eyebrows that were growling. That was a relief.

This was beginning to aggravate Neil. He couldn't understand why such strange things had been happening the past few hours and were affecting his mood. He had been snappish with Deke earlier when he had been reluctant to give Dusty to the training of Gene and then all this unusual energy and strength in his body, especially his legs and arms.

Neil shook his head, fully infuriated at not being able to understand what was going on. That was when the growling noise picked back up. He was about to call under the door and ask Gene if he was doing that when he realized that the growling noise increased when he opened his mouth!

Shutting it back up, Neil froze. He was fully afraid now and the growling stopped. Now he just felt strangely concerned and that was when he noticed a funny feeling on his neck and his head. At first, he thought something was crawling in his hair but when he reached back, he realized that his hair, even on the back of his neck was standing up straight. Not all of it but one long line from the top of his forehead to the back of his neck almost like a Mohawk.

But his hair wasn't wet, and it never stood up like that . . . it was too heavy to. Neil at once realized that this seemed strangely familiar. When he was angry, he could hear the growling and when he was afraid or concerned, his hair stood up. It sounded a little too much like a dog's reaction to fear and anger!

Neil grabbed the doorknob, about to pull himself to his feet when the doorknob broke off in his hand as easy as breaking a thread. Neil stared at it in his palm and stuffed it into his pocket. He would fix it later when he had calmed himself down.

Chapter 41

When the kids arrived at the apothecary, Livonia was shoveling snow on the front stoop so that it was easier to open the door. The snow had been falling steadily all night but now it lay about ankle deep with a thick covering of ice which made it virtually impossible to sink your feet into the snow, so you were practically walking on slippery ice all over the place.

"Good morning everyone," Livonia greeted, smiling warmly at them. "Staying out of the cold?"

Everyone nodded as they stomped their feet to emphasize the truth to the remark. However, Roy and Reed stomped so hard that they broke through the ice crested snow and made a sound thud as their feet hit the platform beneath their feet.

"We're also trying to prepare our thesis and presentations for tonight," Emma explained, just as pumped about the whole thing as Oliver and Deke were.

Deke had missed working on his while he was gone but knowing him, he was undoubtedly already done. Emma was the only one of the girls who showed a deep interest for learning. All the other girls and all the rest of the gang were keen on doing well, but they wouldn't get all bubbly with excitement over the prospect of preparing a thesis to read aloud to everyone.

"Oh, didn't you hear?" Livonia inquired. "The presentations are being stalled until this weekend."

At once, the twins, Zara, Vivian and Eileen all relaxed while the others cocked their heads in puzzlement.

"How come?" Oliver inquired.

Livonia shook her head. "It's the snow. Because it is so cold, and everyone is working double shifts to shovel snow, we're going through much more food, firewood and fuel than usual. The adults . . . or those who can venture out of Hichester in this weather are going to spend the next two days collecting supplies and they don't want to miss the presentations and thesis speeches, so they petitioned the society to hold it off till they returned."

"Oh," everyone remarked, some of them disappointed but most of them relieved.

"But I do have some news for you," Livonia added, at once getting everyone's rapt attention. "Seraphina and Jerry woke up last night, but it was too late to tell anyone. Bobby is still out but from how he is responding to therapy, he should wake in another few days."

The cheers that came from the small group of children was enough to break Livonia's ear drums, so she instinctively put her hands over her ears. Once the cheers had died down, she stepped aside since she knew that the kids would make a dash for the door.

Sure enough, the kids charged through the door, the twins and Vivian getting stuck on the way in with everyone else behind them. While the three worked to get unstuck, everyone else slipped inside by going between their legs.

As they burst into the living room of the apothecary, they saw Jerry and Seraphina sitting on the couch near the fireplace, wrapped in blankets and drinking cups of hot tea. The girls flew across the room to embrace Seraphina as best they could without spilling her tea.

Deke hurried over to say hello, but Jerry grabbed him from behind and squeezed the life out of him.

"We were so worried about you!" Vivian cried.

"We had no idea when you would wake up . . . or if you would at all!" Eileen added.

Zara nodded. "Stole the words right out of my mouth."

Seraphina smiled. "It's not like I was dead! Just a nap ... It definitely just felt like a nap. Livonia told me that we missed the Christmas party."

Everyone slowly nodded, showing their pity.

"You didn't miss much," Roy admitted.

"Didn't mith much?" Reed inquired in his low, gloomy voice. "Jutht the fact that Rodge wath about to kill the two of uth becausth we blew the play and then Thtyl went mithing and the two of them haven't come back from looking for her. Oh, and then there wath the part where Barret gave Neil mehnthith and made him go crackerth but other than that, you didn't mith anything."

Seraphina and Jerry's eyes had begun to grow the moment Reed began to talk and by the end of his small speech, they were bulging.

"It definitely sounds like we missed something," Jerry mused, smoothing his red hair back. "What happened to Whip and Drew?"

Everyone shook their heads. "They haven't returned," Emma replied. "Luckily their parents are gone helping collect supplies outside of Hichester, so they haven't been missed other than by us and at least we know what they're doing. Their parents wouldn't understand."

Seraphina shivered at the thought. "Well . . . Livonia said we'll be able to come home later tonight. Maybe we could have a sleepover and cover everything that's happened."

Everyone immediately nodded in enthusiasm and Deke was the first to speak. "We could have it at our house. Macaroon and Mr. Wetherby went to help the grownups."

"Who didn't go with the grownups other than the kids?" Jerry inquired, suddenly realizing why it was so quiet around the place.

"The kids and the elderly," Zara replied. "Which is cool because that means Mr. Nielson, Mrs. Schneider and Mrs. Keith didn't leave!"

Whip hooted. "This is gonna be great! It's awesome to have you back Seraphina!"

"Thanks!" Both Sara and Seraphina chirped.

All the girls quickly covered their mouths to suppress their smiles, but Whip's eyes only expanded in shock. "Oh no! This isn't good . . . we'll never be able to tell the two apart!"

Neil gave the two girls a crooked smile before jabbing Whip with his elbow. "They're the Seraphinas! Holy noodles!"

* * * * *

The others had been gone for three hours and Neil was fondling with Peanut's ears. "Deke is really going to kill me if this doesn't work," he remarked to the puppy. "He wasn't keen on pretending that he wanted Gene to train Dusty."

Neil had needed a good reason to keep Gene busy most of the morning. In that case he had employed Deke to give Dusty into the hands of their brother with the faked story that Deke wanted the cat to learn how to answer the telephone. They had moved the upstairs extension telephone into Gene's room, so he could work in there rather than the hallway.

Occasionally Neil could hear Gene speak calmly to the cat or the slight ringing noise as the boy taught the cat how to dial. What Neil couldn't understand was how Dusty would be able to lift the ear piece. It had been quiet for the past hour and Neil concluded that Gene was taking a break. Lunch would be ready soon and he would have to release his brother.

Neil grabbed the basket that Eileen had prepared for the pups and began to place each one inside carefully. He was just placing the red puppy in the basket when he heard the pitter patter of feet from downstairs and the front door slamming.

He began to rule out the possibilities of who it was but of course it turned out to be Deke, closely followed by the rest of the gang (or those who weren't chasing suspiciously aggressive girls or temporarily in comas).

"Neil, has Gene left his room?" Deke demanded.

The boy looked from kid to kid, estimating that they probably had run all the way from either Break Neck Creek, or they had done several loops around Hichester before returning home.

"No, he hasn't," Neil replied. "What happened?"

"We dropped by everyone's houses to see if they had seen Gene anytime today. Three people said they saw him at different places and on our way back we saw him sneaking around behind the Schneider's," Zara explained.

"Did you catch the guy?" Neil demanded, suddenly feeling his spirits soar.

There were several heads that shook at this inquiry. "He practically disappeared," Vivian admitted. "I have never seen anyone run so fast!"

"Let's see what Gene has to say about it," Deke suggested.

Neil caught a hint of doubt in his brother's voice. It was obvious that Deke doubted that it wasn't Gene they had seen and heard about. Sighing to himself, he carefully opened the door, making sure to not break the doorknob that he had just fixed.

Everyone poked their heads inside and stopped short. The room was empty and dark. The window was open, and the cold winter air was causing it to flap open and shut. Dusty was curled up next to the telephone, fast asleep.

"You said you wouldn't leave the door!" Eileen cried.

"I didn't!" Neil admitted honestly. "I was sitting there the whole time and Gene never came out for bathroom break or for a snack!"

"Well it was mostly our fault," Zara admitted, considering the window. "We forgot that Gene is practically a genius and would have gone for the easy exit."

The girl hurried across the room and pushed the window closed while the others scoured the room. There was no sign of Gene.

"Well that settles it," Deke remarked. "It is obvious that there is no evidence to prove that Gene wasn't seen sneaking around."

"But he didn't hurt anyone," Neil pointed out. "And until we have significant proof that it was Gene who caused the attacks, I am not going to give up on him."

"Then what should we do?" Vivian demanded, trying to solve the tension between the two brothers.

Neil sighed. "Deke, Roy and Reed, go and contact the Schneider's and get Rodge over here. We're going to have to search for him."

The three hurried off with the girls close behind. Neil however waited when he saw that Zara was looking out the window in confusion. Walking over to her, Neil saw that her eyebrows were down, and she was biting her lip in concentration.

"What is it?" he inquired.

"The window," Zara replied. "It has been raining and icing the whole time we've been gone . . . the reports we heard of Gene sightings have been all day . . . if Gene had escaped through the window early enough to get to all those places . . . the snow and ice would be piled on the floor from being blown in but there is nothing . . . it's like someone just opened the window five minutes ago."

Neil considered the logic and realized that it made crucial sense. "What are you saying then?"

Zara lifted her dark blue eyes and shook her head. "I don't know . . . but it goes to prove that Gene possibly wasn't the one we saw."

Neil felt himself suddenly relax at this prospect but then disappear when a doubt reached his mind. "But what if the window blew open?"

Zara shook her head. "No can do. The wind has been blowing west for the past week! It hasn't changed once, and this window is facing east, and it opens outward, not inward. For the wind to blow open the door even if it was just slightly ajar, the wind would have to get inside the room and blow the window open. But from considering this . . . he either left just a few minutes ago or propped the window open on purpose."

"And why would he do that?" Neil demanded.

Both stopped when they realized what had possibly happened. No one had been at the door for the past few minutes that they were standing at the window. If Gene had hidden somewhere they hadn't checked, he could have slipped out the door without them seeing!

Both charged out of the room and down the stairs. What they completely missed was what Dusty did. Slowly climbing off the telephone table, the cat crawled under the bed and peered up at the boards that held up the bed. There was a soft thudding sound and the cat scurried out from under the bed with Gene close behind.

"Thanks, Dusty," the boy panted, scratching the cat's ears. "It hurts to hide underneath those bed boards."

And with that, the boy grabbed his knapsack, slung it over his shoulder and hurried out the window, closing it firmly behind him.

Chapter 42

"What is your problem?" Zara demanded as she and Neil stood in the hallway with everyone else.

Roy and Reed both had a hand over their left ears and were cringing while Deke was following them, glowering.

"They were in such a hurry that they dialed the upstairs extension instead of the Schneider's so when Dusty answered and hissed into the phone, they lost all feeling in their left ears," Deke replied. "I managed to call Rodge and he said he'll be coming over soon."

"I understand your logic Zara," Vivian pointed out. "But why would Gene want to sneak out without us noticing? We haven't found him anywhere in the house and none of us heard the door close."

Neil shrugged. "Well we were kinda keeping him prisoner. That is enough reason to want to sneak out."

"And besides," Emma pointed out. "How could Gene have taught Dusty to answer the telephone if he was gone the whole time? It takes a long time to teach a cat tricks especially one like

Dusty and considering the twins' situation, Dusty definitely knows how to answer the telephone."

Eileen grinned. "That actually reminds me of the time Gene taught Dusty a trick when we played hide-n-go-seek where he got Dusty to warn him when the coast was clear and safe for him to run for base."

Almost immediately, Zara and Neil exchanged horrified looks. "Dusty!" they cried in unison, causing everyone else to jump.

"What about him?" Reed demanded.

"Gene didn't leave through the door!" Zara cried. "He made us think he did so we would leave the room and Dusty warned him when the coast was clear, and he used the window! Oh, why didn't I think of that!?"

"Well as soon as Rodge gets here we'll find Gene and you'll get to ask him yourself," Deke remarked glumly.

* * * * *

The wind was swirling now, snow everywhere and getting in Gene's hair, eyes, mouth and clothes. He chastised himself for not grabbing a bigger jacket, but he dealt with it. Letting his wings out, he wrapped them about his body which did great to block the wind and snow.

The only thing that was keeping him from getting horribly lost in the white snow was the river to his left. He was following it carefully, mind, and eyes set on reaching the bargemen village. Ever since the suicide bomber attack Gene had been itching to get to the village and find out why Deke went there so often. Of course, he had been so caught up in Christmas preparations, Deke and Neil's absence, and the rumors to the point where he hadn't had time. Now that it was just the rumors and sudden mistrust from everyone, Gene felt he was free enough to venture there.

There seemed nothing but white snow and ice for miles with the river winding back and forth. Gene almost had the urge to take to the skies when his eyes fell on something in the snow. It was dark colored and small but stood out in the deep snow. He wondered that it wasn't buried but he saw that there was a thin layer of ice covering it.

He was just about to break the ice and see, when a strong hand grabbed his shoulder and spun him around. Gene found himself face to face with Walt. Just great!

"What do you think you're doing out this far pipsqueak?" the boy inquired, using his favorite nickname for Gene.

The boy kept his cool and answered calmly. "I was heading to bargeman village. What about you?"

"Oh, don't try to carry on a conversation with me Mecarnin," Walt snapped. "I'm here on specific matters."

"Well it seems to me that you are carrying on a conversation," Gene pointed out. "Just by asking me what I'm doing."

Walt's eyebrows lowered, and Gene felt a tinge of fear. Walt had grown huge in the past year and was even more frightening than Barret who was more a nuisance than a danger.

Gene wasn't prepared when Walt's huge fist clapped against his cheek, causing him to spin and land in the snow. His face stung but it was numb from the cold, so he couldn't feel anything. As he reached up to touch his face, he saw that his mitten had blood on it now.

The boy pushed himself up slightly with one hand and turned to face Walt. Walt was already on top of him and his foot flashed out and struck Gene hard in the ribs. The boy crumbled to the ground, deciding that staying down would be his best weapon.

"Who is the sassy one now Mecarnin?" Walt taunted. "Your big brother isn't here to help you this time. He probably doesn't even want to help you!"

"What is going on here?" a deep, demanding voice boomed from nearby.

Gene slowly lifted his head from the snow to see two tall figures approaching, both completely different. One was huge, muscular and a giant of a man while the other was tall but slender and graceful like.

"If I remember correctly," another voice remarked. "Taunting someone who is weaker than you is no act of justice."

"This one is a troublemaker," Walt pointed out angrily, glaring down at Gene. "You had better steer clear of him."

There was a scoff and the first voice spoke again. "If I remember correctly, you were the one who was causing trouble for this boy. I think it best if you steer clear of him *lad.*"

The man put emphasize on the word "lad" to point out that he wasn't in the mood to deal with him. Walt took the hint for he was no fool and began to walk off but not without hissing something to Gene.

"This isn't over yet Mecarnin."

When the sound of the boy's footsteps died off completely, Gene felt a hand grip his arm and help him to his feet. Gene rubbed the cold snow and ice out of his eyes and face before looking up at his two rescuers.

The giant man had graying red hair and piercing blue eyes. He reminded Gene of an older version of Hummer Nielson. It was Timber Nielson, Hummer's father! The other, Gene recognized right away as Finn Wagner.

"Thank you . . ." the boy started.

Finn smiled sadly at the boy. "I take it that this is a regular thing?"

Gene didn't answer but shrugged. "I guess."

"You guess?" Timber inquired. "Is that yes or no?"

Gene slowly looked up at the man and saw that he was a man who dwelt on particulars. "It is sometimes regular . . . I guess it depends on his mood. Sometimes I go a week without him bothering me."

Finn smiled. "Now that's the Gene I know."

Looking Gene up and down, Timber realized that he liked what he saw. Tall for a nine-year-old with sturdy shoulders, strong arms and legs, confident head that he held high but not too high to show pride. His eyes flashed with excitement and his smile showed kindness. Timber had seen Gene around society but had never had the boy in his own classes since he taught Marine Progress.

"I have heard a lot about you Gene," Timber remarked.

Gene's face at once went serious and he ducked his head. "Probably not all good I suppose."

Mr. Wagner and Timber exchanged knowing looks. They had indeed heard the rumors and that was one of the reasons they had been looking for Gene.

"I know that people are doubting you Gene," Finn started. "But you've got to believe in your own innocence. Only you and God knows if you are truly innocent or not and you'll have to be content with that till the truth comes clean. If you are innocent, show no fear and no worry because you know you are innocent. Have you heard of Colton Schneider, Gene?"

The boy lifted his eyes and nodded vigorously. "He was sentenced to death because someone made up a lie about him and there was no way he could prove his innocence because only he, God, and the man who lied knew that he hadn't done such a thing."

Timber nodded in satisfaction while Finn smiled. "Exactly Gene. He knew he was innocent and died happy, knowing that he was innocent of such a crime. He felt bad for the man who lied because he lived the rest of his life with that lie upon his chest. If you know you are right, then you have nothing to fear."

Gene considered this before slowly nodding. "Thank you Mr. Wagner . . . that helps."

Chapter 43

"You know Whip," Drew remarked drearily. "If she doesn't leave that house soon, I'm going over there and knocking on the door!"

Whip glanced up from where he was sitting beside Drew's bedroom window. After Styl had hastily left the play, they had followed her in a perfect circle around the society, then halfway through Hichester before she finally made a long loop to the Bevor's house where she was obviously staying. She hadn't left the house all night and Drew had taken shifts with Whip to keep an eye on the door.

Styl had appeared at the front door once but had taken one look at the heavy layers of snow and had disappeared back inside. That had been about three hours ago and the two were now at a loss for words.

"I still don't see why we have to watch her anyway," Drew continued, gaining no reply from Whip.

"I am concentrating," Whip replied.

Drew rolled her eyes. "You are watching the Bevor's front door! You're just lucky that I happen to live across the street from them or we would have been sitting outside all night. You never did explain why we are following Styl. We did our part to bring Styl to justice at least within her soul and now shouldn't we let it be?"

"It is more complicated than that," Whip pointed out. "I want to make sure that Styl doesn't do anything rash or possibly find out that Emma is here in Hichester. Besides, I want to know what the grudge is all about."

"Maybe they were childhood friends, and someone chose Emma for a dodgeball game instead of Styl," Drew remarked glumly, slumping on her chair.

Whip pursed his lips but didn't move his eyes from the window. "And you think Styl would wait several years before beating Emma up with a stick and then leaving her in two feet of snow? Where did you learn common sense?"

"Well the way you're going at it," Drew snapped. "We'll be here for years waiting!"

"Oh, keep your knickers on Drew," Whip groaned. "We don't have to wait any longer because Styl has been standing on the front porch for the past fifteen minutes and three seconds."

Drew leapt to her feet and looked through the window pane. Sure enough, Styl was standing on the porch across the street dressed in the same attire she had worn when Whip and Drew first laid eyes on her.

"Why is she taking so long to leave the house?" Drew demanded angrily. "I'm going down there."

Before Whip could stop her, the girl had exited the room and was charging down the stairs. Whip had nothing to do but follow her. When he finally located his jacket, mittens, and snow boots, Drew was already out the door and crossing the street.

Rather discreet, isn't she? Whip thought to himself.

The boy pulled on his boots and hurried out the door, pulling on his coat and mittens as he went. He found Drew standing on the other side of the street behind the tall bushes that lined the front of the Bevor house. The bushes were the only thing keeping Styl from seeing them.

"What's your big plan, Socrates?" Whip demanded, pulling his mittens on. "Walk up and admit we were the ones in the play?"

Drew spun around and placed her hands on her hips. "What makes you think you're so smart, Plato? You were the one with this brilliant idea to bring out Styl's conscience, you decide what we're going to do about it."

"Oh no you don't," Whip snapped. "I was the one who sat most of the night by the window while you kept saying that this whole thing was junk and then you came sprinting out here and almost blew our cover."

"Huh," Drew scoffed. "From the sound of it, you just supported the fact that it is your idea."

Whip opened his mouth to object, but he stopped, mouth open. Drew noticed his pause and slowly turned around. Standing directly behind them, towering over them was Styl!

"Hi . . ." Drew stammered, hearing Whip swallow loudly behind her.

Styl's dark eyebrows lowered as she considered the two of them. "You . . . you were the two in the play! Absalom and Joab! Who wrote the dialogue you used?"

Drew slowly looked over her shoulder at Whip whose eyes were as big as saucers. Should they tell her, or should they remain silent? Considering Styl's sharp look she was giving them, it might be better to act mute.

"Who. Wrote. The. Dialogue?" Styl demanded, taking care to show how agitated she was.

"A . . ." Drew started, hearing Whip freeze behind her. She knew he was afraid that she was going to spill it. "A kid . . ." Drew started. ". . . who writes dialogues . . ."

Whip rolled his eyes. Sure, that would get them out of trouble! Styl's eyebrows went down at Drew and she took another step forward.

"What was his name?"

Whip felt his face get hot. If Drew revealed that it was two people, Styl would guess it right away! However, he wasn't prepared for what Drew said.

"You're right it was a boy . . . He's short . . . fat . . . really a fool . . . I believe his name is Schneider . . ." Drew replied.

Styl nodded slowly. "Schneider? That sounds familiar. I'll find out more about him. Thank you for your assistance."

With that, the girl began to walk past them down the sidewalk. When she was about ten feet away, Whip spun toward Drew and hissed at her.

"I'm not fat!"

Drew smacked a hand over the boy's mouth, but it was too late . . . Styl had heard him! The girl stormed back over and planted herself in front of Whip this time.

"So, you're Schneider! I thought so. Where did you get the words for that act in the play?" Styl demanded, grabbing Whip by the shirt.

Whip gulped loudly as Styl twisted his shirt, bringing her face close to his to emphasize how angry she was. He could feel the heat of the anger radiating out of her. What he didn't know was that the heat was actually coming from himself. Sweat was pouring down his face and his legs felt like putty.

"Uh . . . well . . . I didn't . . . I mean . . . see we uh . . ."

Styl's hand continued to twist the shirt until it was almost a knot. Right when Whip thought she would cut off his breathing circulation, a voice cut the dreadful silence.

"They got it from me."

Styl let go of Whip's shirt, causing the boy to fall down on his rear in the snow. As he fell down, Whip spun around as did Drew to see who had spoken. It was Gene!

"I wrote the words down," Gene continued. "And they read off of it for the play."

Whip and Drew quickly exchanged looks. That was in fact not far from the truth. When they were trying to learn the lines perfectly, Gene had written them down for them while they practiced the movements. In a way, they did get the words from Gene, just not the first time.

Styl strode over to Gene and planted herself halfway between Gene and the other two. "And where did you hear those words?"

Gene didn't reply. Whip and Drew waited with bated breath while Gene looked passively up at Styl. Would he tell her that he had gotten the words from them or would he tell a lie? It was terribly out of character for Gene to tell a lie but that was an option he could take but shouldn't.

"That is confidential information," Gene finally replied.

Drew clapped a hand over Whip's mouth before the boy could let out a snicker. She put her other hand over her own mouth to conceal the look of horror that had appeared on her face. Styl was definitely going to kill Gene now.

Styl took a hard step toward Gene but stopped short when Gene's voice rang out again. "I thought you believed in angels, Styl *Wagner.*"

Whip and Drew's mouths dropped open, making almost a clanking noise. Styl's head snapped back as if someone had just hit her across the head. Her eyes locked on Gene and her eyebrows lowered.

"What are you talking about?"

A smile appeared on Gene's face. "I ran into Finn Wagner, Emma's father and Timber

Nielson. They had a rather peculiar story to tell me about your past with Emma."

Styl's face at once went a chalky pale color. Her hands began to shake, and she bit her lower lip. Whip and Drew slowly hurried over to listen for they were suddenly intrigued by the whole thing.

"Mr. Nielson told me that you are Emma's cousin. Her mother Holly and your mother Fern are sisters. You two grew up together here in Hichester," Gene began, thrusting his hands into his pockets and walking slowly around Styl as if interrogating.

Drew suddenly realized that Gene was copying Styl's behavior toward Emma. If Whip and Drew were able to make Styl see the wrong in her doing through the play, Gene was making her feel vulnerable like Emma was by doing this.

"You both dreamt of joining the society when you got old enough. However, when it was time for your apothecary check, it was discovered that your sea horse fin was damaged and had to be removed," Gene continued. "Emma went on to society and you were sent to Williams boarding school because you couldn't cope with the loss."

Styl slowly nodded. "You've got that much right."

Gene stopped in front of Styl and crossed his arms. "What else did I forget?"

Styl lifted her eyes and pursed her lips hard. "You forgot to mention that my fin was damaged because during the war of the Black Years, I was caught in an attack and was cut seriously. The doctors believed that I was poisoned because I was in a coma for weeks. When I joined the society, Livonia pointed out that by then, my fin had been completely taken over by an infection that was spreading to my bloodstream."

Whip leant over to Drew and whispered in her ear. "That is just like with Neil!"

Gene nodded. "It was possible that you weren't cleaned completely from the wound or you were poisoned. It slowly infected your fin till you couldn't save it. You're not the first person that's happened to Styl."

Styl scoffed loudly. "And I suppose the other people have just lived with such a loss and moved on?"

Gene swiveled his eyes to look Whip directly in the eye. Whip suddenly found himself smiling at Gene for the first time in several days. He knew what Gene was thinking.

"Actually yes. My brother Neil had a serious injury when he was a kid and was thrown into a coma for two months. The coma did some peculiar things to him. I will say this, he wasn't at all pleased when he found out that his wing needed to be removed and got kinda violent about it. Though afterwards, he was able to move on about it," Gene pointed out. "And he has been able to get over it and think of other things."

Styl's head slowly ducked so as to not meet Gene's eyes and she began to fidget with the fringe on her coat. "Well it's different for me."

"Why is that?" Drew insisted in an impatient voice. "If someone who is about two years younger than you could get over it three years ago, I'm sure you can."

Styl shook her head. "It's different because my fin was never removed."

The three kids started in shock. They hadn't realized that this was what had happened.

"Why . . . Why not?" Whip insisted. "It could have killed you! If the infection was that bad . . . why wouldn't it have killed you already?"

Styl shrugged. "I don't know . . . but ever since I found out I've been really uptight about it. I can talk about it, but other people can't without me feeling sudden anger that I cannot control . . . it's like it is not part of me."

"I think it would be better if you had it removed Styl," Whip remarked without thinking.

In a flash, Styl had broken past Gene and catapulted herself into Whip, knocking him to the ground. Drew was too stunned to move but Gene had seen it coming the moment Whip had opened his mouth. Rushing over to the two struggling forms, Gene brought down the hard part of his wrist onto the back of Styl's neck and the girl crumpled to the snow.

Drew leapt forward and drew Styl's limp head out of the snow. She was still breathing so she was just unconscious. Gene helped Whip out of the snow and then hurried to Styl.

"What caused her to do that?" Drew demanded. "It seems too fairylike for a serious infection to cause her to react aggressively toward people! First Emma and now Whip!"

Whip nodded but Gene didn't. Instead he bit his lip and furrowed his brow. "Or maybe it is something that is closer to reality than we know."

"What do you mean?" Whip inquired, sinking to his knees beside Gene.

Gene reached over with one hand and grasped Styl's wrist in his hand. Pushing the sleeve back, he revealed a bright red line that traveled from the back of her hand to the vein in her wrist. Drew and Whip both started and looked at Gene in unison.

"That was just like the one Reed had . . . only his was on his throat," Whip pointed out.

Gene nodded. "I think this is something beyond our knowledge of the human body. We need to get her to Livonia."

Chapter 44

Bruce glanced up from where he was sitting in the library. He had heard the front door open and close and voices chattering and laughing. The voices grew, and Bruce concluded that they were nearing the library door.

When the voices were at the peak of volume, the door opened to admit Drew, Whip and Gene. All three were rosy in the face from being outside and were pumping their arms to get warm.

"Oh, hi guys," Whip called to Bruce and Clint who were the only ones in the library. "Where is everyone?"

Clint looked up and noticed the three. "Gene! There you are. Everyone went looking for you."

Gene smiled as he sat down beside Bruce. "I took a walk to the river, encountered Walt . . . was saved by Mr. Nielson and Mr. Wagner . . . helped Whip and Drew in their dilemma . . . walked with them to society and then back here."

Clint raised one eyebrow while his other went down. "What dilemma?"

"Oh Styl," Drew replied. "We took her to the apothecary to have her fin removed. Livonia shooed us out of the apothecary till after the procedure."

When the girl saw that both Bruce and Clint were looking at her, completely puzzled, she shook her head. "We'll explain later. What are you two doing anyway?"

"Oh, I am demonstrating the hand reader to Clint," Bruce replied. "He missed the party last night, so I promised I would show him a few of my inventions and experiments."

Drew scooted over and watched as Bruce pulled the glove out of his pocket. "I didn't get to volunteer last night. Could you try it on me next?"

"Oh, do Drew first," Clint remarked hastily. "I don't know if I want to put that on until after I'm sure it won't blow me up."

Bruce lowered his eyebrows at the boy but obliged. Drew held out her hand and Bruce slipped the glove on and began to dial. Drew was on pins and needles, almost ready to explode with bubbles of excitement.

"You are ten years old . . . born January 25th, 712," Bruce read. "A negative blood . . . allergic to poison ivy and are of direct Falfinian decent."

Drew nodded vigorously. "Correct to the dot."

Bruce smiled as he slipped the glove off Drew's hand and onto Clint's. He continued to dial before reading the screen.

"Could I read it?" Whip inquired, suddenly intrigued by the demonstration.

Bruce moved to the side and held the screen toward Whip to read.

"O negative blood . . . seasonal allergies . . . of slight Rechuedian decent with a good deal of Uthanian descent . . . You were born March 4th, 702 . . . you are eighteen years old?"

Drew and Gene's eyebrows shot down in confusion while Whip scratched his head in bewilderment. Bruce pushed him aside and peered at the screen. "Must have malfunctioned . . . maybe I pressed something wrong."

"You didn't," Clint replied. "All of that is true."

All four snapped back in puzzlement.

"Uh Clint . . ." Whip started. "How could you be eighteen? You barely look nine . . ."

Clint slowly shook his head. "I know I look nine but I'm really eighteen. It's a strange thing but I grow really slow. I looked like I was five when I was twelve."

Drew and Bruce cocked their heads to the side, but Gene and Whip's faces lost all color. The three could actually see the blood drain from their faces, leaving them sheet white.

"You . . . You age unusually slow?" Whip stammered. "But that's . . . that's . . ."

The boy wasn't able to go on. It was like there was a rock in his throat. Slowly, Gene managed to speak around his own throat rock. "Clint . . . do you by any chance know anything about your genealogy?"

Clint cocked his head inquisitively. "Yeah . . . why?"

"Do you know the names of your grandparents?" Gene inquired.

"Would you know them Gene?" Drew inquired, confused. "Don't you have the same grandparents as Clint?"

Gene nodded. "I do have the same grandparents on our mother's side . . . but I know nothing about my parents or grandparents on my dad's side other than the fact that my father was Frank Mecarnin, my mom was Morgan Mecarnin and my grandmother was named Gianna. I don't even know my mother's virgin name."

Clint shrugged. "Well in that case let me enlighten you. Our grandfather, on our mother's side, is Charles and our mother's virgin name was Morgan Hichester."

Whip felt like a reed slapped him in the face. He slowly turned his eyes to look at Gene, only to realize that the boy was standing there with a passive look on his face, but his lip was shaking.

"You're . . ." Whip swallowed. "Your great-grandfather was Bentley Hichester? Doesn't that make Clint the third-generation male heir?"

All Gene could do was nod before the door of the library flew open and in burst the whole gang, including Seraphina.

"Gene!" Seraphina cried, rushing over to the boy and flinging her arms around him. "How have you been?"

Drew was surprised that Seraphina completely missed the pale looks on Gene and Whip's faces. However, everyone in the doorway were more surprised that Seraphina was greeting Gene that way.

"How are you feeling?" Gene inquired, stepping back from Seraphina. "You've been out for days!"

Seraphina smiled. "Oh I'm fine. It was just a bump."

"Uh Seraph," Vivian remarked bluntly. "You do realize that said 'bump' was a smack that Gene gave you?"

Seraphina raised her eyebrows and waved her hand. "Come on Vi. Even you would know that Gene wouldn't do such a thing! Someone was probably pretending to be him!"

Vivian ignored her as Deke hurried into the room. "Where have you been Gene?" the boy snapped.

Gene was about to open his mouth when Whip spoke up. "He helped us with Styl. We can vouch for where he was."

"Was he with you an hour ago?" Deke snapped.

Whip slowly looked at Drew then at Gene. He dearly wished that Deke hadn't said that. Considering what Gene had done for them and how kind he had acted despite the fact that Whip had treated him unbearably rude, Whip couldn't help but wonder if Gene really was innocent. He was just convincing himself of that when he realized that Gene really wasn't with them an hour ago.

Slowly, he shook his head. Deke nodded and turned back on his brother. "Where were you before that?"

"I was by the river when Walt set on me," Gene replied. "Then Mr. Nielson and Mr. Wagner came to my rescue."

"And what time was that?" Vivian inquired.

Gene stopped a moment to consider what time it was now, how long he had been with Whip and Drew and how long it had taken him to walk back from the river. "An hour and a half ago."

"Where were you between that time and the time you were with Whip and Drew?" Eileen interrogated.

Neil, Zara, Emma, the twins and Oliver stood at the door, watching the interrogation with deep remorse. Gene seemed so frightened with three people towering over him, demanding answers from him.

"I was walking back from the river . . . then I met Whip and Drew," Gene replied.

"And you didn't stop on your way there and hit Ivan?" Vivian snapped.

Gene's eyes grew wide. "What? No! What happened to him?"

"You happened Gene!" Eileen yelled. "We were standing right there and saw you hit Ivan! Luckily you just bruised him and didn't send him into a coma like you did to Seraphina, Jerry and Bobby."

"Eileen that's enough," Seraphina demanded. "Gene didn't knock me into a coma and even Jerry said that it wasn't Gene."

"So, you say," Deke remarked angrily. "But no one can prove it. Gene has no alibi in any of these cases!"

Neil and Zara exchanged looks. It was true, there was no possible alibi that Gene could possibly have. Every time there was an attack, no one was sure where Gene was, or he had no one with him. They hadn't seen Gene hit Ivan; Eileen, Deke and Vivian had.

"Hey guys," Neil finally said, stepping forward and pulling the three kids away from his brother. "Ease it up. Why don't we relax tonight, have a sleepover and talk about it more tomorrow huh?"

* * * * *

"Hey Neil?" a small voice whispered.

Neil spun around on his rolling chair to see Whip standing in the doorway.

"Yeah Whip? Come on in man."

The boy slowly made his way across the room and sat down timidly on the couch. Neil rolled his chair over so that he was sitting near

Whip. "What's on your mind? You've been kinda quiet today."

Whip fingered with his pajama pant tie. He and Seraphina had headed over to their house to get Rodge and pajamas for the sleepover. All the girl were sleeping in Eileen's bedroom in sleeping bags while the boys camped out in the library on the floor and the couches.

There was still a line in the hallway as all the girls were waiting to brush their teeth. As it turned out, they were waiting on the twins who were delaying finishing their showers.

"I . . . I'm sorry about what I said about Gene the past few days," Whip replied.

Neil lifted an eyebrow and leant back in his chair. "That's not the usually mischievous Whip I know. What's got you acting like this man?"

Whip slumped in the couch and let out a disconcerting groan. "It's everything that's going on Neil. I cannot cope!"

Neil smiled and twirled on his rolling chair to face Whip. "Anyone can find that difficult to cope with. Luckily now that Christmas is over, the play is out of issue and stuff, things will lighten up."

Whip shook his head roughly. "It's not that Neil . . . I've found it impossible to cope with anything for the past several days."

The older boy was about to open his mouth to repeat what he had just said but then stopped to consider the situation. "Whip . . . this is not like you. Out of everyone, you are the one who is able to cope with excitement or problems. What has happened?"

"I . . ." Whip began but got no further. The words stuck in his throat and the redness appearing on his face told Neil that he was on the verge of tears. Whip buried his face in his hands and slowly his shoulders began to shake. When he lifted his face, tears were streaming down his face . . . something Neil had never seen in Whip's case.

"The only reason I cannot cope is because I lost Gene's support. He was always like the core in my eyes, holding us together. Now these rumors are going around, and I feel like the core is gone and we're falling apart. I cannot go on without the Gene I used to know," Whip fairly cried. "I don't know why but I am finding it hard to believe Gene's guilt . . . but I still don't know if he is innocent. I am caught between the hammer and the anvil and I need to escape it."

Neil let out a deep breath that he had been holding back for the past few minutes. "Well Whip . . . the only answer I have to that is I understand what you feel like, concerning Gene.

He has always been the one who has held us together and seen us through hard times which is one of the reasons I find it impossible to find him guilty. The other reason is because, even if he is guilty, I cannot turn on him because he is my brother and my love for my brother comes first before judgment."

A smile slowly lit up Whip's tear stained face. "You know you really love someone when you cannot blame them for breaking your heart. I admire your love for your brother Neil but if you really want to help him and us . . . you need to find something to support your theory."

Neil was about to speak but his eyebrows shot down and a strange flicker appeared in his eyes. "Wait . . . do you mean that this whole thing is not just hurting Gene but also hurting us?"

Whip raised an eyebrow in exasperation. "Are you kidding me man? It is hurting everyone who knows Gene!"

"Then that's it," Neil breathed. "Someone is trying to hurt us by hurting Gene. We hurt whenever Gene hurts and so someone is trying to take out our core."

Whip shrugged. "Good thought . . . but how did they convince Gene to do such evil things?"

"That is something I need to talk to Gene about," Neil replied.

The boy had just leapt from his chair when the door opened, and everyone poked their heads inside.

"Hey Neil," Roy remarked. "You had better come armed because Deke is ready to kill you."

"Why?" Whip and Neil insisted in unison.

"Because we cannot find Gene," Clint replied. "And he's not hiding under his bed or behind his door this time. Dusty doesn't even know where he is."

Chapter 45

Snow crunching beneath heavy footfalls was what caused Neil, Seraphina and Oliver to perk up. They had been leaning against the gate in front of the Wetherby house as Zara came running up to them

"Anything?" Neil insisted, concern evident in his eyes.

Zara shook her head. "He wasn't at the river nor at the bargeman village."

Neil slumped back against the gate again, causing it to creak against his weight. "I just cannot believe that Gene would leave without telling us where he was going."

Oliver opened his mouth and Neil lowered his eyebrows angrily. "And don't say that Gene has lost his marbles or I'm going to say that you agree with Deke and the twins!"

Oliver shook his head slowly. "I was only going to say that we're in a tight spot. There is no evidence proving Gene innocent and a lot proving him guilty."

Neil nodded. "I know. You don't have to remind me."

Neil didn't see Zara give Seraphina a quick look and a sign with her hand. He didn't even remember that the girls were there until Seraphina spoke up.

"Why don't you go inside and get a warmer jacket Neil?" Seraphina inquired. "The others won't be back for a while."

Neil was more than ready to object but Zara gave him a nudge toward the door and cleared her throat meaningfully. He allowed the girl to usher him inside before turning to her.

"What is up with you?" he demanded. "You're acting really weird. Everyone is!"

Zara smiled as she closed the door and grabbed Neil by the wrist. "I need to talk with you."

Neil rolled his eyes as Zara led him into the library and closed the door behind her. "It seems that a lot of people are talking to me and most of the time it's not in Gene's favor."

"Well I have some good news for you then," Zara whispered. "I think there is a catch somewhere in all this."

Neil crossed his arms and leant against the wall. "Then please enlighten me," he remarked doubtfully.

"Don't you find it strange that Gene isn't trying to offer an alibi to prove where he is?" Zara insisted. "Whenever there have been attacks, he has no alibi. If I know Gene, he is much smarter than that and would definitely try to prove his innocence which would make his job easier if he were guilty."

"So . . ." Neil inquired, trying to urge the girl to get to the point.

"So," Zara complied. "Gene isn't prepared whenever there is an attack, as if he doesn't know they're coming. If he was behind the attacks he would make up an excuse or an alibi that would excuse him. Also, there's something else."

"What's that?"

Zara quickly crossed the room and closed the blinds on the windows so no one could peak in on them. "No one went into deep detail about the attacks, but from what I learnt from Whip . . . Gene was acting really strange, not reacting to names as if he didn't know them and when Gene ran off, he didn't let anyone see his back till he was out of sight."

At those words, Neil suddenly became attentive. "That could possibly mean that someone is posing as Gene and didn't want anyone to know that said phony didn't have wings."

Zara nodded but Neil wasn't quite convinced. "But who could it possibly be?"

The girl reached into her pant pocket and drew out a small object which Neil recognized as one of the black flashlights that Deke had made with the screwdriver and knife attached.

"I found this buried beneath snow and ice by the river," Zara explained. "It was hidden but reflected the sunlight."

Neil held out his hand and Zara dropped the object into his palm. It was icy cold from being under snow and ice for quite a while.

"What are you trying to say?" he inquired, looking up from the object.

Zara took the flashlight in her hand and held it up. "I asked Deke what the flashlight is made of and he named off this weird name . . . something called *yuthinis* and when I asked Bruce where it is located, he said Kesroc Falfi."

"So?" Neil inquired, not quite following.

Zara waved the flashlight in front of Neil's face. "The material that Deke used to make the covering of the flashlight is bullet and bomb proof! What if the bomber was wearing an outfit of the same material which protected him from the bomb and he survived?'

"That still doesn't prove that Gene wasn't involved," Neil pointed out. "We need to eliminate all information."

Zara nodded. "First we need to ask everyone who sighted Gene during the attacks and find out if there is something similar with each of the attacks. Second, I'm going to ask Bruce to test that cloth he has been working on and find out if there is a remnant of this *yuthinis* on it."

"Why?"

"Because," Zara replied. "There was no sign of any body anywhere near the river so either the person was blown to oblivion or he survived. Also, that bomb attack that Bruce has been keeping an eye also has no record of any unrecognizable person. What if both bombers are one and the same person? Bruce has plenty of evidence to suppose that the bomber came from Kesroc Falfi and that is the exact same place where this flashlight material came from and the possible answer as to how the bombers or bomber survived."

Neil pursed his lips together and fingered his chin. "But why would the same bomber or a guy in league with him bomb an innocent neighborhood?"

Zara glanced over her shoulder as if checking to make sure no one was about before leaning toward Neil. "That I don't know but I will say this: where did Deke get that material for the flashlight? There is no way it could be just a coincidence that Deke happened to have a bomb and bullet proof material without knowing it."

Chapter 46

Neil felt the blood rush to the back of his neck. He was glad that his face didn't get hot as well or everyone would know that he was nervous. Everyone was leaning against the handles of their shovels, considering Neil and Zara skeptically. They had been assigned the job of shoveling the snow off of the platforms at the society since the parents were gone but Neil had pulled the job to a halt.

"You seriously didn't just ask us that did you?" Eileen insisted. "You're asking us to help prove that Gene is innocent? What if he is guilty? Then we'll be covering up the crime and telling a lie!"

Neil was about to turn to Zara for support, but the girl had already taken a stand. "I would like you to reflect on the past three years . . . Who was the one who risked his own life to save Neil? Who refused to leave Vicky behind because he knew it would cost her life and limb? Who was the one who knocked Barret and Walt's heads together when they duck taped the twins to their lockers in school? Who wrote of a 900-word

Religion essay for Whip when he was sick with smallpox?"

There was a pause in her inquiry where everyone was about to reply but the girl wasn't done. "Who risked getting expelled for sneaking into the school in the middle of the night to get Seraphina's text book that she had accidently left in the principal's office? Who risked some physical harm by standing up to Styl to protect Whip and Drew yesterday? Who protected me from serious harm by going against the society rules and risking his own safety when we were attacked by a bomber? Who was able to do all the jobs assigned to him even though everyone ditched him because of one single rumor?"

The pause that followed was not one where everyone was waiting impatiently for Zara to finish. The silence was one of realization, considering what she had just told them. It was true beyond words that Gene had indeed stood up for them numerous times and got them out of close shaves. In truth, they knew that she was right, yet there was still that tinge of doubt.

When he deemed that the silence had gone on long enough, Neil stepped forward and placed a hand on Zara's shoulder. "I will promise you this. If you will support our effort and promise to not come to hasty conclusions should we find

Gene, I will promise to personally deal with him. If he poses any danger to anyone, I will deal with him personally."

Several eyebrows shot up. Oliver looked up from the floor and a confused frown crossed over Seraphina's pretty round face. Naturally, the twins knocked their heads together to consider the situation without anyone else hearing while everyone else pondered this offer within their own minds.

Almost without hesitation, Seraphina stepped up and stuck out her hand to Zara and Neil. "I'll support you in any way I can."

A smile lit up Zara's face and Neil couldn't help himself from smiling. Seraphina had always been the greatest supporter of the brothers and of any antics that either of the brothers came up with, so her choice was expected but a joy nonetheless.

Zara shook the girl's hand before allowing Neil to do the same. Seraphina then stepped to the side to stand beside Zara to reveal that Whip and Drew were approaching.

The two stuck out their hands as well but both their answers were different:

"I haven't known any of you very long, but I feel that with the little knowledge I have of

Gene's character, it is more than likely the right thing to do," Drew replied.

Whilst Zara shook her hand and grinned brightly at her, Whip grasped Neil's hand but didn't shake it. "If it was any one of us in trouble, Gene would agree. So, I'll do it because he would."

A curious look crossed Neil's face. He had always got the impression that Whip drew his crazy character from the twins' demeanor which was virtually true but now that he thought of it, Whip probably built off of some of Gene's bright, energetic but also accepting character. Whip was one of the few of the gang members who accepted problems as if they weren't problems at all.

Neil gripped Whip's hand strongly and patted him on the shoulder, giving him a smile, which spoke his own form of thanks. It took some time of hesitation but soon the twins, Oliver, Denise, Clint, Sara, Emma and Bruce walked up to agree to the conditions. However, Deke, Vivian and Eileen remained behind, refusing to budge.

"I'm sorry Neil," Eileen remarked, her voice proving that she was indeed sorry. "I wish I could agree but I will not risk more people getting hurt. I cannot let our friendship sway my better sense."

The boy felt as if a cold hand clutched his heart. That was the first time that Eileen ever referred to their relationship as friendship. All other times she had spoken and referred to him and the boys openly as brothers or even like cousins. It was obvious that this wasn't a situation to tread on hastily.

"I understand," Neil replied before Zara could shoot out a retort.

Neil swiveled his eyes over to Vivian who merely shook her head. Even though the boy was giving her his best puppy eyes and pale expression, Vivian remained unemotional.

"No can-do Neil," the girl said. "There is just absolutely no way we can prove Gene's innocence and I am not going to put my life and the lives of our friends on the line for one person."

That was also difficult to hear but when Neil turned to Deke, the reply he heard from his brother fairly caused tears to spring to his eyes:

"I owe Gene nothing."

Ten minutes later, the gang finished shoveling the snow and were returning the shovels to the storage building. Deke, Vivian and Eileen had left directly after the conversation mostly because they felt that the tension in the group was directed at them.

Soon the group was sitting on the edge of the Steeple Hall platform, tying on their skates. It was too bitterly cold to fly, and the water was frozen so there would be no swimming.

"Neil," Seraphina whispered, sitting down next to him.

The boy didn't reply, he didn't even acknowledge Seraphina's presence. He was just staring across the ice, his skates on his feet. Seraphina pulled on her first skate and leaving it unlaced, she placed a gentle hand on the boy's shoulder.

"I know you're hurting . . . we all are. What Deke said was the last thing we wanted to hear . . . it might have seemed unfair, but I guess he had a reason to say that."

Neil at once came to life and pushed the girl's hand aside. "It didn't seem unfair. It was unfair! He had no reason or right to say that about his own brother! Sometimes I wish that he hadn't discovered his true heritage and hadn't known about the difference between him and Gene! If he still thought he was Gene's brother, he wouldn't have said that!"

Seraphina shivered at Neil's strong voice and bit her lip. It had been years since the boy had yelled like that . . . since he had found out from Gene that he needed to have his damaged wing removed. However, this seemed more personal. When he had reacted to Gene three years earlier, it had been almost more desperate. Now it seemed that he was beyond that . . . he had passed beyond worry and desperation into a world he wouldn't escape until he could fix it.

The girl placed her hand on his slender hand and stopped. His hand felt uncommonly warm even though he wasn't wearing mittens and it felt funny. For a moment, Seraphina thought that his hand felt like one single muscle. She looked down to realize that he was clenching his leg until his knuckles turned white . . . and for a split second it almost looked like his hand grew in size. After she shook the thought from her mind, she guessed she had just imagined it.

"Gene is still his brother as much as he is yours. A difference in heritage doesn't mean anything. Clint and Sara think of Gene as their brother even though he is only their half-brother. Blood does not connect two people Neil . . . your soul does," Seraphina whispered, glancing at the others. "You know . . . even though I already have two blood brothers in Whip and Rodge, I still consider everyone in the gang as my siblings. It is better to have a larger family than feeling like you have to limit the number of people you invited under your roof."

423

"Well that's not how Deke is looking at it anymore," Neil snapped. "All he is thinking about is proving how wrong Gene is!"

Seraphina sighed and took her hand off of Neil's. Strange enough, Neil regretted snapping at her because he had suddenly felt relaxed and at peace with her hand over his. She seemed strangely calm and sure, even though his world was falling apart.

"Deke is going through a phase," Seraphina whispered. "You went through your own when you first arrived here . . . you have to let it play itself out but always be there for Deke just like he and Gene were there for you during your phase."

Neil slowly looked over at the girl to realize that she was biting her lip, the blood had drained from her face and tears were fighting at her brown eyes. He hadn't realized it, but she actually felt his pain too.

"Gene will probably never have a phase," Neil remarked, forcing a smile.

Seraphina smiled as well but that broke the dam of tears which began to stream down her face. "Probably not."

She reached up with the back of her hand and wiped the tears from her face just before Neil was about to do it for her. The boy felt the back of his neck burn again when he saw Seraphina give a quizzical look at his outstretched hand. Pulling his hand back, Neil looked back at the ice.

"Will you do what you said?"

Neil at once looked at Seraphina, not sure what she had meant. The confusion in his face was evident so Seraphina went into detail.

"Are you really going to deal personally with Gene when we find him? Or was that just to boost everyone's willingness to help?"

Neil shook his head. "I'm going to keep my promise and deal with Gene personally . . . but not in the way they might think. I'm not going to knock him out and lock him up . . . I'll try to talk to him and find out what's going on and if that doesn't work . . . I might have to use force, but I am going to use words before actions . . . I owe Gene that much."

Chapter 47

When Cook pushed the library door open with her toe, she was about to announce that she had cocoa and cookies for everyone but then stopped. Neil, Zara, Sara and Clint had their heads bent over a stack of notebooks that were full of scribbles, personal notes and check lists.

Neil was chewing on the eraser of his pencil while Sara was giving him disgusted looks. Cook smiled. She had become rather fond of Sara, mostly because the girl didn't approve of Neil's peculiar nervous or concentration habits just as much as Cook.

Zara was writing furiously on her notepad while Clint was flipping through a dictionary that was almost bigger than eighteen encyclopedias put together. Cook wisely placed the tray of cocoa and cookies on the table between the piles of notepads and dictionaries. Without any of the kids noticing her, the woman slipped out of the room and closed the door behind her.

"What could be keeping him?" Neil insisted.

Zara stopped her writing long enough to reply. "Cool it Neil. Don't forget that he still has to check with Whip and Seraphina. You're lucky he agreed to do all the running."

"You already checked with me," Sara pointed out.

Clint rolled his eyes. "You know it's not funny Sara. We were talking about the other Seraphina."

Neil nodded before looking over at Clint. "What are you doing?"

Clint continued to flip but managed to answer his brother. "At present I am trying to locate the definition of a word that Oliver used."

"Which was it?" Zara and Sara asked in unison.

"Atypical," the boy replied. "Oh, here it is! It means 'peculiar' . . . Huh."

"What?"

Clint shook his head. "Oh it's just that Oliver said that when he saw Gene attack Jerry he had acted 'atypical and abnormally apprehensive.'"

Neil's eyebrows went down. "What else did Oliver say?"

Clint nodded toward Zara who flipped through her notebook till she came to the page where she had written down Oliver's comments. "I had to translate all his words to English. He said that Gene was wearing a cap drawn low over his eyes, a heavy coat and kept reaching behind his back and fingering the back of his coat . . ."

"What was his 'Professor language' version?" Clint inquired, having become rather fond of Oliver and an admirer of the boy's form of vocabulary.

"Oh, something about 'obscuring below a visor that isolated somebody from considering his eyes and incessantly situated his hand behind his vertebral and fingered his fleece'," Zara replied. ". . . funny though."

Neil rolled his eyes, almost fed up with the mysterious observations that they kept making but wouldn't reveal what they were thinking unless asked. "Why?"

"Because that was almost the exact same thing that Destiny said about when Gene attacked Bobby . . ." Zara replied. "That he was wearing a hat pulled over his eyes and seemed really anxious, nervous and absent-minded and kept fingering the back of his jacket."

"Maybe a nervous habit," Sara suggested.

Neil shook his head. "Gene bites his nails when he's nervous."

"Well we'll have to compare that to Whip and Seraphina's observations once Oliver gets back," Zara suggested.

Almost as if by magic, Oliver entered the room and closed the door, leaning against it as he caught his breath. By the time he had reached the table, the four were bouncing up and down in anticipation. Without a word, the boy placed a notebook before them that was full of notes.

It was typical that Oliver wouldn't bother to tell them everything in words since Oliver barely spoke two words together. This was definitely like him anyway.

Zara and Neil both reached for the notepad, but Neil was faster. ". . . Anxious . . . didn't react to certain names as if he didn't know them . . . Wore a cap . . . Looked uncommonly pale and didn't notice the cold? In winter?"

"Now that is really weird," Clint admitted. "No one in their right mind would wear clothes not fit for winter in this weather. I mean . . . I don't!"

Neil shook his head. "This is really strange . . . he left as if he didn't want them to see his back until he was out of sight . . . and Seraphina writes that she couldn't see any steam coming from his mouth . . ."

"Steam?" Clint inquired. "What does she expect him to be? A kettle?"

Sara quickly gave her brother a hard wallop on the arm before explaining. "You should

430

know by now that you can see your breath when it's cold out and knowing how cold it's been for the past month, they should have seen a stream of breath coming from Gene. What do you think it means Neil?"

The boy shook his head. "I don't know . . . but it all adds up. Whenever Gene attacked someone, he was wearing a cap to conceal most of his head and his forehead and the third time he covered his eyes . . . Zara, did Destiny say how close she was to Bobby when he was attacked?"

Zara shook her head. "She wasn't close to him at all. She just happened to see the whole thing . . . but from what she could tell, neither Gene nor Bobby knew she and Victor were there."

Neil nodded. "That answers my question . . . When Gene was sighted hurting someone without him having knowledge of being watched, he didn't wear a cap until the time when there was a witness: Whip! Whip witnessed Seraphina getting hurt and Gene knew he saw the whole thing. Gene didn't know that Oliver saw him as well as Destiny and Victor."

"What does that mean?" Oliver inquired, startling everyone with his voice.

"The one thing that really tells Gene apart is his eyes," Neil explained. "They are lighter than your usual blue and turquoise color . . . if someone wanted to pose as Gene, they would have to find someone his height, looked like him and have a similar voice and same color eyes."

"That is a lot of requirements," Clint mused.

Neil grinned at his brother. "Exactly! It would be easier to find someone who was his height, looked like him and had a youthful voice . . . but what if he didn't want anyone to know that his eyes were a different color than Gene's, so he wore a cap?"

Sara shook her head. "But why would he only wear a cap when there was a witness?"

Everyone had been listening, not sure what Neil was thinking but now reality dawned on Zara and her eyes grew wide. "Because he knew he would attack Jerry and later Bobby and would throw them into a coma! That way no one would know about his different colored eyes until Jerry and Bobby were awake and by then everyone would have turned on Gene! But because he couldn't knock Seraphina and Whip out at the same time, he had to cover his eyes, so Whip couldn't attest to him having a different colored eyes!"

"But how can we be sure?" Clint inquired. "Bobby is still in a coma and Seraphina nor Whip saw Gene's eyes . . . and Destiny, Oliver and Victor were too far away to see them . . ."

A smile lit up Zara's face. "But Jerry is awake, and he was close enough to see."

"Exactly," Neil remarked, a teasing look appearing in his eyes. "Thank you for volunteering to go ask him, Zara."

Chapter 48

"How is Styl?" Zara whispered.

Livonia smiled as she continued to file through her mess of papers. "Much better. We had her fin removed . . . just like we suspected, it was terribly infected and was almost as bad as Neil's. She'll be asleep for a few more hours."

Zara nodded. "When Jerry is allowed to leave the apothecary, tell him we're having a sleepover tonight at the Wetherby's."

"I most certainly will," Livonia replied. "He was delighted to have a visitor today. No one has really dropped in since Bobby went home."

Zara at once perked up. "Bobby went home? When did he wake up?"

A grave look crossed Livonia's face and Zara almost regretted asking. "He went home this morning. He didn't wake up Zara, he . . . he stopped breathing last night. We tried everything, but he slipped away in his sleep."

The girl at once clapped a hand over her mouth and felt tears sting her eyes. She didn't know Bobby well since he was in stage two, going on to three. It seemed like such a waste for someone on his way to a new stage to just up and die in his sleep without waking from his coma."

Fifteen minutes later after consoling Livonia and Robin, Zara headed back to the Wetherby's with as much haste as she could through the thick snow. The tears in her eyes were icicles and she didn't feel the numbness in her hands.

Bobby is dead, Bobby is dead, it is all Gene's fault. Zara shook her head, trying to push that voice out of her mind but it kept up its steady stream. *Bobby is dead, and it is Gene's fault. He does not deserve your pity or your time. All a murderer deserves is death.*

"Stop!" Zara cried aloud without meaning to.

She stopped in her tracks and kicked a nearby bush, sending piles of snow everywhere. She had the urge to sink to her knees, but she remembered how cold the snow feels on one's dungarees and she wasn't dressed for snow at present.

She kicked the bush again, this time harder and let out a distressed whimper. The whimper was followed by a voice calling her name that caused Zara to spin around. Standing behind her on the edge of the forest was Gene!

The girl had the urge to run over and hug him. That was what she would have done if she ever had a hard day in the past for Gene always helped her ease out of her pain. But now, she almost felt contempt toward the boy who had been missing for over twenty-four hours and was now standing about five feet from her.

"What are you doing here?" Zara almost snapped. "Where have you been?"

Gene shook his head. "I had to go see someone."

Zara felt her eyebrows go down and as she tried to fight them, the voice in her head spoke for her. "Was that particular someone the suicidal bomber? Did you go and tell him that everything is working great and that soon the whole of Hichester will be dead?"

The blood at once left Gene's face and his clear blue eyes widened in stunned horror. Zara was hitting herself inwardly, angry at herself for letting that evil voice in her head speak through her mouth.

"Wha . . . What are you talking about Zara? The suicidal bomber is dead . . . why would you even think that I would want Hichester dead?" the boy asked, his voice shaking violently.

Zara shook her head. "The suicidal bomber might have survived Gene. That is the

436

only explanation for why there was no body found."

Gene paused to consider this but the color in his face didn't reappear. "But he didn't kill anyone . . . no one has been killed yet . . ."

"Bobby is dead!" Zara yelled before she could stop herself.

Without hesitation she regretted it for Gene turned so pale that she thought he would faint. He took on a purple, almost greenish color and she worried that he would be sick. His hands that had been shaking now were shaking so bad that she could hear his clothes rustling.

"Bobby . . ." The boy started. ". . . is dead?"

Zara nodded. "He died last night in his sleep even before waking up from his coma. Livonia doesn't know the reasons, but she thinks his body wasn't able to take the injury and just shut off."

Almost as soon as she finished saying those words, she became aware of the sound of voices and footsteps nearby. With sudden horror, she realized that someone was walking to the grove!

Leaping forward, the girl slammed into Gene, knocking him into the snow. She didn't get up but lay flat on the boy, peering up just slightly so she could see exactly who was walking nearby.

At once she thanked her quick reaction for the persons turned out to be Eileen, Emma and Vivian. Bad idea to let Vivian and Eileen see Gene. Who knows what they would have done if they saw him.

"What's wrong?" Gene whispered, considering Zara's quiet and serious expression.

"Just stay down," Zara whispered, clapping a hand over the boy's mouth. "You've been missing for a day and during that time, Vivian, Eileen and Deke have almost convinced themselves and each other that there is no reasoning with you."

Gene tried to reply but his answer was muffled. Zara looked down at the boy and suddenly stopped. The only thing she could see of Gene that wasn't covered in snow was his mouth, nose and eyes but his nose and mouth were covered by her hand, so it was just his eyes . . . Clear turquoise blue. Staring at her, Zara could see her reflection in his water-like eyes.

There was nothing in those eyes that confirmed any of Zara's doubts. There was only worry, pain . . . concern . . . innocence reflecting from those eyes. Zara remembered the first time she had met Gene. He had tried to save her from Vicky, Barret and Walt's tormenting but had failed miserably. All the same she had felt grateful for his standing up for her even though he had been barely six at the time. She had marveled at the blueness of his eyes and how pink his face had gotten when she had thanked him. It was those same eyes looking at her now . . . nothing had changed . . . nothing had altered those eyes.

Zara snapped out of her thoughts and removed her hand from Gene's mouth. "What did you say?"

"I have to go," Gene whispered, sitting up and glancing around cautiously. "I can't stay here."

"You've got that right," Zara whispered. "We've got to take you to Neil! He's worried sick about you."

Gene shook his head strongly. "I'm sorry Zara but I can't. I have somewhere I need to be . . . I can't let anyone know I've been here."

Zara paused. There was an urgency in the boy's voice and for a moment she was about to suspect him of being guilty . . . but then again, there had been no attacks whilst he had been missing . . . so what had he been doing? He was looking at her now . . . his blond hair covered in snow, his young face giving her a pleading, earnest look.

"I don't know . . ." Zara started.

Gene reached over and grasped Zara by the shoulders. "Zara . . . please do this for me. I know I do not deserve any belief from anyone . . . not even trust but I need you to trust me this single time . . . then you can spend your trust on someone else who deserves it more."

Those words cut deep. If Zara ever wanted to repay Gene for everything he did for her . . . this would be the chance. But those last words he had said hurt; he didn't think he was worthy of her trust.

Shaking her head, she released his sleeve which she had been gripping for the past five minutes. "No . . . I trust you. You had better go before the others see you."

Gene nodded and removing his jacket, he tied it about his waist. Zara considered that the attire he was wearing was suitable for winter weather and he wasn't wearing a cap . . . this was normal.

Reaching into his pocket, Gene pulled out a small piece of paper and held it out to the girl. "Don't open this . . . not yet. Wait until all this is figured out and sorted out. It has all the answers . . . Mrs. Schneider and Finn Wagner gave it to me."

Zara nodded slowly as she took the paper and slipped it into her jean pocket.

"Please don't tell anyone . . . especially Neil," Gene whispered as he pulled his wings out of his jacket.

Zara nodded, and Gene allowed himself to give her a grateful smile. Then with a single strong stroke, the boy took off and disappeared over the tops of the trees.

* * * * *

Neil shook his head. "Doesn't help any that Jerry couldn't tell if Gene's eyes were blue or not. I almost wish that he had knocked off the hat, so he could get a better look."

The boy looked up from where he was chewing a pencil on the library couch. He saw the twins sitting on another couch, Roy clamping a hat onto Reed's head.

"Nope," Roy remarked, taking the hat off his brother. "The hat shield's his eyes and makes his eyes look black."

"Reed's eyes are already black Roy," Whip pointed out. "We're talking about Gene . . . but it definitely makes sense especially if it wasn't bright out, then it would be hard to tell the color."

Zara nodded. "There was no other information he could give me . . . except that Gene didn't seem to react to his name the first few times."

"Hmm," Drew remarked. "If only we could find Gene then we could ask him personally."

Zara felt her face get pink and found a good reason to hide her face behind her hair.

"What makes you think that he wouldn't deny it?" Eileen insisted. "A guilty man doesn't tell the truth."

Vivian was about to back Eileen up when Oliver spoke from behind his book. "But a changeling does."

Everyone at once looked over at the boy. They could see nothing of his face behind the book other than his pile of orange curls. The silence was broken by the rushed entrance of Bruce who at once plopped down between Neil and Seraphina, holding a glass box in his hand. In the box was the piece of cloth he had been working on. Also, in his hand was a long vial of a clear liquid.

"You'll never guess what I just found out!" he announced, his quirky face grinning broadly at everyone.

"That you're part Hintwini?" Roy suggested.

Bruce didn't seem to notice Roy's annoying joke but answered as if Roy had asked him to explain. "I found a poison on the cloth!"

"A poison?" numerous voices chorused together.

Bruce nodded. "A very peculiar one mind you. I have some of it in the vial right here."

Denise raised an eyebrow. "You happened to find enough poison on the cloth to fill that whole vial?"

Bruce shook his head. "Of course not silly! I found a small trace all over the cloth and put it in the vial. It was about a gram's worth, but I was able to multiply the amount using a special chemical."

"A chemical that multiplies things?" Whip inquired. "Why did you never mention this before?"

"It is dangerous," Bruce explained. "It is dangerous to human skin and animals and can only be used on chemicals. Anyway, I tested the poison and there are a wide range of symptoms, but I found them so peculiar that I thought you might want to know. Depending on how much you use, it can cause you to age rather rapidly over a period of time before you go back to normal. It also causes memory loss and some other symptoms that I haven't figured out yet."

Everyone froze. There was something about what Bruce just said that made everyone pause. However, the silence didn't last long when they became aware of another sound . . . the sound of rapid, heavy footfalls on the stairs in the hallway. Everyone stopped and waited as they heard the fast noises near the door and then the door flew open and Deke rushed in.

Eileen, knowing that look on Deke's face as one of horror, she rushed over to him and wrapped her arms around him tightly from behind. She knew that he had experienced numerous nightmares in the past week and he had obviously just woken up from one.

"Deke what's wrong?" everyone inquired.

Deke's wild brown hair was a mess and covered his forehead and the tops of his eyes. The color was gone from his face and he was sweating uncontrollably.

"I saw Gene . . ." he panted.

Zara felt her heart stop whilst everyone else gasped.

"Gene's back?" Roy inquired. "I thought he was missing."

Deke shook his head. "I saw him in my nightmare . . . he was walking out of a fire . . ."

"A fire?" everyone asked together.

"What was burning?" Neil inquired, pushing past the twins to stand in front of his brother. "Deke, did you see what was burning?"

Slowly the boy nodded but his face went a shade paler. "Bargeman village . . . It was in flames! We have to get to Aston Ridge!"

Chapter 49

If any one of the gang members had ever experienced a day that they wish they could wipe from the face of the earth, it would have been the day when they saw the bargeman village in flames.

As the gang approached, full speed behind their skates, they were shocked to discover that the bridges and barges sitting on the bank of the river had burnt down so much that the water about fifty feet ahead of them was melting. Tearing their skates off mercilessly, the kids followed the smell and sight of smoke and the sounds of troubled screams.

The bargeman village was situated next to Aston Ridge, the ridge that separated Break Neck creek and the river from Hichester and its many rolling hills. The thatched houses were built right on the bank of the river, nearest to the soft sand. The kids had always marveled at how mysterious yet welcoming the village had always seemed. Now, it was no longer either but a burning inferno.

Twenty-five houses were up in flames and another ten were on their way there as well. The bargemen and their families were pouring out of their houses like water. The children were crying and the women screaming while the men tried desperately to throw snow and water onto the fire with no avail.

"Roy, Reed, Emma, and Seraphina, you help the women get the children to the sleighs and bobsleds. The rest of us will help deal with the fire," Neil instructed, the paleness on his face reflecting the flickering redness of the fire. "Oh, and Seraphina . . ."

Right then, both Sara and Seraphina turned to look at him and Neil face palmed himself. "The one who isn't my sister!"

Sara grinned and stepped back while Neil turned to Seraphina. "Keep them as far from the fire as possible. It might offset their water prosthetics and it could be fatal."

The women and children had cleared the inferno village so at least the twins and the two girls were nowhere near the flames as they hurried the women and children to the sleighs and bobsleds that were lining the opposite side of the river. Thank goodness those hadn't caught on fire like the barges.

Meanwhile, the others followed Neil as he hurried toward the fire. Grabbing the nearest object that could carry water, they all dipped them into the thawed river and charged toward the flames. Eileen and Deke tore off their heavy winter coats and leapt into the water. The only part of the icy river that was thawed was a large chunk about thirty meters away from the fire where the barges had caught flame. In that case, the two got to work breaking the ice from the hole all the way down the bank up to right where the fire was so that the people on shore didn't have to travel so far for water.

Neil began to hurry to the river for his eighth bucketful when he spied Whip. Hurrying over, Neil pulled the boy out of the way just when a lick of fire leapt in Whip's direction.

"It's too wild Neil," Whip cried over the roaring fire. "We'll never finish it. We'll have to let it burn itself out."

"Or risk catching the forest on fire," Neil yelled back. "How did this even start in the first place?"

"Neil! Whip!" a voice hollered from nearby.

The two boys spun around to see Lyle rushing toward them. He looked terrible. His clothes were smeared with ashes and his hair was a mess. His face was blackened from ashes and smeared with sweat.

"What are you two doing here?" he hollered. "You cannot be here!"

"We've come to help!" Whip yelled back.

Lyle shook his head hard, blue hair bouncing about as he did so. "You're in danger if you're here!"

"Why?" Neil called back, not sure how they could be in more danger than the bargemen and their families.

"Because of them!" Lyle yelled back, pointing.

The two boys turned and felt their hearts leap into their throats. On the flat snowy plain about forty feet from the village was a line of black figures striding meaningfully toward the village . . . Birds of Prey!

"Oh, come on!" Whip cried. "Will it ever be good news?"

Before Neil could reply, he heard a hard thud behind him and swinging around, he saw that five-winged underbeasts had just landed behind him, blocking his exit. With the now thawed river to his right and the burning village to his left along with a cliff, the two were stuck . . . Definitely stuck.

Neil was praying beyond hope that the others wouldn't see and try to help, endangering themselves. Naturally, it was a day where nothing wanted to go the good way. Letting out a screeching yell, Deke leapt from the river and struck one of the underbeasts in the side with his shoulder, knocking both him and the creature to the ground.

Seeing his brother down and threatened by the other four underbeasts, Neil was about to intervene, but Whip had seen the whole thing happening before it happened. Pushing Neil to the side, out of reach of the underbeasts, Whip released his wings.

Neil lost grip on the slippery, melting snow and fell onto his side. He lifted his head in time to see Whip spin on his heel and strike one of the underbeasts in the face. This was great . . . except Whip hadn't anticipated that all four underbeasts would come at him at the same time. Whilst he dealt with the first one, the other three circled around and surrounded him.

Deke was rolling on the ground with the underbeast and couldn't seem to get a grip, though he managed to keep the creature's weapon as far from his body as possible. All this was being watched by Neil who suddenly felt the blood boil in his veins and this time, he didn't let his puzzlement get in the way.

Whip felt his arms pinned behind him by one of the underbeasts and saw that another was coming at him from the side while the fourth was heading to help the first one with Deke. Wiggling frantically, Whip soon discovered that his wings were pinned and in no way a help at present. He was considering stomping on the creature's foot, but he was suspended in the air.

Both boys were feeling that they had made a terrible error and they were soon going to discover what it felt like to be wounded when the most peculiar thing occurred. First, Deke and Whip both heard a muffled yelp and thud from nearby and the fourth underbeasts disappeared from sight.

Directly afterwards, Whip felt his arms released all of a sudden, but this happened so fast that he didn't have time to look about for the creature. About a millisecond after this, the creature atop of Deke was knocked off of him by what appeared to be a foot. Lifting himself to a sitting position, Deke saw that someone had grabbed the underbeast who had been holding Whip and had clobbered the first underbeast with the creature. Still not releasing the underbeast, the dark figure before them swung the creature around and tossed him straight at the second underbeast who had been approaching Whip.

Whip and Deke were now free with a dark figure standing before them. The figure was tall and rather strongly built. His hands were clenched in fists and he was breathing steadily as if he hadn't just tossed a 150-pound creature about. The first thing that Deke realized was that the figure wore no jacket but only a white linen shirt and didn't seem to notice the cold, but the strangest thing was . . . there was a long strip of hair down the back of the person's back and the hair was standing up in fury.

Deke opened his mouth to inquire who the person was when a lick of fire lit up the ground near him and illuminated the person's face. Sun tanned with firm eyebrows and his jet-black hair standing on end . . . was none other than Neil!

But this wasn't the Neil who had been lying in the snow a second ago. He seemed taller . . . bigger . . . and his erect hair . . . the mohawk down his back . . . the almost tense look of his body . . .

However, before Deke could comment on this opening, it all stopped. Neil's body relaxed, and he didn't seem so tall and big anymore. His hair relaxed on his scalp and the hair on his back relaxed as well . . . Now he was back to the normal Neil . . . but there was still the hair on his back and that look in his eyes.

Neil strode over and pulled Whip and Deke to their feet easily as if they weighed nothing. That was when they heard it . . . a faint scream. Spinning on their heels, the three boys realized that the fifth underbeast had disappeared from their sight and was heading toward the unarmed, defenseless bargemen women and children!

Deke feared that someone would do something foolish, but this thought was blown from his mind by a shrill whistle that broke the silence. All three boys jumped to realize that Seraphina had placed herself between the underbeast and the bargemen families. She had lifted two of her fingers to her mouth and whistled, long and sharp.

Whip lifted his hands to his ears, prepared for his sister to whistle again but she didn't . . . instead her whistle was answered by one that didn't sound so near and had a distinctively different sound . . . not as shrill . . . but urgent like a jet plane screeching to a stop.

Just as that noise broke the deathly silence of the cracking fire, louder sounds struck and the underbeast was knocked out of sight. Neil, Deke and Whip blinked as numerous bodies appeared out of nowhere and slammed into the approaching underbeasts.

It wasn't until the silence had been drowned out by grunting, growling and a great deal of yelling before the three boys realized that backup had arrived. A winged figure left the sky and landed in front of the boys: Vivian. A grin was on her face and her hair was windblown.

"Rodge told us that you would need help," the girl remarked.

Chapter 50

"Where is Rodge?" Whip inquired, suddenly concerned about his brother.

A voice caused the three to jump and look up to see a tall figure standing behind them. "Talking about me? I had some business to attend to little brother."

"Well I'm glad you're here now," Deke remarked.

The boy turned to inquire of his elder brother if he agreed but Neil was nowhere to be found. Turning a full ninety degrees, he finally located his brother helping two werebeast kids wrestle an underbeast vulture.

Neil was no longer his usual self. Tense, twice as large and tall as usual with the muscles in his body taut and sweat pouring down his neck, Neil was in the zone. Deke looked to Whip, Vivian, and Rodge just to see if he was the only one who found this surprising. While the three watched Neil in amazement, it was obvious that they weren't as shocked as he was.

"Am I the only one who finds Neil's new behavior unnerving?" Deke inquired in a loud voice.

His loud voice caught the attention of a nearby underbeast who almost immediately charged toward the small group. However, Vivian skillfully leapt at him and knocked him off his feet.

"Yes Deke," she remarked as she pinned the creature down. "You're the only one who finds it unnerving."

Deke lowered his eyebrows and Rodge saw that he was puzzled. "Didn't you notice Neil's recent strange behavior? His uncanny strength and energy? The number of doorknobs he's been breaking? I also noticed that when he was angry, his hair would stand up and he would make this funny guttural growl."

"But I thought Neil was an aerobeast . . . he had wings, didn't he?" Deke inquired, fully confused.

Whip nodded. "But I guess he also had a tint of Werebeast in him too. I don't know anything about Neil's dad but if he was a changeling and your mom was a changeling, it was possible that Neil inherited something from both of them. Besides that, changelings are unpredictable, and each is different."

Deke was about to nod when he became aware of a strange thing. Whilst Neil had been fighting the underbeast, his hair had been relaxed . . . not standing up. However, as Deke looked back at his brother . . . the hair was now standing erect and the sweat began to pour even more vigorously down his back.

Deke didn't know much about Neil's new discovery of being a werebeast, but he did know from what he had heard from Oliver and Denise was that the senses of a werebeast are twice as fast as hearing or sight of any creature.

All at once, it came to him and Deke felt his heart stop. "Neil look out!"

The boy was too far away to do anything in terms of help, but Seraphina was. As soon as she heard Deke's cry, she instinctively rushed at Neil and pulled him out of the way just as a volley of arrows was about to crash into him.

Everyone looked to the sky to see where the arrows had come from. That was when they saw a troop of vulture underbeast archers on the top of the ridge. The creatures drew back their hands and reloaded their crossbows again.

"We have to get the bargemen and their families out of here!" Denise cried.

Before the words were barely out of her mouth, the sound of water splashing sounded behind them. Turning, the gang saw that the twenty-four bargemen were striding up the bank toward them. Each one was armed with his bargeman rod and their head and neck wraps had been discarded.

Just as the group of men reached the top of the bank, another volley of arrows let loose and came hurling in their direction. Almost as if to the rhythm of music, the bargemen spun on their heels and did something with their hands. To the gang members and all the society changelings, it looked like they just spun their rods around their wrists, deflecting each and every arrow. When they stopped, there were a good dozen arrows stuck in their rods.

As soon as the gang got a good look at the arrows, Rodge's large hands gripped Neil and Deke's shoulders. "Whatever you do . . . stay away from the arrows!"

"Duh," Denise remarked sarcastically. "It would kill us."

Rodge shook his head. "Those arrows are partially blunted. It wouldn't do more than snag you, but the tips are poisoned."

Bruce and Clint's eyes widened at this. "That is a perfectly logical reason to stay clear . . ."

The two never finished their observation for at that moment, Vivian, Eileen and Seraphina each grabbed someone and pulled them out of the way. The only ones they didn't get out of the way in time were Rodge, Oliver and Neil.

Naturally, Oliver had seen the girls' reaction and impulsively placed himself in front of Neil. The volley of arrows hadn't been directed at them but at the bargemen again but two of the arrows went astray . . . and one came directly at Neil.

Neil had fallen into the snow when Oliver planted himself in front of him. Now all he could see was the glare of the fire, snow beneath him and a strangled cry from the boy standing over him. All at once, he feared the worst. Forcing himself to his feet, he grabbed Oliver by the shoulder, but the boy wouldn't turn around and let Neil see the damage. However, Neil knew it was bad for the boy kept a hand on his forehead and even though Oliver was keeping himself firmly in front of Neil, the boy could see that there was a small trickle of blood dripping onto Oliver's jacket.

"Olly, you're bleeding!" Neil cried.

Oliver shook his head. "Just a graze."

Soon the whole gang was crowded around Oliver, trying to look at the wound but Oliver tried to push him off.

"Don't worry," a voice remarked from behind them. "He'll be fine once he's dead."

The blood began to boil in everyone's veins while their hands, backs and hearts felt cold with fear. Everyone remained still, crouching around Rodge . . . everyone that is except Neil.

While everyone slowly looked over their shoulders at the speaker, Neil rose to his feet and turned fully around to face the last person he wanted to face at the moment . . . Gene.

The boy was drenched from head to toe from the slushy water he had been obviously trampling through. He wore no hat but there was something about him that made Neil's hair stand up.

"Gene . . ." the boy started, his voice cracking. "You don't have to do this . . ."

The boy raised an eyebrow but then lowered them. "Oh believe me kid . . . I have to."

At hearing Gene's words and getting a good look at him, Zara slowly rose to her feet. Why would Gene call Neil "kid" when it just so happened that Neil was four years older? Also, the dark brown pants and brown shirt he wore was not what she had seen him in earlier that morning.

"Gene," the girl remarked, startling everyone at her firm voice. "Whatever it is you're going through . . . we'll help you . . . just please don't do this."

"I don't think you quite know what I'm going to do," Gene mused with a smug expression. "I guess you think I'm going to fall down in worship of you. Sorry, but that's not the case."

One thing that Zara never forgot was the day Gene taught her how to deal with bullies. The first thing he taught her was that most of the time, the bully or enemy would begin talking and possibly try to confuse you with words before attacking you midsentence. Now, that knowledge was vital here because that's exactly what happened.

The boy leapt across the snow, headed straight for Neil. Of course, the older brother tensed but was prepared to try another pleading entreaty. Neither entreaty nor attack occurred because everyone, but the bargemen were knocked from their feet. The force that had struck them was not that of an object . . . but of a heated energy like a gust of hot wind.

While everyone laid on their sides or their backs, they lifted their heads to see where the gust had come from. What their eyes fell on was nowhere near what they had been prepared for.

Standing firmly on four sturdy legs was the largest creature they had ever seen. Reaching thirty feet in length from nose to tail, about forty feet wingspan with a reddish color to his skin, the creature had a slender noble head resting atop a decently long neck. His tail was about ten of his thirty-foot length and had spikes running down the back.

The next nearest thing that everyone realized was that Deke was standing beside the creature, facing the scene as was the creature. It was as if the boy didn't realize or didn't even care that he looked like a midget beside the huge dragon for that was what the creature was . . . A dragon.

After taking this all in, Gene leapt to his feet again, but the dragon stretched out his neck full length, opened his huge mouth to reveal a mouthful of razor-sharp teeth and let loose a huge cry. The growl sounded like a mixture of a mad walrus, the screech of an owl and the howl of a wolf all combined, added with the strength of a hot wind.

"What in the world?" Whip cried, his jaw dropping at the scene before him.

The boy didn't even take his eyes off Deke and the dragon as he reached down to help Zara to her feet. However, Zara didn't seem to notice Whip's presence either for her surprise was one of realization.

"In the journal," she muttered to herself. "Deke and Eileen's visits to Aston Ridge . . . were to visit the dragon . . . the egg that Eileen's father gave her was the egg of the last remaining dragon!"

* * * * *

Deke had tried to keep a steady serious look on his face, but he couldn't help a smile. It was quite amusing seeing everyone's reactions to the appearance of the dragon. Of course, the bargemen and Eileen weren't surprised but rather relieved at the sight for Gene and Zara's suspicions had been true.

When Eileen's egg had hatched two years earlier, the two had realized that the dragon could either pose a problem or the inhabitants of Hichester and the society might dislike the presence of a dragon. In that case the two had smuggled the creature out of Hichester to the bargeman village. There, the bargemen had agreed to keep the small dragon with them.

Of course, once the creature reached his first year and was too large to fit in any house, the two kids had to move him to the cave beneath Aston Ridge. Luckily for them, the dragon didn't breathe fire so there was no worry about that issue.

Deke was brought from his thoughts by the returning sound of scuffles. The underbeasts and Gene had recovered and were charging for the nearest changeling. Deke saw right away that Gene was going for Neil. Luckily, Gene was not armed with a weapon, so it was merely a fight of fists and tactics . . . but even with Neil's now discovered beast-like strength, Gene was posing a great issue for Neil. Every time that Gene's hand or foot struck Neil, the boy cringed even if it wasn't just a bump. Deke knew from experience that someone bumping you just slightly didn't hurt at all . . . but to Neil . . . it was worse than that.

Deke hurried toward the dragon and scurried onto his back, grasping one of the spikes on the dragon's neck. "Come on Scout . . . we need to help Neil."

The dragon let out a pleased and agreeable growl, but Deke suddenly pulled on the spike, holding Scout back from advancing. Something had caught his eye all of a sudden but now he wasn't sure if he had seen it or had imagined it. Pulling his goggles onto his eyes, he glared through them, trying to focus. There was something that Gene did that really caught Deke off guard. Naturally everything that Gene had been doing for the past ten minutes was out of the ordinary . . . but there was really something strange.

Then he saw it . . . that movement with his foot and left hand. When Neil stepped forward to lay a blow, Gene stepped back with his left foot . . . then when Gene went to return the blow, he stepped forward with his left foot and struck with his left. That was peculiar because Gene was dominant right handed and rarely used his left for fighting . . . in fact, he never used his left hand for making blows and he always moved his right foot before his left.

Deke, so content on watching the peculiarity of Gene, didn't realize that Neil was struggling. The boy had lost his steady footing ever since Gene had pushed him toward a patch of slush that just refused to let him get a grip. Neil concentrated more on keeping his balance then he did about watching out for Gene. This was a mistake but by no means his fault. In a flash, Gene saw Neil's broken concentration and leapt at him. Neil tried to react but slipped, falling to his knees. Gene continued his approach and swinging his left foot around, he prepared to strike Neil hard in the head.

Just when Deke's heart stopped . . . just as Gene's foot was a millimeter from Neil's unprotected head . . . something happened. Maybe Gene lost his footing on the unstable, slippery ground. Perhaps he overestimated his balance and the weight on his one leg was too much for him . . . all the same, his right leg seemed to crumble below him, and he fell to the ground, narrowing missing Neil's skull.

Neil had seen the blow coming and had reached up with one hand to try and block it, closing his eyes as if trying to hold out the fear. Deke and Bruce had both opened their mouths to speak but the words they had been about to say only ended up being squeaks of puzzlement, shock and sudden horror.

When the blow never came, Neil opened his eyes to see Gene lying on his stomach in the snow. He was pushing himself back up, but he couldn't . . . he was pinned, and Neil saw why. Two large metal balls were lying in the snow on either side of Gene with a rope tying them together. The crudely made weapon had knocked Gene down when all his body weight was on one leg and was now holding him down on the ground. Neil didn't even have to touch the iron balls to know that they were at least fifty pounds each or more.

Gene reached back with one hand and grabbing the rope, prepared to cut it. Just when his knife was cutting through the thick rope, another two balls tied together with a rope appeared out of nowhere and pinned him back down, this time pinning his arms down as well.

Everyone had heard Gene's strangled cry of shock when he had first gone down, and everyone had turned to look at the scene. Now, all their eyes lifted to where the roped balls had appeared from. The burning huts had slightly died down, avoiding the forest but they were still burning decently. The weapon that had pinned Gene had appeared from between two of the houses that were still burning uncontrollably.

The fire smothering the two buildings was all that everyone saw . . . Until a dark shape began to appear from the fire like a puff of jet-black smoke, slowly beginning to take on the shape of a human. As the shape continued to draw near, gradually building shape, the size began to grow from tiny to human size . . . even slightly larger . . . at least in width.

Suddenly, the shape stepped from behind the wall of fire and stood there, untouched . . . unsinged by the flames with a pair of wings spreading from his back and a perfect scowl on his face.

Everyone's jaws dropped. It was that kind of moment when you had been doing a math problem, only to realize that you were doing the math problem from the wrong lesson. This was almost exactly the same but much more shocking because this wasn't math and books... but humans and realization.

All eyes looked from the person to Gene lying in the snow, then back again. The only person who wasn't looking back and forth in stunned confusion was Gene. His eyebrows were down, his face twisted into an ugly scowl and his teeth clenched together. For the person who had just emerged from the fire was not your ordinary changeling... it was Gene.

Chapter 51

If there had been no fire, no underbeasts still about, all of the gang members would have spoken their puzzlement openly in words. Now, all they could do was stare with their jaws dangling from their faces and think over and over in their minds that what they were seeing was just a hallucination.

The first person who recovered from his shock was Neil. He had always suspected that it hadn't been Gene who had been attacking residence of Hichester, but rather a phony. Now, seeing two Genes before him confirmed his suspicion. It was also no doubt that the Gene lying before him was not the real Gene but the phony.

This observation never passed to anyone else present at that moment for both Gene and the phony leapt at each other from a standstill. While Gene leapt into the air slightly, the phony leapt to meet him, and they collided head long in the air. The two went spinning out of control, tangled with each other, trying to lay blows whilst avoiding each other until they landed hard in the snow.

Deke was about to tell Scout to assist Gene, but he also realized that more underbeasts were appearing out of nowhere. Tapping the dragon on the side of his neck, Deke pointed to a herd of underbeasts that were approaching the society members.

Neil caught a fleeting glimpse of the huge dragon rushing on light feet to meet the army of underbeasts. However, he was more concerned about Gene and the phony. The two were equally matched by the other and both were taking some serious blows from each other.

The boy was racing to aide Gene when his path was blocked by a massive underbeast hyena. Feeling his hair stand up on end, Neil braced himself for an attack. However, instead of attacking him head on like the underbeasts usually do, the creature began to circle Neil, twirling the dark blade in his hand as if taunting Neil.

Neil was tense. This behavior was out of character for an underbeast and he was on the alert. However, there was something about this hyena underbeast that seemed slightly off from the rest of the underbeasts. Something about his size . . . how he carried himself and the constant eye contact that he gave Neil.

"So," the beast remarked, his voice neither human nor beast but smack dab between the two. "You're the boy I've heard so much about."

The hair on the back of Neil's neck began to stand up while Neil felt the sweat building up on his back and chest. He didn't feel the cold. It was as if being a cheetah werebeast made him immune to the temperatures in the air. However, inside he was burning with fear and rage.

Keep calm, Neil, the boy thought to himself. *Anger is not a sin unless you allow it to overcome your better judgement and use it in the wrong way.*

As the underbeast continued to circle Neil, the boy got a strange sense that this wasn't an ordinary beast he was dealing with. In fact, he might not even be an underbeast. The sense of power, pride and anger that the creature gave off far surpassed the usual, clueless but bloodthirsty attitude of underbeasts.

"May I be so terse as to ask how you came to know about me?" Neil inquired, never letting his guard down for a second.

The creature smirked, a peculiar thing for this underbeast's face was more like a beasts than the rest of the underbeast who only had the ears, tails, wings or fins of beasts while having faces of humans. This creature seemed more beast than human but yet this underbeast was different in every respect.

"Dorsa was kind enough to mention you before Nohte assigned me to this task," the creature remarked. "I guess she deemed it best to inform her comrade-in-arms of the possible second greatest worry."

So that's it, Neil thought. *This underbeast must be Nohte's second hand man just like Dorsa. Great! Yet another bad guy to deal with!*

Neil nodded, but continued to keep his eyes locked on the creature. "Tell me. Why is it that you choose to carry on a conversation in the heat of a battle instead of dealing with me and getting it over with. As I have noticed, you're the first underbeast who has even spoken two words of sense together."

This infuriated the creature and Neil could tell. The air of pride and self-assurance that the creature had been giving off now reverted to anger and disgust. "I am not your everyday underbeast."

Neil almost wanted to roll his eyes. Naturally it was obvious that this creature wasn't your usual underbeast. But he still hadn't answered Neil's first question. However, before Neil could point that out, the creature did just that.

"I am not worried about dealing with you because I know that sooner or later, someone else will deal with you in a more suitable form for garbage," the underbeast sneered. "Besides that, I want to see what you know about your situation. I am always intrigued to see how Nohte's plans end up."

"I happen to be standing on the bank of a river . . . about ten feet from a burning village . . . my comrades are fighting around me, and I have an underbeast walking in circles around me as if he doesn't understand the concept of direction," Neil remarked, hoping that if he got the creature infuriated, he might find the answers he was looking for.

The underbeast pushed that sarcastic remark off with a grunt. "I am talking about your brother's betrayal."

That is a little too far, mister, Neil thought. "You mean my brother's innocence. I know my brother well enough to know that he was nowhere to blame for anything that happened here in the past few days. You planted a phony in our midst in the hope that we would turn on Gene and you could deal with him personally without anyone really caring."

The underbeast raised one eyebrow in amusement. "Impressive. No one believed that you would figure out that part of the plan on your own. Pray continue."

Neil got the feeling that the underbeast was stalling . . . but for what? Besides, maybe Neil could find out the real core of the whole thing by answering the underbeast's questions.

"You made sure that the phony didn't reveal his eye color to anyone so that we wouldn't know that he wasn't Gene. You also sent a bomber to try and kill Gene and Zara or at least harm them, then you purposely caused Zara to lose the flashlight so that we knew that the bomber escaped alive and then the bomber attacked the neighborhood and left behind a remnant of clothing so that we could track him to Falfi and know that the material of the flashlight was the same and possibly make us believe that Gene gave Deke the remaining material to cover himself up."

The last observation he stated about Gene giving the material to Deke wasn't at all what Neil believed. In fact, it didn't make sense, but he wanted to see what the underbeast would say to it.

The creature's eyebrows had begun to go down from the very start of Neil's announcement and by the end, he looked completely lost as if he had been trying to reach the sea and found the desert.

"Flashlight? Remnant of clothing? What are you talking about? Gus was supposed to not leave any trace behind . . . and what flashlight are you talking about?" the creature inquired.

This reply wasn't what Neil was prepared for. First off, who was Gus and for another thing, if he hadn't been supposed to leave any trace, how could he have missed noticing that he had left behind a large piece of cloth from his clothes? And if Nohte or his minions didn't send Deke the material for the flashlight . . . then who did?

The underbeast began to pace, not around Neil but back and forth in front of him. Neil was considering taking the creature by surprise and pouncing, but he was just as curious to figure out the end of this as the creature was.

"That blasted robot," the creature muttered angrily. "I should have named him Fool rather than Gus. How could he have been so dimwitted as to leave a remnant of material behind? And what flashlight are you talking about?"

Neil didn't answer the creature's question for he was thinking of his own. Obviously, Gus was a robot . . . that answered the question as to how he avoided death in the explosions especially if he was made of the same material as the flashlight.

The boy was about to ask another question of the creature when he realized that Gene was still fighting with the phony. It seemed that Gene couldn't get a good leg up on the boy who was his exact height and build. It was as if the phony was powered with super-strength. Neil knew that Gene was stronger than most boys, sometimes even stronger than Neil and he couldn't see why Gene was having trouble.

Turning to the creature, Neil lowered his eyebrows. "Who is Gus?"

The creature had been pacing and concentrating on his own question so when Neil asked, he answered without hesitation. "He's the one you're runt of a brother is fighting."

Neil spun on his heel and looked at the creature who was going head to head with Gene. There had been a time when Gus might have tried to conceal his back but now, he didn't have the time what with Gene coming at him from all sides. Now, Neil had a perfect view of Gus's back.

Protruding from Gus's shirt were two stubs . . . the stubs of wings but they weren't red or bleeding but looked like solid metal.

The suicidal bomber, Neil thought. *He must have escaped the bomb but his wings were destroyed so whenever someone saw him, he had to conceal the fact that he had only the stubs of broken metal wings rather than real ones.*

Chapter 52

Neil felt his heart stop at this revelation. No wonder he couldn't defeat Gus . . . he was a robot! The boy spun around, disregarding the fact that the underbeast was still within ten feet of him.

"Gene! Watch out!" the boy screamed.

Right away, Neil wanted to smack himself for being so foolish. Naturally Gene would look his direction at the sound of his voice, thus lowering his guard and opening up an opportunity for Gus to strike him. This was exactly what happened, and Gus lifted his metallic arm to hit Gene across the head.

Neil dearly wished he had obtained some of those balls and ropes from Gene since there was no way he could cover forty feet in a matter of seconds. Neil knew that Deke and Scout were a good hundred meters away, aiding the gang and the rest of the changelings and there was no one to help Gene within fifty feet. There was only one thing that could save Gene now and that was a miracle.

Forgetting the slush beneath his feet and the underbeast approaching him from behind, Neil fell to his knees and clasped his hands together. The watery snow soaked through his pants but the pain that shot through his legs was never felt for the cold hand gripping his heart was far more painful. If anything happened to Gene, Neil wouldn't be able to go on. He knew that no one would be able to go on. Just as Whip had said the day before . . . Gene was like their core, holding them together.

"Lord," Neil cried aloud. "If You ever planned to perform a miracle this day, let it be that You save Gene!"

Neil had no idea how he could have possibly cried out that prayer in the seconds that it took Gus to draw back his hand to strike Gene. Everything seemed to slow . . . all noise seemed to disappear, and Neil was frozen in a state of pure shock. He could see the metallic hand of the machine draw back and swing toward Gene's unexpecting head. One blow with that powerful arm and Gene would be dead . . . Dead!

Neil clenched his hands harder, causing his knuckles to turn white and his felt tears spring to his eyes, blurring his vision. His blurred vision of the scene before his eyes was one that never made sense to him. Through the pile of tears, all he could see was the dark silhouette of Gus and the light, winged shape of Gene and the blazing red light from the burning village . . . then another color entered the picture.

A long trail of a bluish object flew into view and struck the dark figure of Gus out of the picture. Now it was just Gene standing there and Neil reached up with one cold hand to wipe away the tears. Gene's wide blue eyes and his dropped jaw told Neil that he was just surprised as Neil had been.

Neil then remembered the underbeast behind him and spinning on his frozen knees, the boy was just in time to see some sort of force strike the creature clear off his feet and slam him into a nearby tree, stunning him. Neil looked toward the river where the force had come from and the questions building up in his mind were answered . . . Three tall figures were striding up the bank. Their faces were darkened by the low amount of light but as they crested the bank, the light of the fire lit up their faces and Neil's eyes grew wide.

Before him stood three people whom Neil never thought he would see outside of society: Elys Schneider, Timber Nielson and Rana Keith! For a moment, Neil wanted to rub his eyes to make sure he wasn't seeing things, but he knew he wasn't. The three adults no longer looked like they were in their sixties . . . rather, they looked young again . . . as if they had just reentered their youth!

Rana Keith's dark black eyes alighted on Neil for a split second and she smiled. Then, turning to her comrades, she spoke in a rushed, urgent but uncommonly calm voice. "Timber, deal with the fire, I'll take care of the intruders. Oh, and Elys . . . we need some light down here."

Hearing her first orders, Timber had saluted mockingly with a grin. Elys meanwhile nodded and considered the sky for a moment before hurrying off into the darkness to some destination that Neil did not know of.

When Gene had first see a blast of blueness knock Gus to the ground, he had thought he had just entered death's door. However, he now stood gaping at the tall figure of Timber Nielson who stood on the bank of the river.

Everyone from the gang members to the youngest bargeman had stopped and were staring at the three newcomers. Naturally, everyone's eyes were locked on Mr. Nielson, mostly because they were curious as to how he would deal with the roaring fire.

The man closed his ocean blue eyes and let out a deep breath. He slowly lifted his sturdily built pale hands until they were level with his hips.

Then, he began to bring them forward . . . and that was when it happened.

Eileen had been in the water, still trying to deal with the fire. When Timber Nielson had lifted his hands, she thought she felt the river suddenly start to rush upstream rather than downstream as it is supposed to. She had felt the water with her hand and realized that the water was now moving at top speed now . . . And she felt her heart skip a beat as the water left the river and climbed up the bank toward Timber Nielson!

There were several gasps, a few hoarse screams and plenty of dropped jaws as the river emptied itself to follow Timber's hands. As he continued to lift his hands and bring them forward, the water rose into the air as if it had life and form until about eighty gallons of water was suspended in the air.

There was a pause, everyone held their breath and then Timber spun on his heel, pivoting all the way around. The water followed suit, making a huge suspended ring around the man until no one could see Timber within the column of water. Then it exploded with great force and the water disappeared . . . But only for a second before everyone heard the faint trickle and paddling sound of falling rain.

All hands reached to cover their heads for no one wanted to be soaked in below freezing weather. However, the water didn't land on the changelings, underbeasts nor the bargemen. Instead, the falling rain sound was followed by a definite sizzling, hissing sound and all eyes turned to the burning houses . . . That were no longer burning but just smoking. Timber had doused the fire.

The fire had been the only source of light on the Ridge and now everyone was swallowed in darkness. Only the nocturnal underbeasts and changelings could see even faintly. But the darkness only lasted for a split second for a pale blue light split the darkness like a ray from a flashlight.

All eyes turned heaven words to realize that the line of archers on the top of the ridge were gone and now only one figure stood there, and that figure had her hand outstretched over the side of the cliff . . . Elys. She was holding her hand out, making an "O" shape with her fingers and blue moonlight was streaming from her fingers.

Eyes traveled farther up to see that the dark cloud that had been shadowing the moon was slowly, ever so slowly parting to admit a ray of blue light that traveled straight to Elys's hand, then down to the darkened village below.

There was no darkness now for the blue light from the moon was twice as strong as the fire light had been. Now it almost seemed like broad daylight on the slushy bank.

The light had barely taken over the darkness when Rana Keith strode up the bank right up to the underbeast who was leaning against the tree. Considering the stunned, motionless creature, the woman smiled faintly.

"It's been a long time Grimoth . . . a very long time."

The underbeast tried so dearly to move but he was motionless and probably would be for another twenty minutes. "It won't be a very long time before I finish this Rana."

The woman smiled a forced smile. "You said that last time and I'm still here. Your threats only go so far."

Neil had been watching this exchange, as was everyone else, even the underbeasts (Which was strange because they never stopped long during fights). Though, there was something about Grimoth's calm pleasure on his face that made Neil's skin crawl. The hair on his back stood up and it tingled his skin.

"It's not me you should be worried about this time Keith . . ." Grimoth growled. "But another."

That was the last thing Neil heard the creature say for an ear-piercing sound rang in his ears. It wasn't a sound he was hearing, but his mind practically exploding with the sudden realization.

His head snapped around and landed on the dark figure of the machine, Gus who had been knocked to the snow by Timber's arrival. Now he saw the machine lift one metallic arm and toss something. Whatever he threw was terribly off aim for it landed between two of the bargeman houses, about eighty feet from everyone else.

Neil only heard the beeping noise for a moment before everything became a blur. He felt Timber's ice-cold hands grab him by the shoulders and pull him to the ground. He caught a glimpse of Rana throwing her arms into the air, causing a huge force to knock all the other changelings to the ground . . . and then that rumbling . . . Vibrating sound overtook everything . . . and then darkness.

Chapter 53

There was complete darkness and Neil was sure that his eyes were open. Blinking several times, thinking that something was covering his eyes, Neil began to focus again. There was snow in his eyes, and he wiped it away, clearing his sight. There was that pale reddish light again coming from the small licks of flame that was scattered all over the snowy plain.

The first thing the boy did was look around for the underbeasts and the changelings. He saw several bodies rising and was relieved when he saw that they were changelings . . . but there was not an underbeast in sight . . . not on the ground, nor anywhere. There were a few dead underbeasts littering the slushy snow but only about ten . . . and Grimoth was nowhere to be seen.

Neil saw a huge shape appear and breathed relief when he realized that it was Scout, with Deke astride him safe and sound. The next thought that passed his mind was Gene and he looked around for the boy. Before he had time to even look, he heard a rustling beside him and turned to see that Gene was lying beside him, pushing himself out of the snow.

Gene's face almost immediately went as pale as the snow beneath him and his eyes widened with fright. "No!"

Neil didn't know what had startled Gene and didn't have time to ask for the boy leapt from the snow and slipping and sliding on the slush, charged toward a body that lay in the snow about twenty feet away.

Neil pushed himself to his knees just as he saw the tall figure of Timber rush forward in the same direction that Gene had rushed. Neil stood up, trying to see what they had spotted and then he knew. He felt coldness clutch his face . . . his whole body and that heat rising in his chest.

By the time he and the rest of the changelings and bargemen reached the scene, Timber had drawn Rana Keith's limp head into his lap and had clutched her to his chest. Slowly the man rocked back and forth, crying bitter tears.

"Is she sleeping?" a young bargeman child whispered.

Neil and all the gang members bit their lips hard to fight back the tears. They knew she wasn't, even though the peaceful look on her face tried to suggest it. Her dark, deep black eyes were closed . . . ash and dirt smeared her face and her black hair was drenched in sweat. There was a trickle of blood running from a cut on her forehead and black crusted blood and ash darkened her mouth and nose.

"Oh Rana," Timber whimpered, rocking his comrade back and forth. "Why? Why did you have to face Grimoth?"

Neil heard a faint gasp beside him and knew it had come from Drew and Eileen. He also saw Seraphina clap a hand over her mouth and tears sprang into her brown eyes.

Then, everyone heard that sound . . . that sound that causes your heart to stop beating . . . That sound that wipes away all your hopes . . . the strangled, agonized cry of distress from a young boy.

Everyone looked around to see where it had come from but there was such a large crowd of people, that no one could see over the heads of the person beside them. The only person who knew where that cry came from was Timber. The man leapt from the ground with as much spring to his step as a young deer. He charged through the crowd and flew over to where Gene had been crouching on the ground.

Neil heard another scream and this time he knew that it had come from Whip and Seraphina. The two of them sprinted after Timber and fell to the slush in one motion. They both grasped the ice-cold hands of Elys while Gene held her weak head in his lap.

Her eyes were barely open and kept fluttering shut. She looked virtually worse than Rana even though she was still breathing. She couldn't move her back for during the explosion, she had been tossed from the top of the Ridge and had landed on her back. Her legs were twisted in painful directions and her hands flat on the ground.

"Elys . . . come on stay with us please?" Timber whimpered, the tears running down his face as fast as water runs down a waterfall. "We can't lose both you and Rana."

A faint smile crossed the woman's face and she gently gripped Whip and Seraphina's shaking hands. "Come on Timber . . . that's not the positive person I know you to be. Everyone has a reason for going . . . and I believe I have mine. I served my purpose as I am more certain that Rana served hers. You have to let me go."

The man shook his head, tossing graying red hair all over his face. "Elys please . . . you can't . . ."

Smiling faintly at her life-long comrade, Elys turned her eyes to Seraphina, Whip and Gene.

As her voice seemed to fade and get weaker, everyone felt tears well up in their eyes. The woman looked up at Gene and reaching up with one hand, she touched his cheek with the tips of her fingers.

"So much like Gianna . . ."

If she had ever planned on saying anything else, she was cut off by the deep sigh that left her body . . . then nothing.

Seraphina clapped a hand over her mouth, closing her eyes to the sight. Whip could only bow his head as his shoulders began to shake rapidly. Timber merely stared at the limp body of his friend as Gene clutched her head in his lap and bit his lip, forcing the tears to not burst from his eyes.

Gene slowly rose from his kneeling position and hurriedly wiped the tears from his face.

Deke lifted his own head to realize that a strange light had suddenly flickered in his brother's eyes. In a single moment he saw Gene push out of the crowd and scan the area swiftly but surely. Finally, his eyes fell on something as did Deke's: Grimoth.

The creature was standing just on the other side of a burning area on the grass with a smug look on his face. With a single bound, Gene took a stride in pursuit of the creature, but Deke felt himself call out to Gene.

"Gene no! He's not worth it!"

Gene stopped and turned to look at his brother. Deke felt his body stop moving and his heart seemed to give way. The scene before him was one he had seen before. The blood-stained snow . . . the visible clay ground beneath the slushy puddles . . . the flames licking about the dead grass. Gene's face was streaked with blood and his straight blond hair was crusted with dried blood and dirt.

Deke could barely bring air back into his body when he heard Gene's answer to his protest:

"You would do the same for those you love," he said in a voice that was foreign to Deke . . . a voice that was cracking with pain and sorrow . . . and voice that Deke had never heard out of Gene.

The boy turned on his heel and continued to sprint toward Grimoth. The creature quickly got down on all fours and began to run off into the darkness . . . but he left something behind. Deke felt someone brush past him, only to realize that Neil was charging after Gene. The younger brother continued in pursuit of Grimoth toward the darkened hills, but Neil paused to look at what Grimoth had dropped.

A decent sized piece of metal lay on the ground. It was shaped like a cross but on each tip was a small little light that was slowly blinking red . . . then it slowly began to turn to orange . . . then yellow . . . then green . . .

"Neil get back!" a voice yelled. "It's a timed detonator!"

Now Neil was no fool, but that announcement didn't register with him as soon as it should. He was preoccupied noticing that the yellow lights on the object were now slowly turning a pale green . . . then a brighter green . . . Then it stopped changing color . . .

Whilst this was all happening, Deke had been registering what he had just seen. It was the exact same vision he had witnessed nearly three years prier when he had been in Break Neck for the first time!

Then a memory crossed his mind. In the vision, he had stepped forward, just missing an arrow meant for him and instead the arrow had struck Neil. Deke looked at his older brother who was standing about eighty feet to Deke's left . . . his black hair plastered to his head by sweat and blood. Deke knew that if he stepped forward, somehow an arrow would strike his brother instead of him.

Then the words of Mrs. Schneider entered his mind: *Those things you saw were possibilities of the future, though there is a way to alter them for the better.*

So that's it, Deke thought. *If I move, the dream's perspective will come true and Neil will be killed in my stead.*

Even before Deke could think of whether or not to move or look for the archer, he heard the twang . . . then a whistle of an arrow. He allowed his feet to sink deep into the mucky snow and he closed his eyes . . . waiting for the pain . . . but it never came.

Instead, a body crashed against him and the two fell into the snow.

Almost at the same time, Neil had been trying to figure out who had warned him when Gene crashed into him, sending the boy spinning and sliding down the bank. Neil struck the water, but the coldness didn't bother him as he struggled for the surface. Almost a half second after he lifted his head from the water, he saw everyone running as far from the river as they could while Gene threw himself onto the ground, right over the object and curled up . . . and closed his eyes . . . Then blackness.

"Deke! Deke wake up!" a voice called from far off.

The boy slowly tossed his head, trying to throw off sleep. He felt unusually cold in his back and the tip of his nose and his hands felt numb.

He felt a warm hand shaking his shoulder roughly and he swatted at the hand.

"Stop shaking me," he groaned.

Deke allowed his eyes to crack open to see that Bruce was kneeling next to him, shaking him. Even when Deke swatted him, Bruce didn't stop shaking him till Deke opened his eyes fully and sat up.

Deke slowly looked about and felt the blood leave his face. Lying next to him was a body . . . a tall, strongly built body with dark brown almost black hair . . . and a long wound running down his left arm . . . Rodge!

"No!" Deke cried, scurrying over to the boy and feeling his face.

It was lifeless . . . cold . . . with no feeling. Deke saw the long arrow that lay in the snow next to Rodge . . . the boy had taken the arrow for Deke!

How traitorous the future is, Deke screamed in his mind. *It's one or the other . . . there is no way to avoid a death!*

Bruce was beside the boy in an instant and shook his shoulder. "There is nothing we could have done Deke, he jumped in the way of the arrow before we even knew what was happening . . . but we need to hurry!" the boy cried in an urgent voice. "It's Gene."

Then everything came back to Deke . . . seeing Gene fly down the bank toward the detonator . . . remembered a sort of rumbling bang go off behind him and something hard strike the back of his neck and everything go black.

A detonator . . . the boy thought. *But Gene was trying to smother it . . . Gene!*

Then it came to him. Flying to his feet, Deke didn't even look to see where Bruce was pointing but dragged the boy after him as he charged toward the small crowd. Everyone was kneeling down or those who weren't kneeling were looking over the kneelers.

Deke squeezed through, leaving Bruce to squeeze through on his own. When he came tumbling into the center, he found Whip, Eileen, Seraphina and Neil kneeling on either side of Gene. The boy was flat on his back, his eyes staring heavenwards as if he didn't know of anyone else's existence. His arms were flat beside him, his legs twisted underneath him in such a painful way that Deke couldn't look at them. His clothes were blackened from ash and soot and soaked to the bone. His hands were thin as if he hadn't eaten in months and all the color was gone from his face and his lips . . . He wasn't even breathing.

Deke fell to his knees beside Gene, not bothering to thank Whip as the boy moved over for him. Deke placed his hand on Gene's head and slipped his fingers into Gene's soft blond hair . . . He couldn't even see the blue in Gene's eyes anymore . . . they were glassed over as if they weren't eyes anymore. The color was disappearing from his eyes as if they were paling.

"Gene . . . Please don't do this," Neil was saying through racking sobs.

Deke grabbed Gene's thin hand and gripped it tight. It felt so bony . . . lifeless. "Gene, I'm so sorry . . . so sorry for thinking that you were responsible for all of this . . . I shouldn't have abandoned you like that. Please don't leave us mate . . . we need you . . . I need you to live . . ."

Gene didn't move, but Deke was sure that he felt the boy slowly grip his hand back . . . but ever so faintly that he wasn't sure that it really happened. Then . . . his eyelids slowly closed . . . concealing those turquoise eyes forever.

Seraphina at once pushed her brother to the side and placed her fingers on the side of the boy's neck. She bent over his head to listen for breathing . . . Nothing. Neil and Deke had been waiting with bated breath to hear her result but when she flopped down in agony on the boy's chest, burying her eyes in his shirt, they knew the answer: Gene wasn't coming back . . . not this time.

Chapter 54

Bruce knew that there was distress . . . more of it than distress. It was more like misery that was lingering in the air. The sun was shining brilliantly on the thawing field. There was barely any snow left . . . just patches here and there and the green grass was screaming to come out. A gentle breeze was blowing but none of this was noticed by anyone present.

The boy slowly blinked back the tears in his eyes to look over at where the rest of the gang were standing. Sara and Clint were standing with Styl. Styl had awoken three days ago, fully recovered and having no recollection of her encounter with Emma or with Whip, Drew and Gene. Everyone had agreed that it was best to not bring it up since the girl seemed to have completely forgotten her grudge against Emma.

Bruce had to wipe his glasses for they were fogging up again. Pushing them off his eyes and onto the side of his head, he looked over at the others. Oliver was the tallest kid in the gang, standing in the center, one arm around Emma's shoulders and the other around Silver who was sniffling and crying silently. Destiny was standing slightly behind Emma, burying her eyes in her sister's shoulder.

Seraphina and Whip were standing together. Seraphina had her arms firmly wrapped around her brother from behind, as if trying to hold Whip back. Whip definitely looked like he wanted to run off in sorrow for his face was red and scrunched as his eyes poured out their misery. Seraphina really impressed Bruce for even though tears were gently falling down her face, she was standing firm and brave with a faint sad smile on her face.

Bruce looked back at the gang to see Vivian and Zara. Zara was kneeling in front of Vivian whilst her sister gripped her shoulder gently and bit back tears of her own. Zara's face was snow white and though she was constantly wiping her face dry with her sleeve, her face was pink and her eyes puffy from three days of crying.

Beside the two of them stood Denise who was weeping as well. Denise kept reaching over and gripping Roy and Reed by the shoulder to offer comfort. The two were allowing their tears to flow but weren't sobbing violently like Whip. They were both shaking, and their bottom lips were trembling.

Bruce forced himself to look to the left to where Ivan and Jerry were trying to comfort

Eileen. The girl was sobbing violently into Ivan's coat. Bruce finally looked at Neil and Deke. Deke looked like he was ready to faint, deathly pale with huge bags under his eyes and surrounded by red from constant crying. Neil's face was drenched in tears, but he was standing firm, gripping his brother's shoulders as moral support.

The group was standing on the edge of the river in the same place where Seraphina and Whip's older sister had been buried. Now there were four freshly carved crosses driven into the ground that was still loose from having been dug up then patted down hard.

Bruce slowly passed by the crosses, glancing at the new ones that lined the river:

Elys Emilia Agnes Schneider
Beloved daughter, wife and mother
652-723

Rana Zelasiz Martin Keith
Beloved wife and mother
652-723

Rodge   Edward   Steven
Schneider
Beloved Son and brother
703 – 723

Seraphina and Whip waited until their parents were done before they approached their brother's grave. That was when Neil realized that there was one other grave cross about five feet away. Etched plainly into the wooden cross were these words:

Emilia   Alanna   Catherine Schneider

Beloved daughter and sister

702-720

Neil felt tears spring to his eyes again. Their sister who had been born between Seraphina and Rodge had died the year that Neil, Deke and Gene moved to Hichester! Suddenly realizing that his grief of losing Gene wasn't the only one, he stepped forward and knelt beside Seraphina. Gently, he wrapped an arm around her shoulder.

"It's a comforting thought to know that Rodge and Gene will have each other up there in heaven. I am more than sure that they'll go straight there . . . after all they died defending those they loved and what they believed in."

Seraphina slowly nodded. "At least we knew that Gene was innocent before he left . . . that was a comfort as well."

Neil didn't reply right away and every one of the gang members knew what he was thinking. Oliver was the one who stepped forward and knelt beside Neil. He was still healing from his graze and his head was bandaged up, but he was able to get around. "Now Neil, I know what you're going to say but it's not true. Gene's death was in no way your fault."

"Then why do I feel like it is? I wasn't able to prove his innocence until twenty minutes before his death. If I had worked harder or had been here sooner, I might have been able to prove it sooner and maybe he wouldn't have died," Neil shot back.

"Neil," Zara said, kneeling down beside him, fighting back the tears that were soaking her shirt. "We all feel the same but that's not so. Gene didn't die because we didn't know if he was innocent or not. He died because he chose to put his life on the line to save us. Even if we hadn't doubted him for a second . . . even if there hadn't been that belief that he was responsible for the attacks, he would have done exactly what he did and that was to save you and protect the rest of us by trying to destroy the detonator. Naturally, not everything works the way we want it, but it worked the way Gene wanted it . . . he wanted to save you and he did. That's what Gene lived for . . . to save people. He found it easier than saving himself."

Neil shook his head and bent over, allowing the sobs to overcome him. Seraphina wrapped her arm around his shaking shoulders and pressed her cheek into his hair. Neil allowed her to hug him to her as he let out all the pain . . . all of it.

After allowing the boy to weep bitterly for about five minutes, Seraphina pulled him to his feet and nodding to Oliver, she gently led the boy over to the fourth cross. Oliver grasped Deke around the shoulders gently and pulled the sobbing boy along after Seraphina. When Neil and Deke realized what the two were doing, they tried to fight them, but their misery made them bodily weak at that moment.

Oliver and Seraphina pulled the two in front of the last cross and knelt down respectfully and lovingly near the loose dirt.

Gene Michael Mecarnin
Beloved brother and friend

714-723

"Gene was a special child," Seraphina whispered. "He loved people more than he loved himself. He lived his life striving to make people happy and to make them experience the goodness that he never lived to witness. He was a leader as well as a follower. He led those who needed a leader and he followed those who had superiority over him. He saved us from our pains . . . from ourselves. If he hadn't lived Neil . . . none of us would be standing here today with our dignity intact. He . . . he came to save us from a debt . . . even though he didn't owe the debt . . . because he knew that we owed a debt that we could never pay back: the debt of goodness."

Seraphina heard a whimper and knew that it had come from Deke. She reached over and gripped his shoulder. "Gene wouldn't want you to live in misery like this."

Deke slowly nodded and sniffled loudly. "Gene . . . I don't know if you can hear me but . . . I'm sorry . . . for not being there for you when I should have. You . . . you were always so passive about everything . . . and you took death readily . . . something I could never do. I just want to say that I'm going to miss you little man and . . . I love you!"

Everyone slowly nodded their heads in agreement, whispering their own farewell and fond words to Gene. Whilst they did this, Deke buried his face in Oliver's chest and allowed the boy to grip him tightly.

"Well . . . at least we know that the war machine is gone," Whip remarked tearfully.

"What war machine?" the twins asked in unison.

Whip looked at the two in shock. "Didn't you know? Gus, the robot, was the war machine that Nohte was trying to make three years ago. He must have found a way to power it without human energy since we stole his last 'battery' so to speak."

Deke's brown eyebrows went down, and he scrunched his nose in thought. "Wait . . . if Emma was the last battery, what if he just kidnapped another kid and used him or her?"

"But he had to use changelings," Bruce pointed out. "Because they have a little more 'hardiness' than humans in a way. Where could he have gotten another changeling?"

Zara slowly released Deke's hand which she had been gripping and reached into her pocket. She drew out the small snippet of paper that Gene had given her. She unfolded it and waved it in front of her comrades, revealing that it was an address.

"I think I know where."

* * * * *

"Maybe you should knock again," Roy suggested.

"Be quiet," Reed hissed at his brother. "It ith a delicate buthineth."

Zara swallowed and shifted her weight from one foot to the other before knocking on the door again. She glanced down at the snippet to make sure that they had the right house. After concluding that they did, she lifted her hand again to knock but before she did, the door opened.

A tall, delicate woman stood at the door and smiled at the children. She looked round with child but looked surprisingly relaxed. "Hello, what can I do for you?"

"Um . . ." Zara started, feeling her mind go blank. "My friend gave me your address . . . and told me to visit you."

The woman smiled, noting the nervousness in the children's faces. "What is your friend's name?"

"Gene Mecarnin," Whip answered when Zara didn't.

The woman's facial expression at once changed and her eyes grew wide. "Oh . . . come in then. You must be the children he had told me about. He said you would be dropping by someday soon."

Seraphina, Whip, Zara and the twins were the first to enter the cozily situated little living room. Neil, Deke, Clint, Denise and Eileen followed slowly. Sara had stayed behind with Bruce since the boy wanted to continue on his experiment with the poison and everyone had agreed he needed someone to keep an eye on him. Emma had remained at home because Oliver was still recovering and couldn't go anywhere far for a few days. Vivian had stayed behind because she hadn't finished her essay for the presentation that evening and was neck high in homework.

The woman led the children into the room and called into an adjoining room. "Francis . . . there are some children to see you from Gene."

Almost immediately a tall man entered the room. He was young, just like the woman and seemed rather confident and kind but there was a look of urgency in his face as he caught sight of the children.

"Please sit down," the man said, waving toward the chairs.

The kids sat down, as did the man and his wife. There was a long silence and Seraphina was about to break it when Francis spoke.

"I suppose you have come to see the child . . ."

All the kids raised their eyebrows in confusion and surprise. Naturally the twins and Whip were about to make some sort of sarcastic remark, but Deke interrupted them in the nick of time. "Sir . . . we honestly don't know why we're here. My brother told us to come here . . . so we thought we might come and find out why."

A faint smile appeared on the man's face. "Well in that case . . . you had better follow me."

The children at once rose and followed Francis into the adjoining room. The room was darkened due to the fact that the shades were down over the windows and barely any lights were on. Frances slipped over to a lamp in the corner and switched on a light.

This allowed the kids a better view of the room they were in. It was a small sitting room but in the center was table and stretched out on the table was a body. Having known what they had gone through the past few days, the kids instinctively approached the table slowly. However, once they got a good look at the person's face, they raced forward.

"Vicky!" everyone gasped together.

For it was Vicky. There was no life in her . . . not a single hint of color in her face. The pasty look on her face almost made her unrecognizable but they had recognized her all the same. From the look of it, she had been dead for several days.

"A stranger appeared out of nowhere three days ago," Francis explained. "Just left the child in my path so I brought her back here. No one knows she's here except myself, my wife, your friend and Elys. I've known Elys for several years and knew that she had encountered peculiar happenings like this, so I called her, and she identified the girl. Then she sent Gene to come by as well."

Deke slowly shook his head. "She must have been caught when she stayed behind three years ago to hold off Dorsa . . . Then they used her to fuel Gus."

Seraphina ran her hands over the girl's cheek and hands. "The poor child . . . there is no way we could revive her even if we had found her three days ago."

As she continued to stroke the girl's arm, she suddenly realized that there was a rip in the girl's sleeve. Glancing down, Seraphina felt the color drain from her face as she realized that the rip was a decent size and looked like someone had purposely ripped it. She only glanced up once and that told everyone to look.

"That is the exact same color and shape as the cloth that Bruce found," Zara mused aloud. "I wonder how it could have gotten in the ruins of that neighborhood."

"I think I know," Neil whispered hoarsely. "I think maybe Nohte didn't use her to power Gus right away but decided to use her as bait or for information. I'm guessing that she might have escaped and taken refuge in that neighborhood. Nohte found her and had one of his guys blow up the place to prevent anyone from helping her and she left behind a fragment of her sleeve so that we would track its origin to Falfi . . . then Nohte drained her and left her in Francis's hands in the hopes of frightening us but he didn't know about the fragment."

"But why would she want us to know the origin of the fragment?" Clint inquired. "What is so special about Kesroc Falfi?"

"It must be where she was kept prisoner," Whip remarked. "Probably to warn us . . . and also so that we would know that Nohte might have used *yuthinis* to build Gus which would answer our questions as to how he survived the explosions."

Roy shook his head. "I am full lost. How in the world did Vicky know that Deke had *yuthinis?*"

All eyes swiveled over to Deke who was standing between Neil and Seraphina. Slowly lowering his eyes, the boy fingered the edge of the table. "I received a package of the stuff . . . About five months ago from an unknown sender. The writing was really wobbly, and it explained how to work with the stuff . . . I guess my curiosity got the better of me."

"That explains it," Seraphina breathed. "Vicky must have obtained some of the material and sent it to Deke.

Neil reached over and placed his hand on Vicky's forehead.

"She did her part . . . she knew she would never escape Nohte, but she did her part in giving us the vital clues. I think in the short time that she had around Gene . . . some of Gene's goodness rubbed off on her."

Seraphina wrapped her arm around the boy's shoulders. "There have been too many deaths Neil . . . but I will say this: if Vicky and Gene hadn't done what they did, there would have been more deaths than we could fathom. We have that to thank them for."

What none of the kids knew was that a pair of amber eyes was watching them through a nearby window, a smug grin on the creature's face.

"101 Firebomb, come in," Someone hissed over his radio.

The creature didn't take his eyes off the window but answered the radio. "Yeah I'm here

513

Boss. Everything's in place. They're all in the house. I think there are only one or two of them missing."

"Did you hack into the weather forecasting system?" the voice glitched back.

"I did. They're going to be expecting some rather cloudy weather with no showers. It's all set. Proceed to Hichester."

Chapter 55

There was a round of applause as Zara stepped back into the crowd to stand between Deke and Vivian. She had just finished reading her thesis on the different ways of concealment.

"Good one sis," Vivian whispered, smiling fondly.

Zara smiled back but only half her heart was behind it. The whole time she was reading it, she knew that Deke would step up after her to read Gene's thesis which he had finished Christmas Eve.

"Deke Rasmussen," Mr. Walker called. "The thesis?"

Deke slowly stepped out of the safety of the crowd and stood before the staring crowd. Putting his hand into his pocket, he drew out a folded piece of paper. It was a single piece, wrinkled and crumpled but fondly folded by a sorrowful boy who had tried his hardest to not harm his brother's work.

Unfolding it, Deke glanced once at the title and swallowed. He had promised himself that he wouldn't read any of Gene's thesis until the presentation. Now he wasn't sure if he would be able to read it without choking on tears.

Slowly, biting back tears, Deke read Gene's thesis with his voice breaking as he reached the end:

SAVER
A thesis by Gene Mecarnin

Every day we hear people talking about developments, better ways to do things . . . easier ways to do things. Each and every day we begin to wonder about the different ways we can make our own developments whether they are in our lives or in what we do as a career or a hobby.

The development that I wish to suggest is one that would be beneficial for the society, Hichester itself and even the world beyond our borders. It is a vital rule in the code of SOHE where no one by any means within the Society of Hichester Enterprise should use his or her changeling traits to attack or brutally harm anyone or anything.

There is a significant difference between fighting someone and defending yourself. In fighting someone you are sure to endanger yourself or the person you are fighting, also possibly harming your dignity, purity and love for life. Naturally this is greatly understood. However, the art of self-defense in no way harms yourself or the other person but merely immobilizes the adversary in such a way that would give one time to escape a dangerous encounter with either bodily harm or possible death.

The Society of Anti-Violence Enterprise Renewed better known as SAVER would be such a development on the firm grounds of SOHE where members of the society could train in the arts of self-defense alongside their other activities and classes. SAVER would offer beneficial exercise as well as understanding the art of defending one's self and others from possible danger.

The rules that would be surrounding this branch of SOHE would be simple but strict:

1) Never using one's understanding of self-defense to inflict harm on oneself or any other person unless you or someone else would die or be shamed otherwise.

2) The art of self-defense will be used only for defense but never for attack and wounding someone. The greatest harm you could inflict on someone is unconsciousness.

3) Never forget, that if you are afraid, it means that you are one step closer to bravery.

That last part of the thesis forced everyone to put a hand to their mouths to cover the small gasps of sobs that escaped them. This was lucky because it caused them to not notice the blood drain from Deke's face when he realized that there was a small sticky note taped on the lower corner of the thesis.

Pulling the sticky note off, Deke realized that it was written directed at him:

Dear Deke, I know you will disagree with this thesis and I am counting on it. Though, I will say this big brother: You never have to be one of them because you are one of your own. Love, your little brother: Gene Mecarnin

P.S. Elys Schneider told me about the Room of Righteousness that you visited with Denise at Hanalona. I wish that I could have a chance to see it but... with all due respect, I know that my limited time will not allow it. Farwell, *Prince Deke of Gerhenia!*

At those words, a sudden memory crashed back to Deke: *The wind was silent, the fire blazed firm but the three knew that the other was worthy and stuck through the night to battle the dark who invaded their home and their life.*

The words on the plaque! The fight at Aston Ridge . . . it was all connected! The plaques were prophesies and whenever the prophesies came true, the scrolls told of it. The chamber of Hope was the prophesies of the three of them: Neil, Deke . . . Gene.

A tinge of pain ran through Deke's heart, realizing that Gene would never be there to help them complete the rest of the prophesies . . . he hadn't even had a chance to see the room!

Deke cleared his throat loudly, causing everyone to look back at him. "I know . . ." he started slowly. "That it is rare for someone to comment on your thesis . . . but I would like to make a comment about my brother's thesis. Knowing Gene . . . he probably wrote this knowing that there would be objections . . . especially from me. I wish to make a petition to the headmaster and headmistress of the society: Gene's thesis is in no way an objection to the rules of the society. If anyone followed the rules faithfully, it was Gene. However, his thesis suggests an edition to the society that would do exactly what he would want . . . and what Elys Schneider and Rana Keith would want: protect the innocent from danger. I beg you to consider Gene's thesis . . . and to everyone who knows Gene . . . everyone who is finding it hard to accept his death . . . if Gene was here, he would say that . . . *You never have to be one of them because you are one of your own.*"

There was a soft murmur before the room erupted in loud clapping. Deke knew that most of it wasn't because of what he had just read . . . but also in memory of the boy who had written it.

Deke was about to step down from the podium, but a shrill voice cut his train of thought and he froze.

"No, no, no!" Iris Opal's loud voice cut in.

The tall woman strode over to the podium and practically glared down at the boy standing there. "You know the rules of the Society as well as I do and they specifically state that no form of use of one's gifts outside of the society is allowed!"

"If you had your way, we wouldn't even be able to use our gifts!" Deke snapped, something coming alive inside of him.

Everyone started in surprise. That was something they would have expected out of Gene for he was so outspoken, but Deke was never the kind to be like that . . . and here he was, battling against Iris Opal, completely disregarding the danger of being expelled.

"Watch your tongue boy," Opal snapped, lowering her black eyebrows at Deke. "You are speaking to Iris Daphnia Opal the third!"

"And Gene was one of the best members of the society that this world has ever seen," a firm voice cut in.

Deke and Iris turned to see none other than Finn Wagner standing there. He looked much different from what everyone last saw him. His hair was brushed neatly back, his face no longer puffy from crying nor lean from lack of sleep and eating. In fact, Finn Wagner looked like he had actually decided to come back to the land of the living.

"He was exceptionally brilliant and never broke the rules once," Finn remarked. "Other than the time he broke into the society with the rest of the members but only by doing that could they save an innocent child."

"That does not give him the right to assume that adding a 'defense' mechanism to the society would keep things in check!" Opal snapped.

At that, a loud voice cut in, making Deke shiver for he knew that voice anywhere.

"He never said such a thing!"

Neil strode up to the podium with his eyebrows down in fury. "Gene never mentioned SAVER 'keeping things in check.' He knew that there was no way to stop evil from coming back . . . but by doing what Gene suggested will lower the chances of us dying!"

"The rules of the Society are absolute!" Iris objected. "Breaking of the rules is punishable by . . ."

"Breaking of the rules has never been punishable," Finn pointed out. "I am one of the few people alive who was present when SOHE was first made . . . and there was nothing anywhere concerning punishment."

Iris Opal's eyebrows went down in annoyance. She opened her mouth to say something else, but Neil's voice cut in once more . . . calmer this time but with dominance.

"Actually . . . Gene was the one who wrote that . . . so if he broke the rules . . . it wouldn't really count . . . cause he's . . ."

The boy felt all the fire that had been building up inside of him, deplete instantly like a balloon. He felt a gentle hand on his shoulder and turned to see Eileen standing there with Vivian close behind her. Neil felt a warm hand slip into his and he spun around to come face to face with Seraphina who was looking at him with an encouraging smile.

"He's right you know," Seraphina remarked, turning to look at Opal. "Gene did all of that on his own . . . none of us had anything to do with it. And you cannot punish someone for something as ingenious as this when they're . . . dead."

Iris Opal looked from person to person and saw that she had no one on her side. She let out a deep huff of annoyance. "Fine! But you two boys won't be here for long. Mr. Rasmussen will be leaving for Gerhenia in a week and Mr. Catalani in a few days. If there is no one running this new development, it will have to be closed."

Neil and Deke's spirits dropped to the pit of their stomachs. They hadn't thought of that factor and now, they knew that there was nothing they could do about it. That is, until a soft voice spoke up from behind them.

"I'll do it," Eileen said. "I'll be SAVER's benefactor."

Neil's eyebrows shot up in surprise. Eileen was the last person he expected to stand up for Gene's idea. After how Eileen and Vivian practically denounced Gene just because of the rumors that never turned out to be true.

A swirl of gray hair caught everyone's attention as Vivian stepped up and planted herself firmly beside Eileen. "I will too . . . we owe it to him."

Chapter 56

A pair of knuckles rapped loudly on the door again. Sighing, Neil called an admittance and the door flew open. Bruce fairly flew across the room to only race around the bed so that he was facing Neil and flop a notebook down on the covers.

"Neil you'll never believe what I . . . what are you doing?"

The boy considered the piles of clothes . . . school books and other personal possessions laying in neat piles on the bed surrounding the empty suitcase. One by one Neil was grasping the piles and laying them carefully in the suitcase.

"Where do you think you're going?" the boy demanded.

"Scardihn Caan," Neil replied without looking up from his work.

Bruce rolled his eyes and sat down on the bed. "No seriously Neil, where are you going?"

Neil stopped his packing and looked over at the boy. "I told you: Scardihn Caan. Charles got word from a friend about an amazing school that Clint has been wanting to attend. We all talked about it last night and it's agreed that Sara and Clint are going to attend the school. Deke is leaving in a few weeks to go live with his dad in Gerh so there's no need for me to be here. Mr. Wetherby agreed that it would be good for me to attend the school as well."

"But what about being a werebeast?" Bruce insisted. "Neil, you just discovered that you are a cheetah werebeast . . . how could you leave Hichester District to go to a school where your identity would have to be concealed?"

Neil placed his toothbrush and paste in the case. "Bruce little man . . . I'm doing this because I have spent thirteen years of my life not knowing my family. I've lost Gene . . . and I know I'll never be able to get over it, but I am going to try and spend as much time with my family as possible from now on. For six years I neglected Gene and now I've lost him. I'm not going to make that mistake with Clint and Sara, nor Deke. Deke has promised to visit us often and there'll be visits back here but I've decided to leave at least for a while."

Bruce pulled himself further onto the bed and peered at Neil. "What about Gene? You're leaving him behind here . . . You cannot leave because you miss him Neil! You won't find him in Scardihn Caan!"

Neil slammed a handful of books into the suitcase roughly and met Bruce's eyes. "That's exactly why I have to leave Bruce! I cannot even bear to walk within a half mile of Gene's grave! When Mr. Walker pinned Gene's thesis on the billboard at the very center, I couldn't go back into the hall again. Everywhere are reminders of Gene . . . Everywhere . . . he has touched everyone and everything with his goodness and now it is haunting me. I have to leave before it drags me to grief."

Bruce sighed and nodded. "I guess that is a reasonable answer. But I've got to tell you something before you go."

"What then?" Neil inquired, not stopping to look at the boy.

"I have done some more work on the *yuthinis* that Vicky sent Deke. I was able to narrow down the location to about fifty miles," Bruce explained.

"Really?" Neil inquired, not in the least interested.

Bruce could tell that Neil wasn't listening, so he decided to cut to the chase. "The material came from a place known as Torch Forest in Kesroc Falfi."

Neil had been placing a handful of socks into his suitcase when he froze. That name almost caused his head to snap back. Slowly he lifted his eyes and looked into Bruce's. "Torch Forest . . ."

Bruce nodded. "I told Sara and Crystal first and they almost flat out cried. They wouldn't tell me why but told me to ask you. Does it sound familiar?"

"Like it was part of my name," Neil replied, looking down at the case with sudden sorrow. "That was where I fell . . . and broke my wing."

Bruce's eyes behind his glasses widened so much that Neil thought they would pop out of his head. However, the boy composed himself and picked up his notepad. "One other thing. I've worked more on that poison that I drew from the piece of Vicky's sleeve and have discovered something rather surprising."

Neil had all his attention wrapped on Bruce's every word now, so the boy didn't stop long for a reaction.

"The poison causes serious infection if injected into a wound and the infection grows slowly overtime but cannot be killed. However, if someone takes in the poison whilst eating or drinking something at the same time, the poison passes through the body rapidly and only has slight symptoms of aggressiveness, red marks and fury and is completely harmless," Bruce replied.

"For some reason, Deke found that part intriguing."

Neil nodded. "That sounds exactly like what happened to Reed, Styl and . . . Me . . . is there a way to test a person to see if they have the poison?"

Bruce shrugged. "If you still had the poison in you, I would say possibly but if you were injected with the poison and if Reed and Styl were too, it would be too late by now."

"How come?"

"Because you and Styl acted aggressively when someone threatened to remove your wing and Styl's fin. It was like you were overly, aggressively protective of your infected limb until after the removal and then neither of you showed any signs of anger even at the mention of wing or fin. In Reed's case, if he took in the poison when he was eating that apple, the apple would have caused him to pass the poison harmlessly since it wasn't injected into a wound."

"But how do we know that the poison was in the apple and not injected into Reed?" Neil insisted, testing to see how learned Bruce was in the situation.

Bruce grinned brightly. "I thought you might ask that, so I went to the Wagner Store and asked where the apples had been imported from.

Hummer Nielson told me that they always get eight bushels of apples once every two months from Kesroc Falfi."

That was all Neil needed to hear before the blood drained from his face. "You don't mean to tell me that . . . That Vicky knew that we would send eight bushels of apples and poisoned one of the apples? Why would she do such a thing?"

"Oh, that's an easy question," Bruce replied. "She wanted to open our eyes to the truth about you and Styl's aggressive traits and the unusually dangerous infections that you both suffered from. She probably found out about the existence of the poison when she was a prisoner and decided to tip the scale."

"Stop speaking in riddles," Neil groaned. "What do you mean by tipping the scale?"

Bruce tossed his notebook over his shoulder. "Two similar situations is suspicious enough, but your symptoms were identical. Vicky poisoned the apples because she knew someone in Hichester would eat it, have the symptoms for a harmless poisoning and that would confirm our suspicion of you and Styl's poisoning. Two is suspicious but three is unanimous. At least she didn't inject it into a wound!"

"A wound . . ." Neil breathed. "Styl received the poison through her wound in her fin when she was a child . . . and I received it when I . . . fell . . ."

Bruce didn't speak. He knew that the truth had dawned on Neil and he felt himself cringing inside and out. He would never feel the horror that Neil was experiencing at that moment, but he knew it would have been painful if he had.

"My infection wasn't an accident . . . an underbeast found me in the ravine and poisoned me . . ."

Bruce slowly nodded and reached out with one hand. "Hey Neil, I know this is hard for you to grasp but I have something else to say. For the longest time, Gene always felt guilty about your fall . . . as if he could have changed the outcome. You know Gene, he always blamed himself for things that happened to other people even if he had nothing to do with it. At least now, he will rest in peace knowing that he wasn't to blame for your wing damage. Besides, you have discovered your new genetics. At least you found out before you leave Hichester."

"Yeah," Neil remarked, his voice fading away to almost nothing. ". . . when I leave Hichester . . ."

* * * * *

531

It was a lovely breezy morning when everyone piled into the sleigh and listened to the jingle of bells as Lyle drove them to Break Neck. Sara had pleaded with everyone to not come and see them off at Break Neck but rather bid farewell on the riverbank. She said she couldn't bear long farewells and preferred making them quick and painless. However, the whole gang absolutely refused and piled into the sleigh.

Oliver had been deprived of a seat since the two benches were already taken and overflowing. He was sitting crunched up between the legs of Whip and Clint who were having their lungs emptied by the twins who were sitting atop them.

Oliver had a good view of Deke and Neil which was one thing he was hoping for. Deke hadn't said a word about Neil's choice to leave with his siblings and Neil hadn't objected about Deke's decision to return to his father in another few days and try to fix things.

Honestly, the boy felt that it would do both of them good and he was sure they thought the same. Deke was content with the knowledge that Gerh wasn't far from Hichester, so he could visit the rest of the gang often. Both Neil and Deke had resigned from present participation in SOHE but promised to write the society and its members often.

Deke was making no eye contact with Neil but the look on his face told them that he wasn't upset, at least with Neil for there was a contented, almost excited look on his face and in his eyes. Neil was calm as usual but there of course was a tint of pain in his eyes, either from grief or pain on leaving Hichester.

When the sleigh pulled up on the riverbank of Break Neck creek, everyone was about to move but Crystal spoke up:

"Maybe it will be best if you all just drop us off here. We don't want to hold you and we're just going to catch a cab . . . like Sara said, we don't want to make it a long and painful farewell," the woman remarked, smiling at the kids. "It's not really goodbye anyway, just a 'see you later' sort of farewell."

The twins and Whip wanted to object but Eileen cut in, seeing that Neil, Sara and Clint were all pleading for them to not draw out the farewell.

"That's a good idea. We do have to prepare for school and society assignments tomorrow," she mused aloud, pushing the twins back into their seats. "We also promised Mr. Walker that we would shovel the slush off the platforms today."

Without waiting for an objection or acceptance, the three kids leapt out of the sleigh with Charles and Crystal following close behind. However, they couldn't stop everyone from piling out to give final hugs and handshakes.

Slowly, Neil went down the line of friends, starting with Lyle. Then there was Vivian, Zara, Emma, Denise, Jerry, Whip, the twins, Destiny and Silver. Neil then turned to Seraphina and Eileen and didn't know whether to give them a hug or handshake. Before he could ask, Eileen rushed forward and squeezed all the air out of him with a swift hug.

Seraphina was a little more elusive and gave him a gentle smile before stepping back, averting her eyes from his. Neil saw the girl step over to his sister and give Sara a hug.

"See you Seraphina," Sara whispered.

A mischievous smile appeared on Seraphina's face and she nodded. "You too Seraphina."

Bruce stuck out his hand to shake Neil's and when Neil took it, he felt a small piece of paper press into his palm. When he looked down, he realized that it was a copy of Gene's thesis. The boy couldn't speak but stuffed the paper into his pocket and turned to Oliver.

"See you man," Neil remarked, holding out his hand. "Come on Seraphinas!"

Seraphina and Sara grinned sheepishly at him as they finished giving each other their addresses so as to be able to write.

Oliver took it and shook it strongly. Neil didn't release his hand but reached over and clapped his friend on the back. Oliver would be hard to part with. He had become like another brother to Neil and in a way, Neil always suspected that Oliver knew more about Gene than anyone.

Then it was Deke. Neil shook his hand but then pulled his little brother into a hug when he saw a flicker of grief pass over Deke's face. Allowing Deke to press his face into his chest, Neil held him close whilst the sobs racked Deke's body. Neil always felt like he had deserted Deke and Gene when they were little, never being there to comfort them. Now, he felt that he needed to make up for it.

"We saw this day coming . . . the day when we would have to part," Neil said, holding Deke at arm's length. "At least we won't be parted fully. We'll have each other's memory to speak to and reflect on . . . especially Gene's memory."

Neil stuffed his hand into his pocket and pulling out the thesis, he placed it in Deke's hand

535

and closed the boy's fingers over it. "I couldn't bear to keep it. It's still too hard for me. Keep it . . . maybe show it to your dad . . . he'll find it amusing. Also, before you leave, make sure to visit Gene . . . and Elys, Rana, Rodge and Vicky."

Deke forced a smile and nodded. "I will."

Neil smiled and stepped back, casting a final look at his comrades and family. Then turning on his heel, he hurried after his family who were waiting on the edge of the fog wall. Just when he felt the coldness of the fog touch his face, Neil paused and looked over his shoulder.

He breathed in a final breath of the sweet-smelling air. He caught one last glance of the frozen golden river, his friends and his brother climbing into the sleigh . . . it was a friendly, welcoming sight as his friends all stopped and turned around to face him.

Deke was seated on the floor of the sleigh, looking straight at him with a contented smile on his face, his huge blue goggles resting in his brown hair. Denise was crouching behind him, giving Neil a bright grin. On either side of her stood Zara and Eileen; Eileen calm and shy with a smile on her face and Zara giving him a cheeky look.

Seraphina was perched on the side of the sleigh, her legs dangling over the side. Oliver had his chin and hands resting on Zara's head, giving

Neil the usual "professor look." Beside him was Bruce, looking at Neil through his huge green spectacles and Jerry was climbing into the sleigh, one hand on the side and a calm look on his face.

Neil could only see the tip of Whip's head as he strained to look over Bruce and Oliver's shoulders whilst the twins peered from behind Oliver and Seraphina. It was truly a wonderful sight . . . then it was gone in a swirl of mist.

Epilogue
Eight Years Later

It was one of those usually "buzzing" sort of days in the pub. Everyone was coming in after long days of work for a drink and some chatter. Everyone knew everyone in the pub, so it was like having a huge family get-together.

There was Charles the butcher, a group of his apprentices listening to him with rapt admiration for the heavy-set man. Phil the baker had all the girls' attention as well as most of the mothers. David the lawyer, the banker and the tailor were all silently watching the chatter from their usual positions near the door, smoking on their pipes.

The pubkeeper let out a howl and his serving girl came rushing over. She was a pretty girl with her jet-black hair braided in a single braid and swung over her shoulder. Her bright blue eyes danced with kindness, but she kept a wary eye around. She smoothed out her apron, smearing it with food grease.

"Take this order over to Horas," the man instructed, shoving a plate and a mug toward the girl.

The serving girl grabbed the plate and mug, wrinkling her nose when she realized that the smell coming from the mug wasn't the pleasant smell of coffee but the stench of beer. Turning on her heel, she hurried through the crowded place and placed the meal in front of the lone man in the corner table.

As she pulled out her rag and wiped off the table really quick, she caught a good look at the man. Grim, a giant of a man, he made the girl shiver. His jet-black hair was slicked over his forehead and the back of his head was bald. He had only one eyebrow for the other had been burnt off in an accident the girl had heard of.

A huge scar ran down the bridge of his nose, over the tip and across his lips to his chin. The girl had not heard about where he got that, but it really made him look twisted. The man grabbed the beer with a huge hand, the fingernails caked in dirt, red and callused. The serving girl stuffed the rag into her apron and stepped away, giving the man's set of pistols and battle axes a worried look.

The girl had barely made her way through clearing two other tables when the door of the pub flew open and everyone stopped. The figure standing in the doorway was no one they knew. In fact, almost everyone in town was in the pub that evening, and this man was not one of the few who weren't present.

Instinctively, the girl placed herself behind several people but made sure that she could see well. The man strode in and walked over to the counter. The girl knew that the top of the counter came up to her chest and she was considered to be not a bad height for a girl. However, considering this stranger, he must at least be over six foot because the top of the counter came to his waste!

She saw the man exchange some words with her employer before she saw the pubkeeper point toward the corner table that she had just served. The stranger wanted Horas. Right away the girl felt her face heat up in anger. This man was just another one of those bounty hunters! Horas was known throughout the town and neighboring towns and villages as a renowned bounty hunter leader. He had a band of men who lived to collect bounties and recruit other men to join in.

The man strode over to Horas and said something that the girl couldn't hear but considering Horas's reaction, it was probably some polite greeting for Horas snorted. He said something in reply, but the stranger didn't move, and the girl couldn't tell if he scowled or not because she couldn't see his face.

Considering the man's attire, she guessed that he came from the same stuff as Horas. He wore a pair of brown pants tucked into knee-high leather boots that were caked in mud. He wore a cream-colored shirt that was tucked into the tops of his pants. Over that he wore a brown leather vest that was tied with string down the front. Over that he wore a brown cloak with the hood up and concealing his face. The middle part of the cloak was pinned close to his back by his belt and swung over his back was a deadly looking crossbow and a large knife at his belt.

A short conversation passed between Horas and the stranger before the stranger said something that caused Horas to slam his mug down and stand up. The buzz of conversation stopped, and the girl was finally able to hear the men talking.

"You dare to call me impudent?" Horas growled, reaching one hand toward one of the pistols on his belt.

"No," the stranger replied coolly. "I said that you were *impertinent*."

The girl felt a smile appear on her face. She knew well enough that both those words meant exactly the same, but she wondered if Horas knew that. Apparently, he didn't because he didn't lose his temper.

"I don't care what that means but it sounds bad enough," the huge man growled in his deep Rechuedian accent. "If you have not come here on business, I will ask you to leave!"

"You seriously think that I walked a full five kilometers just to have a friendly conversation? I want to talk to you about that bounty you have been trying to get but have failed," the stranger remarked in a mature masculine voice.

Horas's face at once softened just slightly and he grabbed his things. "Then let's talk outside."

The two men exited the pub, both tossing a coin to the pubkeeper as they went. The conversations at once picked back up and the serving girl got back to work. She brought back an armful of dishes to her employer before wiping off her hands.

"Thanks, my dear," the man remarked glumly. "Would you be so kind and tack this on the wall with the other notices?"

The girl took the sheet of paper and began to pin it to the board. On the board were about a dozen bounty notices, notices on runaways, stowaways, favorite parts of the newspaper as well as local news. Choosing a tack, the girl pinned the paper onto the wall and stopped. She grabbed the paper she had just pinned and pulled it off the wall again, reading it in a hurry.

Let it be known that two fugitives have broken free from their prison cell. Their capturer, Nohte Respure is offering 100,000 yobs in exchange for their capture and safe return alive.

Glancing over her shoulder carefully, the girl shoved the paper into her jean pocket, tore off her apron and made a quick excuse to get some fresh air. She charged out of the pub and to the nearest phone booth. Closing the door behind her, she dialed a number as quickly as she could. Her conversation was in whispered tones, but it seemed urgent.

"Hello, I would like to speak with Lawrence Marks please . . . Brother Lawrence . . . Yes, I know it's too early but . . . But I have some news for Colonel . . . tell her to check the latest notice . . . it should be in this week's paper . . . thanks . . . bye."

The girl hung up and quickly exited the phone booth. Just as she did, she realized that there had been someone waiting outside to use it and looking up, she realized that it had been the stranger. Now up close, she realized how tall he really was. He wasn't huge and hefty like Horas but looked like he could handle himself and a lot of other people. His face was still shrouded in the cloak, but she could see a pair of eyes staring at her.

Quickly moving to the side, the girl charged back toward the pub without looking back. What she didn't see was the stranger following her and when the pub door closed behind her, a smile appeared on his face . . . but no one saw it.

It would be a long time before any of us saw each other back at that place before the fog wall. The last place where we had all been . . . together. Very few people stayed in Hichester. It came to our attention that it wasn't as protected as we thought it was. It was now, open and vulnerable. The monks and nuns in Break Neck reinserted the highly strict requirements, limiting who could enter Hichester and people who were not connected to changelings were asked to leave.

Oliver healed nicely from his head wound, but it never fully left him. He had constant migraines through his teens and would suffer some serious nose bleeds during extreme temperatures but as always, he dealt with it silently. Oliver was one of the few who remained in Hichester alongside Vivian and Eileen who were determined to bring Gene's dream of SAVER to reality.

Vivian has become the person that we all loath. She has made all our dreams come true by bringing SAVER off the pages of Gene's thesis. She operates all the ambassadors who are basically changeling spies who live in different countries for several years at a time, keeping eyes and ears open to anything out of the norm. There are fewer underbeast sightings now . . . but they are still there. People have grown cold toward changelings, mostly because they blame us for the reappearance of underbeasts. We're okay with that, just as long as people don't start siding with the underbeasts.

Eileen . . . hasn't changed. She still keeps a close eye on Oliver, all the elderly and adults of society and keeps Livonia company. For the longest time Eileen was up to her knees in the twins, until Roy moved to Hanalona to be near Deke, leaving Eileen with only Reed to worry about. The two, surprisingly, have gotten along rather well and Reed has slightly broken past his mischief making self. Of course, that didn't happen until after Eileen threatened to tie Reed to the society tower for a week. Reed didn't take this threat seriously until after he discovered the existence of buzzards, hale and lightening.

Deke . . . well he has certainly outdone himself from what we can decipher from Roy's letters. Deke rarely has the time to write, but he does all the same. For three years he was sent to Rechued with Roy to handle his father's campaigns there. When he returned, we still didn't see anything of him for his father kept him under a firm thumb with his duties as the next in line for the throne.

None of us have seen heads or tails . . . or fins of Deke nor Roy for five years straight but from what we hear

545

from Roy's constant stream of letters, not much has changed. We all knew that it would do Roy good to spend some time with Deke and it seems to have finally brought the boy out of his troublemaking self. Of course, on April first he always sends a gag or prank in the mail just for the fun of it.

Before Deke left, Bruce and Clint made it clear that Scout's life was now to be decided considering that he was Hichester's hero and savior now in almost everyone's eyes. Even before the two could suggest Deke taking him, the boy pointed out that Scout is Eileen's responsibility as much as he was when he was an egg. Of course, what Deke doesn't know is that Eileen speaks of how the dragon wasn't meant for her but for someone "worthy" of the creature's loyalty. Naturally, no one knows who that is . . . except maybe Scout himself.

Seraphina was offered Elys Schneider's job at SOHE but declined, even after Oliver took on Rana Keith's job in society and changeling history. She is the one who travels less than anyone else, spending most of her time at home in Catasbanel or in Hichester, keeping Mr. Wetherby company. She was the only one who wasn't over her head in work when Denise's father died and was the only one who managed to attend the funeral. It was probably for the best because Seraphina told us that she had to hide Roy's letter before Denise burnt it to a crisp.

Denise . . . hasn't changed at all. We see her quite often during diplomatic missions. She went with her sister Kailey to Falfi on a diplomatic mission which soon started a rampage of love for politics. She is quite good when it comes to the art of debating as well which drove her father to name her as his successor, instead of Hahn and Hadwin.

When her father was killed on mission, Kailey was sent to Hanalona for safety while the three boys were sent to Catasbanel or Hichester. Soon after they discovered that his death was not on purpose, the three boys returned to Pyralani, but Kailey stayed in Hanalona with Roy and Deke.

Zara has dove into what everyone has now called "Neil's tomb." She rarely talks unless spoken to and when she does speak, it is rarely positive. People were beginning to worry about her while she was on her SAVER assignments. Soon, Vivian and Eileen sent me to help her in Demavanah to ensure that nothing would happen to her, whether it was accidental or purposely inflicted.

Neil was the least of our concerns after he left for Scardihn Caan. He graduated from the university there with a degree in law. He is now renowned as one of the greatest lawyers east of Caan. Of course, he never writes but Sara and Clint make up for it. They say that he has become "what he was as a kid," which I am not quite sure is good or bad.

About eight years after Aston Ridge, Zara and I were visited by an old friend from SOHE, Maeve, who was one of the newer recruits to the elite of SAVER. She had been assigned a job in Steeks but was soon sent to meet up *with us, due to a discovery that Nohte's prisoners weren't as well protected as we thought.*

That was where it started. As we began to grow up, people began to ask us if we would ever go and live a life like that of our childhood. Almost every single one of us denied it, saying that we could never go back to what our life had been when we were kids. In several respects we were right, because the things that we encountered as kids were nothing compared to what we would experience as adults. We were, in the nicest terms. "unprepared."

As ironic as it might sound, whenever we weren't prepared, something huge happened. The truth is, we all thought we would be prepared if something as large as this would happen . . . but we weren't because we were falling apart. It was now time to bring everything back to point one and find out if we could heal the bond that had been waning over the years.

That of course is easy to say from my perspective . . . but it is not easy when all you can do in the midst of it is watch.

The End

Acknowledgements

To Miranda A. Darcy (you know who you are), who was my best pal and fellow childhood detective agent when it came to solving mysteries that never really existed! You have always been a great friend and in memory of that, I based Drew off of you. :)

For Sarah Gracia who steered me in the right direction when I was going the whole wrong way when it came to writing and publishing! Thank you so much for your help and inspiration!

For all those who remember that Christmas when Mom and Dad were in Washington DC! Especially Taylor, Sean, Patrik, Brenna and Aunt Betty!

Last but not least, for the Moore County Philharmonic Orchestra; for a fabulous two years (so far) of fantastic opportunities, fun, and inspiration!

Author's Bio

Sarah Flanagan had always been inspired to read books, especially fantasy and fiction. It wasn't until she was about nine when she took pen in hand and began to write her own stories. The first stories she ever wrote were imaginary sequels to some of her favorite fantasy stories and some short stories of her own. When she turned fifteen, she began her most intense story that would one day take her on a journey of a lifetime. She originally wrote *The Last Victim in Hichester District* as a novel about four friends who entered a boarding school. However, after a week-long personal adventure, she changed the story into what it is now.

Presently, she is preparing to enter her Senior year of homeschooled high school and has become intrigued with her future in college. She is also looking forward to a third adventure with the Mecarnin brothers. When she isn't writing, she is helping with her little brothers or taking long walks and dreaming up more ideas for writing.

Rivershore Books

www.rivershorebooks.com
info@rivershorebooks.com
www.facebook.com/rivershore.books
www.twitter.com/rivershorebooks
blog.rivershorebooks.com
forum.rivershorebooks.com